# The Journey of the Snake

ADAM SMITH

**MILFORD HOUSE**

an imprint of Sunbury Press, Inc.
Mechanicsburg, PA USA

## MILFORD HOUSE

an imprint of Sunbury Press, Inc.
Mechanicsburg, PA USA

For information about special discounts for bulk purchases, please contact Sunbury Press Orders Dept. at (855) 338-8359 or orders@sunburypress.com.

To request one of our authors for speaking engagements or book signings, please contact Sunbury Press Publicity Dept. at publicity@sunburypress.com.

FIRST MILFORD HOUSE PRESS EDITION: December 2024

Set in Adobe Garamond Pro | Interior design by Crystal Devine | Cover by Lawrence Knorr | Edited by Sarah Peachey.

Publisher's Cataloging-in-Publication Data
Names: Smith, Adam, author.
Title: The journey of the snake / Adam Smith.
Description: First trade paperback edition. | Mechanicsburg, PA : Milford House Press, 2024.
Summary: Twenty-year-old Charlotte Savatier returns to Charleston during the American Revolution to avenge the wrongful execution of her affluent parents. Seeking an ally in a ruthless young Brit named Heathcliff, she finds controlling his greed an enormous challenge that could cost her her life.
Identifiers: ISBN : 979-8-88819-259-7 (paperback).
Subjects: FICTION / Historical / Colonial America & Revolution | FICTION / Mystery & Detective / Historical | FICTION / Mystery & Detective / Women Sleuths.

Designed in the USA
0  1  1  2  3  5  8  13  21  34  55

*For the Love of Books!*

For Rita Mae Hines Smith

# Contents

# Acknowledgments

I am eternally grateful to readers Ellen Love Pendleton, Erich Tagtmeyer, and Chef Catherine Reney. A hearty thanks to the team at Sunbury Press: Lawrence Knorr, Katie Cressman, John Jordan, Crystal Devine, and especially to my editor, novelist Sarah Peachey (*The Whispers of War*), whose reasoning would have Mr. Spock, renowned for his logic, green with envy.

# Author's Note

The Wacataw people depicted in this book are fictional, based on the culture of the Siouan language family of Native Americans in the Carolinas, particularly the Catawba. Also, the Americans changed the city name of Charles Town, South Carolina, to Charleston after the Revolutionary War. Since today's readers know this historical gem as Charleston, the author chose to use that name.

*Can you not see*
*The death he wrestles with beside that river*
*No ocean can surpass for rage and fury?*

—Dante Alighieri, *The Inferno*

# CHAPTER ONE

## *The Unlicked Puppy*

I waited on the ship's deck to greet my husband's obnoxious friend, his lawyer, Joseph Bizel. He was late. My constant tears blurred the people on the dock, which was fine at first, as I didn't want to see his face anyway, but when a gust thrust me forward, I lost sight of my footing and nearly stumbled onto the gangway. I cussed in French, luring the stares of the British sailors around me. They were crying, too—not because we shared a common sorrow. The freezing wind had our eyes dripping as steadily as melting icicles.

The sailor beside me blew his high-pitched whistle, a shrill noise that would have made most folks cringe. I found it musical—almost magical, in a Pied Piper sense—how it incited every man to hustle to his station. It meant we were finally setting sail. It meant I could weep real tears—tears of relief, for it appeared that meddling loudmouth Bizel would miss the voyage.

HMS *The Naga*, the frigate Uncle George and I had boarded early that morning, was joining General Benedict Arnold's twenty-three-ship armada in the harbor. *The Naga* wasn't part of Arnold's invasion of an undisclosed rebel city in the south. We were sailing with his fleet for protection from rebel pirates. Our destination was Charleston, where my husband, Major Émile Savatier, had been sent to investigate the murder of a prominent French prisoner of war.

I hadn't seen my husband in three months, and I didn't want to compete for his attention with Bizel, under whom Émile had apprenticed to become a lawyer. So when *The Naga* unfurled her sails, the cold wind became my dearest companion, piloting me away from Old Joe stranded somewhere on the grimy streets of New York City.

*Au revoir!*

We might have been better off missing the voyage. Two days after departure, waves battered the ship as I slept in my cabin, one of ten tiny rooms next to the captain's quarters, five on either side of the deck for the senior officers. My uncle was snoozing, or trying to, on the floor under my hammock. The ship abruptly pitched, sending a ladder-back chair bashing against his head. We figured the gale would worsen, so Uncle George left my cramped cabin to avoid us maiming each other. He took the chair with him—not to sit on, he said, rather to prevent me from impaling myself.

The night turned my porthole window into a black mirror, so I didn't see the massive wave strike the ship's side. I was standing by my hammock, bunching its rope mesh in my fists, when a jolt lifted me and slammed my feet against the floor. The ship rolled exceedingly to one side and stayed in that tilted attitude long enough for the wick in my wall lantern to lose its flame. I knew not to panic. Since childhood, I had suffered random bouts of blindness, so I did what I always had and groped for a place to lay down, but the ship pitched again. It threw me against the hull wall that continued to lean in that direction until it was as horizontal as a floor. I lay still. The wood creaked and squeaked, resonating with the rumbling of the ocean on the other side. Then, a crack as loud as a cattle whip snapped overhead. The ship's bones were splintering. *The Naga* was about to burst.

It didn't, though. The ship righted, spilling me onto the floor. For hours, I played tug-of-war in the dark with my wobbly hammock. It was exhausting, dancing with a wiry demon who, now and again, enjoyed kicking my feet out from under me and sending me on my derrière.

When the sea calmed, I groped my cabin floor for the cape I wore over my nightgown and went topside. The lanterns on the interior rail cast enough light to show men cleaning up the deck, coiling ropes, fussing with sails, and tying things into place. I weaved through the sailors and redcoat soldiers to the bow, where no one was. When the captain fired the signal cannon, the crew shut up and listened for one of the other ships in the fleet to answer with its gun. On land, this was how howling wolves found other pack members. All I heard were the loud slurps of the ocean swells licking the hull. No ships returned fire.

The storm had separated us from the fleet.

Timber creaked behind me, a measured ticking that made me think of a door hinge enduring a thief's slow, creepy intrusion. I looked back. Uncle George stood there. He was a Wacataw warrior, taller than most British, broad-shouldered, with a silver nose ring, eagle feather earring, and face tattoos: A lightning bolt zigzagged from his right eyebrow back across his skull, and five feathers fanned out from his ear onto his cheek. He shaved the right side of his head, the mist giving his skin the sheen of a wet cannonball. Otherwise, he wore his hair long and nearly swatted my face when he flipped it over his shoulder.

"What happened, Charlotte?" Uncle George said in Wacataw, looking up from my feet with a smirk. "Did the storm blow out your lantern?"

In the gloom of my cabin, I could only find my left-footed boot and one right-footed shoe—a slip-on pink mule. I raised my pink mule to hide it behind my boot and immediately stumbled into Uncle George when the ship pitched.

Shouts by the main mast drew our attention, where Captain Nadder and one of his officers had gathered. I recognized him. Lieutenant Williams had shown me to my cabin when we came onboard. He pointed at a snapped boom in the shadows. Lightning had charred one end of the thick dowel, leaving sailcloth and frayed rope trailing. The captain kicked it and the sailcloth folded over, unveiling a man's hand severed at the wrist, palm up, its fingers curled. Uncle George told me lightning had struck a man high up on the mast during the storm, and he had fallen here. They had buried him earlier, plunging his corpse into the sea.

The hand didn't strike me as repulsive or eerie. It looked lonely lying in the shadow, so disassociated from its purpose that I pitied it. Lieutenant Williams grabbed its thumb and, whispering what must have been a prayer, took one giant step to lob the orphan overboard. The trajectory lacked an arc, and the hand struck the back of a man standing at the rail. He turned around.

"Sorry, mate," the lieutenant said.

The man, a few years younger than me, maybe eighteen or so, picked up the hand by the fingers. He didn't wear military garb. I'd seen him several times over the past two days—an important enough passenger to displace an officer and occupy the cabin across from mine.

"Do us the honor, sir," Captain Nadder said to the young man, "and kindly commit that to the sea."

The man dropped it overboard and clapped his hands as if to clear them of ash. A sailor spoke to the captain privately, and the captain meandered off, pointing and shouting to someone in the main mast rigging. Lieutenant Williams stayed back. He spotted me.

"Hello, Mrs. Savatier," he said, lowering his eyes to my pink mule. "I trust the storm wasn't too hard on you?"

"It was as brutal as my childhood dancing master in Québec City," I said.

His smile was short-lived. He turned to the man he'd struck with the flying hand. "Truly sorry about that bad toss, Mr. Bizel," Lieutenant Williams said and hurried to join the captain.

*Mr. Bizel?*

My uncle and I looked at each other. Mr. Bizel, however, had no interest in us. He faced the sea, which had the allure of a black wall.

"Mr. Bizel," I said.

He didn't turn around.

"Excuse me, Mr. Bizel?"

No reaction.

"Bizel, your ear no work?" Uncle George said in his shoddy English.

Mr. Bizel faced us. His eyes were as black as night. A lightning bolt lit up our surroundings, its subsequent thunder vibrating the deck.

"If you don't mind me asking," I said to the young man, "are you Joseph Bizel, the lawyer?"

"I do mind," he said snootily.

Uncle George's snicker blasted hot air on my cold ear. The rude youth amused him.

"Are you Joseph Bizel or not?" I asked.

"Maybe," he said.

"Maybe?"

He scrunched his dark eyebrows, focusing on my uncle instead of me, clenching his right fist. The youth's posturing provoked a grin that widened my uncle's face, revealing his missing front tooth. My uncle hissed through the gap.

"Mr. Bizel," I said, "my—"

"Not too long ago," the imposter told Uncle George, "husbands fit a metal cage over a gossip's head with a device that pinched her tongue in place to keep her from gabbing."

"Me not husband," Uncle George said, hissing again.

The idea to hiss during confrontations came to Uncle George on a hunting trip many years ago. He had stabbed a deer's bloated carcass, and it hissed as it deflated. The noise was so annoying it distracted him. Ever since, Uncle George thought hissing through the gap in his upper teeth added an air of uncertainty about himself that punctured holes in any adversary's concentration. I told him the opposite was true, that he looked dimwitted when he hissed, especially with his tooth missing— which pleased him. After that, Uncle George started to omit verbs and definite articles when he spoke English: He *wanted* people to underestimate him, to think this hissing fool was missing a lot more than a few verbs and a tooth.

The imposter frowned and turned his dark eyes on me.

"Look at those idiots." He pointed his chin across the deck at the captain and his crew. "Obviously, this ship is lost. It's obvious as well that you're the only woman onboard." He grimaced, bearing white teeth with pointed fangs. "I'd wager this ship has over 250 men on it. Imagine what could happen to you out here. Lost at sea with all those men bored out of their trousers."

He closed his eyelids sluggishly, looking, when he opened them, somewhere over my shoulder. Hatred was concentrated in his tight, young face as if the ghost of someone he had recently murdered was taking shape in the darkness behind me. He spooked me enough that I turned to ensure no phantom lurked there.

"I've had enough of this fool," I told my uncle in Wacataw. "I'm telling the captain he's an imposter."

"Hold on," Uncle George said in Wacataw. "Let's think this through. We're going to need an accomplice when we reach Charleston. Someone who isn't a loyalist or a rebel—someone with a British accent. A stranger in town. This unlicked puppy fits that role. He isn't in the military. Or maybe he is. Maybe he's a deserter. Who cares? Whatever he is, he's got the balls of a rutting moose. We could use his cunning."

"Are you crazy?" I said. "For all we know, your unlicked puppy murdered Old Joe."

Uncle George, who disliked Old Joe, shrugged. "Joseph is a blabbermouth. He's also a coward. Our unlicked puppy here isn't a coward. He lashes out when cornered, and Joseph would never corner anyone. Old Joe's probably in a tavern right now."

The imposter's upper lip curled as he studied the shaved side of my uncle's head. Wacataw warriors shaved their heads on their dominant-hand sides so their hair couldn't get snagged in a bowstring or the hammer of a flintlock rifle. I was half Wacataw, half French. My mother was George's sister. When I was ten, I watched my parents hang in Charleston for a crime they didn't commit. My uncle and I knew who framed my parents. He lived in the mansion he stole from them.

We were now on a secret side mission of revenge.

I stepped closer to the youth. "My husband is Major Émile Savatier," I said quietly in English. "His lawyer is Joseph Bizel. Joseph left Québec City two weeks before we did to visit friends in New York." I waved a hand at my uncle. "He was supposed to rendezvous with us at the dock. He never showed." I glanced at the imposter's broad chest. "The new Joseph Bizel seems to have lost twenty pounds, thirty-five years, and his double chin. He also miraculously transformed his greasy gray hair into the stunning black curls of a French poodle." I stepped back, close to Uncle George. "Care to explain?"

The man's eyes were moist from whatever storm was stirring within him. Behind him, lightning flashed in the distance, tiny white fractures forming in the protective shell surrounding our dark world. Overhead, a colossal lightning bolt cracked the sky. It was so white and long and loud, you'd have thought the world was splitting apart, each black half rolling away from the other to expose us to the great light of God—a terror usually reserved for the tenants of eggs who quickly found themselves plopped into a frying pan or a mixing bowl, where they were beaten beyond recognition.

I hoped the storm was done beating on us.

It wasn't. The fractured sky gave way, and rain pelted the dark deck in a torrent of bouncing white pebbles. The unlicked puppy raced for the stairs, knocking me into Uncle George.

# CHAPTER TWO

## *A Ghostly Trick*

He wasn't hiding in his cabin. We checked. Uncle George and I went into mine, where he suggested we let "Mr. Bizel" stew for a few days.

"He'll lose sleep worrying that he could be thrown into chains any minute," Uncle George said in Wacataw. "We have him trapped."

"Trapped? What's to stop him from stabbing us in our sleep?"

"Life."

"Life?"

"He knows he'll lose his if he tries to take ours. The captain'll hang him. I bet he's hiding down in the hold like a rat, agonizing over us telling everyone he's an imposter. Let's see how he behaves under stress."

"I think it's an unnecessary risk."

"*Il vaut mieux hasarder de sauver un coupable que condamner un innocent*," Uncle George said in French, quoting someone; he spoke excellent French—my father taught him.

It was a game Uncle George had forced me to play since I was ten. He'd quote some poet or writer, and I was supposed to guess who. I didn't care who famously said *it is better to risk saving a guilty person than to condemn an innocent one*. It didn't make sense.

"We're not condemning an innocent man," I told him. "That man's an imposter."

He stared, waiting for me to play the game.

"Molière?" I said.

"Voltaire."

To my knowledge, I was the one who lost sleep over the following days. The ship constantly creaked and squeaked, keeping me on edge and making me fear the unlicked puppy was sneaking into my cabin or creeping up behind me. The captain opened a sealed envelope that the fleet's commodore had given him in New York in the event the ships separated. We learned General Arnold's armada was headed for Virginia. The crew of *The Naga* got their bearings and sailed for Charleston. The imposter stayed in his cabin most of the time. At night, the young man never lit his lantern.

I decided to stir the pot on the evening of the third day. Uncle George and I were in my cabin, having returned from the galley with dinner. We ate in my cabin mostly. I told him I wanted to meet with the imposter alone.

"I'm not a physical threat to him," I said, "so he might skip all the manly posturing if you're not there."

My uncle reached behind his shoulder for one of two knives sheathed in a hidden harness on his back and offered it to me.

"I won't need it. If he wanted to kill me, he'd have already done it."

Uncle George left. I knew he wouldn't go far, that he'd follow me.

The imposter wasn't in his cabin. Two Royal Marines stood watch between the walled-off entrance to our quarters and the gun deck. I asked them whether they'd seen Mr. Bizel.

"They say he goes to the hold," one guard said. "He prefers the company of pigs."

"He brings his meals there," the other said. "He won't eat with us."

Sure enough, the imposter was three decks down. With no fresh air, the reek was farmy. He sat with his back to the rails of the pigpen, cradling a wooden bowl of porridge in his lap. He pinched a morsel of meat in the bowl and brought it to his mouth. He could have dined in the solitude of his cabin. He chose not to. Eating in this stench showed the other men onboard that he had nothing in common with them. A ploy that ensured no one spoke to him.

I sat at his side. Steamy breath from several pigs' double-barrelled nostrils heated the back of my neck. Squinting, he observed me. I kept my eyes on people when I spoke with them; afterward, too, when they thought the conversation was over. Their expressions revealed what they thought—the reddish afterglow in a liar's gloating face or how a thief's smirk parts her lips. The young man never entirely looked away, either.

"They fed me rats they caught on the ship," he said. "When we were crossing the Atlantic."

I frowned. "What do you mean?"

"You ever eat rat?"

"I don't think so, no."

"Rat is quite good. I never told them that."

"Told who?"

He chewed loudly, saying, "A gang from His Majesty's Navy dragged me onto a frigate in Liverpool about four months ago. I finally escaped the other day in New York." He pointed a dirty finger at my mouth. "Did you know you can pick the shite out of your teeth with the tip of a cooked rat tail?"

"You mean the cook didn't cut the tail off for you?"

"That's how you eat it." He brought his fist close to his mouth as if he was going to cough into it. "You grab the tail up close to the arsehole."

"Sounds tasty." I flicked a few stems of straw off my dress. "May I ask why they were feeding you rats?"

Grinning, he said, "I crushed a sailor's ribs like a hazelnut, so they chained me in the hold. I swore I'd disembowel the first fool that came near me." He held the bowl out. "Want a nibble?" He spoke pleasantly, his smile enhancing his handsome face. "Mind the biscuit. You could carve your initials into the floor with it."

I ignored the bowl. He was as unpredictable as a cat: Soft and purring one moment, viciously sinking its claws and fangs into your petting hand the next.

"Where's Joseph Bizel?" I asked.

He chewed, not answering.

"Is he dead?"

"I met him in a tavern after overhearing him discuss his trip to Charleston aboard *The Naga*. He was carrying on about how he was going to solve the murder of that French twat. Count whatever."

The imposter scooped up porridge with his fingers.

"And?"

"And I robbed him of his papers and money. I beat him senseless while he was pissing out back and told a group of soldiers that he was a rebel, that I heard the drunkard brag about smuggling the enemy rifles and saying fuck King George."

"They arrested him?"

He nodded, licking his fingertips.

Joseph Bizel wasn't assisting Émile in his investigation. He was merely visiting. It was in his character to exaggerate and brag, though. In my highly biased opinion, he got what he deserved.

"Back in that tavern," he said, "Bizel never said anything about you or your Mohawk friend being on this ship. I gather you value his friendship more than he does yours."

A pig chewed my hair, pulling strands through the gaps in the rails. I felt pinpricks as if a cruel child were behind me with a sewing needle. I leaned forward, gliding my palm along the back of my skull to collect my hair.

"Why would a French slag come down into the hold alone?" he said, eyeballing my chest. "Looking to earn a few farthings, are you?"

He enjoyed insulting people.

"We're looking for someone to work with us in Charleston," I said. "Someone no one knows there—a Brit who isn't afraid to impersonate, say, a soldier or landowner so we can gather information on a corrupt businessman. And put him where he belongs."

"Where's that? The grave?"

I chuckled at the thought of him strangling Donald Pawsworthy, the man who set my parents up and had them hanged.

"A prison ship, I hope, so he suffers miserably."

"Who's *we?*"

"Me and my bodyguard."

Uncle George and I wanted to hide our identities from Donald Pawsworthy. When I left Charleston as a child, I had my father's last name, La Pierre, and today, I had my husband's surname, Savatier. Everyone said I could have been my mother's twin, although I had my French father's light skin and brown hair, so I looked European. I would tell everyone in Charleston what I told *The Naga*'s crew in New York: My bodyguard, George, was an Abénaki. That's what the ship's manifest would say, should anyone snoop. No one would know we were Wacataw, which had an added benefit: The Wacataw were fighting on the rebels' side.

The stranger dragged his biscuit through his porridge.

"I can provide shelter and food for you in Charleston," I said, raising my eyes. "In exchange for your help."

"I want money." He crunched the biscuit, blowing out crumbs. "And I don't care how I get it. That's why I took Bizel's place on this ship, him carrying on about how wealthy Charleston is."

"This man's got money. More than you can imagine."

"I doubt that." He cupped the bowl with both palms. "That's all I've thought about these last four months. Riches. And what I'll do with them."

Dark splotches—stains—soiled the front of his brown shirt. A small tear ran along the underside of his right sleeve. Scuffs had worn nicks in the cuffs of his black trousers, and the fabric around his knees was thin but stiff with filth.

"You could start by buying yourself new clothes," I said. "You dress like a street urchin."

He ignored me, raising the bowl to his lips and tilting his head back. Porridge oozed into his mouth. He used his hand to wipe the inside of the bowl, sucking each finger with kissing noises.

"Do we have a deal?" I said.

"What about your husband?"

"What about him?"

"How will he feel about me beating his chubby lover up and taking his place on this ship?"

"I won't tell him. Not until you prove your usefulness."

"He isn't part of your scheme?"

"He's got enough on his plate. Once we gather irrefutable evidence, he'll help with the prosecution."

"I'm not making a deal." He licked the back of his hand. "I have no idea what your real plans for me are. Set me up as a thief, claim I'm a rebel, get me hanged or shot by a firing squad."

"I can get you the riches you're after. Help me, and I'll help you."

"I don't trust you. I don't trust anyone."

"That's the deal."

I stood. I saw a way to exploit Joseph Bizel's penchant for exaggerating his self-importance.

"Joseph Bizel was working on behalf of the Crown, helping my husband investigate the murder of Major Henrique Baptiste de Montcalm, the Count of Voisenon. They'll hang you for impersonating a man of his importance."

The imposter closed his eyes and rested his head on the fence rail.

"I'm going to walk away," I said. "Am I returning to my cabin or going to the captain's quarters instead? Do I leave here as your partner or your executioner?"

He stood. Clasping the bottom of the bowl with one hand, he reached over the fence and placed it upside down as a crown on the closest pig's head. He held his hand out. This was what men did when making a deal: Shake hands.

"I'm Charlotte," I said, unsure what else to say.

His big hand was sticky with porridge, and mine fit into it as snugly as a mouse's. If it had been a mouse, he would have killed it. He squeezed so hard I thought my bones would snap. I didn't flinch. I held my breath and stared into his black eyes, concentrating on the pigs to help ignore the pain. They were getting loud, hooves scraping the floorboards, grunts, oinks, and a hollow knocking sound as they headbutted the empty wooden bowl. They were upset. They realized someone had played a ghostly trick on them: They were smelling something fabulous in the bowl that wasn't there.

Was this the imposter's clever way of warning me not to make an empty promise?

He stood with his feet far enough apart to adjust his stance as the ship pitched and rolled. If he hadn't let go when he did, I planned to kick his goolies to win my hand back. I held my fingers up. They were stiff and pale from strangulation.

"I guess I'll brush my hair with my other hand tonight," I said, clenching and unclenching my numb fist. "Back on that ship, when you were crossing the Atlantic, did it ever occur to you that if you weren't so adversarial, maybe you might have gotten mutton chops, peas, and a mug of grog instead of rats? Your own hammock to sleep on?"

He shrugged. "I prefer to bring out the worst in people. That way, I know who someone is straight off."

"Can you control that preference?"

He reached for my hand, the one he had squeezed the bejabbers out of, and brought it to his warm lips. He kissed my skin, smiling handsomely again.

"What's your real name, anyway?" I said.

His smile weakened as stronger muscles along his jawline bulged. Those muscles were the ones that expressed anger and hate, and they were much more developed, bulked out by repeat and frequent use. He was so young yet had the bearing of a ruthless old king accustomed to ruling cruelly—mercy and kindness were offensive concepts, tactical elements reserved for schemes and plots.

"Heathcliff," he said.

"Heathcliff. Heathcliff what?"

"That's it. Heathcliff." He raised a forefinger. "But, please, for the duration of our enchanted voyage, call me Joseph."

"Good night, *Joseph*."

"Good night, *partner*."

I walked away. The pigs were still making a ruckus, still angry at the empty bowl.

～～～

Uncle George wasn't in the cabin when I returned. I lolled in my hammock in the dark, thinking about Émile. Sometimes, when we discussed one of his cases, I'd grab his upper arm to emphasize my argument. Feeling his muscles harden through his shirt when he pressed his palm on the edge of a table to push his chair back and look up at me with his sky-blue eyes, when he'd flip his black hair aside, his smile revealing his straight white teeth—it would send a thrill through me that I couldn't tamper. And that was the beauty of a husband: It took absolutely no effort to get him naked.

I had to stop thinking about Émile when Uncle George came into the cabin holding a candle. He could have slept on a hammock with the sailors on the berth deck. He preferred the role of a guard dog on the floor below me. I told him about my deal with Heathcliff and how he got Old Joe arrested—which amused Uncle George.

"Heathcliff's quite intelligent," I said. "He can be exceptionally charming. At heart, though, he's evil. Maybe *evil* is a little harsh. He's intensely selfish and sly."

"In other words, perfect for the part," Uncle George said.

Uncle George insisted, despite our deal, that until we reached Charleston, we needed to be alert more than ever. Heathcliff would assume our guard was down. Uncle George unraveled his bedding and positioned himself so the flats of his feet lay against the door, which opened out.

"Good night, Crow," he said, blowing out the candlelight.

I got the nickname *Crow* as a child in my Wacataw village. It was a bird that never shut up—when eating, roosting, mating, even when it flew away in defeat, a crow constantly cawed. I was known as someone who likewise never shut up. Tonight, I didn't want to talk. The waves rocked the ship, and, hearing them lick the hull, I thought about Émile again, about what we did to each other when we were naked.

I couldn't wait to see him.

I had another uncle in Charleston, Uncle George's youngest sibling, Gabriel. Dr. Gabriel "DuBois" had changed his last name from Harris after returning from a ten-year study of medicine in Paris. To secure a successful career as a doctor in Charleston, Gabriel thought hiding his Wacataw blood was requisite. He and Uncle George, a proud Wacataw, didn't get along.

On the morning of the tenth day after leaving New York, *The Naga* finally approached Charleston. During the voyage, I had stored my trunks outside my cabin in the officers' wardroom because they wouldn't fit through my tiny cabin's narrow doorway. Uncle George traveled lightly, comparatively: My large two trunks to his one. He had more books than clothes. Molière and Voltaire in French; Shakespeare, Milton, and Pope in English.

Since it would take hours to dock, Uncle George and I headed for the galley. We wanted to invite Heathcliff, but he wasn't in his cabin.

He had remained distant, even after our deal. We ate on the main deck, standing at the rail and watching Sullivan Island get closer as *The Naga* approached Charleston Harbor.

When we returned below deck to get our luggage, Heathcliff was sitting on one of my trunks. He stood, duplicating the slouched posture of my uncle. Both men were too tall for the low ceilings. Heathcliff, not surprisingly, didn't have any luggage. He had worn the same pants and shirt every day. He was, however, smartly dressed today in blue trousers, a white shirt, a brown dress coat, and a pair of black shoes. He even combed his hair.

"If captain find out you steal clothes, he cut off your hand and nail it on mast," my uncle told Heathcliff.

"I didn't steal anything," Heathcliff said quietly.

"Then how you wear fancy clothes then?" Uncle George asked, book-ending his question with the same word, boxing Heathcliff in.

"I bargained for them. I told the owner of these shoes and this fine coat that if he gave them to me, he could keep his left eyeball for the rest of his life. And if he threw in the shirt and the trousers, he could keep his right eye, too."

Heathcliff winked at me, suggesting—I think—that he was joking.

"Well," I said, "since you're here, give us a hand with these trunks, will you?"

Heathcliff began dragging the trunk he had been sitting on. I ran ahead and held the wide door open to the gun deck. A half-dozen sailors saw me and stepped up, handily hauling the trunks up the steep stairs.

Tall ships were anchored in the harbor and docked along the city's piers. I recognized St. Michael's and St. Philip's steeples rising above a swarm of red clay and dark slate rooftops. St. Michael's steeple was painted black for some reason. It used to be white. Pillars of gray smoke streamed from the rooftop chimneys, bending during their ascension as if connecting the city umbilically to the massive clouds, stacked white billows, slow-moving and majestic, that towered over the landscape. Perched on the waterfront loomed the city's architectural jewel: The Exchange Building. Built of carved pale stone blocks, it stood out from the rest of the city with its tall windows, columns, and deep archway entrances that funneled seafarers to and from the bustling streets.

I remember the year they finished that building, the year my parents were executed, the year I was taken away from Charleston: 1771.

When we disembarked, Captain Nadder instructed sailors to carry our trunks. We strode directly through the Exchange Building and waited on the landing of the steps that overlooked the intersection of East Bay and Broad Streets. I searched the crowd for my husband. In his last letter, Émile said he'd meet me here.

A black woman in a gray dress with a white apron walked up the steps and, smiling, handed me a note. Her hair was pulled tight to her head in a bun. Her swiftly moving eyes fully took in her surroundings. She lowered those eyes to the note and wiggled her eyebrows. The message was in Gabriel's handwriting:

> *Charlotte, ma puce!*
> *Go with Mahala. She will bring you to my house as the crow flies.*
> *À très bientôt.*
> *Gabriel*

I asked Mahala where my husband was. She didn't reply. I asked again, and she pointed at the note. She had light brown skin and a prominent Roman nose, so I assumed she was, like me, of mixed race, a local who spoke English. Apparently not. I tried talking to her in French, and she turned away. She walked down the steps and climbed aboard a box carriage, a black one drawn by two black horses with one driver, a woman in a black dress with curly dark hair.

It was a curious carriage. At the back, above the twin doors, a wooden dowel ran parallel with the roof's edge from which hung what appeared to be rust-colored rats dangling by their tails. I looked closer. They were made of forged iron. At least a half-dozen of them.

When we rode along Broad Street, the iron rats rang out like cowbells. I parted the black curtain over the door's window. Pedestrians were so used to this noisy carriage that only a few folks looked at us. We passed the statue of William Pitt. William was missing an arm, probably blown off by a cannonball. We turned left when we reached King Street, passing by Tradd Street, and stopped at the corner where Price's Alley led back to Meeting Street.

I smiled, happy that I remembered the streets.

We got out, stepping onto a large brownstone carriage block. Mahala pointed at the large house behind a high red brick wall with a broad wooden gate door. Dr. Gabriel DuBois had done well for himself. A towering three-story structure with a piazza on each floor.

Mahala strutted up the stone walkway. The piazza door opened and a Wacataw man stepped out, the right side of his head shaved. To my awe, Mahala greeted him in English. He passed me, saying *Hello, Crow* in Wacataw. I didn't know him. Uncle George sure did, the men screaming each other's names and hugging with the compassion of long-lost lovers.

So Mahala could speak!

Why the silence?

I was too excited to see Émile to concern myself with her. I stepped up into the piazza, and that's when I saw Gabriel standing inside the house doorway. I froze. Dark semicircles stained the puffy skin under his eyes; the hollows of his cheeks and temples were so sunken you could see the contours of his skull, making his proud cheekbones more prominent. The whites of his eyes were yellowy. We hugged. He was weightless. I would've lifted his heels off the floor if I had leaned back.

He explained in Wacataw how he was recovering from an inoculation procedure. He drew both sleeves back, revealing black sores on his forearms. Wrapping my arm around his waist, we entered the front parlor, and I held Gabriel's hand as he sat on a sofa. The curtains were closed, and no fire burned in the fireplace. A three-arm pewter candelabra on the table in front of the sofa provided little light, the petite flames wiggling in response to our commotion.

"How are you feeling?" I asked.

"I drank my first spruce beer today and it didn't drip out anywhere," he said. "That means I'll survive."

"Where's Émile?" I said in French, walking to the foot of the staircase that went up a few steps to a landing and turned right. "Émile!" I shouted up the stairs. "Émile!"

"Crow," Gabriel said. "Émile isn't here."

"Where'd he go?"

The light in the hall dimmed as someone closed the front door leading to the piazza. The wall behind Gabriel got darker as someone in the hall shut the parlor door. As light receded, shadows positioned themselves behind table legs and staircase balusters, shuddering in step with the fluttering flames, waiting to take over the room the moment the candlelight went out.

"He's not *here*," Gabriel said, raising his hands toward the tall ceiling; when he lowered them, he crossed his skinny, pale forearms. He looked eerily similar to the white skull and crossbones you saw on those black flags the pirates flew. "Not here in this world, I meant to say. He . . . I . . . Oh, my dear Crow, Émile is dead. Poor Émile passed away last week."

I stared at his bony skull, at the frown sunken in loose skin.

I muttered, "He's dead?"

He teared up.

"What do you mean?" I said stupidly.

A charred log lay in the grimy, cold fireplace. I thought how Émile was now a corpse lying alone somewhere, too. The log was in a state of ruin. Instead of bark, burnt, black scabbing covered it, and fire had narrowed the ends to tapers. I wanted to squeeze the burnt log with both hands and crush it—to finish its destruction—but I knew my palms would come away the color of night, blackening everything I touched.

*Émile!*

My frantic hand bumped a statue of a wooden angel on a table, and it fell into the shadows on the floor. The sound reminded me of that ghostly trick back on *The Naga*, how those hoodwinked pigs kept knocking the empty bowl around, sensing something fabulous in it that wasn't there anymore.

# CHAPTER THREE

## Slimy Cannonball

I sat on the stairway. I wasn't sure where to look. I stood, turned in place, and watched my hands move. One slapped the ball post at the bottom of the staircase while the other fidgeted with my collar. I paced. Eventually, I found myself standing by the sofa, hugging Gabriel. His skin reeked of rust. An old rusty pot.

"How can he be dead?" I backed out of his embrace. "I don't believe you."

I sounded irrational, and I knew it.

"His heart failed," Gabriel said. "He was alone when it happened. He couldn't be helped."

I dropped into a cushioned chair and lowered my head. I couldn't hear anyone stirring or talking in the house. Not even Uncle George on the porch. The sofa creaked as Gabriel settled on it.

"How could Émile have had heart failure?" My heart pounded, and the woosh of blood filling my head was so distracting I had to stand to quiet it. "He was twenty-six. He was strong. He was healthy, Gabriel. *Extremely* healthy. No one knows that more than me."

"Weakness of the heart lies hidden, Crow. It suddenly strikes, like when you step on a snake. It's not common for someone as young as him. It's not unheard of, either."

"What was he doing?" I said. "When it happened?"

"What does that matter?"

"It matters to me. Was he running up these stairs here? Eating a leg of lamb? Powdering his wig? What?"

"He was on his way to question a soldier. He said it was one of the guards watching the house where the French officer was murdered."

"And you didn't find that suspicious?" I stared. "Him dying while questioning a witness to a murder?"

"His death was natural, Crow."

"Where was he exactly?"

"Where?"

"Yes. Where?"

"In the street."

"Which street?"

If it was East Bay Street, he was probably robbed by drunkards and killed in the struggle. Gabriel paused, holding back.

"What's with all the questions?" he said.

"Which street, Gabriel?"

"South Bay."

"South Bay?" I spoke hurriedly. "Where on South Bay? Not in front of my parents' house? Where Pawsworthy lives?"

My hands were shaking. I was losing control, like when I would temporarily go blind. My knees shook now, and my breathing was choppy. I suddenly remembered that severed hand on *The Naga*, how it lay alone in the dark, separated from its body—separated from its purpose.

"No," Gabriel said, tamping the air with both hands to calm me. "Émile was found next door by the Gibbes House. The British arrested Gibbes as a revolutionary and turned his house into a military hospital. Émile went to speak with a soldier who was being treated there. I gather he was injured in a skirmish—the soldier, that is."

"It's a little odd, isn't it?" I said. "Émile dying in front of that murderer's house?"

"Next door, actually. I guess it could appear dubious."

"*Dubious?*"

Gabriel shrugged.

"You said he went there alone," I said. "Émile wrote me saying he had an assistant, a sergeant. He wasn't with Émile?"

"I have no idea." Gabriel rubbed his eyes with his bony fingers. "And I didn't say he went there alone. I said he was found alone."

"No. You said he was *alone when it happened*. When did it happen?"

"Today's the thirtieth, so five days ago—"

"He died on Christmas?"

"The night before."

"He died at night?"

He nodded.

"Are you telling me no one in the British Army finds this suspicious?" I said. "A young and healthy officer—a royal inspector—dying alone in the street at night during an inquiry?"

Gabriel exhaled and his lungs wheezed; he had something more than air in there.

"Charlotte, I understand you're upset. Don't take it out on me. One of the soldiers who found him came and got me. I brought his body back here and examined him. He died a natural death."

"I'm sorry to be so rude. I simply can't be convinced that a healthy young man can die so abruptly." I slogged up the stairs. I opened and closed doors on the second floor until I found Émile's room. Stacks of books and bottles of wine characteristically crowded a tabletop. Closing the door, I lay on his bed.

The news was so new I couldn't cry. I wanted to blame someone, to hate someone for his death. There was no one.

Somebody knocked. By the time I turned to look, the door was in motion. I curled my arm under the pillow as Uncle George sat on the bed near my hips. He passed his hand in front of my face, close to my eyes, and I blinked.

"I'm fine," I said in Wacataw.

He cupped his hands in his lap.

"Can we go back home?" I asked.

He knew I wasn't thinking clearly. "We'd have to walk back. That's a brisk 1,300 miles through mountains, forests, rivers, lakes, and Iroquois." He playfully pulled on my earlobe as he would when I was a child, only not so roughly.

"Something's not right," I said. "Émile didn't have a bad heart."

"That kind of death comes out of nowhere, Crow."

I sat up, scooting beside him, my cheek against his arm's broad muscle. I explained how Émile died in the dark next to Pawsworthy's house.

"Don't you find that odd?" I asked.

"Very odd, yes."

"I changed my mind." I tapped his kneecap. "We're not going back."

"We're not?" he said, mocking me with a smirk.

"I'm going to do what Émile would do. Get to the bottom of this. Someone killed Émile."

"Good." Uncle George slapped my knee. "I don't know how many 1,300-mile walks I got left in me."

We looked at each other and laughed.

I thought about my parents, and now Émile—all dead. While he continued to laugh, I finally cried. Uncle George put his arm around me and pulled me close. When I could breathe without shuddering, I looked at him.

"Émile is in your blood, Crow." His fingernails grazed my cheeks, sweeping aside the hair stuck to my wet skin. "Your heart will always keep him alive inside you. So don't worry about him. Worry about something else—getting revenge on Pawsworthy."

He got up, saying he'd get my luggage. I rummaged through my husband's goods. His books were in French, except for the volumes of Blackstone's *Commentaries On The Laws Of England*. He also had a book on botany in the colonies. The wine collection was French, all reds. I turned to his wardrobe, smelling his shirts. I went to the desk by a window overlooking another house inside the compound. I recognized it from Émile's drawings in his letters. It was Gabriel's military hospital.

Émile had neatly stacked blank paper in the center of the desk. I sat and opened the drawers, finding his journal. We both kept journals. He bound the loose pages of his journal with black ribbons tied through holes in the left margin. I read through his final ten or so pages, which ran from December 15 to December 21. He never mentioned chest pains or awkward thumps in his heartbeat.

Not once.

However, on December 20, he canceled dinner with fellow officers, saying that an upset stomach had inspired repeated trips to the chamber pot. At first, he blamed the Duke of Norfolk punch, which he had drunk at dinner the night before with rice and oysters. He suspected the punch was the culprit after learning how it was made. "Unskilled servants (I refused to call them cooks!)," he wrote, "boil egg whites and sugar with sliced lemons and whole oranges, then add cheap rum and soak the potion in casks for months."

But he seemed to have changed his mind, drawing a fine line through the sentences that blamed the punch. Émile never left crossed-out sentences in his journal. He disliked messy journals and notes as much as a cluttered desk. He would remove the page, rewrite it, and insert a clean entry. Leaving the page in was a testimony to how sick he was.

He had drawings in the center drawer, too. He was an amateurish artist. I flipped through the top sketches of rooms and streets that pertained to his investigation. I found more sketches in a lower drawer. Many were of my face. The ones deeper in the pile showed me naked—a close-up of my face and a breast, for example. He drew them from memory. I decided to go through the rest of those intimate sketches later with a glass of his wine.

Émile also painted. His drawings were far better. He had a painting of me, a portrait he painted from memory, hanging over the head of his bed. I managed to chuckle. He hadn't painted me: He had painted the likeness of my mother, albeit a pale version of her.

A sudden feeling of shame and guilt worried me. He sketched me from memory, yet I couldn't remember his face.

I was a terrible wife!

Uncle George and his Wacataw friend came into the room carrying one of my trunks. Heathcliff and a black man followed with the other trunk, placing it at the foot of the bed. Heathcliff left. The other man stopped on his way out to introduce himself as Winslow Welby. He had coal-black skin, high cheekbones, and beautiful teeth the color of lightning.

Uncle George introduced me to his friend, John Peele. John Peele said his family used to live in our village and that they moved to North Carolina when I was a child. We spoke Wacataw, exchanging pleasantries, learning that my mother was the first girl John Peele kissed.

"And also the last," Uncle George said.

Their laughter was so genuine and pleasant that I smiled. I pointed at the painting.

"That's Gail," John Peele said. "Why does your husband have a portrait of your mother above his bed?"

"It's supposed to be me."

"He was a much better lawyer," Uncle George said, his pursed lips holding in his laughter.

"Do you want the painting, Uncle George? To remind you of your sister?"

He shook his head. "I have your mother's image clearly painted in my mind. It can never be replaced."

I didn't want to hear *that*.

The trunk in front of the bed housed my dresses and shoes. I unbuckled the straps and lifted the lid. Instead of reaching inside, I jumped back. I looked over my shoulder at Uncle George, who frowned as he raised his head to peek inside the trunk.

"Isn't that lovely?" I said, waving my hand over its contents.

"*O, amiable lovely death,*" Uncle George said in English. "*Come, grin on me, and I will think thou smilest.*"

Uncle George was trying to keep my spirits up, playing his guess-the-author-of-the-quote game. He taught me to never surrender to emotions and never show you were hurt or vulnerable. He told me that a fake smile was a shield of armor that shuts people out. He was trying to get me to raise my guard. I was hardly in the mood to play along. Still, I knew he'd never give up.

"Alexander Pope?" I guessed, looking over at him.

He winked. "Shakespeare."

"Ah, how appropriate." I widened my hands over the trunk. "Such theatrics."

John Peele kicked the trunk, attempting to rouse its occupant.

"Would someone get Heathcliff?" I said.

John Peele walked out. He came right back, poking his head into the room. "How do you say his name again?"

I told him, and he screamed *Heap-cliff* several times. Uncle George told me John Peele had trouble pronouncing English and French words, especially people's names. About a minute later, footsteps clopped on the stairs.

Heathcliff entered the room without looking at the naked sailor's corpse in the trunk. The body lay on its back, one knee up by his jaw, its upper lip curled into a grotesque snarl that exposed a few tan teeth. Blood had run from his nostrils, dressing his bare chest with a red bib.

"You put us all at risk," I said. "They would have hanged us if they found him."

"You said you wanted my help," Heathcliff said. "This shows how committed I am. Will you hold up your end of the bargain, no matter what happens?"

"This is reckless," I said. "You could have—"

"Charlotte," Gabriel yelled up the stairwell in English. "Someone from His Majesty's Royal Navy is here to see you. A Lieutenant Williams."

"He from *Naga*," Uncle George said in English.

"*They know.*" I glared at Heathcliff, pointing at the corpse. "You fool."

A stampede of footsteps shook the floor downstairs. Lieutenant Williams brought soldiers.

"Hurry," I said. "Take him out of the trunk and hide him."

"Hide him?" Heathcliff said. "Where?"

"His body nasty," Uncle George said. "With shit and piss."

I slammed the trunk's lid and fastened the buckles. Lieutenant Williams marched into the room.

"Mrs. Savatier," he said. "We meet again." He acknowledged Uncle George and Heathcliff with a nod.

"What brings you into town, Lieutenant?" I said.

"You do. Or rather, your clothes do."

He turned toward the doorway and waved a redcoat soldier in. He carried a large cloth sack over his shoulder. The soldier dropped the sack on top of the trunk beside me. Another soldier walked behind him, armed with a rifle and a fixed bayonet.

"Ma'am," the lieutenant said, "why would a woman abandon her dresses and gowns and shoes? I thought nothing was of more value to the fair sex than her garments."

"Why are you insulting me with clichés?" I said.

"I didn't mean to insult you." He shook his head. "A sailor is missing from our ship. Did you lot help him leave?"

Not unlike members of a Shakespearean chorus, we all said *no* at the same time.

"The captain thinks he deserted." Lieutenant Williams pointed his chin at the trunk. "Did he pay you to smuggle him out in that trunk? Empty your clothes out to make room for him?"

I glanced at Heathcliff. His dark eyes glared at me, and the hate muscles along his jawbone were as pronounced as the knuckles on his fists.

"I'm the wife of a British Army officer," I said. "Why would I ever help a deserter?"

"Why did you leave your clothes in your cabin?" Lieutenant Williams asked.

I turned and opened the sack, pulling out a gown.

"Lieutenant Williams," I said. "The storm toppled my trunks and scattered these clothes everywhere, and I was so frazzled at the time that I stuffed everything back in. This morning, I asked George to unpack and reorganize everything." I tapped the fastened buckles on the trunk with the toe of my shoe. "I haven't had a chance to open my trunks yet. I had no idea my clothes were even missing." I threw the gown at Uncle George, wrapping his face. "You'd have to ask him why he left half my wardrobe behind."

The lieutenant looked at Uncle George, who clutched the gown with both hands.

"Me so hungry this morning," Uncle George said, his missing tooth making his smile appropriately goofy. "I bring clothes in cabin and forget to fold."

Lieutenant Williams nodded, looking at me. "I believe you," he said. "I had to ask."

He and the two redcoats headed for the stairs. I waited for the front door to thud before turning to Heathcliff. Uncle George closed the bedroom door.

Heathcliff raised a palm to hush me. "That idiot in the trunk was on his way to get permission to lay ashore when I stopped him. I offered to buy his fancy clothes." Heathcliff paused, pointing his chin at me. "You said I looked like a street urchin, remember? I told him I'd get the money from you. So we went to your cabin. You weren't there. I couldn't pay him, and he threatened to tell the guards that I stole his clothes."

Heathcliff clasped his hands, his left one squeezing his right thumb. "He tried to blackmail me, too. He told me he heard us talking in the hold. He was going to tell the captain everything."

"So what?" I said. "I never mentioned any names."

"He heard me say I deserted in New York. He knew I wasn't Bizel." Heathcliff stepped toward me. "That corpse should give you confidence that I shall do anything to help you." He glared at Uncle George. "Let it also be a warning. I won't let anyone rob me of my chance of being as rich as possible."

"I no understand," Uncle George said. "Marine guards no hear you kill him?"

Heathcliff scratched his chin. "If you press your thumbs into the throat below this bump," he said, tilting his head back, "strangulation is a quiet affair so long as you keep their feet off the floor."

He grimaced, pretending to choke himself, and all I could focus on were his pointed white fangs.

~

I believed Heathcliff. He'd have been hanged if the sailor revealed he was a deserter. I doubted he would risk everything and murder someone over clothes. Late that night, we dressed the corpse in a dead soldier's uniform from Gabriel's hospital, and Uncle George dumped him in the Ashley River. Uncle George said we were co-conspirators now, bound by our commitment to each other.

Haunted by Émile's death, I hardly slept. I still couldn't picture his face. If I loved him, I'd have been able to see him in my mind as clearly as any dream. The guilt and shame of not remembering made our marriage seem worthless, a farce, merely a play on a stage—when it wasn't.

I had breakfast with Gabriel, Mahala, and Winslow in the second-floor dining room. We stirred strawberry jam into our porridge, which we ate with gingerbread. Mahala was a free black. So was Winslow. They worked for a wage and lived in bedrooms on the third floor. Hired right after Émile arrived to handle the increase in hungry mouths, she cooked for the household and the hospital. Winslow assisted her occasionally. He was otherwise a carpenter and mason.

Heathcliff joined us, having slept in the hospital somewhere. He sat down next to me, reaching for a slice of bread.

"And *who* are *you?*" Gabriel said, staring.

No one had introduced Heathcliff to Gabriel yesterday.

"Heathcliff is our guest," I told Gabriel in French. "Uncle George's and mine."

"Is he indeed?" Gabriel said haughtily.

"I was going to pass it by you first," I said. "I guess I forgot. After learning about Émile, I—"

"My house is your house," Gabriel said, softening his tone.

Hearing the word *house* worried me for some reason. I realized why: Eventually, I'd have to sail back to Québec City without Émile and live alone in our house. It wouldn't be *our* house.

Nothing was *ours* anymore.

I heard Uncle George yelling in the hallway in Wacataw. A redcoat soldier stood in the doorway, his face glowing pink.

"Hello, Sergeant," Gabriel said to the soldier. "Come in."

The sergeant raised his hand as he approached, holding an envelope.

"This is Sergeant Dawson," Gabriel told me, "of the South Carolina Royalists. He worked with Émile investigating the murder of Major Montcalm."

"I came here earlier," the sergeant said. "Your obnoxious Cherokee sent me away."

"I don't have a Cherokee," Gabriel said.

"I'll rephrase myself. That man with the face tattoos told me to go away." He smiled at Mahala and me. "He didn't use the words *go away*. What he said in English—what little English he spoke—was so vile that decency forbids me from repeating it in your presence, ladies."

The fermented stench of ale piggybacked the sergeant's breath. That was what probably provoked Uncle George's rude rebuff.

"Well, anyway," Sergeant Dawson said. "Colonel Balfour said he didn't care if you were entertaining King George himself—he wanted this letter delivered to Mrs. Savatier." He handed me the envelope. "I'm assuming you're Émile's wife, ma'am. That's from Lieutenant Colonel Nesbit Balfour, Commandant of Charleston."

Taking the envelope, I smiled. I didn't open it.

"Your husband was honorable, ma'am," Sergeant Dawson said.

I had no desire to discuss Émile with someone who'd been drinking. The awkward silence alerted Gabriel to my discomfort.

"Thank you, Sergeant," Gabriel said, standing and walking him out the door.

I cracked the seal. Heathcliff leaned in, his cheek near mine, to read the letter. It was brief, requesting my *presence appear, sharply, at 12:00 today before the Commandant of Charleston and the Board of Police on the second floor of the Craven Bastion.*

Heathcliff sank his fangs into a hunk of gingerbread, no doubt thinking what I was: They found the dead sailor floating in the river, and *The Naga*'s crew had identified him. Maybe someone saw Uncle George dump the corpse last night. Followed him back here. This was an inquiry into his murder.

"What does Balfour want?" Gabriel said, sitting.

"He doesn't say," I said.

My stomach felt as if someone had slashed it with a hunting knife, hot mush gushing out. I glared at Heathcliff, and he looked away, spreading jam on his bread with the heel of a silver spoon and munching quietly.

"I imagine he wants to discuss Émile," Gabriel said. "He was greatly respected and admired. They probably have some of his belongings to give you."

"If it's not too much trouble," Heathcliff said, leaning over his plate to address Gabriel, "could I get a pot of tea?"

I was so angry I couldn't look at Heathcliff. I got up and brushed by his chair. I had to squeeze my elbow tight to my ribs to stop it from striking the back of his head as I stomped toward the door.

At exactly noon, I entered the expansive room on the second floor of the Craven Bastion, a two-story brick building at the end of East Bay Street shy of Governor's Bridge. Sergeant Dawson sat at a small table opposite a longer one that seated five men behind whom a tall pendulum clock loomed. Two men wore redcoat military uniforms. The others were colonists. The officer in the middle spoke, saying he was Lieutenant

Colonel Nesbit Balfour. He swept his hand at the table across from him, indicating I was to sit next to Sergeant Dawson.

"Mrs. Savatier," Colonel Balfour said, "let me introduce these gentlemen. They are members of the Board of Police. To my left is intendant general James Simpson, and next to him is Mr. Alexander Wright. To my right is Mr. Robert Powell. On the end is Major Donald Pawsworthy of the South Carolina Royalists."

Tiny white lights exploded in my field of vision as if someone had grabbed my ears and bounced my face off the tabletop. I glared so intensely at Pawsworthy that I had to flatten my palms on the table to steady my dizziness. I had hated Pawsworthy all my life yet never met him. My hands trembled. I felt queasy. There must be a moment before the cannon launches its ball, when the gunpowder begins to sizzle, when pressure mounts, when the cannon trembles—that moment of unease when it realizes it's about to hurl its guts out.

"Mr. Simpson is leaving Charleston next month," Colonel Balfour said. "Mr. Wright and Mr. Powell are entrenched here, I assure you. They concern themselves with civil law. You can approach them anytime. Your husband, God rest his soul, regularly reported to Major Pawsworthy. You will do the same. Major Pawsworthy will serve as the liaison between you and me."

*Émile worked with Pawsworthy?*

Why didn't Émile mention this in his journal? I was baffled. I came here expecting to be arrested for, or at least questioned about, the sailor floating in the Ashley River. I had no idea what Balfour was talking about.

"Report what to you?" I said.

Colonel Balfour glared at Sergeant Dawson. "You haven't spoken with Mrs. Savatier?" he said.

"My schedule this morning was very pressing, Colonel," Sergeant Dawson said. "I apologize, sir. I mean to say, sir, that I assumed your note this morning explained the purpose of this meeting."

Red creases zigzagged along Sergeant Dawson's cheek. Perhaps the imprint of a pressing nap.

"I see," the colonel said, sighing. "Mrs. Savatier, we all respected your husband. I considered him a friend. He told me that he learned more about arguing law from you than from anyone else. He was especially impressed by how thoroughly you studied case histories. What I found intriguing was how you researched the personal histories of your opposing lawyers so that you knew as much about them as you did a criminal's background."

I had no idea what the purpose of this meeting was or why Colonel Balfour was even talking about me. I thought it wise to play along.

"Québec has two legal systems funneling into it, sir," I said. "We have both French Customary Law and British Common Law. A rich resource of historical precedents. And every law, every crime, and everyone has a backstory, so proving guilt lies in finding the point where they all converge. That requires research."

Colonel Balfour nodded, saying, "Émile told me you and you alone made him a confident lawyer. He said you argued law better than him, in fact."

"I think Émile was deliriously homesick when he told you that, sir," I said, forcing a smile. "I'm merely his—" I stopped myself. "I was merely his assistant."

It was heartwarming to learn Émile talked so highly of me. Had my hatred for Pawsworthy not corrupted my passion, I would have started crying.

"He told me," Colonel Balfour said, shaking his head, "how you singlehandedly solved the murder of two girls in Québec City."

"I did it *singlehandedly* because no one cared enough to investigate their deaths. One girl was Abénaki and the other a poor farmer." I glanced at Pawsworthy. "The offenders were a soldier and two fur traders. What they did to those girls was unspeakable. Émile prosecuted them."

"Émile also told me," Colonel Balfour said, "that when you arrived in Charleston, he was going to put you to work in the investigation of this case." He pointed at Pawsworthy. "In honor of Major Savatier, Major Pawsworthy has suggested I fulfill your husband's wishes—at least in part—by having you take his place as a royal inspector to catch the killer of the French officer."

"Me?" I could hear my voice rise in pitch.

Colonel Balfour nodded. "I created the position of royal inspector specifically for this investigation."

If Pawsworthy only knew who I was!

Why didn't Émile tell me he worked with Pawsworthy? We wrote each other letters every week. And why didn't Gabriel tell me this? Long ago, I had told Émile how Pawsworthy set my parents up and murdered them. Before he left Québec City, I had advised Émile not to tell anyone who I was, especially my connection to Gabriel. I knew Pawsworthy was a socialite, that their paths might one day cross, and if that murderer knew Émile was married to the daughter of Dr. Jacque La Pierre and his wife, Gail, he would make life difficult for him. I had explained to Émile how no one in Charleston knew Dr. Gabriel DuBois was Wacataw.

I was certainly relieved to learn that I wasn't being arrested for the murder of that British sailor. That relief was offset, compounded, by an appointment of this importance. It was overwhelming.

"Me?" I said again.

"Yes, you," Mr. Powell said; he spoke in a respectful tone, not a condescending one.

"Do you accept the position?" Colonel Balfour asked. An eager smile appeared on his handsome face.

"Sergeant Dawson has your husband's notes," Pawsworthy said. "You'll be given those. You'll also have Major Savatier's office on the first floor here in the Craven Bastion with access to whatever resources you need for your investigation."

"My gender," I said, facing Colonel Balfour, "prevented me from becoming a lawyer, but it didn't stop me from working closely with Émile. He insisted I deal directly with opposing counsel. Men in back rooms, in chambers, in hallways. They never made it easy for me. I accepted that. I developed a hardened reputation because of it, and the more success we had, the more they hated dealing with me. So I know more than anyone that no one will take me or my inquiries seriously. Without Émile, I would need a small platoon of armed soldiers to force a man to sit down and listen to me, much less answer me. Unfortunately, I would disservice the Crown if I accepted the position."

I noticed Simpson and Wright whispering while I spoke, giggling even.

"Well, a small platoon you shall have." Colonel Balfour raised both palms. "How many is a small platoon, in your estimation?"

"It was hyperbole, sir," I said.

Those who understood that word chuckled; Pawsworthy and Dawson weren't among the amused.

"I rather think having a dozen of His Majesty's armed soldiers at your side would put the fear of God in someone," Colonel Balfour said, laughing as he turned toward Pawsworthy, seeking agreement.

Wright and Simpson were chitchatting again.

"You will be paid a wage, of course," Colonel Balfour continued, "which we can discuss with Major Pawsworthy afterward. I—"

"Shut up," I said, pretending to be angry.

Colonel Balfour opened his mouth, staring. He stood, the flats of both hands spread on the table as he bore down on me. He was quite tall.

"What did you say?" he said, his face more crimson than when he had laughed a moment ago.

"I wasn't addressing you, sir." I jerked my head at his colleagues. "I'm talking to Mr. Wright and Mr. Simpson. Shut up when we're talking."

Colonel Balfour turned his head, projecting the anger he had for me at them. He sat down.

"Your colleagues are perfect examples of men not taking me seriously," I told Colonel Balfour.

"I agree." Colonel Balfour whispered something to Wright and Simpson. "The war is taking a toll on everyone, Mrs. Savatier, and these gentlemen aren't handling that stress very well. Kindly excuse their behavior."

"Of course, sir." I looked the men over, stopping at Pawsworthy. "I would have to have absolute freedom to ask anyone anything. I've discovered you can never tell where an investigation will go. It can be as deceiving as the path a snake makes. The snake's journey slithers left and right, going places you can't anticipate—sneaky places, dark places, places no man will want me to be. I could meander through any one of your back doors. Do you really want me to go there? I can promise you this: If I take this journey, I'll have my fangs out."

"My gracious," Colonel Balfour said. "You're an even bigger powder keg than your husband said. I've signed a special order." He raised a document. "An Order of Compliance, which Émile had as well. It allows you to access any home, law office, physician's office—whatever record or interview you need. No one can ignore you. That includes the military. It gives you the power to arrest as well."

He held the document out, and Sergeant Dawson jumped up, the tops of his thighs hitting the underside of the table so that it jutted forward with a screech. Sergeant Dawson practically jogged the space between our tables and returned, setting two documents before me. "That other document is a pass," Colonel Balfour said. "You can come and go from the city whenever you want."

"So I can question anyone?" I said. "No one is outside my authority?"

"Only King George," Colonel Balfour said. He looked to his right and left. "Can you gentlemen think of anything else Mrs. Savatier might need?"

"When Major Savatier was appointed royal inspector," Pawsworthy said, "I wrote to the governor of Québec, General Frederick Haldimand. I wanted his assessment of Major Savatier. You know the general, Mrs. Savatier?"

"Of course," I said. "He's Émile's superior officer." I frowned. "Who also happens to be his cousin. They're both from Switzerland—before joining His Majesty's army, that is."

Colonel Balfour glanced from Pawsworthy to Dawson and rolled his eyes, his lips pursed in apparent frustration, saying, "Everyone seems to be related to everyone else these days."

Pawsworthy lowered his head and began thumbing through paperwork while Sergeant Dawson looked off so he could scratch behind his ear: Pawsworthy and Dawson were related.

"So it appears," I said.

"General Haldimand spoke highly of Émile," Pawsworthy said.

I fantasized about shoving burning coals into Pawsworthy's mouth, forcing them down his fat throat with a sword.

"Mr. Pawsworthy," I said, not addressing him as major. "My husband arrived in the Province of Québec before General Haldimand was appointed to the governorship. He fought and was injured defending Québec City when the Yankees attacked in '75. Bravery moved my husband up the ranks, not nepotism—"

"Mrs. Savatier," Pawsworthy said. "I wasn't suggesting anything of the sort."

"Then why bring his cousin up at all?"

"Merely to share the general's confidence in you. General Haldimand admired your dedication to your husband. That's why I'm confident you'll be equally dedicated to this investigation."

I felt that hot mush leak out of my gut again.

Why would these prominent and influential men place the British military's international reputation in the hands of an unknown woman, however "great" her reputation? Merely out of respect for Émile?

Was I right to question their motivation?

Maybe not. But experience taught me researching the background of the magistrate overseeing your case was always a good idea. In that spirit, I had skimmed through Émile's journals to get his assessment of Balfour. Émile praised Balfour as an intelligent and open-minded commandant whose management of this strategic military city prioritized the army's strict control over the citizens without sacrificing their material needs. In other words, he was fair.

Balfour would never disgrace his honor or the British Army's reputation with some underhanded treatment of a respected officer's widow.

On the other hand, I had every reason not to trust Pawsworthy.

Also, being the sole woman in South Carolina's ten-thousand-member men's club called the British Army may have weakened my confidence.

"Mr. Pawsworthy," I said. "It's not lost on me that my husband was given this investigation because he was a native French speaker. As a French speaker, he made the British military's investigation into this embarrassing murder appear impartial. I believe it was the appropriate posture to take. But he's dead now, and His Majesty's Army already proved their dedication to impartiality. There must be a hundred officers who'd cherish this appointment. Why me?"

"Mrs. Savatier," Colonel Balfour said, not allowing Pawsworthy to reply. "The enemy's parties are everywhere, making the general state of the countryside distressful. Officers and their regiments can be called away at any time without warning as battlefields shift. You would remain in place no matter what happens, uninfluenced by the events in the war theater. And I agree with Major Pawsworthy's assertion that your dedication to your husband will inspire your commitment to this investigation. Major Savatier would be proud knowing you picked up where he left off."

I nodded.

"Can you think of anything else you might need to help you work on a sound footing?" Colonel Balfour asked me.

"I can think of something that would come in mighty handy."

Everyone stared.

"And what would that be?"

"A penis," I said.

I wasn't trying to be funny—I wanted to project the difficulty of my appointment—but my answer provoked full-throated laughter.

"Let me be clear about this investigation," Colonel Balfour said, his complexion still colored by the warmth of his delight. "Although this murder is a military matter, your husband said he was also looking into the possibility of a local citizen having a role in it. That's why I have involved the city's Board of Police. These gentlemen and all their connections in Charleston and across the countryside, including those of the other board members who aren't here, are at your disposal. Please keep in mind that three months have passed. His Majesty finds it humiliating enough that he has to answer to the enemy's royal court. It's exacerbated by the fact that Major Montcalm was also a French count, and we don't have an answer. Do whatever you have to, Mrs. Savatier, to find the murderer of Major Montcalm."

I had to take the position if I wanted to remain this close to Pawsworthy—if I ever wanted to see him suffer on a prison ship.

"I'm honored to serve the Crown, sir," I told Colonel Balfour.

"Well done, Mrs. Savatier," Colonel Balfour said. "Does anyone have anything more to say?"

"Yes." Pawsworthy looked at me. "I ask that Sergeant Dawson work with you. He worked closely with your husband. He'll be able to answer any questions you might have to get caught up on the investigation." Pawsworthy raised his eyebrows. "I hope you find my suggestion agreeable?"

"I agree wholeheartedly," I said. "I, too, have a request."

"Do tell," Colonel Balfour said.

"I want to pick the soldiers for my private platoon myself."

"I thought we were humoring ourselves," Mr. Wright said; he had to say something after being told to shut up. "You actually want your own soldiers?"

"Yes. You and Mr. Simpson proved my need for them, wouldn't you agree?"

"We do," Colonel Balfour said hurriedly. "Keep the Order of Compliance you have for now. Go to the State House tomorrow morning and I'll rewrite it to include your power to draft soldiers whenever needed. Major Pawsworthy can help you select them." He looked over his shoulder at the clock, then stood. "Gentlemen. Mrs. Savatier. Thank you for coming."

As everyone started shuffling off, Pawsworthy asked me to stay.

"Solving this murder is of the utmost importance," Pawsworthy said, coming out from behind the long table.

"I get that."

He dismissed Sergeant Dawson, telling him to wait downstairs to show me my office. No one else was in the room. I moved to the front of my table, placing my city pass and the Order of Compliance in a leather satchel I wore at my side. Pawsworthy stood a little closer to me than necessary. He was shorter, so I had to look down. His belly stretched the fabric of his white vest, its buttons challenging the thoroughness of his tailor's threadwork. If one of those buttons popped free, it would strike me with the force of a musket ball.

"The Board of Police," he said, "and all of Charleston, including you, my dear, will look swimmingly in the eyes of King George and Parliament if we solve this disgraceful murder quickly."

I had no idea what *swimmingly* meant.

"What happens in Charleston doesn't concern me," I said. "I'm from Québec City. And that's where I'm going when this is over. And it'll be over only when I find the murderer."

I wanted Pawsworthy to think I had no interest in Charleston. I doubted I'd return to Québec City—I no longer had a home. His gray pig eyes studied me.

"When can I select my soldiers?" I asked.

He stepped closer and would have rubbed me with his belly if I hadn't inched away.

"You don't need soldiers."

"I wish I had a few right now." I hurried to the other side of the table, ensuring it stood between us. "I want to pick them myself. And I don't want any more South Carolina Royalists. One drunkard is enough, thank you. Oh, listen . . ." I placed my fingers behind my ear, imitating one of Uncle George's dramatic acting gestures. "I can hear Colonel Balfour out in the hall. I think I'll ask him. I don't need you."

I headed toward the door.

"Stop," he said. "Meet me at the Watch House at three o'clock tomorrow."

"Where's that?"

I knew where it was. However, having Pawsworthy think the city was foreign to me, having him think I would characteristically blurt out my ignorance, allowed him to underestimate me.

"It's across the street from the State House on Broad Street."

"How about we meet earlier, say, at noon? That way, we can satisfy this urgency to find the murderer."

"Fine," he said.

He placed a hand on his hip, an authoritative gesture that brought his potbelly into focus. I felt my face sour. He noticed my disgust, and the network of tiny blood vessels branching across his chubby cheeks grew less noticeable as his face flushed.

"Let me give you an incentive," he said through gnashed teeth. "If you don't find the murderer soon, I'll find one for you."

He had the irrational rage of a rabid dog.

I knew Émile would never frame an innocent man, which is what solving a murder quickly seemed to entail. Is that why Émile was found dead near Pawsworthy's house? Had Pawsworthy threatened Émile similarly?

"In fact," Pawsworthy said. "I have a suspect in mind."

"Who?"

"Your husband's best friend, Dr. Gabriel DuBois."

My surging anger had to have colored my face as rosy as his. The murderer who had framed my parents now threatened to set up my uncle. Then, a terrifying thought paralyzed me: Pawsworthy had recognized me. He saw my mother's features on my face and figured out who I was! He knew, too, that I was related to Gabriel. That was why he chose him.

I expected him to drive the knife deeper and twist, saying nasty things about my parents. He didn't. He saw that I was frightened, though. A smirk fattened his cheeks. His pale complexion returned and, bereft of rage, he nodded with the petty smugness of someone who had just won a card game.

"I suggest you get to work immediately, my dear." He walked away with his nose in the air. "Or you'll be living in the street before you know it."

He was merely a bully. He wanted to put me in my place right from the start. What better way to shock and torment me than to fully display the repugnancy of his corruption? He wanted to scare me.

That meant he hadn't recognized me.

Or had he? Was this a game to him?

The uncertainty made my whole body tremble, and my mouth got slimy because it knew I was about to throw up a cannonball.

# CHAPTER FOUR

## *Dirty Rag*

My shaking knees had me negotiating the steps as if ice covered them. I calmed my nausea by rationalizing that Pawsworthy couldn't have recognized me: He had cleared the room of witnesses to talk privately with me, to find out whether I was corruptible. When he discovered that I wasn't, only then did he promise to frame my "husband's best friend." He didn't say *your uncle,* nor did he mention my parents.

Had I agreed to solve the crime quickly, we'd have left the building arm-in-arm and been on our merry way to a tavern where we'd show the ceiling the bottoms of our beer mugs. Ultimately, Pawsworthy knew that, without evidence, I could never tell Balfour he had threatened to frame Gabriel. That was why he had strutted off so smugly.

"Thanks for waiting, Sergeant Dawson," I said, coming off the steps.

Sergeant Dawson and I walked to the back of the building, where a soldier unlocked a door and handed me the key to Émile's office—my office now. It was a reading room with oak desks, candelabras, ladder-back chairs, bookcases, and a wall of split logs adjacent to the fireplace. A tall window overlooking the wharves allowed ample light into the room. A spider web sprawled across the lower left windowpane.

"Where are my husband's notes, Sergeant Dawson?"

"In that desk." He pointed. "The one closest to the window. He kept everything in the bigger drawers on the right."

I sat, waving for him to take the chair opposite my new desk.

"Call me Dawson," he said, sitting. "My friends call me Dawson."

I opened the drawer. Oddly, Émile's notes were in English. He usually wrote in French. On the upper right of the desktop was an inkwell and quill in its stand. On the upper left corner sat a thin stack of blank paper. Émile always kept his paper stacked in the center: Someone had sat here and made room on the desktop to read Émile's notes. I skimmed through the pages, looking for Pawsworthy's name. Émile mentioned him once in the opening pages, saying Pawsworthy was a Board of Police member and the top militia officer involved in the investigation. Sergeant Dawson's name appeared a few times, too.

"Has Major Pawsworthy gone through my husband's notes?"

Dawson paused, musing whether he should answer.

"Ah," I said. "He has. Has he taken any of them?"

"I doubt it."

I glimpsed down, darting my eyes back on Dawson. He looked at the cabinets below the bookcase, fiddling with a button on his red coat.

"How are you related to Major Pawsworthy?" I asked.

Covering his mouth with his palm, he rubbed his beard stubble.

"He's my uncle. My mother's brother."

"That must be nice. I wish I had an uncle."

He didn't contribute a response.

"My only relatives, besides my parents, are my aunts," I said. "Two hags who live together in an apartment over their shop on *Rue Saint-Louis* in Québec City. One bakes bread all day and the other makes cheese. They're like fucking mice."

Inner pressure caused his cheeks to bulge. He tightened his lips to suppress his laughter.

"They got gray-black mousy hair, too," I said, "that's pulled so tight to their heads their big pink ears stick out. The older one—they call her *Chewy*—she's even got whiskers."

He buckled with laughter. I laughed, too.

I walked to the cabinet he was looking at and pulled both doors open. A stack of candles, a metal tinder box, a few ledger books on their sides, two drinking glasses, and a glass decanter of caramel-colored liquor. I set a glass on the table beside Dawson and filled it halfway.

"Whiskey," I said, smelling its harsh fume.

"Scotch," he said, correcting me; he raised the glass to his nostrils. "Your husband had fine taste."

I took the decanter back to my desk and sat. "Were you with my husband the night he died?"

He didn't hesitate or look off. "I wasn't, no."

The office door opened.

"Mrs. Savatier," a soldier said. "There's a young man here to see you. Mr. Heathcliff."

I imagined Heathcliff came to find out how my meeting with Colonel Balfour and the Board of Police went. Very brave of him, seeing as he could have been named in a conspiracy to murder. Heathcliff shut the door, dragging a chair next to Dawson.

"Dawson," I said, "meet my assistant, Heathcliff. Heathcliff worked with Major Savatier and me in Québec City."

Dawson raised his glass, nodding to Heathcliff before taking a sip.

"The major never mentioned you," Dawson said.

"Why would he?" Heathcliff said.

I told Heathcliff how Colonel Balfour had given me my husband's job as the royal inspector tasked with finding the murderer of Major Henrique Baptiste de Montcalm. I explained my Order of Compliance, taking it out of my satchel to show Heathcliff. From Heathcliff's raised eyebrows and frozen shrug, I could tell he wanted to know whether there had been any inquiry into the missing sailor. I subtly grinned and shook my head. He relaxed in his chair.

"Sergeant Dawson of the South Carolina Royalists will be our colleague," I told Heathcliff. Grabbing the quill, I pulled the pile of blank paper close. "Now, Dawson, kindly tell us everything about the murder."

One glass of scotch later, we learned that on the night of September 3, 1780, an unidentified loyalist overheard two men arguing at The Jester's Mate, a tavern on East Bay Street. They spoke English, and one man had a French accent. During their spat, the Frenchman said he had to leave Charleston that night and return to Martinique, where his regiment was. Afterward, the loyalist followed the French spy outside, flagging down soldiers who arrested him. The soldiers returned to the tavern with the loyalist to capture the spy's co-conspirator. He was gone. They imprisoned the French spy in the Provost Dungeon beneath the Exchange Building, where he told the guards he was a major in the French Army and a nobleman, so they alerted their superiors. Out of respect for a fellow officer, Colonel Balfour ordered his soldiers to move Major Montcalm to a rebel's house the British had seized on Queen Street and to place guards there. The following morning, the guards found him in his bedroom naked, bound upside down in a cushioned chair with hundreds of tiny cactus needles stuck in his face, hands, the bottoms of his feet, and his genitals. Bloodshot eyes. Bruises on his limbs. The brown stem of a plant with little needles was in his mouth, bound shut with a white cloth.

Brutally torturing and murdering a French officer, a prisoner of war, was a disgrace to the British military. The abused body was too embarrassing to be seen, so Colonel Balfour had it burned. Incredibly, no one thought to get the loyalist informant's name.

I looked out the window at the ships along the piers. The strings in the spider web had collected dust, meaning the web had been there a long time. That meant Émile had been avoiding this room. This room offered no privacy. Pawsworthy had snuck in and read Émile's notes, the decoy ones written in English. I had seen Émile's actual notes in French in his bedroom at Gabriel's house. That's where I'd keep my notes, too.

"I have some news that might interest you," Dawson said, staring at his empty glass.

"What's that?" I said.

"It's something Major Savatier and I were working on." He sat back and crossed his legs. "A private named Simon Fowls was the guard on duty at the Provost when Balfour's soldiers came to get Montcalm and move him to that house on Queen Street. Montcalm spoke with him. He's the one who reported Montcalm was an officer and a count. By the time your husband arrived in Charleston, Fowls had been temporarily reassigned to a company delivering mail to Cornwallis in Camden. Your husband ordered the commander at the Watch House to have Fowls report to this office the moment he returned to Charleston. These little inconveniences were what always delayed our investigation. I tried explaining that to my uncle." Dawson uncrossed his legs and drummed the tops of his thighs—an indication the scotch had invigorated his spirit. "Anyway, the commander informed me that Fowls returned yesterday."

"Have you spoken to Fowls?"

"No."

"Where is he?"

"He's scheduled to report for guard duty at five o'clock at the Provost," he said.

The pendulum clock on the wall behind Dawson said it was a quarter till three. I wanted Heathcliff to see how wealthy Charleston was.

"That gives us more than enough time to tour the town," I said.

I stood. Heathcliff walked to the door and opened it. Dawson didn't get up.

"Come with us," I told Dawson.

"I'd rather not."

He wanted to stay behind with the free scotch.

"Let me help you, sir," Heathcliff said.

Heathcliff stepped toward Dawson and, grabbing his hand, jerked him to his feet.

"A friendly word of advice," Heathcliff said, pulling him close. "Always do precisely what Mrs. Savatier asks of you without hesitation."

Heathcliff must have been squeezing Dawson's hand. Dawson's scrunched nose and open mouth expressed agony, but he didn't scream—that would have been unmanly. Shortly after, Heathcliff stepped back. He bowed, gesturing to me in the hall.

"After you, sir," he said to Dawson.

Dawson's thumb appeared stuck inside his palm. His crimson hand looked as dysfunctional as a boiled lobster claw. I chuckled privately: Heathcliff's abuse might inspire Dawson to quit.

We walked along East Bay Street and cut across Queen Street to Meeting Street, stopping to look at the magnificent homes. Their architecture was unique to Charleston, finely crafted two- and three-story houses with piazzas on each level. Tall palmetto and crepe myrtle trees lined the streets, the snakeskin bark of the myrtles in a constant state of peeling. Some homes still showed damage from the siege in May, either fire or wreckage from cannonballs. Eventually, we reached South Bay Street, where more rows of stately houses faced the harbor and the Atlantic Ocean beyond.

I stopped in front of my parents' mansion, the one Pawsworthy stole from them. The three-story house had piazzas on each level. To the right was a dirt road hardened with crushed oyster shells that led to a stable house in the back. A tall Bermuda stone wall surrounded the property. As a child, I played on the second-floor piazza, where my father's office was. My parents and I would sit there in cushioned chairs in the mornings and watch the sun rise over the Atlantic Ocean as ships sailed in and out of the harbor.

"That house is beautiful," I said.

"That's my uncle's house," Dawson said.

Where I expected a boastful tone, I detected a begrudged one—resentment.

"He owns two more around the corner on Meeting Street and another on Tradd. And he's eyeing one across from St. Michael's on Broad Street."

"Eyeing?" I said.

"He finds a suspected rebel's house, a nice one, then gets his friend John Cruden to sequester the property. He also owns a few plantations in the low country." He nodded toward the Cooper River. "Not to mention several ships."

I glanced at Heathcliff, who wiggled his eyebrows. I approached the Bermuda stone wall surrounding my parents' property, stopping at the open entry. A smooth stone walkway led to the looming white mansion with black shutters. The iron gate that swung between the two high stone columns was missing. My father's German blacksmith forged the elaborate ironwork. I ran my finger inside one of the upturned iron wall mounts that once held the hinges.

"His Majesty's soldiers appropriated our gate," Dawson said, "and melted it into horseshoes. You can't find a scrap of metal anywhere in Charleston these days."

I turned and faced him. "Where was my husband found?" I asked. "Exactly."

If Dawson knew Pawsworthy was involved somehow with Émile's death, his guilty knowledge would have prompted him to at least glance at my parents' house. He didn't. He blinked, cocking his head.

"Over there, in front of the Gibbes House," he said.

We walked toward the spot.

"You spent more time with him than anyone else," I said. "Was he ever feeling sick? Did he complain about chest pains?"

He shook his head.

The road was a mosaic of crushed seashells and dirt, and you could see eroding clumps of horse dung everywhere. The idea that Émile lay here alone, huffing this vile dust, smelling horse shit as he died, was infuriating. I disregarded the lessons Uncle George had taught me. To remain calm. To never get emotional.

"Where were you that night?" I asked angrily.

"I . . . Let's see. I started at The Bloody Knuckle. I had a late dinner there. Then I went to The City Tavern. I came back home here, and that's when two soldiers told me the major had collapsed in front of the Gibbes House."

"Pretty convenient," I said, "him dying when you're *supposedly* not around."

"I wasn't here when it happened, if you're insinuating foul play."

"I'm not insinuating anything," I said. "What concerns me is your absence. You were the only person working with him, so why weren't you with him that night? Why *weren't* you here to help with the investigation?"

"The major preferred to work alone."

"Why? Did he suspect you were filing secret reports back to your uncle?"

He scrunched his face, not answering. Heathcliff had been pacing behind me. Now he stood at my side.

"I knew Émile better than anyone," I said. "If he had confidence in you, he would have worked closely with you."

"So what are you so worried about?" he said. "If what you suspect is true, that Major Savatier didn't trust me, I couldn't have worked closely with him. And if I didn't, how could I have anything to report to my uncle—if that's what I was doing?"

He coughed into his fist, a smug expression flowering his cheeks. "And, believe me, *Mrs.* Savatier," he said with a smirk, "you don't know your husband as well as you claim to."

Heathcliff shifted his eyes from Dawson to me.

"What does that mean?" I said.

Dawson shrugged, winking at Heathcliff.

"What do you mean by that?"

"What do you think I mean, *Mrs.* Savatier?"

He affected a chuckle when he pronounced *Mrs.*, haughtily hinting that Émile may have been unfaithful.

Dawson was a drunkard. Drunkards drank because their spiritual cups were empty and unfulfilled. Getting drunk daily was an attempt to achieve spiritual fullness by substituting it with physical pleasure. A spiritually happy person doesn't chase satisfaction *every day*. Threaten the empty man's fake happiness and he will say hurtful things—take his drink away and you'll see firsthand how mean he is. I had forced Dawson to admit he was at a tavern while Émile was dying alone in the street, and Dawson resisted with a smear against Émile—ultimately to hurt me. I'd never believe Émile cheated on me.

Dawson walked away, heading through the open gateway. I wanted the names of the two soldiers who saw Émile collapse. I began to chase after Dawson when Heathcliff bunched my hair in his fist and yanked me back on my heels, hugging me to him.

"Play your role in our scheme, you fucking slag," he said, tightening his fist, drawing the point of my nose high in the air. "We have a deal. You fuck this up for me and I'll bash your brains out and paint that fancy front door up there with your blood, yeah?"

Heathcliff released my hair. I didn't scamper away. I wasn't afraid. I stood with my back still close to his chest, my eyes fixed on Dawson swaggering up my parents' house stairs as if he owned the place. Turning, I faced Heathcliff. I was close enough to feel the heat of his breath on my forehead.

"If you have something to say to me, no matter how nasty it is, simply tell me. Physical pain won't intimidate me. If you ever touch me again, I'll cut your hands off and have George throw you in the Ashley River alive."

He showed no emotion. His dark eyes studied mine. I combed my fingers through my hair, shaking my head to fluff my locks out as best I could without a mirror or brush.

"How's my hair look?" I asked the brute.

"What?"

"My hair. You messed it up. We're going to talk with the guards at the Provost, and I can't show up with the hair of a fucking slag, now can I? How's it look?"

"Spectacular."

"Good." I pointed up the road. "Let's go."

I walked on. Heathcliff stayed back, following. I stopped when I turned onto Meeting Street.

"Come on," I said, waiting for him to catch up. "Let me ask you something. Have you ever had to shit in front of other people? Not behind a bush somewhere. Right out in the open in front of everyone?"

He pondered my question, nodding slowly. "As a small child, yeah."

"How'd it make you feel?"

"Jumpy."

"Well, that's the feeling I get with you walking behind me. So stay at my side, will you?"

A sergeant at the Exchange Building led us down the stairs to the Provost Dungeon. The raw sewer stench intensified with our descent. It was a dimly lit red brick cavern with flickering lanterns on the walls. Even the vaulted ceiling was constructed of red brick, well-crafted archways reminiscent of cathedral basements I'd seen in Paris. The sergeant pointed Private Fowls out to us. He was one of three soldiers seated at a rickety table that wiggled when they slapped playing cards down. I introduced Heathcliff and myself.

"Who are you?" he said, still seated, wrinkling his nose at me.

"Royal Inspector Charlotte Savatier, appointed by Colonel Nesbit Balfour, Commandant of—"

"You're French, ain't you?" His voice almost squeaked in disbelief. He appealed to the sergeant behind me. "What's a bloody French woman doing here? Is she—"

"French Québec," I said. "We've been part of the British Empire for about seventeen years. Private Fowls, I need you to stop asking questions and concentrate on answering mine. The sooner you answer, the sooner you can go back to playing cards."

"Who is this bird?" he said to the sergeant.

The sergeant shrugged and shook his head.

"She represents the Crown," Heathcliff said, reaching inside my satchel. "Here is an Order of Compliance issued by the Commandant of Charleston demanding your submission to her inquiry, sir."

He unfolded the document and showed it to Private Fowls, who stared at the red seal. His eyeballs didn't shift.

He was illiterate.

"Refusing to answer Mrs. Savatier's questions is analogous to telling King George to fuck himself," Heathcliff said, neatly folding the document and handing it to me. "I wouldn't advise that, sir, not if you're happy with the present length of your neck."

"Do what they say, Fowls," the sergeant said curtly, his boots scraping granules of dirt on his slog back up the stairs.

"What do you want?" Private Fowls said.

"You were here the night the two guards came to get Major Montcalm," I said.

"Yes. That dandy hated it down here. But when I told him that guards were going to take him to a private residence for house arrest because he was an officer, he got scared. Suddenly, he loved the place. He wanted to stay." Private Fowls laughed, showing yellow teeth. "He thought the guards were going to hang him. He swore he wasn't a spy. That he was here in Charleston to meet someone he knew before the war. A business partner."

"Business with the enemy?" I said. "That's treason. Did he name this business partner?"

"Yeah. I remember it because it was an odd name. Rag."

"His name was Rag?"

He chuckled, nodding.

"Was Rag in the military?" I asked. "Did he mention a rank?"

"Rag wasn't in no army. He said Rag *live here ten year*. I remember how he said it. He never put an 'S' on *years*. He never put an 'S' on nothing in English. Is that a French thing?"

"Yessss." I practically hissed the word to emphasize my pronunciation of the "S." "Did he have a first name? Or was Rag some nickname?"

Another chuckle.

"Yeah. *Dirty*. I think he said that was his first name. Dirty Rag."

He and his comrades laughed heartily. Heathcliff set his jaw, the muscles along the side of his cheek pulsing under the skin. I could see from his clenched fist that he wanted to smash the private's brains out.

"Private Fowls," Heathcliff said calmly. "Was his last name Rag, or are you playing with us? Before you answer, remember that we report directly to Colonel Balfour and I'll happily mention any help you give us, naming you specifically."

"His last name was Rag," Private Fowls said, suddenly solemn. "I don't remember his first name."

"Your neck is safe for the moment," Heathcliff said.

We turned and walked up the stairs. On Broad Street, I told Heathcliff I was impressed with his self-control. Where I expected him to shake the sarcastic private's head about by the hair, he showed reserve.

"A man named Earnshaw once told me you can catch more flies with honey than vinegar," Heathcliff said.

"He was right. How'd it feel, choosing to be nice to someone who didn't deserve it?"

"I didn't feel anything. It was an act."

We didn't speak on our way back to Gabriel's house. I wanted to ask Gabriel if he knew a man named Rag. Mahala told me he went to a field hospital in the low country. He'd be gone overnight.

The following morning, I went to the State House for my revised Order of Compliance. Colonel Balfour had it waiting for me with soldiers at the front door. I hiked to the Horn Works, the fortress housing the gateway into and out of Charleston, at the other end of town and returned to the Watch House fifteen minutes before my meeting at noon with Pawsworthy. A swarm of soldiers stood in the street, haughty men armed with rifles and loud voices. Their volume lowered as I approached. I stood with my back to them. I was a hen in a den of horny roosters, chicken-scratching the dirt to keep busy.

Nearly a half-hour later, Pawsworthy and Dawson came down Broad Street from the direction of the Exchange Building. They were late.

Pawsworthy was in the lead. I focused on him with a hunter's eye. As he crossed the street, I fantasized about shooting him.

I recalled what Uncle George taught me. When you fire a lead ball or an arrow at a moving target, you're shooting into the future. You anticipate your victim's path and shoot toward a specific space ahead of him. He will run into the projected trajectory of your lead ball or arrow and drop dead.

"Hello," Dawson said.

"Let's make this quick," Pawsworthy told me. "I've got transport ships to meet."

I threw my hands up.

"How's this for quick?" I said, walking across Broad Street toward the State House.

"Where are you going?" Pawsworthy shouted. "What about picking out your precious soldiers?" Pawsworthy pointed at the soldiers beside him—spies, no doubt, preselected by him.

"I already got my soldiers this morning," I said, walking backward. "Captain Merryman at the Horn Works gave me three huge grenadiers from a Scottish regiment. They are the biggest men you've ever seen."

I went into the State House. Rag owned a business, or used to, with Montcalm. A business owner who'd lived in Charleston for ten years had to own a house. That meant he paid taxes. The one thing the British were experts at was taxing people, places, and things. And by things, I mean everything. If you had a closet, they taxed that as another room. They taxed the glass panes in your windows. They probably began assessing taxes in Charleston the same day they took it back from the rebels, even before they started cleaning the streets of the war debris.

None of the local clerks were working today; every bureaucrat was from England, and they couldn't find any land or tax records of a man named Rag. I doubted they knew where to look. I decided to go to the Exchange Building. Everything that came into or left Charleston on a ship went through the tax inspectors at the Exchange Building. Those men had daily interaction with locals. I asked a soldier where I'd find a tax inspector, and he brought me outside to the wharves. He said the assessors sat at small tables along the walkway.

"It's warm and sunny for January," he said. "Too nice to be inside."

The first taxman I approached seemed far more interested in the motion of my breasts than the sounds of my voice. After I showed him my Order of Compliance, he took his eyes off my chest long enough to inform me he had arrived three weeks ago from Liverpool and wasn't familiar with anyone in town. I moved on to the next taxman whose table stood in the shade of a large palmetto tree. This man had a neat row of thick ledgers that stood like books on a bookshelf, an inkwell, and three different-sized quills lined up on his tabletop. And his eyes didn't stray from mine.

"I was wondering whether you could help me?" I said.

"Ah." He smiled. "A French woman. Not too many of you around here these days. Are you a pirate working for the British Crown?"

We both laughed.

"I'm looking for someone," I said.

"You've come to the right place." He waved at the crowds on the docks and ships in the harbor. "We have an abundance of *someones* here today."

"This someone is a businessman named Rag."

"Ah. You must mean the one and only Wragg family. That's *Wragg* with a '*W*,' yes?"

"Yes," I said, guessing.

"Are you having something shipped? You'll need a certificate from the intendant general of—"

"No. I'm looking for a specific Wragg."

"Which Wragg?"

"The one who's been living here for ten years."

"That will be Francis Wragg. He's considered a newcomer. The other Wraggs in the family have been here since the beginning of time."

He placed a finger on the spine of one ledger, tilting it back, and yanked his hand away as if a bee had stung him. He flapped that hand.

"Those damn palmetto fronds." He jerked his head toward a stack of them behind his chair. "I sliced my finger on one this morning. It was rather windy last night, I gather."

He pulled the ledger out with his other hand and opened it flat on his tabletop, slowly turning pages.

"Francis Thomas Wragg, Cabinetmaker, Legare Street." He smiled, looking up from his ledger. "Is that the chap?"

"It is," I said, guessing again.

It was a start, anyway.

"I dare say the war has hurt his business," the taxman said.

"So you know him?"

"I know everyone," he said.

"What's your name?"

Standing, he bowed.

"Byron Bêche."

"*Bêche*," I said. "That's French."

"It means shovel, doesn't it?"

"*Oui*."

"I guess I'm a shovel of sorts. I'm a Royal Tax Assessor. Always digging into people's finances. I'm also an inspector for the superintendent of the port, making me one of the most hated men in Charleston, and you display immense bravery, ma'am, speaking with me for more than two minutes."

We laughed as he sat back down.

"I'd offer you a chair but I don't have them anymore. Angry ship owners or their captains kept throwing them in the harbor."

I pointed to his ledger. "Tell me about Francis Wragg."

"As I said, his business is in a slump. No matter, really. He's quite wealthy. He owns a beautiful house facing the west, and he sits on his third-floor piazza every night sipping from his barrel of rum and watching dreamy sunsets." He tapped the open ledger with his knuckles. "He receives a barrel from Barbados every three months or so."

"I'm jealous," I said. "I live in a house in Québec City made out of ice. We have to uncork our French wine bottles and hang them upside down in front of the fireplace to defrost them, collecting slow drips on our waiting tongues."

He smiled.

"Do you know where he lives on Legare Street?" I said.

"Two houses down from the big white house the British junior officers have taken over," he said. "You can't miss that place. Those chaps are louder than drunken pirates."

"I'm so happy to have met you, Byron."

"I haven't heard anyone say that in years. Certainly not a woman."

"My name's Charlotte Savatier. Colonel Balfour has given me the title of royal inspector. I'm working with the Board of Police to find the murderer of Major Henrique Baptiste de Montcalm. May I call upon you, *Mr. Shovel*, if my inquiries need any more dirt dug up?"

He looked down, closed the ledger, and stood. "I am at your service, *madame*."

"And I yours, *monsieur*," I said.

I entered the compound at Gabriel's house through the gate on Price's Alley. Mahala was in the kitchen house, chopping carrots. It was a small two-story brick building between the main house and Gabriel's hospital. A central chimney with back-to-back fireplaces separated the first floor into two rooms, the larger kitchen on the right and the smaller laundry room on the left with a washtub. Stairs in the kitchen led to the second floor. I told her I needed something to nibble on, and she pointed her knife at an open clay pot of strawberry jam on the table and said to toast some bread.

She told me Gabriel had rented a house for George and Heathcliff on Archdale Street, and they moved out about a half-hour ago. I walked to Archdale Street and, after inquiring at five houses, found their new home. Heathcliff said Uncle George was at the Horn Works, so Heathcliff and I went to Francis Wragg's house. Heathcliff banged the knocker on the piazza door. Half a minute later, he pounded a little harder. The door was locked, so I walked alongside the piazza, backed up a few steps, and sprinted high enough to wrap an arm over the railing. I pulled myself onto the piazza and opened the door for Heathcliff, but he was gone. When I turned around, the door to the house creaked open. Heathcliff stood on the threshold.

"The back door isn't locked," he said.

I called out Wragg's name as we passed by finely crafted tables, plush sofas, cushioned chairs, canopy beds on the second floor, high-boy dressers, and glossy wooden chests. The rooms were clean and clear of clutter. They were also clear of people. We didn't find anyone in the house until we reached the small bedroom on the third floor.

A naked man was bound upside down in a cushioned armchair next to the fireplace. I stepped close to him. His chest wasn't heaving. He was dead.

This had to be Francis Wragg.

His legs were bent at the knees, hanging over the top of the chair so that his feet faced the wall. A wide strap was wound across his thighs and around the chair, holding his legs in place. His back was where his behind should have been, his head hanging down where his knees should have gone. A strip of cloth was wrapped several times around his head to keep his mouth shut. A white glove, a right-handed one, rested on his genitals. His eyes were open.

I unwound the cloth binding his mouth. His swollen lips resembled two gorged earthworms. I separated them and saw a brown plant stem on his tongue.

"This is exactly how Major Montcalm was found," I told Heathcliff. "In this type of chair. The same position. Look at all the tiny needles in his skin."

Heathcliff wasn't interested. "I've got better things to do than stare at a naked corpse."

"You can leave any time."

He left.

I knelt. Little needles bestubbled the man's flesh, mostly on his face. His skin was ashen gray, flecked with irritated patches of pink and red, and black and blue bruises from a beating. I raised the glove. The same needles riddled his penis. I peeled back the foreskin, and the mushroom cap bristled with them. They also covered the bottoms of his feet.

A stack of finely threaded, luxurious white handkerchiefs was in the top drawer of a bureau across from the bed. A pair of scissors lay in a jewelry box. Standing at the fireplace, I rubbed the edges of the scissor blades on a brick, dulling them. I carefully tugged needles from his face using the dull scissors as tweezers. I removed about one hundred, laying them on the handkerchief I had positioned on a small table beside the chair. Using the scissors, I pulled the stem out of his mouth. It had the same needles sprouting from it. Maybe I could identify the spiny stem later with Émile's botany book. I placed it in the same handkerchief.

A small pile of ash was on the rug by the foot of the chair. I looked at the fireplace behind me. Someone had emptied a bed warmer on the brick hearth. That little mound of ash had a few thick sticks that hadn't completely burned. The curious sticks had tiny hairs (roots possibly) growing off them. Ash was spilled across the table, too. When I folded the handkerchief to place it in my satchel, enough ash soiled the luxurious white fabric that you'd have classified it as a dirty rag.

# CHAPTER FIVE

# This End of Eternity

When I came through the back door of Gabriel's house, Mahala stepped out of the sitting room, a quaint space for cards or fireside tea and conversation on a settee and cushioned chairs.

"My pork belly soured," she told me. "So I'm heading out to borrow some."

"Borrow?" I said.

"Well, trade." She raised a clay butter pot, and a skunk stench rode the breeze her hand generated.

"Your butter smells sour, too," I said.

"It's cannabis," she said. "Similar to hemp. You smoke this, and it calms your mind. I think of it as a warm bath for your thoughts. It makes you hungry, too. You should try it. You could put some meat on those bones of yours."

"Why don't you just go to the Beef Market?"

"Don't ever go there." Her advice came with a shake of her head. "Go to the Lower Market on Tradd Street. It's better. Get to know the black women vendors. They have connections to plantations and can get you anything—well, not now they can't. The markets closed hours ago."

She explained how the markets opened at sunrise and had to shut down by 11 A.M. She said if vendors at the markets operated outside those hours or sold to someone without a permit, they risked losing their license to sell, and all their goods would be confiscated. She said Colonel Balfour forced everyone to get a permit from the Board of Police to buy anything, too. The military had tight control over all the markets in town. They didn't want goods falling into rebel hands. She said I needed to get a permit.

I went to my bedroom and read through Émile's journal, looking for Pawsworthy's name. He wasn't mentioned. Maybe Émile had no need to mention Pawsworthy because Pawsworthy didn't have an active role in the investigation, and since Émile reported to him in person, why mention him?

I wanted to ask Gabriel why he didn't tell me Émile worked with Pawsworthy. That wasn't a minor oversight. I found him on the sofa in the front parlor, scribbling a list. He glanced up, saying hello. I was about to sit in one of the cushioned chairs when I recognized the wall mirror at the foot of the stairs. That mirror used to hang in my parents' bedroom. It had a wide twisted iron frame made by that German blacksmith friend of my father's. I couldn't believe I hadn't seen it before.

"How'd you get this?" I spoke French; French kept the presence of Émile close.

"Get what?"

"My parents' mirror." I stepped closer to my reflection.

"From Pawsworthy," he said.

"*Pawsworthy*?" My face flushed in the mirror. "Why would you even talk to him?"

He got up and stood beside me. "Don't get upset." He looked into the mirror at me. "I had Mahala handle the transaction. Pawsworthy knew your mother and father looked at themselves in this mirror every day, so he kept it. It gave him a certain smugness seeing himself in it. I hear he collects petty things that used to belong to his victims."

"Victims?"

"Your parents weren't the only ones. He schemes and plots and cheats people out of their homes and businesses. So many people owe him debts. Recently, he's become superstitious. This mirror began to frighten him."

"How do you know this?" I squinted, strengthening my focus. "You two are on such intimate terms that he confides in you?"

"One of his slaves, Hannah, told Mahala." He ignored my sarcasm. "Hannah eavesdropped on Pawsworthy when he was talking with his pastor. They belong to a church that believes in predestination, where God chooses who goes to heaven and who goes to hell *before* you are born. And it seems his pastor has the holy insight to foresee where someone will end up in the afterlife." Gabriel rolled his eyes, chuckling. "Years ago, he told Pawsworthy that he was predestined to go to heaven."

"So no consequences for acting immorally in this world?" I glanced at Gabriel's image in the mirror, pivoting to face the real version. "You're saying that's why he does whatever he wants to people. He knows he's going to heaven regardless."

He nodded. "Hannah overheard him tell the pastor that he thought he saw an Indian woman's reflection in the mirror when he was shaving. He said it could only be one person, Dr. Jacque La Pierre's wife. He told the pastor that the mirror used to belong to her. The pastor told him evil spirits could come back from the dead—from hell. It seems the pastor controls his flock by spooking them. Anyway, Hannah hates Pawsworthy, so she began to torment him. She waited a week before telling him she had seen an Indian woman's face appear in the mirror while cleaning it. Hannah said Pawsworthy told her he had seen the Indian woman, too, that he knew her when she was alive, and he told Hannah to toss the mirror out. That clever woman told Pawsworthy that if he destroyed the mirror, he would trap the evil Indian's ghost on this side of it, freeing her to haunt him forever—even follow him into heaven."

"So how'd you end up with it?"

"That bastard had Hannah move it to the outhouse, where it was utterly useless." Gabriel shook his head. "Ask yourself: Who looks in the mirror while they're in the outhouse?"

"That's disgusting. Putting their mirror in there."

"That's why I paid Hannah to steal it." He straightened the frame. "I had Mahala pay her. Hannah waited till Pawsworthy threw one of his rum parties and told him afterward that one of his guests stole the mirror and that he had better pray that it never breaks, wherever it is. She told him if it ever broke, he'd start to experience bad things."

Gabriel laughed.

When he said *bad things,* I got a bad feeling. I realized why: I remembered Émile was dead. *I had somehow forgotten.* Sudden tears blurred my vision, and I, too, saw my mother in the mirror. Not my actual mother or her ghost: I saw her in my cheekbones, in the shape of my full lips, in my dark eyes, the identical eyebrows, my jawline, my proud chin. I wiped my eyes with the back of my forefinger, with that bold knuckle there at the base.

"The last time I looked in this mirror was the morning I went to their hanging," I told Gabriel, sniffling. "Uncle George was late getting here from Québec City. I wanted to make sure I looked pretty. I knew I'd be the last thing they'd ever see, and I wanted them to be proud. That's what you do, right, when you go see your parents die—look respectful? I said goodbye to myself the way I planned to say it to them in this mirror and walked out the door for the last time."

I heard a creak, and we darted our eyes around the room. The creak sounded again, wood cinching against the tight grip of a nail. Was that the noise a ghost made prying itself from mirror glass—the birth cries of transitioning from a supernatural world to a natural one?

No. It wasn't. It was the sound Winslow made slowly treading the stairs. He carried an iron pot with both hands clasping the bail handle. It brimmed with ash from the upstairs fireplaces.

"Watch out," he said, stepping off the stairs, "this is as hot as the sun."

He shuffled into the hall, shifting weight from one foot to the other as if he were nine months pregnant. Gabriel stepped into the hall, saying he had work to do. I walked with him across the compound to his hospital, a one-room-wide, three-story structure. The open room on the first floor had about a dozen beds, all occupied by soldiers. They didn't suffer from battle wounds alone. The ones I could see by the door also had smallpox, their skin riddled with little bumps.

We climbed to the third floor, where Gabriel sat in a high chair at a tall table long enough to fit a human body. He lifted a towel spread over the marble top, revealing a severed human forearm. It was a man's arm, hairy-side down, with large pustules dotting the flesh. A tray held scalpels and strips of linen cloth. Rust-colored splotches stiffened the fabric, apparently dried blood. I pointed my chin at the severed forearm.

"What are you doing?"

"Trying to collect blood from the pustules for inoculation."

"From a dead arm?"

"It was alive an hour ago."

Splicing an abscess with the blade of his scalpel, Gabriel soaked up black ooze with the strip of cloth. He stood and faced the tall cabinet with glass doors. Several surgically severed forearms lined the shelves with their underbellies facing up. He took another forearm out. It was older: Dry, shriveled skin; gray, stiff fingers with fingernails the color of frosted glass. He said he had treated the forearms with something that prevented maggots from burrowing into the flesh. He pointed his scalpel at a few black pustules.

"I used this one to inoculate myself," he said.

"You put that nasty pus in your body?"

He shook his head, saying the arm was far fresher at the time. He stood and walked across the open room to his office. I eagerly followed. He faced a tall bureau with fifty small drawers, all numbered. Each had a U-shaped brass pull handle with a number painted onto the drawer front. I pulled a drawer open that was level with my chin. Drawer number thirteen.

"What's in these?" I asked.

"The lower-numbered drawers where you're standing go back several years. They contain elements I rarely use these days. Crystals, spices, ground bones. The drawers with the higher numbers contain useful elements. Copper and iron wires, magnets, salts, glass tubing, needles."

He pulled open Drawer Forty-eight and took out a few long needles, telling me how he was designing a medical device that used rods and magnets to clamp blood vessels to stop the flow of blood while he sutured battle wounds. We walked back to the marble table.

"Alright, Gabriel," I said as he sat. "Why didn't you tell me Émile was working directly with Pawsworthy? Better yet, why didn't Émile tell me that himself?"

Gabriel put his needles down. "I asked him not to."

"Why?"

"Pawsworthy read his letters," he said. "I didn't mean for him to keep a secret from you. But the less Pawsworthy knew, the better."

"He read Émile's letters?" I felt queasy. "The personal ones I wrote to him, too?"

"You can bet on it. He'd want to know everything Émile did." Gabriel sneezed into his elbow. "Before Émile left Québec City, I sent him a letter through John Peele, not the mail service here. I asked Émile not to tell you I had written him. I asked him not to mention I was related to you in his letters to Colonel Balfour or Lord Cornwallis. I said it was fine to mention he would be living with me and to tell them we met in France years ago. I insisted he not tell anyone that he was married to my niece. Everyone thinks I'm French, that I'm DuBois, and I want to keep it that way. He kept his word. He didn't tell you?"

I shook my head.

I didn't tell Gabriel that I had asked Émile not to tell anyone Gabriel was my uncle—my secret was justified, though. Uncle George and I were planning on destroying Pawsworthy.

"Émile never even mentioned Pawsworthy in his journal," I said. "He kept it here in his bedroom. That's awfully odd, especially considering how rude and confrontational Pawsworthy is."

"I don't know anything about his journal," Gabriel said. "But I warned him not to mention Pawsworthy in his letters or his notes. He could argue those were official documents and use them against him— get Sergeant Dawson to corroborate some concocted story. Pawsworthy has a unique skill of corrupting anything anyone says or does or writes and uses it against them. Of course, Émile didn't like him to begin with because of what he did to your parents."

"What about your friends Mahala and Winslow?" I said. "Have you confided in them? Do they know we're related?"

"Of course not. They think you're my friend's wife."

"Did you tell them Uncle George is your brother?"

He paused, studying me, realizing my reputation as someone who never stopped talking meant I also asked endless questions.

"They think he's your bodyguard. And they think Heathcliff is his boorish lover boy." He looked at me and shrugged. "Speaking of those two, I found them a two-story shack on Archdale Street. It's a cute little place."

"I heard."

"I even paid a year's rent in advance." He laughed. "George is difficult to get along with. He's unpredictable. If I say the wrong thing, I might end up with one ear. As for your friend, Heathcliff, he should be sleeping with the Gypsy Lady's horses."

"The Gypsy Lady?"

"It was her carriage that picked you up at the Exchange."

"So one guy's not stable, and the other belongs in a stable," I said in English. He turned a forearm over and rubbed a large black pustule with the padding of his thumb. Switching back to French, I finally said, "The Board of Police gave me Émile's position of royal inspector."

He stopped what he was doing and stared, nodding. "That's an extraordinary honor, Crow." I explained how Pawsworthy cornered me alone afterward, how he threatened to frame Gabriel. I shook my head, still taken aback by Pawsworthy's arrogance. Gabriel went back to prodding the pustule.

"You're not worried about Pawsworthy setting you up?" I asked.

"My life is in your hands, Crow." He grinned his bony grimace. "There's no one I trust more."

I kept silent—until I realized he had complimented me to shut me up. So I immediately began telling him how I feared Pawsworthy had recognized me.

"If Pawsworthy knew you were Gail's daughter," he said, "you'd never have made it back here. His ruffians would have already thrown a blanket over your head and dragged you onto one of his transport ships. And you'd never be seen again."

"Why do I get the feeling you get along with Pawsworthy?" I said.

He paused. "He's on the Board of Police."

"So?"

"I'd rather avoid a conflict, so I'm civil with him."

"How can you mention his name and the word *civil* in the same sentence? That's like spreading shit over cinnamon toast and eating it."

"He's always looking for ways to weasel people out of their property," Gabriel said. "He'll even break the law to do it—as you learned firsthand. Several years ago, Pawsworthy told me I didn't look French. I said my mother was from French Catalonia, and she descended from the Moors. He hadn't a clue what a Moor was." He slid an elbow onto the table, leaning on it. "After the British took over Charleston, he kissed all the right asses. He's got monopolies on certain products my hospital needs, such as candles and soaps. The war causes shortages of everything, obviously." He sat back and widened his hands. "Look. The British are seizing rebel-owned houses and plantations across South Carolina. I'm friends with the ones who've had their property taken away—Thomas Heyward, the Pinckneys, the Rutledges, Dr. Radcliff. They're imprisoned in St. Augustine. Anyone associated with them can be investigated. Pawsworthy works closely with those in charge of these property appropriations. I don't want him seizing mine."

I couldn't blame Gabriel for not wanting to swap his house and profession for a prison colony—or worse, a prison ship. He wiped the corner of his mouth with the back of his finger and examined it.

"So tell me," I said, "if Pawsworthy has no idea you're Gail La Pierre's brother, and you get along so *civilly*, what's the bad blood between you two?"

"We've no bad blood."

"Then why would he target you—frame you as the murderer out of all the scoundrels in Charleston?"

"He's not targeting me. He's targeting you. He knows you live in my house. He's making it personal, using me to upset you. He upsets you, then sets you up for something. That's how he operates." Gabriel picked up a long needle, piercing one of the black boils on the underbelly of the severed arm. "So whatever you do—for both our sakes—don't let him get under your skin, Charlotte."

He stood, placing the severed arms inside the glass cabinet. He scrubbed the tabletop with a brush in a small bucket of soapy water, wiping the table with a dry rag. On the floor beside the glass cabinet stood a wide, tall clay pot. It was Wacataw pottery with its tell-tale black and brownish-gray finish. Two black snakes climbed along the outside, their thick bodies arching off the pot beneath the lip of the opening to create two loops that acted as handles. I peered inside. Slick bullfrogs with gold-colored eyeballs were jostling for position, rudely climbing over each other with long toes.

"You catch these yourself?" I asked. "They're usually sleeping underwater this time of the year."

"Winslow got them," he said.

He reached into the pot for a frog and laid it on its back on the table, placing a rag over its head. He squinted and pierced its heart with a long needle. When it stopped kicking, he placed the body on a cedar shingle and dug the scalpel's blade into the frog's abdomen, separating the hip and legs from the torso. Gabriel wrapped the legs in a small linen towel, discarding the torso in a bin.

"Where's Émile buried?" I asked.

"The military cemeteries are in the low country," he said, grabbing another frog and covering its head with the rag. "But I insisted that Émile be buried at Saint Philip's. I pleaded with the clergy. I told them you were arriving any day. That being surprised by your husband's passing was bad enough. Making you travel into the dangerous countryside to mourn at his grave wouldn't be fair."

"In the graveyard or the cemetery?" I used the English nouns.

He picked the long needle up. "There's a difference?"

"A graveyard is on the same grounds as the church. A cemetery stands on its own."

"The cemetery, then," Gabriel said, piercing the frog's heart. "Across the street."

"How about my parents? Where are they buried?"

Gabriel's fingers relaxed in tandem with the dying frog's legs, and he lowered the needle. I already knew that Gabriel had told his mother— my grandmother, Jane Harris—that he arrived in Charleston a week after my mother and father were hanged. Uncle George said Gabriel lied. He said Gabriel was in town and never attempted to comfort or defend their sister. Gabriel thought if the elite class of Charleston knew he was the criminal Gail La Pierre's Wacataw Indian brother, his medical career would have ended before it began.

"I never found out where they're buried." He moved a rag in circles over the polished marble tabletop, absorbing frog blood. "Or if they even got a burial, Crow. I couldn't bring myself to ask. I was so afraid I'd be ostracized by the town." He preferred to observe my clasped hands instead of my face. "I've been working hard ever since to make things right. No one's wrestled with their conscience in this family more than me."

Liar or not, I could see he was still troubled by my mother's death a decade later. I came around the table and hugged him, holding his bony head close, which shuddered when he sniffled.

"There's one person to blame for all our misery, Gabriel," I said, stepping back.

"Stay away from Pawsworthy, Crow. He's more powerful than ever."

"We'll see about that," I said. I pulled the linen handkerchief soiled with ash from my satchel and unfolded it on his table. I told Gabriel how Wragg and Montcalm were tortured.

"You should see what these things do to the skin," I said.

He reached for the handkerchief and I seized his wrist.

"I know better than to touch anything," he said. "I was moving the cloth to get a better view."

"Did Émile ever discuss his investigation with you?"

"He'd occasionally ask me about people here in Charleston. Tavern owners. Warehouse owners. Dockworkers. Where someone lived."

"Were you friends with Francis Wragg?"

"Never met him. I knew he was a cabinetmaker."

I pointed to the handkerchief. "Do you think they're from a cactus?"

"I'm not aware of cactus needles causing any horrific skin irritation. Outside the initial pain of the puncture wound, that is." He tapped his forefinger on the tabletop. "You could ask Dr. Garden. You remember him, don't you? He was great friends with your father."

"I do. I also remember his children, Harriette and Alex. We used to play together. Since the Gardens are still in Charleston, that means they're loyalists, which means they're acquainted with Pawsworthy. Which means—"

"Which means they might recognize you."

"Exactly."

Gabriel scratched his bony chin. "There's a botanist up north on the Santee River. Thomas Walter. He might be able to identify this plant."

"Is he a loyalist or a rebel? I don't want to go to his estate with redcoat soldiers and get shot."

"Living between Cornwallis's army in Camden and the British garrison at Charleston, I'm sure he claims he's a loyalist. The rebels captured his wife's brother after the Battle of Black Mingo. Honestly, though, you never know which side someone's on these days."

I folded the handkerchief and returned it to my satchel. I glanced inside the big crock. The frogs were slapping the walls of their dark prison and, seeing me, ribbited loudly. The world they once knew was out of reach. They could only stare at my face with gold eyes, the circle of light behind my head appearing as a false halo.

I told Gabriel I needed fresh air and left.

~~~

I strolled to St. Philip's Church, to the cemetery. Gabriel had erected a tall slate gravestone for Émile with a carved angel face crowning the top, wings flowing down both margins. *Major Émile Gaston Savatier* was chiseled into the stone, his birth date and the date he passed below. There was ample room beneath his script, a blank slate, that descended into the disturbed dirt. Was that space for me, for carving my name and my dates? I didn't need that much room. Summing up my existence would take the undertaker's cold chisel less than two inches of inscription.

At first, I thought I would have cried visiting his graveside, seeing his name. I didn't. I *knew* he was dead, yet I felt, absurdly, that he was off with his regiment somewhere, and he'd be back home soon. Pretending that felt good. I wanted to hug him again. I wanted him to hug me. To love me.

I had brought a blanket and wrapped myself in it, sitting on the recently turned patch of yellowy-brown dirt. Émile arrived in Charleston on October 3. He came here without me. When he determined Charleston was safe from rebel attack, he sent for me. After he left Québec City, I had this image of him with his black hair and blue eyes looking up at me, smiling.

I had that perspective of him because that was how we interacted. I thought on my feet, pacing, while he thought sitting at a desk—looking up at me. He was genuinely interested in what I had to say; he listened out of respect. We were still facing each other in that manner, me looking down, him looking up—only now, a dark barrier permanently separated us. I'd *never* see him again.

That, finally, was what made me cry. And that's when it happened.

I lost my sight.

I went blind.

I didn't panic. I knew to close my eyes and lie down. I pulled the blanket over my head.

I started suffering bouts of blindness right after I lost my parents. After my parents were arrested, they were held in the city jail for a month. I had no other family in Charleston, so Dr. John Radcliff, a close friend of my father's, took me in temporarily while we waited for Uncle George to arrive from Québec City to pick me up and take me back. He was serving with the British Army there. My mother had written Uncle George right after the arrest.

On the day of their execution, April 11, 1771, the entire town, it seemed, had gathered at Gibbes Wharf to watch. Dr. Radcliff refused to go. He told me that Donald Pawsworthy was the most awful man on earth, that he set my parents up. Pawsworthy had asked my father to treat six of his slaves who had a fever. After a week under my father and mother's care, Pawsworthy arrived at my parents' house with town constables and accused my parents of stealing his slaves. The slaves, who were either paid or threatened by Pawsworthy to lie, said my parents were hiding them with the promise of passage to a runaway camp in a Georgia swamp. It turned out that they were acting. They weren't sick.

Dr. Radcliff said my father could have prohibited the slaves' testimony since slaves couldn't legally testify against a white landowner, but my father and mother were abolitionists. Pawsworthy knew my parents wouldn't object to their testimony. They testified that my parents had been helping slaves escape for years. The court found my parents guilty and condemned them to death.

Dr. Radcliff lived on Broad Street, in the city's center, and I watched from a second-floor window as crowds made their way down King Street to get to the gallows on Gibbes Wharf. I snuck out and ran home. Our house was diagonally across the street from Gibbes Wharf. Pawsworthy hadn't "bought" the property yet. No one was in the house.

After changing into my fanciest dress, I squeezed through the mob and stood close to the gallows. My mother and father were each flanked

by two big men who ushered them forward into the nooses. My parents'
heads were cloaked with black hoods, so they couldn't see me. I had gotten dressed up for nothing. Their clothes were filthy and wrinkled. My
mother had always been clean and orderly.

I looked up at the adults spewing spittle, yelling, their fists pumping.
I closed my eyes. A cheer rose from the mob. I opened my eyes to see my
parents dangling from their respective ropes. Their arms were tied behind
their backs, but their ankles weren't bound. My father stoically hung
still. My mother fought. She kicked and swayed, and the awful people
laughed. She found her mark and wrapped her legs around my father's
waist. Blinded by their hoods, their love thrived in darkness. It's what
connected them. It's all they had left.

The terrible people mocked my mother, saying she was a typical sav-
age trying to save herself. That wasn't what she was doing. I could see
the back of her head bulging through the hood as she leaned with all her
strength. Absurd as it was, she struggled to lift my father's body so he
could breathe and live. And it worked. I saw it work. For a little while,
anyway. Her body went limp first and fell away, swinging, and that's
when my father started kicking, trying to grope for her in the darkness
with his feet. But he ran out of air, and his legs drooped.

Gradually, the mob's evil joy ran out of life, too, and people stopped
jumping and hollering. Someone grabbed my upper arms and jerked me
so hard into the air that my top molars smashed against my lower ones,
and my ears started ringing.

It was Uncle George.

He didn't say a word. He cradled me in his strong arms and stomped
through the crowd. He usually dressed the same as a colonist. Not today.
He had come to town as a Wacataw warrior. He wore deerskin pants, but
he was shirtless. He had painted his torso, face, and throat blood red with
a black circle around one eye, a white one around the other. The shaved
side of his head was painted red, too, and his long black hair fluttered
with his eagle feather. He even polished his silver nose ring. I could see
the head of one of his snake tattoos on his shoulder. Uncle George had
two black snake tattoos. They started in the small of his back, winding
in opposite directions up his shoulder blades, their heads resting on the

balls of his shoulders. The one I saw wiggled its tongue at the crowd as his arm flexed. Uncle George towered over the people around him, his jaw set as he plowed through the mob, knocking anyone—man, woman, or child—aside.

Uncle George told me we were stopping at Dr. Radcliff's house to let him know he had found me. The world slowly darkened as we pounded through the streets. By the time we got to Dr. Radcliff's, I couldn't see. I didn't tell Uncle George. Not yet. I wasn't sure what was happening. Uncle George set me down. I heard him knock on the door. I was dizzy, so I sat on the ground. I started bawling, slapping the air, trying to find something to hold.

"I can't see!" I screamed.

Uncle George rushed me inside, where Dr. Radcliff examined me. He had me look at the ceiling, and I felt a breeze on my face as he waved something in front of my eyes. The heat of a candle flame warmed my cheeks. He said my pupils responded to the light, but I assured him I couldn't see. I felt that breeze again as something fanned my face. I didn't blink.

In the end, he was as baffled as Uncle George and me. They set a small bed up by the hearth in his front parlor. I eventually fell asleep. When I woke, I could see. Uncle George whisked me out of town.

We spent the rest of that month in my Wacataw village near the North Carolina border. I suffered a few more bouts of blindness, each randomly occurring. Uncle George thought emotions caused my blindness. He hated emotions, as contradictory as that sounds. My loss of sight was proof that emotions clogged your thinking, he said. My grandmother, Jane Harris, said my blindness was God visiting me while I was awake. In Wacataw, God is called He Who Never Dies.

"God speaks to us in dreams," she said. "Darkness is the paper He Who Never Dies writes on and dreams are His words. So if He Who Never Dies was going to talk with you when you were awake, He'd blind you. It makes perfect sense. Consider yourself lucky."

I didn't share Grandmother's optimism. By her reasoning, if He Who Never Dies wanted to talk to me when I was awake, He should have shown me images since those were His words. He never showed me anything other than a darkness darker than the blackest places on Earth.

Something went wrong inside me the day my parents died. A door opened somewhere, a door that's supposed to be shut when you're awake. It was open now, and I had walked through it and down into the valley of sleep. Or maybe God's holy darkness seeped out that open door and coiled itself around my eyesight.

But why?

I didn't understand.

Eventually, I learned to cope with my blindness. I had no choice. After all, you can't untwist yourself from God. I discovered my sight always returned after I slept; sometimes, a nap would suffice, and other times, I had to sleep through the night. As I grew into adulthood, the bouts persisted. Then I met Émile. I never had a bout of blindness in the last four years. With Émile gone, the darkness had come back.

I curled up at the foot of Émile's gravestone, cloaked in the blanket. I thought about the stoneworker chiseling my name below my husband's, about the little flecks of marble that would sail into the dirt. If you collected them in your palm, you'd be holding the full weight of my existence; if you put the flecks back, little piece by little piece, all evidence of my existence would disappear.

Was that what was happening inside me on the other side of my eyes? Were fragments being put back piece by piece? Bricks in a wall that ultimately blocked the outside light? Is that what He Who Never Dies was up to in here?

I fell asleep thinking that.

Sometime later, I awoke. It was dark and cold. I could see. Candlelight glowed in houses whose curtains weren't yet drawn. When I returned to Gabriel's house, I grabbed the round mirror on the vanity in my bedroom and brought it downstairs to the front parlor. Wall lanterns and candelabras lit up the room, and logs burned in the fireplace. I stood before my parents' mirror. Holding the round one in front of my face, below my eyes, I pointed it at the larger one, and it opened a circular corridor of mirrors that tunneled into eternity, a tunnel of identical reflections becoming smaller and smaller, darker and darker. That's where Émile was, somewhere along that snaking corridor, lost and alone and heading the wrong way for the distant tiny other end, that black dot.

I wanted him close to me. If I kept a candle burning at night on this side of the mirror, if, by day, I corralled the sunlight inside this room by opening the door and pulling the black curtains back as far to the sides of the windows as possible, would that turn him around? Would the light lure him back to this end of eternity, where I was?

Would his smiling face appear in the glass someday, close enough to kiss and remind me what he looked like?

# CHAPTER SIX

## *The Lover's Jolt*

At breakfast, Gabriel announced he would cheer me up with a dinner party. He had designed a feast that would take Mahala and him until tomorrow to execute. I didn't know he was a chef, too. John Peele apologized for missing the festivity. He had to leave town on a mission for Gabriel. Mahala said Gabriel's complex menu required a larger dining room table, so I heard Winslow hammering across the hall all day. Mahala warned that we were forbidden to peek inside the kitchen house or the dining room.

They served dinner the following evening. Two teenage boys with wiry red hair, a cellist and a pianist, played next to the blazing fireplace. Gabriel stood at the head of his new table, asking us to sit. However, no one wanted to.

"Please," Gabriel said in English, spreading his hands over the feast. "They won't bite."

I was the first to sit since the party was in my honor. The others followed, chair feet humming across the area carpet. It was apparent that the chef was also a doctor. Gabriel had taken parts from different animals and re-assembled them to create a winged creature. Even our plates were odd: They weren't the customary ceramic or pewter round platters but rectangular wooden planks. Gabriel used his dinner knife as a pointer.

"These are frog legs," he said. "The torso is a duck breast braised in duck fat and fresh sage. Its nipples are soft-boiled clove buds. To the left and right of the torso are thin slices of cured ham from Virginia, splayed out in a fan pattern to give the impression of feathered wings. I've run thin arm bones from the breast to the wingtips to lend the wings a degree of realism. As you can see from the cute little black hands, those are raccoon bones. The creature's head is Mahala's pork sausage, which I sculpted into tiny skulls before baking them. Their wigs are dried dandelion flowers."

"They look like those flying things in Greek mythology," I said. "They had the body of a lion, an eagle's head and wings. What were they called?"

"Griffins," Uncle George said. "Them call griffins."

"How would a blabbering baboon like you know that?" Heathcliff said, one eyebrow raised.

I'm sure Uncle George read about griffins in Shakespeare or one of the ancient playwrights.

"Exactly," I said, nodding to Gabriel. "A griffin. A tortured baby griffin."

"Tortured?" Gabriel said, holding a hand flat to his chest. "How dreadful. My intention was to create a whimsical meal."

"Whatever it is," Winslow said. "It smells delicious."

"What's this?" Heathcliff pointed to a small bowl north of his plate; everyone had one.

"Ah," Mahala said, who sat at the other end of the long table opposite Gabriel. "I made that. It's almond cream. You thicken almond milk by heating it. My father showed me that trick. It's how he made molasses for his rum recipe. He'd slow-boil sugar cane juice. I added the shavings of a tangerine rind. You dip the duck in it."

"Gabriel," I said, "dining on frog legs is nothing new. However, we usually cook ours. These legs are raw."

He raised a bony forefinger.

"Not for long, my dear."

He pointed at two dark wooden boxes on either side of the table, each supported by four tall piano legs. Heathcliff sat opposite me. Between Winslow and him stood one of the boxes; the other box was between Uncle George and me on this side of the table. Wires ran from the boxes to the underside of the tabletop.

"Those boxes contain Leyden jars," Gabriel said. "Has anyone heard of a Leyden jar?"

No one had.

"Leyden jars contain electricity," Gabriel said. "Everyone is familiar with electricity, I hope?"

"Yas," Uncle George said. "Before they make love on rug, man and woman kiss for several minute. Then she get on hand and knee with man in back. When he touch woman he get sparked. That *electrickity*."

Everyone laughed at his butchery of the word.

"That's called *static electrickity*," Gabriel said, and his ghoulish smile widened his face. "This." He pointed to the box next to Heathcliff. "This is a thousand times stronger than that lover's jolt."

On the corner of the table between Gabriel and Heathcliff were six brass levers nailed in place. The top of each lever had corkwood attached to it.

"Watch closely, Mr. Heathcliff," Gabriel said.

He pinched one of the corked ends and lowered that lever so that it slid snugly between the prongs of an iron clip, also nailed to the table. That instant, a white spark flashed and the frog legs on Heathcliff's wooden plate rose, kicking violently. Heathcliff jumped back. He glared at Gabriel, his upper lip snarled in horror.

Gabriel raised the lever out of the clip, stopping the flow of electricity. The frog legs went limp and slapped the plate delicately. I glanced at Mahala, who was a co-conspirator in this bizarre menu. She struggled to restrain her smirk and failed. The ginger-haired cellist stopped playing, throwing the pianist off. The boys stared at the floor, snickering, their faces flushing. Gabriel waited for them to resume their duet.

Each frog's hip was pinned to the wooden board, leaving the legs free to kick about. Our plates were nailed in place. I peeked under the table and saw wires running to each plate. Heathcliff slid forward. He lowered his face to inspect the legs, and Gabriel lowered the lever again. A brilliant spark flashed and the frog legs sprang to life, their feet raised high and spread widely, trembling as if in sexual ecstasy inches from Heathcliff's plush, wet lips.

"The legs will stop moving when they are cooked," Gabriel told Heathcliff.

"Monster!" Heathcliff shouted.

He pounded the frog legs with the bottom of his fist. The impact rocked the table, and a long white tongue of almond cream leaped out of Heathcliff's bowl and licked the air. It splashed across his meal, igniting more sparks. We rocked in our chairs, laughing. The musicians stopped playing again and cackled with laughter, too. We watched Heathcliff shake. His hand was stuck to the plate, somehow. Gabriel lifted the lever, and Heathcliff yanked his hand back.

"I meant to warn you not to touch the plate while the lever is engaged," Gabriel said. "If it makes you any happier, that's a relatively mild shock compared to a lightning bolt."

"You call that mild?" Heathcliff stared madly at Gabriel, flapping his hand to rid it of its misery.

Gabriel lowered the levers one by one, connecting each with its corresponding clip, and the frog legs around the table rose in concert, spreading and shaking. The long toes on my frog legs slowly curled and closed into an uneven fist. The legs smoked and turned brown as they stiffened. Gabriel raised the levers. He pointed to the glasses with tall stems, each half-filled with red wine.

"I discovered this wine in France," Gabriel said. "In the tiny town of Saint-Émilion." He raised his glass. "*Bon appétit.*"

Uncle George was the first to dig in. He cut into the duck breast, dipped a forked morsel into the almond tangerine cream, and moaned with delight. He sipped the wine, nodding his head.

"Crow," Gabriel said in French, "does your English friend here know we're related?"

"No."

"Good." Gabriel chewed a slab of ham and pointed his fork at his brother. "I got something to show you, George." He spoke in English. "It's been a while since we've seen each other."

Uncle George nodded without speaking.

My father practiced medicine in Philadelphia before moving to Charleston. He had married my mother there, who was eighteen or nineteen. He took fifteen-year-old Gabriel into his home as a son. Gabriel studied medicine first with my father and later with Benjamin Franklin, who introduced him to the French physician Jean-Paul DuBois.

During the French and Indian War, Uncle George and Gabriel joined opposite sides. Uncle George was a British guide and warrior in the northern colonies, including Québec; Gabriel sided with the French. He and Dr. DuBois joined the French Army as surgeons. In 1760, three years before France lost the war, Gabriel and Dr. Dubois left for France so Gabriel could enroll at the Academy in Montpellier. In 1771, with a physician's degree in hand, Gabriel moved to Charleston, reemerging as Dr. Gabriel DuBois. Gabriel and Uncle George didn't speak for fourteen years.

"You remember Benjamin West, the painter?" Gabriel asked Uncle George. "Back in Pennsylvania?"

Uncle George munched on a slice of ham, perhaps remembering. I believe he was studying Gabriel, no doubt wondering why he was taking him on a journey into the past.

"Yas," Uncle George finally said in English.

Gabriel dug his fingers into a balled-up napkin before reaching into a leather bag on the floor beside his chair. He handed me two bundles of heavy paper. I unfolded them. They were large sheets with similar drawings—several sketches of the same scene—of military officers gathered around another officer who had fallen from an injury. In the foreground was an Indian on one knee, looking heartfeltly at the injured officer. The drawings were well done.

I handed them to Uncle George.

"Benjamin has become quite a celebrity in London, painting portraits." Gabriel nodded at the drawings. "He's King George's favorite, I hear. Ben sent me those more than eight years ago. He told me in his letter that he needed an Indian for his painting, so he drew you, George. He used sketches of you from the Pennsylvania days." He switched to French. "That's you in the foreground. He included your face tattoos. Look closer, George. He painted the Wacataw black snakes."

Uncle George's eyes widened as he beheld himself. I got up and hugged him, then I kissed his cheek.

"He made you look handsome," I said, seizing the opportunity to tease Uncle George. "Oh, the magic of art!"

"Those are sketches of the actual painting that's hanging in some parlor in London," Gabriel said in English. "The painting's much bigger, of course. He calls it *The Death of General Wolfe*. It was a favorite at the Royal Academy."

"I was at that battle," Uncle George said in French. "On the Plains of Abraham, but I wasn't near Wolfe when he died. I never even met him."

Realistically, the snakes in the drawing weren't as detailed and girthy as the tattoos on Uncle George's back and shoulders. He said getting those tattoos was the most painful experience of his life, that he'd rather get scalped than go through that again. Wacataw elders gifted black snake tattoos to warriors. They were a badge of honor.

The drawings seemed to dissolve any tension between my uncles.

"Keep those, George," Gabriel said. "Ben wanted you to have them." He held up one frog leg and nibbled off a morsel. "Back in Philadelphia, I used to watch Jean-Paul DuBois and Ben Franklin electrocute things—even each other. Once, Jean-Paul brought a chicken back to life by electrocuting it with Leyden jars. He smothered it to death first. He immediately jolted the creature with electricity and then put its beak in his mouth. He breathed into it several times, electrocuted it again, then breathed into it until, *voilà*, the bird came back to life. It jumped up and began flying around the room, desperate to get out of there."

"He brought a dead chicken back to life?" Heathcliff said. "You're lying."

"I saw him perform the fête several times," Gabriel said. "I've done it myself."

"I'd love to see that," Heathcliff said. "You giving a chicken the lover's jolt."

Gabriel's ghoulish grin tightened his thin, sickly skin to his skull. "Maybe you will one day."

Winslow raised his wine glass and said, "Here's to *electrickity*."

They laughed and drank.

I didn't. I was having trouble eating. We were dining on this imaginary bird as part of a whimsical dinner meant to cheer me up over the loss of Émile—whom I always called *mon ange*, my angel. I knew my thinking was irrational, but putting a creature with artificial wings inside my body made me feel guilty, as if I was trying to *replace* Émile, my angel, with something fake.

Dessert was a chocolate soufflé, a new French creation, a recipe from Gabriel's close friend, Antoine Beauvilliers, a young chef in Paris. Émile loved chocolate. A surge of sadness rose from my chest with the power of electricity, flooding my eyes with tears: *Émile would never get to taste a chocolate soufflé!*

I pushed the back of my spoon mournfully through my soufflé cup. Gabriel saw my tears.

"It can't taste that bad, does it, Crow?" he said.

## CHAPTER SEVEN

## *Curtain Call*

After saying good night to Uncle George and Heathcliff on the first-floor piazza, I went to my bedroom. My door was open. I was surprised to find Gabriel there. He stood at my desk with his back to me. My notes on the murders, in French, were on the desktop. I didn't care if he read them, but he could've asked first. I approached him quietly to scare him with a tickle when, startled, he spun around. We collided, and the bouquet of dried flowers he held crushed against me.

"I'm so sorry," he said, stepping back. "I thought I'd brighten the room with a bouquet."

"Of dead flowers?" I laughed.

"At this time of the year, I arrange dried flowers throughout the house," Gabriel said. "They are all from our gardens."

"It's very thoughtful," I said, although I didn't understand how that morose assortment could brighten anyone's world.

Well, maybe Heathcliff's.

The stiff, brittle blossoms trembled as he arranged them in a white and blue vase on my desk. He knelt and picked up several rust-colored rose petals and some tiny white florets of baby's breath. He left.

I opened a bottle of wine from Beaune, France—my father's hometown. Sitting at the desk, I opened the drawer and took out Émile's drawings. A few sketches were of my face. Most were of me naked: A view of me from behind, standing; one of me sitting with one knee up close to my breast, my sensitive areas tastefully inked with the darkest shade.

Others had me looking down at him, the inclusion of my breasts and the point of view suggesting I was straddling him. I went through the drawings repeatedly, finishing the glass of wine.

I took my clothes off and brought the drawings to my bed, where I placed the rectangular pages one by one on the blanket, creating a paper quilt. The pattern reminded me of snakeskin scales. Émile had slept in this very bed, between these very bedsheets, and rested his head on this same pillow. My paper quilt of his sketches was the closest I would ever get to having Émile's hands on my body. I slid between the sheets, noticing my forearm had a thin cut from the rose stems.

At some point, I began dreaming of Émile. We were in my village, swimming in the Catawba River. We were alone. He walked out of the water and sat back on the clay embankment. I followed, sitting naked on his wet chest. He smiled up at me and scooted between my legs. I felt his warm mouth there, but he vanished and a breeze chilled my wet skin. Suddenly, I was standing by the river with the flat of my hand pressed against the side of my pregnant belly. I was pregnant with Émile. He was being reborn through me, and when I gave birth, he was a toddler with an adult head full of black hair, but I couldn't see his face. He started running. We were inside a house—my parents' house in Charleston. I was in their bedroom, and he stomped up and down the stairs. I noticed he no longer had a head. I shouted for him to be quiet, but he couldn't hear me without a head, so his ruckus got louder.

I woke up sweating and hugging a clutch of his papers. I heard crows cawing on the piazza. I got up and drew aside the curtains. The sky was beginning to glow with that same ugly gray color of those lifeless forearms in Gabriel's hospital. Two big crows spotted me in the window. They pumped their wings, flying away and screaming at the dead sky.

Slipping a cape over my nightgown, I headed down Tradd Street to the Ashley River. The tide was high and I walked into the cold water and bathed. On my way back to Gabriel's house, I saw smoke coming from the chimney of the kitchen house. No one was in the kitchen, so I hung my cape and soaking gown over the backs of chairs and stepped closer to the fireplace to dry off. Someone was in the room above me. Footfalls on the wooden stairs prompted me to cover my front with my cape. It was Mahala carrying a bundle of herbs.

She didn't appear put off having a naked woman in her kitchen. Without speaking, she opened the cabinet door behind her and tossed me two folded linen towels. I dried off and put my cape on.

A large black iron box stood on the table, a type I'd never seen. Thin trails of smoke rose from tiny vent holes on the sides. Before I could ask, she told me she smoked meat in the contraption. She said she placed an iron pot of hot coals inside over which she laid moist chunks of applewood or cherrywood. The rising smoke both flavored and slowly cooked the meat hanging inside. But this smoke didn't have the musk of burning wood. It reminded me of a skunk. The oven box shook on its own, shifting slightly over the tabletop.

"Whatever's in there is still alive," I told her. "Is it a skunk?"

"It's a raccoon," Mahala said, laughing quietly.

"That's cruel."

"On the contrary. I'm not cooking it. I'm putting it to sleep before taking its life." She raised her hand, showing me what I thought were herbs. "I put a few buds from a female cannabis plant on the coals inside the box, along with some special mushrooms, all to soothe the creature." She pointed to a blue and white clay bowl. "I added some of these lemon thyme leaves stems to the mix. They're soaking in opium water." She pointed to a large butcher knife beside the bowl. "Gabriel gave me a thermometer, and I'll warm my knife blade in hot water to the same temperature of the raccoon's body, which he said was around 100 degrees, and I'll cut its throat with that so he doesn't feel death coming. I don't want to hurt him. Or frighten him. When the time comes, his mind will be high up in the clouds anyway—from the cannabis and opium and mushrooms."

The cannabis is what stunk of skunk. She said she got seeds to grow it from Portuguese sailors. I fanned my nostrils and faced the fireplace, wringing out my drenched gown with knuckled fists, the droplets hissing when they hit the hot hearthstone.

"Why wouldn't you talk to me when we got off the ship?" I asked her.

"Gabriel told me not to. He said you talked a lot. That you'd ask me endless questions about Émile. Gabriel didn't want you learning about your husband's passing from a stranger."

I smiled. "Did he say I talked *a lot* or *too much?*"

Mahala laughed and raised a hinged door on the roof of the iron box. She offered the raccoon a sprig of opium-laced thyme, and he gripped it by the stem with his tiny black hand. Mahala shut the door.

"Why didn't Gabriel meet me in person?" I asked. "Because of how sick he looked? Or was he too weak?"

She studied me for a moment. "Why don't you ask him yourself?"

"How you answer will tell me what makes you loyal to Gabriel: The money he pays you or your friendship."

"For a moment, I thought we might be friends," she said.

"We can be."

"You remind me of my knife blade, warming up to me before you stick it in, yeah?"

"I'm being honest with you."

She frowned, nodding slightly.

"Gabriel's trying to stay out of the public arena so he doesn't risk spreading the pox he's trying to inoculate himself against."

She pinched a thyme sprig and, without tapping the stem on the bowl's rim, slipped the wet leafy end between her lips, sucking on it. She pinched another and offered it to me.

"No, thank you."

"Any more questions?"

"Yes," I said. "You want some help preparing this meal?"

"You ever slit a raccoon's throat?"

"Not a living one," I said. "We usually chase them up a tree first and shoot them. But I've been cooking and hunting since I was three years old. I've skinned or slit the throats of dead chickens, swans, geese, ducks, pigeons, possums, snakes, frogs, hogs, buffalo, wolves, goats, sheep, deer, moose, elk, bears, turtles, seals, dolphins, alligators, and fish of every denomination, including sharks. I've bitten off the heads of crickets, a salamander, a nosy mouse, and a snapping turtle—the turtle was on a dare. I've also stabbed an insane horse to death and a rapist named Zechariah Barker."

"Oh, heavens," she said. "You do talk a lot. Can you peel a simple onion?" She picked one from a wooden bowl on the table and rolled it toward me.

"I doubt it," I said, stopping its wobble with an open hand; for fun, I rolled the onion back and added, "We eat onions with the skins on up north."

She grinned and bowled it toward me again. "Well, Frenchie, down south we don't. You'll find a knife on the hutch shelf behind you."

~~~

Mahala wanted to bleed the raccoon and marinate the meat for a day before braising it, so I had dinner with Uncle George and Heathcliff at their house. Afterward, we walked through the city. The sun was setting, but it wasn't quite twilight. Soldiers were dismantling an iron fence separating an upscale home from Meeting Street; others took the wheels off a wagon in the street in front of the gate to strip the iron rims. The homeowner, an older man who informed the soldiers he was a loyalist, pleaded with them to spare his property. A lieutenant stepped up and politely explained the British Army needed the man's metal for hobnails and horseshoes. The lieutenant sat the frustrated owner on a carriage stone and explained how iron, steel, and pewter were scarce because of the war. As the lieutenant spoke, a soldier knelt at the feet of the unlucky loyalist and cut the steel buckles from his fancy shoes.

I walked away immediately. I didn't want that soldier slashing the silver buckles off my shoes. Heathcliff and Uncle George followed. I told them how I used to play in Price's Alley at night with other kids. We raced down the dirt road barefoot, dodging bats and jumping over mounds of horse dung. Unlike the streets, Price's Alley didn't have lamp posts, so the darkness made the piles challenging to see. When one of us stepped on a turd, she'd scream—especially if it was fresh. Those ones oozed warmly between your toes.

Drunkards came out as night fell, mostly soldiers traveling in larger packs, staggering and singing. As we came down Ellery Street, several soldiers had formed a line off the road to piss. They were arching their streams of urine, competing to see who could reach the creek—a boyish game I didn't need to behold. We were crossing Governor's Bridge heading along East Bay Street when a lone drunken soldier muttered something.

We ignored him, but he began to walk backward, trying to keep up with us.

"You lot think you're better'n me, do ya?" he asked, tripping. His voice chirped when he landed on his ass.

We stopped, and Uncle George picked him up.

"Cheers, mate," the soldier said. He steadied himself, focusing on Heathcliff. "Why ain't a strapping lad like you in the army?"

Heathcliff ignored him, looking down the length of the bridge. The soldier staggered forward and put his arm around Heathcliff's shoulder.

"You can enlist in my regiment," he said. "Come to the Horn Works and ask for me. Sergeant Linton."

Heathcliff shrugged him off so violently the man stumbled. It took a few seconds before he realized he'd been rebuffed. Rage flushed his face, but before he could act, Heathcliff shoved him. Uncle George stepped up, grabbing the soldier's arm to steady him.

"He drunk," Uncle George told Heathcliff. "That like hitting baby-child."

Other soldiers were crossing the bridge, coming toward us. I pulled Heathcliff by the elbow, and we started walking away while Uncle George convinced the drunkard to do the same.

"I didn't want him touching me," Heathcliff said. "But what upset me most was his name."

"You were offended by his name?" I said. "That's why you shoved him?"

"I hate the name Linton," Heathcliff said.

"You almost push him off bridge," George said, coming up behind us.

"Damn that fool."

"You've got to control yourself," I told Heathcliff. "Look. At first, I thought you were a shallow brat who hated mama and papa because they didn't give you an easy life. But the more I watch you, the more I realize you probably never had parents. Not ones that loved you, anyway. George called you an unlicked puppy—"

"I no think that anymore," Uncle George said. "I think girl break Heapcliff's tender heart and make him into crying sad little boy."

Heathcliff inhaled deeply to invigorate some nasty response. I cut him off.

"I don't care what makes you tick." I threw both hands out at him. "I only care about our deal. You want money. That we can get you, but we all have to work together. You've got to stop being yourself when you're in public. You can't lash out at whatever displeases you, which is apparently everything. What if I acted that way? What if I pulled your hair or shoved you whenever I disliked something you said?"

"You'd be a lot happier," he said. "Lower your expectations, and nothing will frustrate you."

"So I should attack Pawsworthy since I hate him? We'd never get his money."

"I should branch off on my own." Heathcliff slowed, increasing the distance between us as we walked. "Head to Virginia."

Uncle George stopped walking. Then I did.

"You made a bargain with Charlotte," Uncle George told Heathcliff. "Your word means nothing?"

"How do I know *your* word means anything?" he said. "Either of yours?"

"I've proven myself by not exposing you as an imposter on *The Naga*," I said. "That was actually my uncle's doing. He saw potential in you." I jerked my head toward Uncle George.

Heathcliff blinked. "Uncle?" Surprise raised the pitch of his voice. "This arse is your uncle?"

"I'm entrusting our secret with you," I said. "To convince you we're sincere."

Uncle George stepped close to Heathcliff. "How do you plan on running away?" Uncle George flipped his long hair over his left shoulder. "I doubt you're going to sneak aboard a ship after your recent experience at sea, so you'll travel by land. The guards will question you if you try leaving through the city gate. I've been with the British Army for twenty-five years. I can come and go as I please. You can't. You can't prove who you are. Even if you sneak by the garrison and float up the Cooper at night, there's a civil war raging out there. You'd eventually run into a militia. I hear the rebels sit enemies on a fence rail, naked, tying you in place, and parade you around on their shoulders till your cock and balls wear off. Then they dip you in hot tar and feathers and hang you. If you run into a loyalist militia, and they hear that pretty accent of yours, they'll shoot you as a deserter. The Brits have promised slaves freedom, so runaway slaves are attacking farmhouses and plantations. Think you can take on that angry mob? If you head into the wilderness, the bears or the wolves will get you. If they don't, you'll starve to death in these forests. But if you make it far enough north, the Cheraw will find you. They'll invite you into their houses for a meal, but once they learn how cynical and mean you are at such a young age, they'll break your legs and leave you in a swamp. If you go west, the Cherokee will get you. You don't want that, believe me. If you go south, you'll run into the Yamasee. The Yamasee hate the British. They'll skin you alive and use your hide for a water pouch. Your skin's a wee darker than the other Brits, but it's still see-through when it dries. They'll be able to see how full the pouch is when they take it with them to shit. You'll be perfect for cleaning up after."

I felt my cheeks balloon as I held back laughter.

"Hang on a second," Heathcliff said to Uncle George, fury roasting his face the color of his hot tongue. "How is it that you suddenly speak perfect English?"

I snorted under the pressure of abrupt laughter, and Heathcliff glared at me, wise to my sneaky role in the conspiracy.

"Your baby talk has been a play-act all along?" Heathcliff asked Uncle George.

Having heard the word "play," Uncle George lifted his eyebrows excitedly. I sensed a quote was coming, something from a playwright— Molière, or possibly the Grand Master Shakespeare himself.

"*All the world's a stage*, you dolt," Uncle George said, curtsying a bow as if answering a curtain call, "*and all the men and women merely players.*"

# CHAPTER EIGHT

## Smells Like Satan

I met with my three Scotsmen and discussed our trip north to visit the botanist Thomas Walter. I asked them to hire a local scout who knew the safest route to the Santee River. I didn't tell Uncle George of my travel plans. He'd talk me out of it.

The day before the Scotsmen and I departed, I brought Heathcliff much of Émile's wardrobe. Heathcliff was taller than Émile, so I adjusted the hem of his trousers; otherwise, Émile's clothes outfitted the ruffian with an air of sophistication. I sat him at his dinner table and snipped his hair. I told him I needed my assistant to dress spiffily. He stood, pulling the red silk vest down and standing straight as a soldier, chin out as I instructed.

"Look how cute you are," I said. "No one will ever suspect what a raging ass you are on the inside."

I pinched his cheek and he tried to swat my hand but my recoil was too fast. The breeze his swipe created fluffed my bangs, and I knew that had he struck my wrist, he would have broken it. He was in a foul mood. Far more foul than usual. He staggered to an armchair by the fireplace and collapsed in it. No fire burned. He leaned back with an elbow on the chair's armrest, which was odd. He was the uptight type who sat stiffly on the edge of a chair, alert, ready to stomp on the first shadow that moved.

Was he getting comfortable in my company?

He appeared pale and tired. He rolled his sleeves up, and his skin was sweaty. His face, too. He wasn't sweating a moment ago. And it was chilly in this room.

"Are you alright?" I asked.

"Don't be concerned with me."

I looked closer. Tiny bumps pimpled his arms, including a thin cut with a rash surrounding it.

"What's that?" I grabbed his wrist and pointed to the cut. "What is this?"

"I got that at Gabriel's house." He tugged his sweaty arm out of my grip. "The second night there. The ghoul was putting a bouquet of ugly dead flowers on the table by my bed in the hospital. I went to grab the flowers to stomp on them when we ran into each other and I got cut by rose thorns."

"Rose thorns?"

I looked at my arm where Gabriel had also run into me. My cut didn't have an accompanying rash, though.

"That bastard," I said.

"Who?"

"Gabriel."

"Why? What'd he do?"

"He's infected us. Well, not infected. He's inoculated us."

I told him those rose thorns were tainted with smallpox pus. I explained how my father would inoculate someone by taking a thread laced with pus from a sick person and packing that thread into a healthy person's open cut.

"When you take pus from an infected person," I said, "from someone who's rebounding from the sickness, when it's in its weakest phase, and introduce it to a healthy person's body, the healthy body fights it and makes you immune. But it isn't foolproof. Some people still die during inoculation."

Gabriel knew I'd never agree to be inoculated. I wouldn't allow myself to be sick for however many days it took to recover. I needed to travel north—I needed to find Montcalm's murderer or Pawsworthy would come after Gabriel.

Did Gabriel have that much faith in me?

Or did he have some underlying scheme, a counter-move against Pawsworthy, so he wasn't worried about me finding the killer quickly?

All I could see in my mind were those pale gray forearms in Gabriel's glass cabinet with big black pustules. Is that what he put in us? Did he lace the tips of the rose thorns with that gooey pus?

Nasty!

I suggested Heathcliff recuperate at Gabriel's hospital. He suggested I get out of his house, so I did. Mahala was in the kitchen house, smoking that skunk-smelling cannabis from a white clay pipe. She said Gabriel should be back before dark, or sooner, that he had gone to aid injured German troops outside the city gates.

I spent the afternoon in my room rereading Émile's notes and reviewing a botany book, hoping to find the needle plant so I didn't have to go north. I read witness descriptions of Major Montcalm's body. They might as well have been describing Wragg's corpse.

I heard a commotion outside. A bang—the wooden gate door slamming. A man shouting—Heathcliff.

I peered out my window. Heathcliff stumbled toward the hospital but stopped when Mahala yelled through the open kitchen house door, telling him Gabriel wasn't here. Heathcliff sat on the kitchen house steps, looking grumpier than ever. Mahala appeared on the threshold behind him, pulling her white clay pipe from her mouth so she could blow out a cloud.

"You're the grouchiest man I've ever met," she told Heathcliff. "But I got a remedy for you." She lowered her hand. "Here, boy. Suck on my white pipe."

I expected him to tell her to do the same, but he showed remarkable reserve—merely turning to look up over his shoulder at her.

"It'll relax you," she said.

"Why the hell would I want to relax?"

She laughed, taking another draw on the pipe. A moment later, Heathcliff spoke up. "Will it relax my stomach?"

"No. It relaxes the soul."

"I could smoke that pipe all day and it would have no effect," Heathcliff said. "Because my soul's in someone else's body."

Mahala bent down and blew a great cloud at the back of Heathcliff's head. The smoke curled around his cheeks and met at the front of his face in an all-enveloping billow. He gagged and furiously fanned his nostrils with an open hand.

"That smells like Satan's fart," he said, standing and facing her. "How can you suck that into your mouth, you foul witch?"

He slapped an open palm to his abdomen and trotted toward the outhouse. I returned to my chair, listening to the merriment of Mahala's impassioned laughter. I went back to my books. However, that's when Gabriel arrived: Heathcliff screamed for him to get the fuck out of the carriage, threatening to bash his skull on the outhouse's stone step and shake his brains out into the shit bucket.

I ran outside.

The Gypsy Lady's carriage was parked in Price's Alley. She and Gabriel were bringing injured German soldiers into the compound. Heathcliff stood in their way. The Gypsy Lady shouted at Heathcliff in her foreign tongue, pulling a pistol from her waist. To my astonishment, Heathcliff shouted back in her language. Whatever he said made the Gypsy Lady laugh. He continued to yell furiously in her gypsy tongue, pointing to the rash on his forearm. She lowered her pistol, talking to him calmly. Waving her off, Heathcliff staggered toward Gabriel.

"Heathcliff," I said, coming up behind him. "You can settle your differences with Gabriel afterward. You're going to need his help to get through this inoculation stage."

"Differences?" he said. "I puked my spleen out back there. You call that a *difference?* I call it attempted murder."

"*Au contraire,*" Gabriel told Heathcliff. "I'm trying to save your life." Gabriel turned to me. "How are you feeling?"

"Perfectly fine so far, you rotten sneak," I said.

"I feel like shite," Heathcliff said, crouching to rest his palms on his knees.

Gabriel asked the Gypsy Lady and Mahala to bring the injured soldiers into the hospital.

"You need to come with me," Gabriel said quietly to Heathcliff, stepping around him.

Heathcliff wouldn't let anyone touch him. We followed Gabriel into the hospital and climbed to the third floor, where Heathcliff stopped to catch his breath, his palms against the door jambs. Gabriel had three beds lined up. Uncle George was lying in one, asleep.

"George agreed to be inoculated days ago," Gabriel said quietly. "Especially after I took him for a ride through the garrison on the other side of the Horn Works. Many British and German soldiers, including their women, and the runaway slaves in their camps, have either the pox or some fever."

"He didn't tell me he got inoculated," I said.

"He didn't want you to worry," he said.

"My father inoculated George and me with cowpox. That doesn't protect us?"

"That was over a decade ago."

"My muscles feel like that gypsy's carriage ran over me," Heathcliff said.

"How is it that you speak her language?" I asked him.

"I gather I spoke it as a child. I understood it the moment I heard it."

"I thought you were from England," I said.

He snickered. "Actually," he said, "I'm a prince in disguise."

Heathcliff stumbled, his knee buckling, and Gabriel and I reached for him. Seizing his elbows, we ushered him toward the bed next to Uncle George, but he shook us off and laid down on his own.

"Mr. Heathcliff," Gabriel said, "you're going to get very sick—sicker than George and Charlotte. The cowpox inoculation they got years ago might lessen their present infection. But you're undoubtedly going to get the full brunt." He pointed to the window. "I'll leave the windows open. The air is cold at night, but it's fresh and that's good for your health. Don't worry, we'll keep the fire going."

"Why didn't you ask for my permission?" Heathcliff said, tendons in his neck protruding as he sat up on his elbows. "Before you poisoned me?"

"Would you have consented?"

"Never," Heathcliff said weakly.

Uncle George groaned in his sleep. Heathcliff laid back and fell quiet. Gabriel and I sat in chairs by the fireplace. For the next twenty minutes, the two sick men performed a morbid concert of snoring, wheezing, and moaning. Gabriel said my inoculation may not have taken hold with one poke from rose thorns. He suggested he pack an infected thread in my cut, which he wanted to slice wider. I declined with as little grace as possible.

Heathcliff shouted something in that gypsy language, and Gabriel and I sprinted to his bedside, standing between his bed and Uncle

George's. Heathcliff's face was wet with sweat and his eyes were squeezed shut. From his intonation, he seemed to be arguing with someone in a dream. He got loud and woke up Uncle George.

"What'd he come from?" Uncle George said, yawning.

Heathcliff was speaking in that foreign tongue.

"I wonder what he's saying," Gabriel said.

"It izz da devil," a female voice said behind us.

The Gypsy Lady stood in the doorway. She came toward us, her boots kicking the hemline of her black gown. The fabric had to be dense with grime to collapse so fast. That's why she wore black—to hide how filthy her clothes were. Mahala had told me the gypsy transported injured soldiers to and from Gabriel's hospital, often picking soldiers up off battlefields or wherever a skirmish broke out. She handed Gabriel a piece of paper. A demand for payment, perhaps, for her body count.

"Who's the devil?" I asked her, jerking my thumb at Heathcliff. "Him?"

Heathcliff continued to clamor.

"Da devil izz talk-ink through him."

Her accent was thick. She placed the flats of her hands on the bedding and brought her head close to his. Heathcliff erupted with a spew of guttural words and spittle.

"He say Cathy got thrown out of heaven." She pointed her skinny finger at me. "You Cathy?"

I shook my head. "Charlotte."

She closed her eyes, listening to Heathcliff grumble between gasps. "You know 'dis Cathy?" she asked Gabriel and Uncle George, shifting her gaze between them.

They shook their heads. The Gypsy Lady and Gabriel stepped away and strolled toward the stairs, her ankles kicking her heavy dress. Heathcliff's body relaxed, and a tear leaked from his closed eye, a singular drop that snaked into his bushy hair.

"*What a hell of witchcraft lies in the small orb of one particular tear,*" Uncle George said.

If that quote meant Heathcliff was a deeply disturbed young man, I agreed. My knowledge of Shakespeare was limited, but it was more than what I knew of Milton or Pope; however, I knew Milton wrote about paradise, about losing paradise. Such poetry had to include hell, witches, and weeping.

"I know this one," I whispered so the Gypsy Lady wouldn't hear me. "I'll wear that hag's nasty black dress for a month if I'm wrong."

He chuckled.

"It's Milton, isn't it?"

He shook his fat head. "Shakespeare."

"*Merde*," I said.

I sat on the bed by Uncle George's feet. He kicked at me, saying he had to get up.

"Where are you going?"

"To rip that dress off the Gypsy Lady," he said. "I can't wait to see you in it."

I pushed his feet back onto the bed and took the handkerchief from my satchel to show him the needles and the stem.

"The tread-softly plant has those little needles," Uncle George said.

"I've stepped on those barefooted," I said. "I've picked their flowers, too. They're nothing compared to what these things do to you. This plant is the connection between these murders and Pawsworthy."

"Pawsworthy?" Gabriel said, standing next to us now.

The Gypsy Lady had left soundlessly.

"He's involved," I said. "I haven't figured out how yet. But that's why he insists I solve Montcalm's murder immediately—so I don't investigate him. I don't believe King George is in a rush to tell the French who murdered their major—not when they're at war."

Heathcliff gagged and wheezed, still asleep.

"And now there are two murders to solve," I said. "How can I rush that?"

"You can't," Gabriel said.

Three murders, when I included Émile.

"But if I don't, he'll blame you, Gabriel."

I decided to tell Uncle George about riding north with the three Scots. "I have to leave right away. For Gabriel's sake."

"You can't go without me," Uncle George said. "It's too dangerous, Crow."

"You're too sick to go," I said. "Besides, I have the Scotsmen. Big ones. I'll be safe."

"Four of you against a rebel militia?" Uncle George said.

"*If* we even run into one. I can't worry about that assumed event. We're riding fifty measly miles north. Through loyalist territory."

"You're going right through Goose Creek," Uncle George said. "That's where the Swamp Fox is, the rebel Marion. He's terrorizing British regiments. I've spoken with soldiers at the Horn Works, Crow." Uncle George wiped his wet face with a damp rag. "Rebel militias are raping and murdering loyalist farmers, then burning their farms. And loyalists turn around and do the same to rebel farmers. No one's safe in South Carolina. You and three soldiers can't stand up to a militia. But I know that country. I grew up traveling secret routes—from here to Pennsylvania."

"Well," I said. "I've been talking to people at the Horn Works, too. Captain Merryman told me those particular Scots I selected were skilled fighters. But more importantly, they're Scotsmen who have sworn to fight for an English king. Their Scottish honor is at stake, making them beyond trustworthy."

"And you believe that?"

"Is it not your Wacataw warrior pride that earns you the respect of the British, too?"

He fell silent. I needed to say something Uncle George would appreciate.

"And they're strong, Uncle George. The captain said he uses those Scots as carpenters because they don't need any tools. They can push nails in with their thumbs."

Uncle George knew I made that up, and he choked on phlegm laughing.

His gagging reminded me of Heathcliff choking on Mahala's satanic pipe smoke. That made me think of Émile lying in the street huffing powdery dried horse shit and dirt, dying alone in the dark, and I was suddenly so angry I could feel my face turning the color of blood.

# CHAPTER NINE

## Pardon My French

Gabriel had displayed sneaky characteristics by poisoning Heathcliff and me with smallpox. I had to be sure I wasn't wasting time visiting Thomas Walter, so at sunrise, I snuck up to Gabriel's office and searched his wall of drawers for the suicide plant. I found nothing.

I walked to the Horn Works and met my Scottish soldiers and their local guide, a small bearded man named Norman, for the trip to Thomas Walter's house. The Scots were all privates: Ewan McKie, Ronnie Carnegie, and Douglas Ferguson.

The last time I had ridden a horse was in October, so after a few miles, my thighs ached from stretching. But the longer I rode, the more my muscles acclimated. We reached the plantations in the Goose Creek area with no sign of the infamous Swamp Fox. After another hour, we stopped at a farm to water and feed the horses. Children, both boys and girls, were building a wooden post-and-rail fence in a field beside the main house where a woman stood in the yellowy clay dirt that was her front yard. No men were in sight. She didn't return Ewan McKie's greeting but pointed her chin at a small barn, saying some hay was in there for our horses.

"You British took all my sheep," she said. "So we got nothing for you to eat other than sweet potatoes, but you got to pay. Otherwise, you're welcome to eat the hay, too."

"We brought provisions," Ewan said.

"There's a creek yonder," she said. "But I'd take those fancy red coats off before you kneel and start slurping. Those coats seem to magically attract lead balls from the woods." She nodded to me. "Or you can send her. They won't shoot a woman."

I walked the horses to the creek and, true to her word, no one shot me. We didn't stop again until we were fifteen miles north of Moncks Corner. Norman brought us to a small tavern where we stayed the night. We ate a thick pork stew, and they had several crocks of ale. I didn't. Drinking ale with men you didn't know was a bad idea. I slept in a small bedroom while the men slumbered in a barn.

We rose before sunrise. The owner, a hefty man, was stacking split firewood from a sprawled pile on the floor beside the fireplace. Norman was talking with him, and he stepped away as I approached. Prior to our departure, I had gotten money from the military attaché at the State House. I paid the tavern owner for the lodging. We rode another three hours or so north until we reached the Santee River, where Norman stopped at a few farmhouses before learning where Thomas Walter lived.

The botanist was alarmed to encounter redcoats and a woman with a French accent at his door. Anxiety brought wrinkles to his forehead, and when I produced my Order of Compliance, he turned as red as the wax seal, distraught, it seemed, at the sight of Colonel Balfour's signature.

"We are not here to arrest anyone," I told him. "I want your help identifying a certain plant I've come across."

I watched his tense cheeks relax. His distress was an admission that he was at least a rebel sympathizer, if not an outright militiaman. His face changed to its previous tallow-white color, and he invited us inside.

The Scots declined the invitation, saying they needed to care for the horses. Norman wanted to join us, but I told him to assist the other men, adding that my royal investigation required a level of discretion that excluded him. I wasted no time explaining the effects of the needles on human skin to Thomas Walter, sparing the details of the murders, and warned him not to touch them. Unfortunately, the esteemed botanist couldn't identify the needles. Using tweezers, he removed a dozen of them, placing the collection in a glass tube. I folded the handkerchief and returned it to my satchel.

"I'll ask my colleagues about this plant," he said. "But it may take weeks. I have to write them. It's dangerous to travel right now."

I told him to write to me at Dr. Gabriel DuBois on King Street in Charleston. We had ridden all this way for a ten-minute conversation that yielded nothing. We rode faster on the return trip. By noon, we reached the farmhouse where we had stopped the day before. The children had finished the fence and were playing on it. The house door opened, and the woman called everyone inside. She slammed the door loud enough that it echoed across the open field.

When Private Ferguson drooped forward and fell off his horse, hammering the top of his skull into the road, I realized that that wasn't the door slamming but the boom of a rifle. We dismounted, and Ronnie Carnegie and Ewan McKie grabbed their rifles and powder horns from their saddles. We ran to the house, finding the door locked. Lead balls splintered the clapboards, shattering a windowpane, too. Neither man panicked. Ewan McKie coolly nodded to the barn and we followed. He ran fast for a large man.

As Ronnie opened the wide barn door, he and Ewan were met with lead balls from the dozen rebel militiamen waiting for us. The smoke from the rifles was so thick I couldn't see anyone. The billows rolled by, and I saw the two Scots sprawled on the ground, their limbs awkwardly twisted the way only death can mangle a body—utterly indifferent to how hideous and humiliating a corpse lay. The rebels deliberately hadn't aimed for me. They had known who comprised our party. I turned, looking for Norman. He wasn't flailing on the ground or lying dead; he wasn't running across the field to escape. He calmly walked into the house, the hostess nodding and smiling nervously as she closed the door behind him.

Norman was a rebel.

All but two of the militiamen walked past me, not one of them acknowledging my existence. A skinny one with long blond hair began pointing and issuing orders I couldn't hear. My ears were ringing from the rifles. I was gagging on the lingering stink of gunpowder when two militiamen grabbed me by the elbows and pulled me into the barn. One of them shut the door.

They looked the same age, thirty or so. The shorter one demanded I hand over my satchel. I lifted the strap over my head, giving it to him. He opened it.

"You work for Balfour?" he asked, looking up from my Order of Compliance.

"I am his special appointee investigating the murder of a French prisoner of war, Major Henrique Baptiste de Montcalm."

I thickened my accent to convince these belligerents that I was French.

"You're French?" one man said.

My plan was working.

"I thought the French were on our side," the other said meanly. "You're a traitor."

"I am a British subject from Québec City," I said. "We speak French there. I am not a citizen of France. I am not a traitor."

I was their enemy and a woman. I was doomed.

There was no talking my way out of this; I had to concede, with great agitation, that talking—my trademark characteristic—wouldn't help me. One man stayed in front of me while the other moved behind me.

"We'll hand this over to Marion," the man holding my Order of Compliance said. He folded the paper and stuffed it into the satchel before tossing it on the dirt floor.

"What about her?" the other man said, his voice close to my ear, his hand moving up the outside of my dress.

"If the French lady cooperates," the man in front of me said, "we'll let her go."

If I fought back, they'd beat me up, possibly knock me unconscious or break some bones and do whatever they wanted anyway. I was defenseless, and any noise of a scuffle could lure the other men in here.

And I didn't want *that*.

I needed these two to stay close together.

"Can I have my satchel?" I asked, speaking softly. "I'm going to need my handkerchief."

The man behind me picked up the satchel, peeking inside first. He handed me the handkerchief. I unraveled the linen cloth. The tiny needles sparkled in the sunlight streaming through the crack in the wallboards. The brown stem was there, too, as innocent as a cinnamon stick.

A deep grin created wrinkles across the forehead of the man in front of me. The man behind me raised my dress and pressed himself against my behind. I teasingly face-smushed the man in front of me with the handkerchief, suddenly pushing the cloth hard with my fingertips into his eyes. He let out a chirp, and I spun and face-smushed the other man, pressing the fabric into his eyes, too, rubbing his face as hard as possible. The stem fell inside the collar of his shirt. He blindly slapped my forearms as I jumped aside, losing the handkerchief in the fray.

Both men squeezed their eyelids and screamed into their palms.

"I can't fucking see," one man yelled.

"What did you do to me?" the other cried.

"Oh, oh, oh God, make it stop."

They scratched their faces, trying to scrape the needles out. One man dug visible lines in his skin so deep that blood filled the trenches and dripped down his chin. I had never seen anything agitate men so intensely. The poison these needles possessed was crueler than any snakebite or spider venom. Each man, trying to outdo the other, began calling me awful things—but, honestly, I doubt they could hear each other, such was the heightened volume of their unrest.

The other rebels could hear them, though, and they'd come running any moment, so I grabbed my satchel from the dirt floor, ensuring that it contained my documents, and darted to the back of the barn. I kicked and kicked one of the vertical boards until it broke away and fell outside. The gap was wide enough to squeeze through. I crept to the corner and peeked at the farmhouse. Two soldiers were jogging down the road toward the barn, rifles held horizontally. Norman was on his horse, galloping past the barn on the road to Charleston. The men inside the barn were still miserable, wailing between groans.

The "creek" was a wide river that flowed southeast. I suspected that farm lady had called it a creek—despite its large size—because it led into a much bigger waterway, the Cooper River, which snaked its way to Charleston. I walked into the cold creek and began swimming.

My dress absorbed water immediately, the added weight hindering my swim. The struggle would wear me down and I'd drown, so I swam toward the shore and began crawling along the bottom with my nose above water when several booms from rifles sounded. Gunsmoke rose in white clouds from the bank on my left. The rebels were shooting at me from the bushes.

Kicking my shoes free, I wiggled out of my dress. The dress drifted to the surface in an expanding, slow-moving ball alongside me. I wrapped the satchel strap around my neck and dove underwater. I knew I couldn't stay in the cold water. My fingers were already stiffening. My muscles would harden next. I surfaced and swam the sidestoke. Soon, the tree line disappeared and a field opened up. I crawled onto a patch of sunlight on the bank, shivering, and dried off by rubbing the warm dirt into my skin.

Plowed fields stretched for at least a mile. A large barn wasn't too far from the river. Beyond it loomed a huge white house. I looked for the kitchen house. That was where the laundry was washed. A two-story red brick building stood close to the plantation house. It had two doors, one at either end. That was it. I hoped to see a clothesline flagged with large white sheets, a tablecloth, or a few dresses.

I wasn't so lucky.

This close to Charleston, the British Army had seized the property of everyone not loyal to King George, so a loyalist had to own this property. Black men were working near the barn, repairing a wagon. I didn't see horses or livestock, but the British Army wouldn't have taken every horse. That would provoke hatred and discord.

It was a warm afternoon with little wind, but I still shivered from the river. With my hands clasping my elbows, I approached the barn from the rear, walking along a pathway that cattle had worn over the years on their way to drink at the river's edge. I needed a horse. My documents were wet, though. If I unfolded them to show the plantation owner, demanding a horse, I would smear the ink and render the page illegible. The paper had to sit in the sun or by a fireplace and dry.

And I had an obvious and more significant problem.

I was naked.

Once again, talking wouldn't help me.

The large door at the back of the barn was closed. I pulled on a rope that ran inside through a hole, and it raised the wooden block inside that unlatched the door. I partly opened it and peeked through the gap. It was too dark to see, so I slipped inside. I squatted there until my eyes adjusted to the gloom. I heard what I wanted: A horse snorted.

Creeping deeper into the interior, I saw three stocky field horses in a wide fenced-in area and an elegant brown stallion in a stall to their left. He chewed hay docilely as I approached, unimpressed with me. I searched for something to wear. Anything. A man's breeches. A man's shirt. I grabbed a stiff blanket hanging over a stall door and wound the scratchy fabric around me, covering my breasts and my derrière. I spotted a length of rope hanging from a nail on a post. The rope was wet and greasy, and as I tied it tightly around the blanket, it bled drops of filth. My legs, from heel to thigh, were exposed.

No saddles were in sight. Men's voices, sonorous and confident, approached. I opened the stall gate, leading the horse out far enough that I could climb the gate's railings as if they were ladder rungs. He snorted several times as I rode him toward the exit. I passed two black men who were discussing a wagon wheel that one held between his knees. Their conversation ceased, and they gawked at me. I smiled, speaking French loudly and cheerfully.

*"C'est une journée magnifique pour une balade à cheval, n'est-ce pas messieurs?"*

(*It's a magnificent day for a horse ride, wouldn't you gentlemen agree?*)

The men stepped back, one holding an open palm to his mouth, the other releasing the wheel that rolled briefly before wobbling and collapsing. My horse trotted into the sunlight, my wet hair slapping my exposed shoulders in thick cords. Men and women of both races gathered there, dumbfounded. I might have looked foolish in my pauper's dress. Still, I composed myself honorably. I bunched the horse's mane in my right fist while laying the flat of my left hand on my naked thigh and sat with a general's confident posture, my chin raised as I gazed off into the distance, pretending I knew something that my daft audience didn't.

No one tried to stop or shoot me, and no one asked what the hell I thought I was doing. I could, however, feel the wet rope around my dress loosening, so I took advantage of my spectators' astonishment, which had seduced them into a stupor. I kicked my heels into the horse's ribs and galloped fast along the road to Charleston, twenty or twenty-five miles away.

Plenty of time to fix my miserable dress.

# CHAPTER TEN

## *The Undamned*

The temperature dropped with nightfall, compelling me to stop at a farmhouse. I presented myself as respectfully as my filthy appearance allowed. A concerned older woman ushered me inside, where I stood by her hearth and explained my outfit and my situation in the room's welcoming warmth. She told me that her husband and sons had died in the war. She gave me what she could spare: A pair of her husband's trousers, a nightgown to act as a dress over them, and an apron to cover the gown. She had no spare shoes, no saddle for my horse, and nothing to feed me. I rode to the Horn Works wrapped in a ragged quilt.

The soldiers stopped laughing at my apparel when I told them their loyalist guide betrayed us to the Yankees who massacred Ewan McKie, Ronnie Carnegie, and Douglas Ferguson. No one knew whether Norman had ridden through the city gate. I told them to arrest the damned traitor if he tried to leave or enter the city and to notify me of his capture. It was nearly ten o'clock.

I left my weary horse in their care and walked to Gabriel's house. I wanted to check on Uncle George, so I didn't change my crude attire. Gabriel had hung black curtains to divide the room, apparently allowing him to work without his candlelight disturbing Uncle George and Heathcliff. Gabriel must have heard my slog up the stairs. The curtains parted, and his face glowed in the yellow orb of a three-tiered candelabra, which he placed on the table between the two beds. The flames flickered in the open window's chilly breeze.

Uncle George rolled onto his back, mumbling in his sleep. His soul was in the hands of He Who Never Dies. He crossed his forearms over his stomach and began pleading desperately, squeezing his sweaty shirt, his knuckles protruding like they wanted to tear through the skin to get out of his body and get away from God. Uncle George struggled to explain himself, abruptly screaming, gasping, and groaning—all the behavior of a mortal in the presence of a superior Being.

In his youth, Uncle George had hunted runaway slaves. He was exceptionally good at it and was well paid. But then he disappeared for over a year: He had fallen in love with a runaway named Betty Polk. They lived in western Georgia in a farmhouse until Cherokee trackers took Betty away while Uncle George was hunting. He returned to find Betty's empty dress stabbed to his front door with a Cherokee blowgun dart.

Uncle George returned to the North Carolina plantation to bargain with the owner, who had initially contracted Uncle George to capture Betty. He refused to meet with George. The people on the plantation told him he had already sold Betty, and they had no idea where she had ended up. Uncle George searched for two years. He never found her. One morning, however, the folks at the North Carolina plantation found the plantation owner lying in an open field. He was missing his head. They never found that, either.

Uncle George never slept well again. Worry and guilt consigned him to the full terror of He Who Never Dies. His was a restless sleep, he told me. Gabriel nudged a book on the bedside table. *Le Misanthrope*, by Molière.

"It's this stuff," he said. "He's reenacting the French and English garbage he reads all day."

"No," I said. "This is how he sleeps since Betty. He asks He Who Never Dies every night before he goes to bed to have no mercy on his soul. He begs God to make him suffer the tormented sleep of slaves who've had their spouses and children sold out from under them."

Gabriel looked at his troubled brother and shook his head. "I'm against slavery, as you know," he said. "But everyone has them. Wacataw, Cherokees, whites, and blacks. Why—"

"Betty was pregnant," I whispered.

Gabriel looked at the floor, and his bony hand clenched his forehead.

"How's he taking the inoculation?" I asked.

"Better," Gabriel said. "He had a fever of 103 all day. He's down to 99. He'll be fine."

He nodded toward Heathcliff. "Your English friend, on the other hand, isn't doing well."

Heathcliff's nostrils barely expanded and shrank. His curly, slick hair looked blacker, contrasting the paleness of his wet flesh.

"How are you feeling?" Gabriel asked. "Your cowpox inoculation may have made your body immune to this pox. That's exciting to see. I'll make a note of it. But even though you show no signs, you could have spread it to others."

Gabriel looked at my outfit and bare feet. He wrinkled his nose. "Why are you dressed like that?"

I quickly recapped my day: the attack on my soldiers, the would-be rapists, my debut as a horse thief, and the farm lady's charity.

"Aren't your feet cold?" Gabriel said.

"Yes," I said.

"That was reckless," Uncle George said in Wacataw, having awoken.

"What was?" I said.

"You got those soldiers killed." He turned on his side and rose on one elbow. "You should never have taken that trip with only three men. I told you."

"We were ambushed by a militia who knew our number in advance, Uncle George. If I had more men, that only means they would have formed a larger militia to ambush us with."

"So now you're a military tactician," he said, lying back down.

"What did you find out?" Gabriel asked. "About the needles?"

"Nothing."

Uncle George laughed.

"But Thomas Walter will write me when he finds out what they are," I said, leaning in to shout at the side of Uncle George's stupid face.

"And when will that be?" Uncle George asked. "This June, perhaps? July?"

I wished I still had those itchy needles; I'd have stuck them into the tip of his huge nose and watched him slap at it furiously with both hands for the next ten entertaining hours.

Suddenly, Heathcliff gagged as if he had inhaled a ladle of water. His eyes never opened, but he thrust his hips in the air, back arched, obviously suffering extreme internal pain. He abruptly collapsed. Gabriel held the side of his forefinger close to Heathcliff's nostrils, lowering his ear to Heathcliff's chest, his eyes shifting as he listened. Uncle George sat up, legs over the side of his bed.

"Come quickly," Gabriel said to me.

I followed him through the part in the curtain. He stopped at the large chest on four piano legs that held the Leyden jars.

"Help me carry this next to him," he said.

Gabriel raised the chest's lid at Heathcliff's bedside and fiddled with levers and wires. He held up two wires with pincher clips at their ends.

"What are you doing?" Uncle George said, spreading his hands over Heathcliff's body. "He's dead. He's got no heartbeat."

"I told you before"—Gabriel glanced from his brother to me—"I saw Jean-Paul DuBois do this. I've done it myself. We smothered chickens and brought them back to life by breathing into their beaks and jolting them with electricity."

He told me to tear Heathcliff's shirt open, and before I could even try, Uncle George reached in with one of his knives and cut the front of the shirt and yanked it off his torso. A large pustule grew where the thorn had punctured the skin on Heathcliff's arm. Gabriel attached one pincher clip to Heathcliff's left nipple and the other to the skin at the bottom of that chest muscle.

"I've gotten the muscles of dead frogs and severed human arms and fingers to move," Gabriel said. "Why not a heart? It's a muscle."

Gabriel half-turned, facing the Leyden jars. He lowered one lever, and a bright bolt of electricity arced between the pincher clips. Heathcliff's body stiffened. Gabriel raised the lever and put his ear to Heathcliff's chest.

"Take over here," he told me. "Hurry. Grab that lever."

He hurried to the other side of the bed, facing Uncle George and me, pinching Heathcliff's nose with one hand and holding his mouth open by tugging on his chin with the other.

"I saw Jean-Paul breathe into a soldier like this in a field hospital." Gabriel's eyes widened with excitement. "Then blood shot out the bullet hole in his chest." He nodded at the lever. "I'll stand back while you lower that lever and give him a jolt. Then I'm going to breathe into him four times. I'll stand back, and you lower the lever, wait two seconds, and raise it. I'll breathe into him again, and so forth. Go!"

I lowered the lever and electrocuted Heathcliff. A tiny streak of lightning arced from the nipple clamp, and his legs and arms stiffened. I raised the lever, interrupting the electricity, and his body relaxed. Gabriel pinched Heathcliff's nose, lowered his mouth over Heathcliff's, and breathed into him many times, both men's cheeks ballooning. He stood back, and I jolted Heathcliff. Gabriel breathed into him. I zapped him again. Heathcliff started coughing. Gabriel unclamped the clips from Heathcliff's skin.

Uncle George lowered himself off the bed, getting closer, face to face with Heathcliff. Heathcliff opened his eyes and shoved Uncle George away. Heathcliff sat up, his face scrunched into a snarl.

"What are you lot staring at?" Heathcliff said to us.

"You're alive." Uncle George placed his palm against Heathcliff's cheek, and Heathcliff slapped his hand away. "You did it." Uncle George looked at Gabriel. "You brought him back from the dead."

"I wasn't dead, you cow," Heathcliff told Uncle George. "I was having a nightmare."

"A nightmare?" I said. "What do you mean?"

Heathcliff's jaw muscles flexed as he gazed hard at the orgy of shadows that the flickering candlelight cast upon the walls.

"I dreamt I was in hell. There were flames all around me, as close as the darkness around us now. It was so hot. Horrifically hot. As hot inside me as the heat all around me."

"You're describing your fever," Gabriel said.

"And possibly the electrocution," I said.

Uncle George pointed his chin at Heathcliff, saying, "That wasn't a nightmare, you ass. You were dead."

"I can't address the part about you going to hell," Gabriel said. "But I can assure you as a doctor that you had no heartbeat and you weren't breathing."

"How could I be here talking to you if I died?" Heathcliff said angrily.

"Heathcliff," I said, jerking my head at Uncle George. "That man is a Wacataw warrior. This other man spent ten years at the academy in Montpellier. They are both experts in determining whether someone is dead. Gabriel had me repeatedly electrocute you like those frog legs at our dinner party. He put his mouth on yours and breathed into you. It took several tries, but he brought you back from the dead."

"I felt ghosts around me," Heathcliff said, his face sterner—which I didn't think possible. "They were telling me to leave. They didn't want me there. They threw me out of hell. A giant blackbird swooped down." He felt his left chest muscle. "It sunk its talons into me, piercing my chest, and flew me away from the fire. I flew over a foggy bog, what had to be the moors back home, close to the ground. The bird was going to drop me there, but the next thing I knew, I was here." He glanced at Uncle George. "Staring at your ugly fucking face."

Uncle George laughed, but his smile abruptly stopped. He looked at me, winked, and jerked his head to his left—signaling me to be wary of danger. He lifted one candle from the candelabra and flung it into the darkness toward the door at the top of the stairs.

"Uhhh," a man groaned in the dark.

Unsheathing his big knife, Uncle George rolled off his bed and disappeared into the darkness. I heard a knocking noise and a muffled cry. Uncle George walked into the light, pulling Dawson by his hair behind him. Dawson wasn't wearing his uniform. I could also smell booze on him, not surprisingly. Uncle George let him go.

"Why are you spying on us?" I said. "Your uncle sent you here to sneak about?"

"I wasn't spying," Dawson panted. "I came here to tell you to report to Major Pawsworthy at his house tomorrow morning at eight."

"What for?"

"He wants a report."

"On what?"

"On everything you've been doing. Including those three soldiers who got killed."

I was sure Uncle George's mocking eyes were glaring smugly at me.

"You forgot how to knock on a door?" Gabriel asked Dawson.

"I did knock," Dawson said. "Downstairs at the other house. The lady there said you were up here."

"So you snuck up the stairs?" I said.

"I wasn't sneaking," he said, his words slurred. "Out of courtesy, I stopped at the door because you were obviously busy with some surgery." He nodded to Gabriel. "Or was that witchery?"

No one answered that stupid question. Dawson shifted his eyes to Heathcliff. "My uncle would love to talk with you. He's obsessed with predestination."

"What's that?" Heathcliff said.

"The belief that God predetermines if you're going to heaven or hell," Dawson said, "before you're born. My uncle knows he's going to heaven. So whatever he does in this life doesn't matter. It won't affect the ultimate outcome, he says."

"How can he be so sure?" I asked.

"About twenty years ago, Pastor Barnacle told him he was predestined to go to heaven," Dawson said. "These days, my uncle's beginning to doubt it, though. He was at some costume party not long ago and stopped to piss on the way home when someone screamed at him and he fell off Roper's Dock and almost drowned." He nodded at Gabriel. "Your Gypsy Lady was passing by and pulled him from the water. He thanked her and she told him there's no need to thank her since she was putting off the inevitable. She said if he had drowned, he would have gone straight to hell."

"You said he was going to heaven," I said.

"That's what he tried to tell the Gypsy Lady. That hag said whoever told him that was full of shit. She said she could foresee these things." Dawson chuckled. "She told him she couldn't see the reflection of the stars in the dark water after pulling him out of it. That meant in God's eyes he was invisible, that he had no place in heaven and never would."

"And he believed her?" I asked.

"They had never met," Dawson said. "She didn't know anything about his belief in predestination and that's what spooked him. He's been a mess ever since."

I eyeballed Gabriel. I suspected he set Pawsworthy up with the Gypsy Lady. Gabriel was far more cunning than I thought. He knew I was observing him, so he moved his eyes off Dawson and met my stare, and a smirk brought some plumpness to his bony face.

"No need to worry," Dawson said, looking from Heathcliff to me. "I'm not going to tell my uncle about what happened here. I don't want to deal with him obsessing over Heathcliff. He's got enough obsessions as it is. I personally don't believe in any of that predestination nonsense."

"My limited exposure to your uncle," I told Dawson, "has shown me that he's so arrogant he can't keep his mouth shut. We'll find out soon enough if you're like him."

Dawson rolled his eyes, saying, "I'll see you in the morning." He pivoted to leave but stopped, facing me again. "Is that all you do? Trick people into liking you and then treat them terribly once they're no longer any use to you?"

"Yes," I said sarcastically. "That's all I do."

He left the room. He was much louder going down the stairs than his artful ascent. Heathcliff looked deathly pale. Gabriel fetched him a dry blanket, insisting that he stay the night under his watch. Uncle George said he was unwilling to sleep next to the Englishman whom the devil had spoken through once before, who had just died and gone to hell—and come back.

"I'm getting out of here," Uncle George said.

I followed him downstairs.

He handed me a knife. "Keep this under your pillow. Dawson is dodgy. Drunks tend to sneak into women's rooms when they're asleep."

Uncle George went home, and I went to the kitchen house. I washed off the road grime with a linen hand towel and a kettle of hot water, then went to my room. Someone had lit a fire for me. I thought I would have been exhausted enough to doze off immediately, but I couldn't sleep. I lay in bed trying to remember Émile's face and failed. I got up, dressed, and, sliding George's knife into the cloth belt of my dress, went for a stroll through Charleston. I headed down King Street toward the harbor, toward South Bay. I stopped across the street from my parents' house, near the spot where Émile died.

A yawn crept over me, and I inhaled a shuddered breath, my eyes watering. Blinking away my blurry vision, I saw Norman, the guide who betrayed us, coming out the front door of Pawsworthy's house. He was with two soldiers. Pawsworthy stood inside the foyer, nodding his fat face and patting Norman's shoulder. The soldiers saluted Pawsworthy, and he closed the door.

The soldiers weren't arresting Norman, as I had instructed. One put his arm around Norman's shoulder, laughing loudly as they pranced down the stairs.

Was Norman a rebel double-spy, tricking Pawsworthy?

Or was Pawsworthy a rebel spy and traitor, too?

A familiar stench stole my attention—the acidic vapors of booze breath. I gripped the handle of the knife.

"Spying on my uncle?" Dawson said. "So much for knocking on doors, eh?"

"Hardly." I turned and faced him. "I'm studying a crime scene."

"What crime scene?" He slugged from a green bottle.

"This is where Émile was murdered," I said.

"Now he's been murdered, eh? But why study a scene at night? What can you possibly learn in the dark?"

"You learn how someone can sneak up behind you. Even someone as drunk as you. Is that how Émile was killed?"

Norman and the two soldiers were coming down the walkway. One of the soldiers held a lantern. The three men were obviously friends, walking in a tight pack to hear each other as they joked. The soldiers I spoke with earlier at the Horn Works wore red coats with blue facings; these soldiers had red coats with yellow facings—the uniform of Pawsworthy's South Carolina Royalists.

I stepped in front of Dawson, placing him between Norman and me. I didn't want Norman to see me. I wasn't going to confront three men on a dark street this late at night. I inched closer to Dawson. Too close.

"What are you doing?" Dawson said.

"Who's that man behind you? The one not in uniform?"

He half-turned. They had marched out the doorless gate and headed toward Meeting Street, laughing, walking fast, eager for a drink perhaps.

"Norman?" Dawson faced me. "You can't possibly think he's the murderer?"

"Who is he?" I asked, backing away.

Dawson slugged from his bottle, staggering across the street. He stepped through the gateway.

"Who is he?" I yelled.

"My brother," he said, heading for the house.

I ran along South Bay, turning up Meeting Street, intent on following Norman. I'd come back afterward with soldiers and arrest him. I didn't see him anywhere.

Pawsworthy had learned about my murdered Scots from his spies at the Horn Works. That's how he knew I was back in Charleston. That meant he also knew I wanted Norman arrested. Yet, instead of jailing him, he escorted the damn murderer out his front door like he was a cherished dinner guest—as effortlessly as the devil letting Heathcliff out of hell.

Whatever Pawsworthy planned for me tomorrow morning, it wouldn't be good.

## CHAPTER ELEVEN

## *The Suicide Plant*

I deliberately missed Pawsworthy's eight o'clock meeting. Around a quarter after nine, Pawsworthy and Dawson came to Gabriel's house. Winslow met them at the door and was about to escort them to the parlor. I didn't want Pawsworthy to see my parents' mirror. I called out to Winslow as I walked down the hall.

"Let's take them to the sitting room," I said. "A fire's burning there."

The sitting room, of course, was next to the back door that led to the compound—my quick escape. Winslow and I walked side by side ahead of our unwanted visitors. I moved closer to have a *tête-à-tête*.

"These men are rats." I watched his face for an expression that might betray his emotions. He stared ahead, not even glancing at me. "I don't want to be alone with them. Will you stay at my side? The fat one has a reputation for being a lecher." I detected a smirk forming, but he coyly walked faster and opened the door to the sitting room.

"Of course, Charlotte," he said.

Pawsworthy and Dawson sat in the embroidered armchairs. Winslow and I settled on the settee. I waited until Pawsworthy took a deep breath, preparing to speak, and beat him to it.

"Your nephew Norman is a rebel spy. That fact is in my report to Colonel Balfour. Are you aware he's a spy?"

The fatty folds collaring Pawsworthy's throat began to shake. "Listen here, you can't—"

"Yesterday," I said, "your nephew had my military escort slaughtered when he betrayed us to a rebel militia. Afterward, your nephew rode to

Charleston and rendezvoused with you last night. Before you answer my next question, I want you to know that I am officially representing His Most Gracious Majesty King George the Third, sovereign ruler of the British Empire. Are you, Major Donald Pawsworthy of the South Carolina Royalists, also a traitor?"

"You arrogant fucking tramp." His plump fist hammered the arm of the chair. "I put you in charge of this investigation. I can easily remove you, too."

"No, you can't. I'm acting under Colonel Balfour's authority, not yours. You are merely a militia soldier who, from what my people tell me, has seen more action at the buffet table than the battlefield."

I glanced at Dawson and spotted a grin. Did he enjoy me abusing his uncle? He did, which meant he harbored a loathing for him—leverage I might use later. Winslow, however, inched away from me. "Are you a traitor, Pawsworthy?" I asked again.

He struggled to sit forward, wiggling in place. "You're deliberately keeping me in the dark. Why? Why did you meet with Thomas Walter? You left Charleston without notifying me of your plans. Why isn't Sergeant Dawson more involved in the investigation?"

"When did you find out I was going to Walter's home?" I said.

"After I noticed you were gone. I asked Captain Merryman where you went."

"Do you expect me to believe it was a coincidence that our guide was your nephew? I told you about my Scotsmen. Which means you bribed someone in Captain Merryman's office to keep you informed of my plans. Once your spy told you I intended to go north with my Scots, you planted your nephew as my guide."

"You think Thomas Walter has something to do with Montcalm's murder?" Pawsworthy said, not addressing my accusations.

"No," I said. "Émile had a glass jar at Dr. DuBois's house containing dozens of tiny needles taken from Montcalm's body. I brought those to Thomas Walter to see whether he could identify the plant."

"That's impossible. We had Montcalm's body destroyed long before Émile arrived here."

"Someone had the awareness to collect and save those needles," I said, "and gave them to Émile. If you want to believe I traveled through the Swamp Fox's backyard to deliver an empty glass jar to Thomas Walter, you are free to do so."

I hadn't officially reported Wragg's murder. So it would be interesting to see whether Pawsworthy mentioned Wragg—it would mean he had to have had a hand in his murder. Pawsworthy's knee began to pump as he pondered who could have given Émile evidence and not told him about it.

"What good is that going to serve, identifying the plant the needles come from?" he asked.

"Let's say you and your charming nephews enjoy going to New Spain in the winter to escape the cold," I said. "And it turns out that Thomas Walter says the plant comes from New Spain. I'm going to suspect you and your nephews are the murderers."

Pawsworthy pursed his lips, rolling his eyes. He showed no unease about being accused.

"Is Norman's last name the same as yours?" I asked Dawson.

"What the hell else would it be?" Dawson said.

The drunkard was getting testy—or was his rudeness a show of defiance to impress his uncle?

"He could be your half-brother," I told him. "Your father could've made love to some prostitute. Or Norman's last name could be Pawsworthy. Your mom's bastard child before she met your father."

"How can you say such an awful thing?" Dawson said, his lips puckered in disgust.

"My sister was an honorable woman, Charlotte," Pawsworthy said, not looking at Dawson.

"Don't call me Charlotte," I said. "We are not on informal terms."

I wasn't sure I could rely on Winslow: He had inched even farther away. I stood.

"I'll be right back," I said.

I went upstairs for paper, ink, and the knife Uncle George had given me. I placed everything in Émile's leather carrying bag and returned. Winslow hadn't left the room in my absence. Adjacent to the wall by the fireplace was a card table with chairs. I used that as a desk. I dipped my quill in the inkwell.

"Major Pawsworthy, Sergeant Dawson." I looked from one to the other. "Are either of you militiamen aware of Norman Dawson's treasonous involvement with the enemy? You first, Major Pawsworthy."

"I'm not answering your questions," he said. "Are you out of your—"

"Duly noted." I logged his statement into my journal. "Be aware that I'll recommend Colonel Balfour hang you, both or either of you, if you lie to me. Mr. Winslow Welby, a free man, is a witness."

Telling Pawsworthy I would have him hanged gave me a thrill that reminded me of the rush of drinking whiskey with your naked man when things start to heat up.

"Who's going to take his word over mine?" Pawsworthy said, dismissing Winslow with a chuckle.

Winslow's eyebrows lowered and his lips tightened. He despised Pawsworthy.

I pointed my chin at Dawson. "How about you? Are you aware that your brother is a traitor?"

"Hell, no."

I wrote that down.

"Major Pawsworthy, I was with Sergeant Dawson last night on South Bay Street. I saw you talk with Norman Dawson at the door of your house. He left with two of your Royalist soldiers. For the record, Sergeant Dawson identified him as his brother. What did you and your nephew discuss?"

"I don't answer to you," Pawsworthy said.

"You're breaching my Order of Compliance. Colonel Balfour wanted me to keep him apprised of significant discoveries in my investigation. Conspiring with a traitor is significant—"

Pawsworthy slapped the arm of his chair. "Why are you interrogating us? Shouldn't you be focusing on catching the murderer?"

"At the moment, I'm trying to catch who murdered His Majesty's Scots. For all I know, you sent your nephew to kill my Scotsmen and me to sabotage my royal investigation into the murder of Major Montcalm."

"Why would I appoint you as an inspector and then try to kill you, you idiot?"

"That very appellation answers your question," I said, raising my chin.

"What?" Pawsworthy's frown united his chin with his neck fat. "What does that even mean?"

"When you realized that I wasn't, in fact, an idiot, you tried to assassinate me to end the investigation so you could fulfill your promise to frame Dr. Gabriel DuBois for the murder of Major Henrique Baptiste de Montcalm. So you know, I have been keeping a journal for Colonel Balfour, a written record of your criminal schemes."

"You told Colonel Balfour that I—"

"Not yet. But I write down everything. Names, places, secret meetings, even what people wear. A person's appearance is telling." I raised my quill and pointed the feather end at him. "A filthy neck, for example, turns a white shirt collar the color of a tobacco smoker's teeth. That outer filth tells me a lot about a man's inner personage."

Dawson covered his sudden smirk with his palm to cork his laughter. His red complexion was a testament to how intensely he held his breath. Winslow cupped his palm over his grin, too, pressing so hard his knuckles emerged. Pawsworthy squinted, his tight lips deepening his frown.

"You," I said to Pawsworthy, "threatened to frame the owner of this house if I didn't find the murderer within your timeline. But you don't want me to find the murderer, do you? You're connected somehow to the killer. You may even be the killer."

There. I said it. I had stomped into the wolf's lair and kicked him in the teeth. He jiggled to the edge of the chair, grunting as he stood.

"Leaving so soon?" I said.

Dawson stood, too. Winslow remained seated, observing. Pawsworthy strutted to my makeshift desk. Overnight, I developed a few tiny red dots on one arm—flare-ups from the inoculation—none as developed as Heathcliff's; still, I used my quill to point out a few on my wrist.

"Don't come too close. You might catch the pox."

He backed away. "You don't fool me. Tell Colonel Balfour about Norman all you want. I'm not responsible for that stupid sneak. But I'm sure of one thing. You'd never tell Balfour you suspect I'm the murderer. It's not true, and without proof, you'd discredit yourself and he'd get rid of you immediately. And if that happens, my sweet little dear, you're mine."

"My report states that you spied on me," I said quickly, unsure what he meant about me being his; was that a colloquial English expression indicating he'd come after me, or did the creep mean he'd somehow enslave me? "You discovered that my Scotsmen and I were traveling north and you planted your nephew as our guide. He ambushed us, murdering three British soldiers. Those are provable facts. Good luck explaining them to Colonel Balfour."

"I had no idea he was going to set you up." Pawsworthy shook his head. "If that's what he did." He glanced at Dawson. "Can you believe this lady?"

"Where did your soldiers take him last night?" I said. "Where is he now? I've issued a warrant for Norman Dawson's arrest."

He shrugged. Dawson kicked at something on the rug.

"I'll give Colonel Balfour my report today. I'm reporting that you refused to describe your meeting with Norman Dawson and that you refused to tell me where your soldiers are hiding him. You *will* answer Colonel Balfour, or you'll find yourself in the Provost imprisoned with rebels who hate your guts, of which you have a robust supply."

Pawsworthy clenched his fists. "Norman is a double agent. He's presently heading north on a mission."

"Does Colonel Balfour know he's a double agent?"

He shook his head.

I laughed. "I see. A double agent who arranges the murder of British soldiers? A double agent who tried, but failed, to arrange the rape and murder of His Majesty's royal inspector—*me*?"

Standing, I brought the two pages of my notes with wet ink to the fireplace and set them on the mantel to dry. I turned and faced Pawsworthy.

"You are the most dishonorable man in Charleston," I said. "Get out of Dr. DuBois's house."

"You're throwing *me* out?"

"Yes. It'll be in my report."

"You little—"

"Get out."

He shuffled to the card table and reached for the quill. I also had small sheets of paper for writing reminders. After scribbling on one, he returned to where he had been standing. He didn't want to hand me the note, wary of the pox. I picked it up.

*Third house on the right on St. Philip's Street after Liberty Street.*

"What's this?" I said.

"A test of your will. You might call it a turn in the . . . aw . . . aw, how did you put it?—oh, yes, the snake's journey. You might call it a distraction that makes you stray off course." He chuckled. "That's Eliza Breckenridge's house. I know her. She's the woman your dearly departed husband was fucking before the idiot fell dead in the street."

I swooned in a hot whirl of humility, hurt, and rage. I concentrated on the note. I memorized the streets and, turning, dropped the paper into the fireplace. It started burning in the air, the edges turning into wings of flame, a fallen angel crashlanding on hell-hot coals.

That's when it struck.

Suddenly.

Instantly.

I went blind.

I didn't want Pawsworthy and Dawson to know I couldn't see. I was utterly vulnerable. I concentrated on remaining calm. I "stared" at the fire, pretending to sniffle, wiping nonexistent tears with my forefinger. The trick to locating a fireplace mantel without giving away your blindness was to lean the underside of your forearm on it—not to grope for it with your hand.

"Your passion for this investigation seems to be motivated by your love for Émile," Pawsworthy said. "Let's see how strong that motivation is now."

I kept my back to him, forearm on the mantel. "Get out," I said.

"How about these rude French people?" Pawsworthy chuckled. "First, they invite you in for a fireside chat, then they throw you out."

"I didn't invite you in," I said.

"Let's get out of here," he said.

His feet pivoted, the leather soles giving the floorboards a good sanding. They stomped out of the room, heels punching down the hall.

"He's a cruel devil, Charlotte," Winslow said, and the settee creaked as he stood, his voice close behind me. "You're playing with fire."

Gripping the mantel's edge, I rested my forehead on my knuckles.

"Pawsworthy is a tiny campfire burning on the banks of a river," I said. "And spring will be here soon, bringing the melting snow from the north. Everyone knows you never build a fire beside a rising river."

"I'll see you later, Charlotte," he said.

I heard the door close.

My bedroom was above me. Another stairway was across the hall, a narrow one behind a door. I groped my way up those stairs to my room. Pawsworthy was right. I would never tell Balfour about his connection to the murders without proof. I wouldn't mention Norman either. Not yet. First, I'd torture Pawsworthy with worry, let him believe I told Balfour about Norman, and let him agonize over why Balfour hadn't mentioned his nephew. He'd lose sleep knowing he could be thrown into chains any minute.

Pawsworthy couldn't have been more wrong about my motivation, though. My hatred of him kept me going, not my love for Émile.

And I hated him more than ever.

~~~

I woke from my nap an hour or so later. I opened my eyes and was relieved I was no longer staring into the black mirror of my soul—I could see! However, I was still looking into a mirror of sorts: Émile's lousy painting of me. I had slept on my covers with my head at the foot of the bed.

I loved Émile. To imagine him lying naked with another woman—his face between her legs, or his hands gripping her hips from behind—that was a cruel pain. Pawsworthy was a depraved liar, so until I interviewed Eliza Breckenridge, I wouldn't think further about it. I wouldn't accept he had been unfaithful.

My first thought, as I combed my hair in the mirror, was, despite having refused to think about it, *did he cheat on me?*

I decided to keep busy. I checked on Heathcliff. He wasn't in the hospital. I found him sitting at the table in the kitchen with a massive carrot in his hand. Chewing sloppily, he stared at me with dark half-circles under his eyes. No hello. Not even a nod. His hair was unkempt. He looked older, meaner, and empty of humor. I pointed to the carrots in a box of sand beside me.

"I think these are for the horses," I said. "They're old and limp."

"Damn the horses," he said.

"You feeling any better?" I said, leaning my shoulder on the door jamb.

"I've been up and down those stairs more times than a whore's stockings." He pointed his carrot at the outhouse next door. "To shit and puke."

"You look—well, you look exactly like what you are: Someone who's come back from the dead."

"That's why I'm eating a root vegetable. Neither of us belong here. We should both be underground."

I genuinely laughed. "Was that . . . was that a joke, Heathcliff?"

"You thought it was funny?" he said with a snarl, and orange drool snaked through his beard stubble.

"Yes. It was witty."

"Then, yeah, it was a damn joke."

What a grump!

Gabriel stopped by the kitchen house. He greeted Heathcliff in English, getting no salutation in return.

"Winslow says Pawsworthy blessed us with a visit," Gabriel said in French.

"Uninvited," I said, also in French. "He didn't stay long." I briefly recapped the meeting, including how I ensured he didn't see my parents' mirror. "I doubt he'll ever come back."

"You provoked him?"

"I treated him with the same disrespect he gives me," I said, coming out of the doorway and joining him in the compound.

"I suggest you stop. Or tell George to cut his throat. Pawsworthy doesn't go away. He's a greedy man with odd fixations." He studied me for several seconds, finally smiling. "You're not going to give up. I can see that. At least don't provoke him publicly. Scheme secretly, Crow."

"Crows aren't known for their stealth," I said.

He didn't respond. I stared at the dirt.

"I wanted to keep riding to our village," I told him. "When I was up by the Santee."

"Our villages are gone. There are no more Wacataw in South Carolina."

"It's hard to grasp," I said quietly.

Last summer, Colonel Rawdon told our people to sign a loyalty oath to King George if they wanted protection from rebels. The Wacataw chose instead to side with the Yankees and moved from South Carolina to North Carolina. The British and their loyalists looted our homes and fields and burned every village. This created conflict in my marriage—so much that I couldn't discuss it with Émile.

"John Peele spoke with my mother recently," Gabriel said. "Things are changing."

"What do you mean, *changing*?"

"General Big River might be coming south. Don't repeat that."

My grandmother, Jane Harris, argued forcefully to have General Big River elected as our leader after King Klow abdicated when the war began. General Big River's wife was Sally Big River, the daughter of the daughter of the most powerful Wacataw leader, King Higler himself. Jane Harris had succeeded in keeping the female royal line of Wacataw rulers.

Our family's allegiance was split, though. Most Wacataw, including my grandmother, were on the rebels' side; my uncles and I were with the British. One thing was certain: None of us would ever raise a hatchet against a fellow Wacataw.

"General Big River can't stand up to the British Army," I said. "So why would they come back with all these British here? There's a solid line of redcoats from Camden to Savannah. And I know for a fact that a fleet of soldiers landed in Virginia with General Arnold. I sailed with them. So did he." I pointed a thumb at Heathcliff.

"And a huge British fleet landed here in Charleston a week before you did," Gabriel said. "Unloading troops. I inspected as many soldiers as possible to ensure they were fit for duty."

He smiled—or rather, he grinned. Why would he bear a sinister grin if he was proud of his official position? He looked dodgy and dishonest. I disliked Gabriel being deliberately vague. I had no idea what he meant by *things are changing*, or the significance of it, and I told him so.

He shrugged. "When John Peele gets back, the three of us should talk."

I also had no idea which side John Peele was on. I wasn't so sure about Gabriel's allegiance, either. Those two could get us all hanged.

Heathcliff stomped across the wooden floor, feet dense with anger, and the slam of the door shuddered the still air.

"Leave off, ya frogs," he shouted from the other side. "All that bloody yapping!"

We both laughed. I changed subjects and asked for Gabriel's thoughts on the murders. Besides the torture and the needles, I told him I couldn't see any other connection between the murders. The nearly three-month interval between the two was baffling. Unless there had been another similar murder that the military wasn't aware of. Local doctors could have encountered a tortured victim and, unaware that their victim was killed exactly as Major Montcalm, didn't report it to the military.

Gabriel hadn't heard of murder victims tortured with needles. Charleston had many other doctors, at least thirteen prominent ones, not including those in the low country. Gabriel said he'd make a list. I was determined to question them all.

First, I needed soldiers. I went to the Horn Works. A Major Bannery informed me that Captain Merryman had succumbed to smallpox. He introduced me to an Irish regiment. Ordinarily, most men greeted me with a smile and a courteous nod, and immediately, their eyes dropped to other places. To their credit, these Irishmen were polite enough not to directly look me over so I didn't feel as naked as a flapping fish. I asked for volunteers, and everyone raised his hand. Ultimately, I handpicked eight of the toughest-looking lads, one of them an accomplished boxer.

I told them I'd return later and walked to Uncle George's house. He was squatting shirtless by the fireplace. He said he had just bathed in the Ashley. I explained my mission, assuring him that an Irish troop would accompany me this time.

"Send Heathcliff into the State House while I'm gone," I told him. "Have him research as much information as possible on Pawsworthy's wealth. Heathcliff can be charming, convincingly so. Émile has a nice carrying case made from leather that Heathcliff can bring along to look official. I didn't bring it, obviously. It's in my bedroom."

"What's he supposed to tell the clerks?" Uncle George said. "That he's working for you?"

"Yes. I'll write a letter that allows him to research whatever interests him. I'll leave it on my desk in my bedroom for you."

"How's he feeling?" Uncle George asked.

"Who?"

"Lazarus."

"Oh," I said. "He's back to being himself. For example, Gabriel and I were having a quiet conversation, and he slammed the door in our faces."

~~~

Accompanied by my Irish soldiers on horseback, I began interviewing the thirteen doctors in Charleston. We had an unproductive start. We wasted the morning tracking down physicians who weren't home. Gabriel insisted we eat lunch at his house, which was convenient since King Street was a central location from which to branch out. We covered Charleston in a day and a half. No doctor in the city had encountered a victim riddled with needles.

By the time we headed into the countryside, a few soldiers complained they were lightheaded. The farther we traveled from Charleston, the more the sickness—what seemed to be smallpox—spread through my troop. Three Irishmen fell so ill on the fourth day they couldn't ride on horseback. After six days of sleeping in barns and military tents, visiting doctors' homes, military hospitals, military field hospitals, and private homes, I lost seven Irish soldiers. Though none died, each became too weak to travel. I had to leave them in the care of the doctors I interviewed. I was down to one soldier, Sergeant Patrick O'Regan, the boxer.

I remembered Gabriel telling me I could be contagious. I wasn't sick, though, so how could I have been infecting these soldiers?

Early on the morning of the sixth day, Sergeant O'Regan and I were fifteen miles south of Orangeburg, passing through a small village of farmhouses. When I reached the third farm, I realized the armies had taken all the livestock. I also noticed no people were around. I stopped at one house, knocking on the door. No one answered, so I went inside. It was a small one-room square house with a staircase that led to another open room on the second floor where a family of six, husband and wife and children of various ages, lay huddled on the floor under blankets. They were dead.

They had some form of the pox, their faces and hands covered with pustules—large ones, though. I stopped at the next house. A family of seven, all dead, also lying huddled under blankets. They had large pustules, too. Every house was the same. Seven houses in total. Dead families with large pustules: Five white, two black.

Outside Charleston, we entered a camp of German soldiers. It was there, in the early morning, that I met Dr. Daniel Tagtmeyer, lead physician of the Hessian army. He said his company discovered a torture victim riddled with needles during a raid on a plantation on the fifth of December last year.

We were sitting in his tent on cozy chairs that had once belonged to a well-off landowner; clearly, these weren't military-issued. Dr. Tagtmeyer spoke excellent English. He stroked his blond goatee, recalling how he had examined the corpse of the plantation owner, Barnabas Bancroft, more out of curiosity than duty.

"We found him naked and upside down in an armchair," Dr. Tagtmeyer said, his sky-blue eyes peering through his round wire eyeglasses.

I raised a finger, interrupting him. "Are these his chairs, by chance?"

He shrugged, rubbing the cushioned arm of his chair as he would a lover's bare thigh. "What use is a chair to a dead man?" he said, gently squeezing the soft fabric.

"None," I said.

"So. This unlucky Barnabas chap had the tiny needles sticking into his skin—especially his face. The condition of his eyes, thoroughly bloodshot, made me examine his throat because many times severe coughing will cause the blood vessels in the eyes to rupture. His throat was inflamed but I couldn't determine why. The cause wasn't the tiny needles. That is to say, he had a plant stem in his mouth like a small cigar, although it only affected his tongue and lips, not his throat. So, something else caused the throat irritation. What, I have no idea. Did your victims have hemorrhaged eyes and red throats as well?"

"The man I found had bloodshot eyes, yes. I didn't think to examine his throat. The British military destroyed Major Montcalm's body shortly after it was discovered."

Dr. Tagtmeyer squinted, examining the faded dots on the back of my hands.

"I was recently inoculated for the pox by Dr. Gabriel DuBois. Do you know Dr. DuBois?"

"I've heard of him," he said. "A gallant professional. He and that gypsy woman risk their lives saving injured soldiers." He chuckled. "He's so good many soldiers don't want his help."

"What do you mean?"

"Most of his patients recover from their injuries." He leaned toward me to share a secret. "And therein lies the problem: He returns them healthy and fit for duty, ready to rejoin the fight. But no one wants to rejoin the fight."

"So he does too good of a job?" I said, my smile inspired by family pride.

"*Genau.*"

Dr. Tagtmeyer sat back.

"What about this Barnabas Bancroft? Did anyone in his household witness his murder?"

"The slaves had all run away," he said. "We found his mother tied up in the kitchen house."

"Alive?"

"Quite. A dead chicken and its feathers were on the table. She had been plucking—"

"Where is she now, at this plantation?"

He nodded. "Practically speaking, however, I don't see how she can survive there. She doesn't even have a kettle to boil water in."

"Where is this plantation?"

"On the other side of the Cooper, opposite Charleston." He scratched his beard. "Sail up the Wando River and turn right into Hobcaw Creek. Ask for the Bancroft Plantation as you go. But you mustn't travel there. The Swamp Fox is in the area. He attacked Wando Landing. Captured thirty Brits and loyalists. Officers, too."

"Why would this swamp rat stick around after an attack?" I said. "Why risk getting captured?"

He shook his head and shrugged. "I can't speak to military tactics." He raised a forefinger. "However, I can tell you this much: I have an idea what this needle plant might be."

I sat forward. Now I was the one squeezing the chair's arm.

"You ever hear of a place called New Holland?" he asked.

"Of course," I said, not wanting to appear ignorant. "It's either an island, an island continent, or a huge peninsula somewhere south of China, yes?"

"Close enough. I know some Dutch explorers who used to go there. They were cutting their way through the hillside, shirtless in the heat, hacking down these broad-leafed plants with their donkeys in tow when they began to itch madly. The donkeys started stomping the earth. At first, they thought they were fire ants, but the pain was a thousand times worse, and there were no ants in sight. One of the donkeys finally ran over a cliff and killed itself to end the misery. A shirtless man threatened to join his four-legged companion but was restrained by his colleagues. The cause turned out to be the broad-leafed plants with their tiny needles. They said their flesh itched and burned for two weeks. My friend said he could still feel the needles in his back after two years. The local tribesmen told him the needles never lose their potency, not even the dead dry ones. They call it the Suicide Plant. I think this is that plant."

"So someone brought it to Charleston from New Holland," I said, thinking aloud, "to torture people."

"That's a lot of work that also takes a lot of time—sailing it from there to here, that is."

"Hatred is a powerful motivation."

A soldier opened the flapper door to the tent, spoke German, and left.

"Well," Dr. Tagtmeyer said, slapping his thighs once before standing. "I have to leave. The plague is devastating our troops. The British troops, too, including the camp followers—utterly sick with disease."

Before I left, I told him about the village I had come through, where everyone was dead. He said he knew about that place, that a plague had wiped them out practically overnight. All armies were avoiding that road.

"That gypsy woman won't go there, either," he said. "She's quite remarkable. Nobody from either side will shoot at her. She can come and go as she pleases because she will stop for *any* injured soldier. That's why she has those rat bells. So everyone can recognize her."

The same German soldier poked his head into the tent, speaking German.

"I must go." Dr. Tagtmeyer saluted me. "*Auf wiedersehen, Frau Savatier!*"

"*Au revoir, monsieur le docteur Tagtmeyer!*"

Outside, Sergeant Patrick O'Regan had collapsed between the front legs of his loyal horse. He saw me and tried to smile. The pores of his pale face were weeping tears of sweat. I explained who he was to Dr. Tagtmeyer, and he instantly instructed two German soldiers to help him to his feet. Sergeant O'Regan assured me he would persevere, employing his Irish vernacular and wit to dismiss his affliction as a temporary case of *the trots*. They dragged him backward by his armpits, and the heels of his boots left trench marks in the dirt, two parallel paths that suggested invisible snakes were pursuing him.

# CHAPTER TWELVE

## *German Chicken*

I stopped at the Horn Works for more soldiers. Another officer was sitting at Major Bannery's desk, spooning through cornmeal porridge. The three soldiers he was speaking with stepped aside as I approached. The officer stood and introduced himself as Captain Thompson, informing me that the major was in the infirmary.

"Oh," I said, trying to mimic British elocution, "that's perfectly awful news."

I reached for my Order of Compliance. This was the first time I had unfolded the document since drying it on the kitchen house's torrid hearthstones, and the crisp paper's crinkle produced the only noise in the room. I held it at arm's length.

"I don't need to read that." Captain Thompson showed me his palm. "Your reputation precedes you."

I quickly folded my Order of Compliance, the crunch sounding like I'd stepped on a pair of eyeglasses.

"My Irish soldiers have caught some kind of sickness," I said.

"And I'd wager they're all going to die," Captain Thompson said.

He picked up his breakfast plate and a teacup and relocated them to a table against the wall behind him. The soldiers shuffled to the far side of the room before dashing out the door. Based on the speed of their departure and Captain Thompson's nasty tone, I suspected gossiping soldiers at the Horn Works had slandered me as contagious—or worse, Bad Luck.

"Why are you so rude?" I said. "I'm not that Gypsy Lady in the black carriage with rats hanging all about. I'm His Majesty's inspector—"

"At least she *saves* lives. Quite the opposite of you."

I could see the bottoms of my eyebrows forming a horizontal line in my field of vision—a testimony to my displeasure with the ill-mannered man.

"I need a small company of soldiers to accompany me up the Wando to Hobcaw Creek, Captain. I'll also need a boat, obviously."

"The Swamp Fox is on the loose there. I wouldn't advise—"

"Why does everyone keep mentioning this Swamp Fox? He's not the legendary Robin Hood. He's a murderous rebel thug, Captain."

"A rebel thug who'll annihilate a small party of kingsmen."

I took my Order of Compliance out again. Reading from it, I informed him that *anyone refusing to comply with royal inspector Charlotte Savatier's demands would be hanged.*

Captain Thompson shouted, "Sergeant Bostwick!"

A sloppy man limped through the doorway. Sweat darkened the armpits of his white shirt, and he was paler than your average pale Brit.

"The Maiden of Death is back for more souls," Captain Thompson told the sergeant. "Prepare a party of heavily armed soldiers and a few boats to sail across the Cooper River." He looked at me. "Or shall we call it the River Styx?"

"Aye, sir," Sergeant Bostwick said lethargically, coughing into his fist.

"Cough in the other room," Captain Thompson told Bostwick, who shuffled off.

"I see how this works," I said. "When an enemy of the Crown deliberately kills our troops, he is awarded the sleek name of Swamp Fox. But when a woman, who is His Majesty King George the Third's royal inspector—when she, through no fault of her own, has soldiers die alongside her, she is labeled *The Maiden of Death.*"

"Come back tomorrow and ask for Sergeant Bostwick," he said snootily. "He's coming down with a sickness, so he's the perfect man to lead your mission, whatever the bloody hell it is, *Inspector.*"

I left my horse at the Horn Works and walked to Uncle George's house. Heathcliff was sitting across from him at their dinner table. They looked healthy.

"You look terrible," Uncle George said to me.

"Well, isn't that nice of you?" I said, falling into the closest chair.

"*The more we love our friends,*" Uncle George said, one hand theatrically held aloft, "*the less we flatter them; it is by excusing nothing that pure love shows itself.*"

"That sounds like an excuse a man would make," I said. "One who's been called out for taking his wife for granted."

He tapped his finger on the table, waiting for my answer. This time, I was sure I knew who authored his quote. Uncle George told me that the poet Jonathan Swift's father died when he was young, and his uncle raised him. Telling the truth to someone you love, even if it's uncomfortable—as he just had—was the clue.

"Swift!" I said gleefully.

My uncle squeezed my hand warmly. "Molière!"

I pulled my hand free and slapped his. I could see the bottoms of my eyebrows again. "Why would you quote a French writer in English? To trick me?"

"*Oui, mon bébé,*" he said, reaching in to tug on my earlobe, and I bit his thumb, which was salty with grime.

"I'm afraid I have something to confess," I said, wiping my mouth on my sleeve.

"Oh?" Heathcliff said, suddenly interested in my presence.

"You were right, Uncle George."

"About what?"

"About drawing attention by traveling into the countryside with imperial soldiers."

"You were attacked again?" Heathcliff asked.

I told them about the Swamp Fox capturing soldiers along the Wando River. I also mentioned how Major Bannery and my Irish soldiers had fallen ill. Of course, I proudly announced the discovery of the Suicide Plant and my mission to question the owner of Bancroft Plantation.

"I don't want to get any more soldiers killed, though," I said, adding that the soldiers at the Horn Works had dubbed me *The Maiden of Death*.

They laughed at me.

"I sent him into the State House during your absence," Uncle George said, pointing his chin at Heathcliff. "Exactly as you wanted."

"How did that go?"

"He owns a lot of property," Uncle George said. "Quite a few ships, too. We've been keeping an eye on the docks. One of his transport ships came into port today from Barbados. Pawsworthy unloaded twenty kegs of rum and five thousand pounds of sugar. They were loaded onto wagons and brought to his warehouse on East Bay Street."

"But here's what's odd," Heathcliff said, glancing at Uncle George. "They loaded one barrel of rum on the first wagon. One, mind you. And that horse struggled up the incline of the alleyway that leads from the docks to East Bay Street. After that, they loaded five barrels at a time on a wagon."

"So?" I said.

"That first barrel was extremely heavy," Uncle George said.

"That barrel didn't contain rum," Heathcliff said. "Rum doesn't weigh that much."

"Is it possible the other barrels were empty?" I rested my forearms on the table, moving aside a dinner plate streaked with dried blood. "So they stacked five to a wagon."

"I thought that, too," Heathcliff said. "So I helped them load one of those barrels to see how heavy it was. It was filled with rum. It swished around."

"They didn't want him near their wagons." Uncle George nodded at Heathcliff. "They pointed about six bayonets in his face and told him to back off."

"Charlotte," Heathcliff said. "That first barrel had to be filled with gold."

"They tripled the guards at the warehouse, too," Uncle George said.

"I'm certain they'll sneak that barrel to his house late tonight." Heathcliff paused, squinting as he mused. "If I was Pawsworthy, I couldn't sleep knowing my gold sat a few yards from a harbor full of ships ready to sail away with it."

"Or it could be lead for musket balls," I said.

"Why hide lead in a cask?" Uncle George said.

"It's for the rebel army," I said.

"If they move that barrel tonight," Heathcliff said. "We'll know it's gold."

"Not necessarily. To Pawsworthy, lead could be more valuable than gold. If the rebels win the war, and Pawsworthy can prove he helped them by having secretly provided them munitions, they won't seize his property and put him on a prison ship. He's playing both sides, using his rebel nephew Norman as his go-between."

"Now I simply have to find out what's in that cask," Heathcliff said.

"I don't want a barrel of gold," I said. "I want *everything* he owns."

"Well, he owns a lot, Charlotte," Uncle George said.

Heathcliff pushed a stack of papers at me, notes he'd made at the State House. I read through the top ones, learning Pawsworthy owned at least five houses in Charleston, two plantations in the low country, four taverns, a transport ship, four schooners, a warehouse on East Bay Street, and thirty Narragansett Pacers on a third plantation."

"What's a Narragansett Pacer?" I asked, glancing up from the papers.

"A breed of horse from New England," Heathcliff said, jerking his head at Uncle George. "He asked around at the Horn Works. They're fast and sturdy, bred for traveling over rough terrain. But they also make excellent endurance racers."

"Pawsworthy was turning his plantation on Rantowles Creek into a Narragansett Pacer race track," Uncle George said. "Today's races are short and fast-paced. He designed races that would last much longer using these Narragansett Pacers. It appears he has a huge import rum business and planned on selling cocktails to the crowds at these longer racing events."

"Cocktails?" I said. "What's that?"

"That's what I asked the owner of The Jester's Mate," Heathcliff said. "It's a drink a French fur trader in New York invented. He mixed rum and limes and other shite in his mug, stuck a rooster feather in it, and called it a cocktail."

"Pawsworthy was creating a sporting club," Uncle George explained. "Then the war ruined those plans."

"Or rather," Heathcliff said, nodding, "the war postponed them. He sailed his entire stable of Narragansett Pacers to Barbados. He didn't want them falling into the hands of the army—any army."

"Barbados?"

"Yeah. It's a Royal—"

"This is the stuff of gossip, not record books," I said. "How did you get all this information?"

"I tracked down your friend Byron, the tax assessor," Heathcliff said.

"How do you know about him?"

"I read your notes on your desk," he said.

"You speak French?"

Heathcliff jerked his head at Uncle George, saying, "He does."

"You aided in the invasion of my privacy?" I asked Uncle George.

"I translated what I read—that Byron was a royal tax assessor and a—"

"I said for *you* to fetch Émile's bag and the letter I'd write—"

"Hush!" Heathcliff said, the bottom of his fist pounding the tabletop. "Our sole purpose for banding together is to steal Pawsworthy's riches, yeah?"

I glared at him.

"So what's it matter if I looked at your notes?" he said. "It's not as if I was drooling over those lewd drawings of you naked." He lowered his eyes to my chest.

"We need to find out what's in that heavy cask," Uncle George told me, quickly returning to our original discussion. "If it's lead, you can tell Colonel Balfour. He'll arrest him. Pawsworthy has no legitimate reason to hide it."

I stood and collected Heathcliff's papers. As I shuffled them into a neat stack, I uncovered one of Émile's intimate drawings of me. I pulled it from the pile and floated it across the table toward Heathcliff.

"You should keep a handkerchief handy," I said. "To collect your drool."

Tucking the rest of the notes under my arm, I stomped past him and left.

~

After changing my clothes, I walked to the docks on East Bay, looking to rent a small boat: The Maiden of Death had decided to go to Bancroft Plantation without soldiers. Eventually, I found a Pee Dee Indian calling himself Pee Dee Amos, who took me to Hobcaw Creek in his canoe for a fee. Though the Cooper River was rough, we negotiated the high waves steadily since we both knew how to row.

After two hours of stopping at farmhouses and plantations along the Hobcaw, we found the Bancroft Plantation. Mrs. Bancroft was inside a small house twenty yards from the plantation house, which was in ashes. She refused to open her door and spoke to me through a closed window. I pressed my Order of Compliance against the glass, demanding she come outside. When I pulled the paper away, I found myself staring at two black holes at the ends of her pistol barrels.

Pee Dee Amos spoke Wacataw.

"That crazy lady's hands are shaking like a wet dog drying off," he said, standing behind me.

"I know," I said, looking over my shoulder at him, "one twitch of her trigger finger and I'll lose my face."

When she heard me speaking Wacataw, she screamed and wiggled her pistols, telling us to climb back into our wobbly little canoe.

"You're making a critical error," I told her. "Colonel Balfour will seize this property."

"There's nothing left to take," she said, her voice breaking. "So clear out of here, you half-breed guttersnipe."

Once I was back in Charleston, I went to the Horn Works and told Captain Thompson to send soldiers immediately to the Bancroft Plantation, bring Barnabas Bancroft's mother back to Charleston, hold her in the Provost Dungeon overnight, and deliver her at nine o'clock to my office at the Craven Bastion. I drew a map with her exact location.

From there, I went to Eliza Breckenridge's house on St. Philip's Street. I stood across the road, observing. The house to the left of Eliza's was a tavern. I could see another tavern a few houses down. For some reason, I had imagined Eliza living in a beautiful home, expecting her to be a strong woman of character, perhaps a wealthy widow.

Eliza's house, however, was in shambles.

Some clapboards on the front of the house were warped or missing, exposing the inner skeletal frame. The piazza had no door, and I could see several women sitting in chairs, chatting, passing a green bottle around, an occasional burst of laughter rising above the chatter. During my brief vigil, three men came out and one went in. They all had the same style of white pants, although their shirts varied in color and tailoring—off-duty soldiers. The Horn Works was a few blocks away.

This was a brothel.

I crossed the street. At the piazza steps, I asked the women if they knew Eliza Breckenridge.

"She's busy putting a loaf in the oven, sweetie," one woman said, provoking cackles from her colleagues.

I turned and left.

It would have been utterly out of character for Émile to use a prostitute. Émile had fought for legislation in Québec City to stop prostitution. He lost, of course. Still, he raised money from wealthy citizens and churches to establish a home for women, to lure them away from prostitution, and to free them from the economic dependency of selling themselves. Women ran that home, women who tried to teach business skills and promote self-respect and self-reliance.

You can never claim to know what's in another person's heart, but I couldn't see Émile demeaning a woman for sexual pleasure. Pawsworthy was lying. He was a cruel man who enjoyed hurting others.

Or, possibly, I had married the most deceitful, lying, two-faced hypocrite bastard this side of the Atlantic.

It was forty-five degrees the following morning, according to Gabriel's thermometer outside the kitchen house door. I wore a shawl for the walk to Archdale Street. Heathcliff was stacking firewood inside the house. Crazy George, Heathcliff reported, was taking his usual bath in the frigid river.

"They moved that heavy barrel last night," he said. "They put the wagon in Pawsworthy's stable house and left it there."

"I need you to go to someone's house," I said. "The third house on the right on St. Philip's Street after Liberty Street. Get a woman living there named Eliza Breckenridge and bring her to the Craven Bastion."

"Why don't your soldiers do it?"

"Please. Go get her."

He wiped his wet forehead with the hairy side of his forearm. "Eliza Breckenridge," he said. "I read that name in your notes, on a page with your husband's name at the top. There was a question mark under her name, too. What's her connection to these murders?"

Of course, I remembered Heathcliff grabbing the back of my hair, warning me not to let my vendetta jeopardize our acquisition of riches.

"That's why I drew a question mark. Pawsworthy told me that's the woman my husband was seeing. Why—"

"By *seeing*, you mean *fucking*?"

"Pawsworthy is paying or blackmailing her to say that," I said. "Why would Pawsworthy tell me about her? So I'd be so discouraged I'd give up the investigation. And why would he want me to give up? He's connected somehow. He never thought I'd figure that out, so he's trying to break my spirit. But Eliza Breckenridge may know something that can help prove Pawsworthy's connection. She might even know if Pawsworthy's connected to my husband's death. That would be treason, punishable by death."

"Then Balfour will seize his property," Heathcliff said. "And we'll get nothing. I warned you. You let your husband's death ruin our chances—"

"And I warned you not to threaten me," I said. "I never said I'd tell Balfour. We will blackmail Pawsworthy and take all he's got. Discovering his secrets is how we break him. So kindly go get Eliza Breckenridge."

I walked out without saying goodbye. It made no sense to say hello or goodbye to that sweaty pig. Heathcliff was perpetually miserable, manipulative, and morose. A man utterly intolerant of empathy or sympathy. What humored him was anyone's guess. Even his rare spurts of happiness, if you could call them that, were a reaction to someone else's misery or a performance.

Hence my reason for not using soldiers to get Eliza: After a brisk arm-in-arm saunter across Charleston with Heathcliff, she would, by the time she reached my office, enthusiastically confess her innermost sins if it would free her from that fiend's clutches.

I went to my office and started a crackling fire. The split wood, in a peaceful state earlier, was now exposed to its arch-enemy, fire. It was fundamentally changing its character before my eyes, self-sustaining its destruction in becoming what it hated.

The crackling was soon interrupted by a fast-paced drumming of footfalls out in the hall, the abrupt shuffle of someone being hurried by a tormentor's pushy hands. The door opened, and a pretty young woman rushed in with Heathcliff on her heels. Heathcliff, squeezing her bicep, turned and kicked the door shut. He directed her into a chair opposite my desk. A rip on the shoulder of her right sleeve displayed frayed threads.

"Eliza Breckenridge," I said from behind my desk, "how do you know Major Donald Pawsworthy?"

"Who the hell are you?" she said.

I glanced at Heathcliff. He was suddenly interested in something on the other side of the window behind me. How could Heathcliff drag her here and not tell her who I was or why I wanted to interview her?

"Answer the question," I told Eliza.

"Never heard of him."

"Listen, sweetie," I told her. "You have fallen from paradise and landed in hell with us. You can only return to a state of grace by telling the truth."

"I wasn't in no state of grace, trust me," she said, shifting her eyes off the floorboards to meet mine. She looked at the cabinets, the books, and the tables with chairs around them. "What is this place?"

"It's my debriefing room."

"Really? What's it for?"

I thought she was mocking me. She wasn't. She was sincerely waiting for an answer. Placing both elbows on the table, I rubbed my temples with closed eyes.

"Why would Major Pawsworthy say he knows you if he doesn't?" I asked.

"Beats me."

I studied her. What an improbable choice of words—particularly from someone who took a stroll with Heathcliff.

"Do you know Sergeant Andrew Dawson?" I said.

She puckered her lips and shook her head meditatively, mulling over the name. She wasn't the meditative type. She was lying. She saw me glaring at her.

"I know a lot of soldiers, lady," she said, her drab expression suggesting it would be fruitless to go over the list.

I turned in my chair, remarking Heathcliff, still at the window. He adapted rapidly to his new life, taking advantage of the unfolding events. He was an opportunist playing his own game behind my back.

"Did Mr. Heathcliff tell you why he brought you here?"

"Mr. Heathcliff?"

She was either slightly drunk or, sadly, stupid—or both.

"That man," I said, jerking my head at Heathcliff.

"Oh, him."

"Did he hurt you? Rip your dress?"

I touched the shoulder of my dress where hers was torn. She turned her head, and her chin receded into her throat as she spoke to the rip, chuckling, noticing it for the first time.

"I must have done that last night," she said. "Me and the girls got a little drunk and—"

"So Mr. Heathcliff didn't threaten or hurt you?"

I didn't instruct Heathcliff to hurt her. I had expected him to—it was his nature.

"He ridiculed me, but, no, he didn't hurt me none. He didn't have to. He paid me to come here."

She raised her face to him with a defiant look that said she wouldn't play her part in his scheme. Apparently, Heathcliff didn't pay her enough. He slithered to the fireplace and grabbed a split log from the stack. He turned, glaring at the back of Eliza's head. His stare met mine, and he reluctantly tossed the log on the fire. An ember the size of a peach pit tumbled onto the hearthstone. A black crust tried to form around its orange heart, but the parent fire pulsated waves of heat over the little ember, keeping it bright, keeping the black crust isolated to a few dark scabs here and there. It wouldn't last. I knew better than anyone that the orphaned ember could never hold back the darkness. That darkness would entomb the orphan as it grew cold to its core, turning it into a blind orb.

Boots pounded on the floorboards in the hall. The door opened. Two soldiers entered, flanking an older woman. Mrs. Bancroft looked harried. Her black and gray hair was in a bun above her head, sprouting arched bows that fell in all directions like a landscape water fountain. Splotches of filth spotted her white dress, resembling the hide of a dairy cow, and the hem had absorbed grime from the floor of the Provost Dungeon, forming a dark ring.

The soldiers weren't from the Provost. They wore the uniforms of Pawsworthy's South Carolina Royalists. Pawsworthy had intervened. I thanked the soldiers and they left, closing the door. Recognizing me, Mrs. Bancroft began to speak. I ordered her to hush and sit at one of the tables. I sat back in my chair.

"Is Pawsworthy a client of yours?" I asked Eliza.

I glanced at Mrs. Bancroft, observing her reaction to hearing Pawsworthy's name. She raised her head attentively.

"No," Eliza said.

"What about Major Savatier?"

"Which one is he? Your husband?"

"Pawsworthy told me you were fucking him," I said, glancing at Mrs. Bancroft, whose eyes darted between Eliza and me.

"It wasn't nothin' personal," Eliza said, biting her lower lip. "Every now and again, we'd do it." She shrugged, nibbling on a fingernail, her eyes somewhere over my shoulder. "Usually after he'd had a few at the tavern."

I didn't believe her. No matter how drunk Émile got, he would never sleep with a prostitute. He found prostitution repugnant. If he had struck up a relationship with another woman here in Charleston, fine, that would be a reality I'd have to acknowledge. He would never degrade a woman by paying to sleep with her. It was fundamentally against everything he stood for. The irony of a prostitute disgracing Émile's name— the name of the man who would have tried to help her, to raise her out of poverty and disgrace—was frustrating.

"There's a slight problem with your story," I told Eliza. "My husband didn't drink."

Émile, of course, did drink. In fact, Eliza's face was taking on a crimson hue that, if it kept enriching itself, would have ended up the color of our favorite red wine from Beaune, France.

"Why would you lie about sleeping with my husband?" I said. "Did Pawsworthy put you up to this?"

Heathcliff stepped forward, his hand coming up to grab her hair or slap her. She crouched to the right, away from him.

"Heathcliff, don't. Let her be." I pointed my chin at Eliza. "Why did Pawsworthy tell you to lie to me?"

"I ain't going to talk about him," she said. "You'll get me into awful trouble, lady—trouble nobody on earth would want. All I got to say is, no, I didn't fuck your lousy husband. I don't know nothing about the man. Never laid eyes on him. Why don't you ask Pawsworthy yourself? Please leave me out of this. Please."

As I suspected, Pawsworthy was trying to demoralize me, to take the enthusiasm out of my investigation so I would fail. It conclusively meant he had something to do with these murders and didn't want me to discover what it was. Eliza was studying the floorboards.

Mrs. Bancroft spoke loudly, "Why in God's name am I here?"

Heathcliff, standing behind Eliza, turned toward her. "Hush, you filthy cow," he said. "You'll have your chance to talk soon enough."

"I don't understand why you didn't have the soldiers bring me directly here," she said to me. "Instead of sending me to that prison."

"Mrs. Bancroft," I said. "Yesterday, I took the time from my schedule to travel to you, to question you in person, but you sent me and my Pee Dee guide away at gunpoint. After insulting us."

She fell silent, examining the ceiling suddenly, fiddling with her messy hair.

"Eliza," I said. "You need to stop drinking and stop working at that house."

She nodded solemnly.

"What if you came and worked for me?" I said, confident this is what Émile would want me to do. "I have a place for you to stay."

"What would I do?"

"You'd assist me. My only requirement is you can't drink spirits."

"I'd like that."

Heathcliff walked deeper into the room, grabbing a table and dragging it alongside Eliza. He went to the cabinet doors beside Mrs. Bancroft, bending to open one. He took out the decanter of scotch and a glass, filling a third of it, and placed it on the table beside Eliza.

"What's this?" she said, glancing down.

Heathcliff grinned, his sharp white fangs quite prominent.

"A celebratory drink," he said. "For your new job."

"Cheers."

She slugged the scotch in one gulp, holding the glass out for more. So long as she drank, her life would never change.

"You can go," I told Eliza.

"I can leave?" she asked happily, slamming the glass down.

Heathcliff stepped toward the door and opened it. She hustled past him. Down the hall, someone whistled, and I heard her tell him to pleasure himself in a thicket of thorny rose bushes. Heathcliff closed the door. Nodding to Mrs. Bancroft, he waved a hand over the chair Eliza had occupied.

"Please, Mrs. Bancroft," Heathcliff said with a handsome smile. "It's your turn in the interrogation chair."

"I'm fine where I am, thank you," she said.

"I strongly advise you sit right here, love," he said calmly, tapping the back of the chair.

Her raised eyebrows were an appeal for me to intervene. I nodded at the empty chair. She stood and crept toward it, maybe hoping the closer she got to the chair, the farther Heathcliff would stray from it.

That wasn't the case.

"Do you have any idea who killed your son?" I said to her.

"No," she said, sitting slowly. "If I did, I would have directly reported them to the soldiers at the Horn Works."

"Your son was murdered in the same grotesque manner as Francis Wragg and Major Henrique Baptiste de Montcalm. Did your son know these men, Wragg and Montcalm?"

"Yes," she said, nodding fast. "We both did."

"What about Major Donald Pawsworthy?"

"Of course."

"Of course?" I said, mocking her. "Why 'of course?'"

"He's a successful merchant and plantation owner. He's famous in Charleston and all the low country."

"So you know *of* him? You don't know him."

"No. I know him. I've known him for twenty years. Why?"

"Stop asking me questions. For every question you ask from this moment on, you'll spend another night in the Provost."

"And this time I might tell all those stinking rebels there that you're a loyalist," Heathcliff said.

"What do you want from me?" she said, ignoring Heathcliff, her proud posture wilting into a slouch. "They murdered my son. My husband died fighting rebels. I have nothing left in this world. Everything on my plantation has been robbed. Everything. My livestock, my food, even my furniture, books, and clothes. My slaves are gone. They ran away with the King's army. They burned my home to the ground. I live in a shack. And now this happens." She threw her hand out at me. "How is it that I, a lifelong loyalist, sit here in a British city being interrogated by a *French* inquisitor and her *English* wolfhound? Does it get any crazier than this?"

"We live in a country at war," I said. "Where everyone wants to take something from someone else. In all wars, militants impart atrocities on each other."

"A mob of runaway slaves destroyed my plantation. Not a militia."

"I thought the Hessian army raided your plantation thinking you were a rebel?" I said.

"They knew I was a loyalist. It didn't matter. Those greedy Germans wanted to ransack my place. The slaves showed up afterward while I was burying my son."

"Did you recognize any of the slaves as yours?"

"I did, yes. But the Germans didn't leave anything for them, so they burned my plantation out of spite."

"I suspect they had a more dignified reason for burning your plantation, Mrs. Bancroft."

She rolled her eyes, dismissing my rationale.

"You have to be aware," I said, "that slaves have been told by the British that they will be freed when the rebels lose the war, so why would they stay on the plantations?"

"Which makes the runaway slaves *loyalists* like you," Heathcliff told her, chuckling.

"How's that for crazy?" I said, also adding a chuckle.

She darted her gaze between Heathcliff and me.

"Where did they find you two?" she said.

I assumed by *they* she meant the British government in Charleston. I told her how Colonel Balfour and the Board of Police appointed me. "As for him," I said, glancing at Heathcliff. "I met him on a frigate during a raging storm in the Atlantic. Not long afterward, he died in a military hospital, and the doctor brought him back to life by electrocuting him and breathing into his face. He went to hell when he died—briefly, before he was brought back to life, that is." I nodded to Heathcliff. "Isn't that right, Mr. Heathcliff?"

"You didn't bring me back," Heathcliff said nastily; I couldn't tell whether he was playing along or being earnest. "I was *thrown* out of hell."

"Think about that for a moment, Mrs. Bancroft," I said, seizing the opportunity. "You have to be a mighty awful person to get thrown out of hell."

"You're both devils, as far as I'm concerned," Mrs. Bancroft said, her little fists tight. "And to hellfire you'll return."

"Speaking of fire," I said. "Earlier, you said *they* burned your house, meaning the slaves. You also said *they* murdered your son. You think the slaves murdered your son?"

"No. He was murdered before the Germans or the slaves got there."

"Who's *they*?" I asked.

"I don't know. It's an English expression, I guess. I meant whoever did it."

"But you said *they*. So there was more than one person?"

"I'm not sure."

"Who tied you up? A group of men? One man?"

"They put a hood over my head from behind."

"*They?*"

"Whoever. They. Him. I couldn't see."

"Did you fight back?"

"My first instinct was to get the hood off my head. The moment I raised my hands, they slipped the rope around one wrist, jerked it behind me, and tied my other one."

"So whoever tied you up had a level of expertise."

"They even tied me to the chair."

"What were you doing at the time?"

"I was sitting at the table in the kitchen house, plucking the feathers off my last chicken."

"No one spoke to you," I said, "while you were being tied up?"

"Not a peep."

"Did you hear lots of footsteps or a few?"

"I don't remember."

"Does your kitchen house have a dirt floor, brick, or floorboards?"

"Floorboards."

"Think. You are being tied to the chair. Do you hear footsteps? More than one person's footsteps?"

"I didn't hear anything."

"Whispers?"

She shook her head.

"How about the door? Did you hear that close?"

"Yes. I remember hearing the latch click. I was afraid it was a pistol getting cocked."

"How long after you were tied up did you hear the click?"

"Immediately, I guess."

"So one person exited if the door closed that quickly," I said. "You must have screamed when the hood went over your head. No one tried to silence you?"

"I screamed, of course, for help. No one told me to shut up, and no one came to help, either. There was no one to come besides my son. They must have already gotten to him."

Tears magnified her blue eyes.

"Why do you think you weren't killed, too?" I said. "Why did the killer go to the trouble of putting a hood over your head?"

"I reckoned that's what criminals did."

"Your son's killer knew you, that's why. Or at least he didn't want to be identified by you later on. The killer has something against your son, but not you."

"They were brutal, these killers. I heard Barnabas screaming. Begging for mercy. Apologizing for something."

I felt my eyebrows rise on their own. "Apologizing?" I said. "So he offended his killer somehow. This was revenge. What was he apologizing for?"

"He never said." She wiped one eye with the padding of her thumb. "He stopped screaming after that."

"How long were you tied up?"

"A couple hours, I reckon."

"The Germans untied you, is that right?"

She nodded, saying, "Yeah—after they robbed everything. They even took my door hinges and the buckles in my shoes."

"What did you do after they freed you?"

"I ran into the house to find Barnabas. Upstairs to his bedroom. That's where the Germans said his body was. I found him on the floor naked. He had been tortured. My poor boy was mutilated. His skin was red as a sunburn, and they stuck little needles in him. Everywhere. Hundreds of them. His face, his hands, his backside, his . . ." She dropped her face in both palms, weeping quietly.

"So your son knew Pawsworthy, too?"

"Of course," she said, sniffling, using the side of her forefinger to gather what her nostrils couldn't pull back in.

"Someone in this world hates your son and Wragg and Montcalm so much that they butchered them," I said. "Who would do that? Pawsworthy? Is that why he put a hood over your head?"

She paused, lowering her head, and the thin skin of her eyelids betrayed the swift shifts of her eyeballs within—the panicky behavior of a schemer.

"Mrs. Bancroft," I said softly, "if you start lying to me, I'll have Mr. Heathcliff throw you into the Provost naked. Honestly, I don't want to do that. Work with me. I'm trying to find who killed your son."

She raised her head, nodding, exhaling loudly.

"Montcalm was at our plantation," she finally said. "The night before he was arrested in Charleston."

"Why was he here, a French officer in enemy British Charleston? Is there a spy ring?"

"Good lord, no. They were all friends before the war."

"I live in Québec City, Mrs. Bancroft. I have friends in New England who are rebels. Friends from before the war. The last thing I'd do is visit them."

She blinked at me. She glanced at the door. Heathcliff noticed, too, and stepped in front of it. She clenched her hands in her lap.

"Am I going to get in any trouble for this? For having Montcalm at my home?"

"Mrs. Bancroft, I want to find your son's murderer. Nothing more."

"You got to promise—"

Heathcliff stomped toward her.

"Before the war," she said, showing Heathcliff her palm, "my son, Mr. Wragg, Montcalm, and Donald started a rum company in Barbados."

"What's the name of this company?"

"Mount Gilboa Distillery. When the war started, they continued to sell rum—to both sides. Montcalm sold to the French, and the others sold to everyone here and in Great Britain. But the war began to take its toll, especially with those Yankee pirates stealing everything. That's why Montcalm was here. The profits were slim. He wanted to sell his part of the business. So did Francis Wragg."

"Who else was at this meeting? Pawsworthy?"

"All the owners, yes. They set the business up so that no owner could heir his percentage of ownership to someone other than the surviving owners. When one of them died, his ownership would go to the other owners who would pay the deceased's estate whatever his share was worth."

"Do you think Pawsworthy is killing off his business partners? You said yourself the war is hurting sales. With them dead, he'd pay their estates little to nothing."

She kept her head up and chin set. Hers was a concentrated expression that showed she sincerely contemplated that possibility.

"If Donald wanted his partners out of the way," she said, shaking her head, "he wouldn't have to kill them. He could accuse them of being rebels and use his friend John Cruden to seize their property. With them out of the way, he could take the rum plantation. He's not doing that. And I simply can't see Donald killing his partners. Pawsworthy's not a killer."

"You think highly of him?"

"I do, yes."

"Maybe you're in on it with him?" I didn't believe that, but I wouldn't let anyone compliment Pawsworthy and not suffer for it.

"I'd never kill my son," she said through sudden tears, her voice chortled.

"Pawsworthy would," I said. "It's a lot of work proving Wragg and your son were rebels. It's a lot easier and faster to kill them." I waited for her to contradict me, but she didn't. "Do you know anyone else who'd want Wragg, Montcalm, and your son dead?"

"No."

Pawsworthy had to be the murderer. Unwittingly, Mrs. Bancroft had implicated Pawsworthy in treason: He was selling goods—rum—to the enemy by conspiring with a French officer, Major Montcalm. And she was my witness. She just didn't know it. I clapped as a baker does to free his hands of flour.

"We're done," I said. "You can go."

"Go?" she said. "Go where? Not back to that dungeon? I beg you, please, I—"

"Go home."

She stood, and Heathcliff opened the door. A soldier stood there, his back to us as if standing guard. He turned, a surprised look on his face. His uniform had the yellow facing of the South Carolina Royalists.

"Sir," Heathcliff said to the soldier, "if eavesdropping excites you, you could better satisfy that deranged pleasure by standing outside the window of the nearest brothel."

The soldier's face flushed, and he strolled away. Heathcliff slammed the door, causing Mrs. Bancroft to flinch. "But"—her nose wrinkled— "but how am I supposed to get home?"

"Why don't you ask your friend Pawsworthy if you can borrow a spare ass?"

She turned to leave. Heathcliff stepped into her lane.

"Not so fast," he said.

"What now?" Her meek eyes struggled to hold his weighty stare.

"What happened to the chicken?" Heathcliff asked.

"The chicken?" Her little fists pulsated with frustration. "What chicken?"

"You said you were plucking a chicken when the killer put a hood over your head."

"I was," she said with a self-righteous promotion in her tone.

"Well, what happened to it?"

She pursed her shuddering lips, remembering. "The fucking Germans ate it."

# CHAPTER THIRTEEN

## *The Maiden Of Death*

On my walk home, I thought about Pawsworthy staging the grotesque murders so they would appear to be the demented work of a cruel lunatic. Also, I didn't believe Heathcliff paid Eliza to come to my office. I suspected he paid her not to tell me something she told him on the way there.

I opened my desk drawer in my bedroom and pulled out the stack of blank paper to update my notes when I discovered a letter in Émile's handwriting. The letter was backward in the pile; that is, the side with writing on it was facing the bottom of the drawer. It was addressed to me, dated December 23, 1780. He never mailed it. I realized he never intended to. I would have arrived here long before that letter arrived in Québec City. He had left it here, hidden, for me to find.

In the letter, he described an angry Pee Dee man who'd been stopped at the city gate because he didn't have a license to operate a wagon, nor was his wagon registered at the State House. The incident didn't interest me as much as the odd symbol at the bottom of this hidden epistle. Émile had drawn the letter U, a capital one, with the number four inside the U. I had also seen this same symbol drawn on one of his note pages, dated December 21, 1780. He drew it in the middle of the page. The notes above the U-4 symbol described how Gabriel would operate on soldiers from any regiment or militia—British, Germans, loyalists, and rebels; whites, blacks, and Indians, too.

I could not see how the symbol of the U with the four inside it was connected to the information in the note written on December 21 and his letter a few days later. However, there was something quite obvious about the U-4 symbol. In both incidences, in the letter and his note, Émile had written two words in English below the symbol, "for you."

Exactly what was for me?

I did notice a discrepancy. Émile traditionally wrote his number four with an open top, 4; but the four in his symbols had a closed top, 4.

Why?

And who writes a letter he never intends to mail? Who hides a letter in a pile of blank papers knowing the person he's addressing it to will arrive in person in a matter of days? Why not leave it out in the open?

Someone who knew he was going to die, that's who—someone who didn't want his killer intercepting his letter.

I had breakfast with Mahala. Duck eggs fried in duck fat with red rice and a delicious gingerbread with orange peel and caraway seeds. We sat by the fire at the table in the kitchen house since it was chilly outdoors. Winslow came in and handed me a letter from Captain Thompson, addressed to *Her Eminence, The Maiden of Death.*

The nerve of this man!

It said Mrs. Bancroft had drowned in the Cooper River near one of the docks on East Bay Street. Her skull was bludgeoned, and she had black hair snagged in the fingernails of her right hand.

I pondered who had black hair.

Dawson.

Pawsworthy.

Heathcliff.

Also, every Indian and African in the land under sixty.

And probably half the drunks on East Bay.

I crumpled the note in my fist when armed redcoats stormed the compound, yelling. I ran outdoors. Pawsworthy and Dawson were dressed in military garb. Pawsworthy ordered about a dozen soldiers into the hospital. They terrorized the patients, eventually forcing several outside in their white gowns. Next came Gabriel with his wrists in iron shackles. Pawsworthy watched me approach.

"I'm arresting DuBois for treason," he told me.

"Treason?" I said, hearing my voice rising in pitch.

"He's openly operating on rebel soldiers. In clear violation of the law."

Pawsworthy nodded to his soldiers and told them to take Gabriel to the Provost. I stepped in, squeezing Gabriel's bony shoulder.

"I'll get you out, Gabriel," I told him in French.

"I'm confident you will."

Doors slammed and boots clopped along the piazza as soldiers marched into the main house. I didn't want them seizing my notes on my desk. Those notes included details of my investigation into Pawsworthy. I ran inside, climbing the back steps to the second floor. Three soldiers stood in the hall outside the dining room. No one was in my room. I stuffed my papers into Émile's leather carrying case and looked out the window. Dawson had lined the injured rebel patients up in front of the kitchen house. Opposite them stood more of Pawsworthy's soldiers. Clutching the carrying case, I ran downstairs.

"What the hell are you doing?" I said to Pawsworthy, coming at him at full stride.

He tried to ignore me, so I stood directly in front of him. Greasy black hair flaked with dandruff stuck to his forehead.

"Stand back," he said, "or I'll arrest you, too."

He drew his sword from its sheath, ushering me aside with the outside of his forearm. Seven injured rebels stood hunched inside their baggy white gowns. One soldier sat on the ground, revealing an ankle wrapped in a white bandage with bright red blood. Pawsworthy told his soldiers to aim. He raised his sword above his head, lowering it fast as he yelled, "Fire!" Thick white smoke from the thunderous rifle blasts filled the air between the soldiers and the rebels. The ghostly cloud floated toward Price's Alley, revealing sprawled bodies—except the one soldier who had been sitting. No one had aimed at him. A white cloth wrapped around his head, the bandaging covering one eye so that only the working one darted around the compound. He appeared oblivious to the corpses.

Pawsworthy nodded to Dawson. Dawson withdrew his pistol, cocking the hammer as he approached the man and shot him in the head.

Blood and something yellowy smacked against the brick wall; blood also squirted back out the hole in the man's skull, brightening Dawson's white pant legs from the thighs down.

"Don't look so stricken," Pawsworthy said to me. "Those men were dead the moment they arrived. They would've been put aboard a prison ship when they left this hospital. Nobody survives a prison ship."

"You're a weakling," I told him.

He glanced at the leather case at my side. "You'll need to pack more than that little bag, my dear." He looked up at the house behind me. "I'm fixing on making this place mine. I'll rent it to our regiment, horse stable and all."

He lowered his gaze to my breasts, his pig eyes shifting from one to the other, ogling me. What kind of person murders defenseless men and immediately turns his attention to sex? The door to the house opened, and Winslow stepped out, coming toward me, looking along his shoulder at the corpses.

"Seize him," Pawsworthy said to his soldiers, pointing his sword. "I'm detaining all DuBois's slaves."

"Dr. DuBois doesn't own slaves," I said. "Everyone living here is a paid worker. Winslow is a free man."

Winslow smiled, revealing his lightning-white teeth.

"Well, sir," Pawsworthy said to Winslow. "You best pack your bags, too."

"Don't go anywhere," I told him. "This property doesn't belong to Pawsworthy. Not yet." I faced Pawsworthy. "I know the law. You can't seize this property if John Cruden hasn't officially sequestered it. You have arrested and removed Dr. Gabriel DuBois. Do you have evidence that he is a traitor?"

"Of course," he said, chuckling arrogantly.

"Enough to convict him, that is?"

"Enough to *hang* him."

"Good. That means you have no further business here. I am an official representative of His Majesty King George the Third, and you are interfering with the King's wishes for me to solve the murder of Major Henrique Baptiste de Montcalm. I'll challenge your claim on this property on behalf of the King, forcing you to work your procurance through the court. Even your corrupt friend Egerton McClain won't be able to help you. Leave these premises immediately. I have work to do. Urgent work."

Egerton McClain was a magistrate and the former attorney general of the South Carolina colony. He was a member of the Board of Police as well. Heathcliff's notes showed McClain's signature as a witness was on every one of Pawsworthy's recent property deeds. Why the same witness every time? Pawsworthy had to have either been blackmailing him or conspiring with him. That's how Pawsworthy had been able to amass so much property since the British took Charleston nine months ago.

Calling Egerton McClain corrupt irked Pawsworthy. I struck a nerve. His eyebrows scrunched. I glanced at Dawson, where a smirk fattened his cheeks. Pawsworthy sheathed his sword and told Dawson to gather the troops and leave the property.

"What about all these bodies?" I said.

"You deal with them," he said with a snicker. "You're the Maiden of Death."

## CHAPTER FOURTEEN

### *Wedding Bells*

The tax assessor, Byron, wasn't at his makeshift office on the docks. He was inside the Exchange Building in a first-floor office, door open.

"*Bonjour*," I said, clasping my hands as I entered. "I have one quick question, Byron: Did you process that recent arrival of Major Pawsworthy's rum from Barbados?"

He was seated behind a desk with open ledgers sprawled before him. He looked over his round wire-rimmed glasses and whispered, "Kindly close the door."

I did so.

"Around here," he said, winking, "we never say that man's name above a whisper."

"More specifically," I whispered, "did that rum come from Mount Gilboa Distillery?"

Nodding, he said, "In fact, the captain happily reported he didn't see one Yankee pirate ship *en route*."

"*Merci beaucoup*."

I turned to leave. I stopped. Mahala's iron meat-smoking oven was on the floor in the corner.

"You know Mahala?" I asked, nodding at the metal contraption.

"I know everyone," he said with a grin. "Dr. DuBois is my physician. That's where I saw Miss Mahala's oven. It's quite an invention, flavoring meat with smoke. I have an appointment with a blacksmith later today to make five such ovens based on this prototype. I plan to sell them to ship cooks from my roost on the docks. If the five sell, I'll contract the fabrication of more."

"Does Mahala get a portion of your sales? Or are you an invention thief?"

"We have a commission agreement pending."

I bowed my head, smiling. "You are a man of honor, as I suspected." I studied him for a moment: He had a lot of connections; maybe I could do future business with him. "Have you seen Dr. DuBois's Leyden jars?"

"What's a Leyden jar?"

"They generate electricity. He cooks frog legs with it."

"He cooks with electricity?"

"Yes."

"There's no future in that. People will think it's the work of the devil."

I chuckled. "I've seen it work." I opened the door. "When I'm done with this investigation, we should ask Dr. DuBois for a demonstration."

"You just proved it's the work of the devil," he said, laughing.

"I did? How?"

"There's the word *demon* in *demonstration*."

I rolled my eyes. "Do you want to see how they work or not?"

"I'd love to," he said.

"I'm going to insist on a commission agreement beforehand," I said, winking.

"Naturally."

Colonel Balfour's house was at the other end of East Bay Street near my Craven Bastion office, diagonally across the street on the other side of Governor's Bridge in what was probably the most beautiful mansion in Charleston, the Pinckney House. Constructed of dark British bricks and local black cypress, it had four large columns out front with two sets of stone stairs that led from the ground to the central front door on an elevated main floor, like the Gibbes House.

An officer answered the door. A young woman was behind him, passing from one room to another. She paused, curiosity drawing her attention to me. She nodded *hello* and moved on.

"Sir," I said to the officer, handsome, perhaps thirty years old. "I'm looking for Colonel Balfour."

"I'm Colonel Balfour's aide," he said. "You must be Major Savatier's wife, Charlotte?"

"How'd you guess?"

"I can't name a French-speaking woman other than you who would have a reason to call on the Commandant of Charleston—not to mention Émile constantly spoke about you. I had immense respect for your husband. He was a very by-the-book officer but also quite funny. He once sewed my stockings together at the heel." He laughed, remembering. "I nearly broke my big toe trying to stuff my foot in."

"A pleasure to meet you," I said.

"I'm Captain George Benson," he said. "I'm afraid Colonel Balfour isn't home presently. He's meeting with a cantankerous colonel who came all the way from Camden. He's upset that Colonel Balfour supplied his regiment, the 23rd of Foot, with new uniforms *back in November*. The colonel is demanding new uniforms for his regiment now."

"Is not having new uniforms a morale issue for the colonel's soldiers?" I asked. "Or does this colonel want to see the dazzle of bright new uniforms getting ripped to shreds on the battlefield?"

He chuckled. "It's not worth the risk," he said. "Coming to Charleston to bicker. There are bandits and rebels behind every tree between here and Camden."

"You're telling me. I recently escaped a rebel attack outside Moncks Corner."

"I heard. Your Scottish grenadiers were killed. You're quite brave."

"Captain," I said, raising my chin and holding that dignified posture long enough to capture his stare. "I have a problem I need to discuss with Colonel Balfour. It will only take a few minutes. When will he return?"

"He's throwing a party here tonight. He'll be back before four to ensure everything is spot on."

"I'll come back."

"I'll tell him to expect you, ma'am."

"Thank you," I said.

I turned and walked down the stone stairs, pausing when a woman's voice flowed out the window, piggybacking a cross-breeze.

"Who was that girl?" she said; she didn't share Captain Benson's British accent.

"Émile's wife," he said.

"Is she from Charleston?"

"Québec City. Why?"

"She looked familiar," the woman said.

"I wouldn't have noticed, my darling," he said. "For I look at no one but you."

Her lofty giggle floated over my head as I continued my stony descent.

An hour later, a British soldier came to the house with a written invitation to Colonel Balfour's party that began at five o'clock.

I went to Uncle George's house and sat at the dinner table across from Heathcliff. Uncle George asked what was wrong with me. "You have that look of hopelessness," he said, "that Heathcliff's mother must have had when she first saw what she gave birth to."

This commentary elicited a chuckle from Heathcliff. I couldn't discern whether his mirth was sincere. I explained how Gabriel had been arrested for treason and how Pawsworthy executed the injured rebels. I told Heathcliff I wanted him as an ally at Balfour's party. Pawsworthy would undoubtedly be there, so I needed someone on my side. Taking Uncle George would have been a distraction. No matter how well dressed he was, his nose ring, ear feather (which he only took off to replace), and face tattoos would have stood out as much as a wedding cake at a funeral.

"There's nothing in this for you," I told Heathcliff. "I need your help as a friend, if I can call you that."

His dark eyes studied me. Heathcliff was a conniver, so it wasn't easy to read him. For him, a simple human friendship was an unreasonable concept. Selflessly helping someone was meaningless. He looked up from my breasts to the bun at the top of my head. Was he having sexual thoughts, dreaming of tit-for-tats, gripping my bun with my head in his lap? Or was he measuring the level of his disdain for me?

"You never had a friend back home?" I finally asked. "I'm not judging you or your upbringing. I've never met anyone who doesn't want friends. Why is that?"

After a pause, he said, "You can befriend one special person in such a deep and personal way that all other relationships are superficial. I'll illustrate what I mean. Dr. DuBois showed me his magnets. He showed me how they have polarities. How the north pole on one magnet is attracted to the south pole on another magnet—so attracted that they stick together as one. I had a friend who was that close. Only one. Dr. DuBois also showed me how the identical poles on magnets repelled each other. No matter how hard you try, you can never get them to stick. That's how I interact with all other people. Only one person is my polar opposite. I am repelled by everyone else. And—"

"And they are repelled by you," I said.

"Exactly."

I nodded, frowning as I considered this other person he had been close to, which had to have been a woman—that woman named Cathy that the Gypsy Lady heard Heathcliff talking about in his dream, the girl that was thrown out of heaven. Heathcliff was taking their break-up hard. Abnormally hard.

"Enough of the poor-me talk," Uncle George said. "You going to help or not?"

"I'll go to the party," he said. "I want to see who attends these gatherings. Who the wealthy people are in this city."

"*Merci*," I said, standing to leave.

Instead of *you're welcome*, he said, "If you ever ask me a personal question again, you'll risk splitting your skull against my knuckles."

This from the nosy cur whose prying eyes canvassed naked drawings of me? He watched me glance at Uncle George beside him, who reached in and slapped Heathcliff's head with enough force to shake his black curls. Heathcliff didn't flinch or blink. He knew from my shifting eyes that the slap or a punch was coming, and he didn't care.

Heathcliff dressed sharply for the party: Black shoes, Émile's red imprint pants, a matching vest over a white high-collared shirt, a black overcoat, and a powdered wig. He wrapped a white linen stock around his neck with a fancy knot.

"Where'd you get the wig?" I asked.

He prefaced his reply with an eerie grin, so I showed him my palm.

"Don't answer that. I'll pretend you bought it."

Balfour's front door was open, and as we entered the high-ceilinged foyer, I handed the redcoat soldier-butler my invitation. My finely combed hair was in a tall updo, and I wore a formal, fancily embroidered olive-green dress with a white collar so that my cleavage didn't show. I didn't want men leering. Nor had I intentions of lingering here. I wanted to speak with Colonel Balfour and leave.

We followed the couple in front of us down a spacious hallway and up a flight of stairs with masterfully carved woodwork and arched windows on the first landing. The ballroom, whose tall ceilings seemed to amplify the musicians and the people trying to talk over them, was at the front of the house. Despite the room's enormous size (it had to be over thirty feet wide), I immediately spotted Pawsworthy. He was hard to miss. He and Dawson stood behind a long buffet table outfitted with one of his wooden rum casks in the center, the ends of their table adorned with tall blue and white clay vases sprouting towering stocks of dried seagrass. Both men were in full military garb. They were making their rum drinks—*cocktails*—for the crowd.

"There he is," I told Heathcliff, pointing my chin at the other side of the room where Colonel Balfour stood beneath a massive painting of two white horses on their hind legs, battling each other.

Colonel Balfour, bewigged and in military regalia, stood beneath the painting, talking with an older man smoking a white clay pipe.

"Thank you for the invitation, Colonel," I told Balfour, waving a hand over Heathcliff and introducing him as my assistant.

Colonel Balfour told the pipe-smoking man that he'd be with him shortly. The man blew out a blueish-white billow of tobacco and walked through it.

"Captain Benson said you had stopped by earlier wanting to talk privately," Colonel Balfour said. "Pray tell, you've solved the murder."

"Almost. There seems to be several murders, all related to Major Montcalm's. But I'm here to talk about something else."

"Oh?" he said, raising his eyebrows.

I couldn't be too pushy. As I learned on the day I met Balfour, he was short-tempered.

"Major Pawsworthy," I said, head tilted back, "has arrested my host, Dr. Gabriel DuBois, on charges of aiding the enemy."

"Apparently, this DuBois has been operating on enemy soldiers, healing them. That's treason."

"He's a doctor, sir. He sees a human body that needs fixing, so he fixes it. They are not wearing uniforms in his eyes."

"He should get spectacles," Heathcliff said.

Colonel Balfour chuckled; so did Heathcliff. Heathcliff wasn't helping. I wasn't surprised.

"Dr. DuBois was a dear friend of my husband's. He's a loyalist, sir. Dr. DuBois cares for injured soldiers so he can study their anatomy. If he heals them, he notes how and why his methods succeed. He does the same for his failures so he doesn't repeat them. The knowledge he gains from his medical studies will help His Majesty's Army in the future. Ultimately, the rebels he heals are sent to prison ships, sir. A Hessian doctor recently told me Dr. DuBois was too good. He said Dubois heals our soldiers so well they are returned to the war sooner than they'd like."

Balfour slugged back whatever was in his mug. "To hell with the Hessians," he said under his breath.

I looked around. A few of their green-coated officers colored the crowd of red uniforms.

"Please, sir," I said. "Release Dr. DuBois from the Provost. For the moment, his French accent might keep him safe. They think he's on their side. But if anyone recognizes him—he's a loyalist—they'll kill him. As I said, he was a dear friend of my husband's. I can attest—"

"I can place Dr. DuBois on parole," Colonel Balfour said. "And have him released immediately."

"Can I use my Order of Compliance to demand his release?"

"Of course." Colonel Balfour studied me. "You're a very brave and devoted woman."

"To the King as well, sir," I said.

"Pay close attention to what I'm about to tell you. I've had enough of this insurrection. The rebels are forcing loyalists in the backcountry to side with them. Those who don't are brutally murdered. I'm determined to make examples of traitors. This Dr. DuBois has signed a loyalty oath, correct?"

"Of course."

"If he violates parole, I'll personally hang him in a very public manner. Mind you, Pawsworthy will be watching him. He has many friends. Many eyes will be on him."

"He'll never heal another rebel, that I can assure you."

He nodded to someone behind Heathcliff, a stunning black woman in an elegant royal blue gown, her hair tied tightly in a cone-shaped updo. Raising his right hand to take her arm-in-arm, he motioned to step toward her.

"I have another request, Colonel," I said. "A rather bold but deserving one."

"Oh?"

"In light of the sacrifice my husband has made for the war and the King—a sacrifice I am willing to make as well—I humbly and formally ask that you sequester Dr. DuBois's house and give it to me, Charlotte Savatier, proud widow of Major Émile Gaston Savatier."

I pursed my lips and bobbed one affirmative nod. Strands of my bangs bounced in front of my face and clumsily poked my eye with their tips. I could see Balfour struggle to contain a smirk.

"I have no reason to return to Québec City without my husband," I said. "He is buried here and I want to be by him."

Colonel Balfour rubbed his chin, observing me. "Do you see that young man over there by the fireplace?" Colonel Balfour pointed. "The one holding a glass of my finest *uisge beatha*."

"Your what?"

"Scotch," Heathcliff said, translating.

I glanced at the man, nodding.

"His name is John Cruden. Lord Cornwallis appointed him the commissioner of sequestered estates, giving him the power to seize property. And I have the power to order him to sequester Dr. DuBois's estate and give it to you."

"Will you do so, sir?"

"You had better solve these murders."

"No one wants to solve them more than I," I said. "Besides the King, of course. And you."

He waved his hand and called out to John Cruden, who stopped his conversation with two officers and strutted over to us. He looked twenty-six years old, no more than twenty-eight. Colonel Balfour introduced me and told him to give me Gabriel's house and his hospital. Immediately.

"Process the paperwork by tomorrow," he said.

John Cruden said he'd come by the house tomorrow afternoon. Colonel Balfour dismissed Mr. Cruden, who returned to his fireside chat.

"How will Dr. DuBois feel about you taking his property?" Colonel Balfour asked.

"I'm not sure," I said, rolling my eyes. "I can always sell it back to him—for the right price."

"Such perspicacity," Colonel Balfour said, squinting. He wagged a finger at me. "You know Pawsworthy has his eye on that place."

"He can buy it as well—also for the right price," Heathcliff said.

"More perspicacity." Colonel Balfour winked at me. "Keep an eye on your assistant. He's as cunning as you."

Heathcliff stepped aside to let the colonel pass.

"He gave you both properties," Heathcliff said.

"As I had hoped." We walked side-by-side through the crowd. "I gave him the excuse he needed to keep the military hospital running without openly confronting Pawsworthy. Colonel Balfour knows how good DuBois—"

"Charlotte!" a woman shouted.

The young woman squeezed my shoulder, an excited smile revealing perfect white teeth. She was holding a mug of Pawsworthy's cocktail. It was the young woman I saw earlier at the Pinckney House.

"Charlotte La Pierre!" the woman shouted. "Is that you? *It can't be!*"

People stopped talking and gawked. I had to fight an impulse to punch her throat, a crippling strike that Uncle George taught me. I desperately searched the crowd for Pawsworthy. He stood by the fireplace, chatting with John Cruden. Pawsworthy's fat face was red—not from his cocktails, either; he must have learned I owned Gabriel's property.

"It's Harriette," she said, her volume inspired by the content of her mug. "Harriette Garden."

I feigned a smile. I could only hope greed consumed Pawsworthy's attention, making him deaf to Harriette Garden. Pawsworthy's lackey,

Dawson, wasn't far away. He stood behind the buffet table. He wasn't serving anyone a cocktail.

"Alex is coming home in a few weeks," Harriette said, still loud. "Around the middle of March. He'll be so excited to see you."

Harriette Garden, her brother, and I were childhood friends. Their father was Dr. Alexander Garden, also a botanist and a good friend of my father's. I had avoided consulting him about the suicide plant. I didn't want him or his family to recognize me. Harriette's brother, Alex, was a few years older; Harriette was nineteen or so. As children, she and I ran through the streets barefoot, dodging bats and piles of horseshit on Price's Alley.

She stepped in to hug me, and I imitated Uncle George, producing that hissing noise he made with his missing tooth. She backed off, her smile tightening into an uncomfortable frown.

"You have mistaken me for someone else," I said, stepping back and thickly laying on a French accent. "My name is Charlotte, *oui*. Charlotte *Savatier*." I threw in some French. "*Je ne suis pas celle que tu crois.*"

I hoped projecting a foreign language into our conversation would widen the gap between us and distance any association she made between me and the Charlotte La Pierre of her past.

"I . . . I . . . I'm so sorry," Harriette said. "I thought . . . You look rather like the Charlotte I know. Or knew. But that was so many years ago when we were kids."

Captain George Benson stepped forward, coming up next to Harriette.

"*Capitaine*," I said. "Nice to see you again." I turned to Heathcliff and introduced him.

Captain Benson put his arm around Harriette's waist.

"My fiancée, Harriette Garden." He smiled. "Harriette, this is Émile's wife."

I smiled and dipped a slight bow.

"*Enchanté*," I said.

"Excuse me," Heathcliff said, addressing Captain Benson. "Are there any wines here? I don't fancy rum or scotch. Rum's what unscrupulous sailors drink, is it not, sir?"

"The kitchen's in the basement," Captain Benson said. "There's wine in the storeroom down there. Ask one of the servants. They'll get it for you."

"Cheers," Heathcliff said, drawing me away by the elbow.

Heathcliff didn't drink, so I knew it was a pretense to get me away from Harriette. We went to the first floor via the stairs in the piazza at the back of the house overlooking the garden and took another set of stairs to the basement. The kitchen door at the end of the hall was open. People were preparing the banquet, clanging metal pots and trays, shouting and laughing. Heathcliff opened the door to our right and poked his head in.

"This must be the storeroom," he said, looking back at me over his shoulder. "I'll be right back."

I wanted to leave. "You don't drink. What the hell are you up to?"

"I got to piss."

"Classy."

I waited in the hall. After about five minutes, my tolerance for pacing ended, and I opened the door to tell Heathcliff to hurry up. Heathcliff stood over a soldier sprawled on his back. The man wasn't moving, and he bled from his lower lip. I stepped inside, closing the door. The soldier's red coat was draped over the back of a chair by a table.

"Don't tell me he's dead," I whispered hoarsely.

Heathcliff shook his head. "I merely bounced his face off the wall." He kicked his opponent's hand. "Do you recognize this ass?"

I shook my head.

"It's the drunkard from Governor's Bridge."

"The guy whose name you disliked?"

"Yeah. Linton. He recognized me. He said he would have me arrested for attacking a kingsman."

"What was he doing in here?"

"Imbibing."

Heathcliff pointed to a whiskey bottle on the sill of the open window. This small room had one window across from the fireplace. No fire presently burned. Floor-to-ceiling cabinets covered the walls, and I opened a few at random. Blankets, soap, candlesticks, candleholders, oil lamps, plates, and glassware. Bottles of whiskey, rum, port, and Madeira.

I grabbed an off-white blanket, unraveled it in the air with a flap, and cast it over the floorboards.

"Roll him onto it," I told Heathcliff. "And get as much blood on it as possible. We want the scene to be shocking."

"What?" Heathcliff said, reluctant to follow my directions.

"We need to create palace intrigue," I said, waving a hand over his victim.

"Palace intrigue?"

"Yes. We have to silence him forever."

Heathcliff knelt immediately, taking the man by the throat with both hands. I slapped his shoulder.

"Not like that. We silence him with shame, with an *affaire du cœur*. Something so scandalous that this man will be too embarrassed to identify you in the future." I pointed. "Take his pants off." I stood back to imagine the point of view of the next person coming through the door. "Better yet, pull them down around his ankles."

Heathcliff peeled the man's trousers along his hairy legs until they bunched around his shoes. He rolled him over, his manly parts on display. Meanwhile, I reached for the whiskey bottle on the sill. I yanked the cork out with my teeth and spit it out by his face, splashing whiskey over his body and the blanket. Placing the bottle by his head, I stood back.

"On second thought," I said. "Remove his shirt as well."

Heathcliff placed his heel on the man's neck and, leaning in, grabbed his shirt by the collar and ripped it off his torso with violent tugs. He tossed the shirt out the open window.

"*Voilà*," I said, clapping my hands once. "We now have a drunken tryst gone scandalously wrong."

A rush of footsteps in the hallway shook the door in its frame as the servants hauled the party's repast upstairs, the heavy fragrance of baked pork and clove somehow pushing its way through the closed door.

"Imagine if we got caught standing here," I said. "What people would say!" I nodded to the window. "Let's go out the window."

"All right," Heathcliff said. "You first."

Gathering the skirt of my dress, I said, "Open the window a bit more."

He didn't step toward the window. He sprinted to the fireplace and groped through the cold ashes until he found a chunk of charcoal. Not sure what he was up to, I stepped toward the door, ready to block anyone's attempt to open it. He rolled Linton over on his side, his naked buttocks facing me. Crouching over the man, Heathcliff drew two solid black circles side by side on the same ass cheek, the upper one. The artist tilted his head left and right, deciding to draw a line above each circle. He had drawn eyes and eyebrows that magically transformed the man's derrière into a glum face, with the crack being the mouth—a tight-lipped one with a dark hairy frown—and the lower ass cheek acting as a broad chin. The artist stepped back, nodding with apparent satisfaction.

"Now they'll think something unspeakably depraved transpired in this vile chamber," he said, his wet eyes widening as he admired his deranged artwork.

"You must really hate this Linton fellow back home," I said, stepping toward the window.

"You have no idea," he said through gnashed teeth.

He turned and opened the door a foot or more. Anyone walking by could see directly in, assuring Sergeant Linton would be discovered before he regained consciousness—a brilliant maneuver. While I began to climb out the window, Heathcliff crossed the room to join me. He paused briefly to whip the charcoal into the fireplace, where it struck something metal that chimed with the same faint ring of a distant church bell—wedding bells possibly, as far away as England herself.

Bells that had been ringing in Heathcliff's ears ever since he left his homeland, driving him mad.

# CHAPTER FIFTEEN

## *Hunger Pain*

After getting my Order of Compliance from my bedroom, on my way out the back door, I told Mahala and Winslow how Balfour gave me permission to free Gabriel. It was dark when I presented my document at the Exchange Building. I asked the guard to bring Dr. DuBois up from the dungeon. I didn't want to go into that disgusting pit. About fifteen minutes later, a soldier came up the stairs with Gabriel.

"*Merci, ma chère,*" Gabriel said.

Outside, I planned to tell him I owned his property and how he was on parole under penalty of death if he touched another rebel, but he spotted the Gypsy Lady's carriage and headed for it. Mahala must have sent the carriage. I held the door, helped him climb inside, and sat beside him. The tiny interior lantern dimly lit John Peele sitting across from us. He told Gabriel that he had sailed their ship down the Cooper.

*Their ship?*

Why would they have a ship?

The carriage started to roll, the metal rats clonking as we turned down Broad Street.

"Everything's ready?" he asked John Peele, blowing his nose into a stiffly crumpled handkerchief.

"The ship's anchored in the harbor," John Peele said. "I registered the cargo and itinerary with the port inspector. He's also the royal tax man. Byron . . ." He held a document in his lap, studying it. He moved his lips, trying to pronounce what he was reading. Gabriel had told me before that he was teaching John Peele English. "Beh . . . Buh . . . Bah . . ." John Peele stuttered. "Besh-ah, Bush-uh, Beck-ee, or Bach-ah, or . . . damn this." He looked up and spoke Wacataw. "How do you say his goddamn name?"

Gabriel leaned over the paper. "It's pronounced *besh*. It's French."

John Peele looked at Gabriel with a wrinkled nose. "French? Why is a damn French word in with English writing?" he said in English, chuckling. "Anyway," he said in Wacataw, "he gave me a letter on your behalf. I gave that to the intendant general, who signed the back of the export certificate, clearing my passage to London. They think we're shipping rice."

"While you were gone, I rented the warehouse on East Bay." Gabriel coughed into a tight fist. "Tomorrow night, we'll bring my patients there. We'll board them the next night."

I gasped in frustration. "What the hell are you talking about?"

Neither spoke. They looked at each other.

"I'm establishing a hospital ship," Gabriel finally said.

"A hospital ship?" I didn't understand. "Why would you take patients from a hospital and load them onto a ship that's a hospital? To make them seasick, too?"

"You'll know soon enough, Crow," Gabriel said.

"You'd better not have any rebel patients," I told him. "That's a condition of your parole. Balfour will hang you if you do."

Gabriel puckered his mouth and clapped his bony hands, pressing both forefingers against his lips as if to hush me.

～～～

The next day, John Cruden and I sat at the card table in the sitting room. Gabriel was in his hospital. I hadn't told him about taking ownership of his property; I'd wait until it happened. John Cruden slid the deeds with official wax seals toward me. The witnesses, Egerton McClain and Alexander Wright, had *already* signed them. I signed the documents—one for this house, the other for the hospital.

"Both properties are yours," John Cruden said.

"Thank you."

He sat back, crossing his arms. "It's sad, the way your husband went."

I raised my eyebrows. "What do you mean?"

"I was there the night he died. I was at Donald's."

"Major Pawsworthy's?"

"We had finished a late dinner. I stayed on and had a glass of port and some cheese. When I was leaving, that black carriage showed up, the one with the iron rats. I was on the landing at the top of his stairs, which gave me a clear view of the street. She stopped in front of the Gibbes House and dropped Émile in the street."

"Dropped?"

"He staggered out and fell, and she just rode off. She left him there on the ground. I didn't realize it was Émile at the time. I thought it was an injured soldier or a drunken sailor. The Gypsy Lady came back, and this time Dr. DuBois got out of the carriage. He looked rather sick himself. At first Émile resisted Dr. DuBois. Émile had a pistol. DuBois wrestled it away and eventually Émile gave up."

"I thought two soldiers found Émile in the street?" I sat forward. "They recognized Major Savatier and ran to get Dr. DuBois."

"Who told you that?"

"I think it was Captain Merryman," I said, not wanting to disclose it was Gabriel.

"No. A few soldiers on watch stepped out into the street and tried to help, but Dr. DuBois dismissed them. Then the Gypsy Lady and DuBois lifted Émile into the back of the carriage."

"Why would they drop him in the street only to come back and pick him up?"

"That's what I wondered. Maybe she was supposed to drop Émile off at Dr. DuBois's hospital but dropped him off at the Gibbes House by mistake, so she returned with DuBois to bring him to the correct hospital. That's what the soldiers thought. They said Émile looked awfully sick."

"I heard he died of a heart attack. Right there in the street."

"I know for a fact he didn't die in the street."

"I guess he must have died at the hospital here," I said, pointing my chin at the back door.

"I heard he died that night, yeah."

I was doing my best to act calm. Why would Gabriel lie? Uncertainty fogged my thinking. Maybe it wasn't uncertainty but the distrust and shock of betrayal that had me reacting like I'd been slapped.

"Well," John Cruden said, standing. "I hope owning these houses gives you a good start in life."

I nodded. "Thank you, Mr. Cruden. Stay healthy!"

I escorted him to the back door, and I would have collapsed with weak knees if I didn't have the door jamb to lean on.

Why didn't Gabriel tell me Émile was sick?

Why would he lie about how he died?

I avoided Gabriel for the rest of the day, skipping dinner, too, not wanting to confront him until I calmed myself emotionally. Around eight o'clock, I was ready to ask him to explain what happened the night Émile died. I walked to his third-floor operating theatre. He sat in his office, candles burning in the candelabra on his desk. Perhaps he was writing a letter to someone about his stay in the Provost. My first thought was emotional: I should have let the fucking liar rot down there in that stinking dungeon.

"Hello, Charlotte," he said in French, looking up.

I was too fidgety to sit. I paced the room, looking at the endless drawers that were neatly numbered, each concealing minerals, chemicals, herbs, secret medicines, and specialized gadgets.

"I was wondering, Gabriel," I said, "exactly what—"

I froze. I stood on the far left of the wall of little drawers, where the lower-numbered ones were. Each brass drawer handle was U-shaped, and the number for each drawer was inside the dip of the handle, inside the "U." I was staring at drawer number 4.

I was staring at the *for you* in Émile's last letter and his note.

This was a closed "4," not the open 4 that Émile would have written.

"What were you wondering?" Gabriel said, eyebrows up.

"I was wondering if there was anything left over from supper. I fell asleep and missed dinner." My eyes were stuck on Drawer Number Four. "I wish I could describe the hunger pains I'm having right now."

"That pain is easily fixed."

"Is it?"

"Do you want me to make you something?" he asked, returning his quill to its stand.

"No, of course not." I faked a chuckle. "I thought there might be extras left over. I'll go pick through the kitchen house." I stepped away from the drawers. "Sorry to have bothered you."

Returning to my room, I sat at the back window in the dark, watching and waiting for Gabriel to leave. Around ten o'clock, he left the hospital and entered the house. When he went into his bedroom down the hall, I grabbed a small candleholder and snuck into the hospital.

I held the small candle high and opened Drawer Number Four.

Tucked between several small pods of nutmeg seeds was a rolled-up paper tube. I pinched the tiny scroll between my thumb and forefinger and, resting the candleholder on the top of the bureau, unraveled it with shaking hands. It was in Émile's handwriting:

*Charlotte, mon amour, cherche-moi!*

(*Charlotte, my love, find me!*)

# CHAPTER SIXTEEN

# How Angels Bathe

Did this mean Émile was alive?

No. Several people, including Colonel Balfour, attended his funeral. Winslow and Mahala said they saw his corpse.

*Find me . . .*

John Cruden said Émile looked awful. Émile was deathly sick. He knew he was dying. He also knew I was on the way to Charleston. If he died before I arrived, he wanted me to discover *something* about him. Hence his note. His note was like a lead ball or arrow that you shoot at a moving target, aiming in front of your victim so that he runs into it.

Émile's letter was a shot into the future.

Targeting me.

*Find me . . .*

There was only one logical starting place.

I ran behind the kitchen house, opened the tool cabinet door, grabbed what I needed, and left. At Uncle George's house, I stood in his kitchen and repeatedly yelled "hello" to wake Heathcliff and him up.

"You have to help me with something," I told them.

"At this hour?" Heathcliff said.

"Help with what?" Uncle George said.

"My quota for selflessly helping others has exhausted itself," Heathcliff said.

"Come with me, please," I said, turning and walking away.

"Why won't you tell us what we're doing?" Uncle George said, following me.

"If I tell you, you won't help me."

In the cemetery across from St. Philip's Church, I handed Uncle George a shovel. I held the other. I carried a small lantern, placing it beside Émile's gravestone. I told Heathcliff we'd switch off when one of us got tired. I stabbed the earth with the blade of my shovel and tossed a pile of dirt to my right.

"You're digging up your dead husband?" Heathcliff said.

Uncle George handed his shovel to Heathcliff. "I'm not going to disturb the dead," he said in English.

"You'll put a bad man in his grave," I replied, "but you won't help take a good one out?"

"What's the point of digging him up, Crow?"

I explained Émile's 4-U symbol.

"Émile knew he was dying," I said. "He didn't know where he would be buried. He wanted me to find his grave. I have to dig him up and find out why."

A tree bough loomed above us, leafless, swaying in the breeze, and moonlight cast a crisscross of shadows over Uncle George's face as if his head were inside a fishnet. Heathcliff stood beside him. In the phantasmagoria of shifting light, I couldn't tell whether his smile was an approving grin or a mocking smirk.

"If you're not going to help," I said, tossing a shovelful of dirt on their shoes, "go home."

"Go home?" Heathcliff stepped up and drove his shovelhead into the ground. "And do what? Your childish outcry in the kitchen sent sleep to the devil for me."

We began digging. Uncle George watched the cemetery entrance, ready to alert us of anyone's approach. It was a chilly night. Low clouds drifted inland from the ocean, a scattering of them at first. The deeper we dug, the more the clouds gathered overhead until we lost the moonlight. That's when the flickering little lantern shone brighter. When Heathcliff told me my arched back looked like a shitting dog's, I jumped into the grave to dig more comfortably. He followed.

The rain started as droplets and grew larger until a downpour thickened the dirt into slick mud. Uncle George scooped out a small cave in the pile of dirt beside me, placing the lantern there to protect it from the rain. Our shovelheads thudded on the wooden coffin lid. We scraped the dirt wall where it was pinning the lid at the corners, and Heathcliff climbed out.

Mud covered the lid now, enough to weigh it down. I knelt and used my hands to scrape what I could onto the shovel head. Gabriel had paid for a high-quality hexagonal coffin. As my palms ran over the polished wood, its wet contours reminded me of the slippery curves of a man's hard thighs and sweaty hips. The downpour splattered muck on my face.

I climbed out of the grave. I lay across the muddy ground and reached back into the grave with the shovel to pry the lid. Heathcliff knelt beside me with his shovel and helped raise the lid. The stench was as you'd expect from a corpse. Uncle George held the lantern in one hand, his other acting as a roof over it. Black fabric lined the coffin's interior, making it too dark to see. I turned and slid feet-first into the coffin, placing a foot on either side of Émile's legs. Uncle George lowered the lantern.

A sheet of black silk cocooned Émile. Crouching over him, I groped for an opening and peeled the cloth away from his face. A lightning flash showed Émile in a white light that was brighter than any sunshine I had ever seen, and what I saw would have made other people jump out of the grave. It brought me to tears. I collapsed, sitting on his lap as I had many times when we made love. Thunder as loud as cannon fire shook the air, and I could feel him tremble where our bodies joined.

"*Mon ange*," I screamed in French, bawling so much it was hard to breathe.

Large pustules, black with rotten blood, covered Émile's beautiful face. These weren't the little bumps of smallpox. I tugged the sheet farther to the side. Big pustules covered his torso—the same ones I'd seen on those dead families in the farmhouses south of Orangeburg. Leaning forward, I placed my elbows on either side of his neck and hovered over his face to see him better. His eyes were gone. When I raised my hands, dead flies encrusted my wet palms. Maggots had eaten his beautiful blue eyes. I shook my hands free of the carcass husks and hugged Émile, lifting his body to mine. He was as weightless as a toddler.

"Oh, *mon ange*," I screamed, squeezing him, rocking him; I knew I sounded and looked hysterical. I didn't care. I screamed in French: "*Mon ange! Mon ange! Qu'est-ce que Gabriel t'a fait putain?*"

(*My angel! My angel! What the fuck did Gabriel do to you?*)

Holding Émile's head in my hands, I looked over my shoulder at Uncle George, lightning revealing glimpses of his grimace. Even Heathcliff was aghast, his mouth open, dark eyebrows scrunched. He seemed more interested in me and my reaction, not poor Émile's condition.

"Look what he did to my angel!" I yelled at them in English. "Ohhhhh." I spoke to Émile, wailing in French: "Ohhhhh, my lover, my angel, you should be alive. You should be alive and here with me." I stared at the sky and squeezed my eyes, screaming to He Who Never Dies in French, "Oh, God, my God, what did Gabriel do?"

Another loud crack of lightning lit up our encampment in bright white light, the thunder shaking the ground with the impact of an entire forest falling at once.

"Gabriel lied," I said in English, looking at Uncle George. "Émile didn't die of heart failure. That bastard murdered him."

"Gabriel could have inoculated him," Uncle George said, "and it went bad."

"An inoculation for what?" I felt my hair sticking to my muddy face. "Have you ever seen a disease do this? This is a full-on infection of something sinister. Émile wanted me to see him. He wanted me to see what Gabriel did to him. But why? Why would Gabriel kill Émile?"

Still hugging Émile, I stood, lifting him with me.

"Help us out," I said.

"Help you *what*?" Uncle George said.

"I'm taking Émile with me. I'm going to lie him next to Gabriel on his bed and demand an explanation from that fucker."

"Hand him to me," Heathcliff said, reaching down.

Alas, my fiendish friend to my rescue!

I pivoted so Heathcliff could grab Émile, and Heathcliff nearly fell into the coffin with us. Lightning flashed and I saw Heathcliff stumble back, his silhouette a black ghostly cut-out of himself as he swayed his arms to regain his balance.

"He's missing an arm," Heathcliff yelled. "I tried to grab it, but it's not there."

"He's what?" I said, confused.

I lowered Émile's body into the coffin, squeezing his shoulders and his biceps, groping my way down his arms in the dark. His right forearm was missing, cut off at the elbow.

*Surgically cut off.*

I stood and stumbled back, remembering those forearms in that glass cabinet in Gabriel's hospital.

"Get out of there," Uncle George shouted deliberately in English so Heathcliff could understand. "You're not going to carry a naked, disease-ridden corpse through the streets of Charleston. Balfour will remove you from the investigation. We'll lose every advantage we have to steal Pawsworthy's wealth and get our revenge."

"He's right," Heathcliff said. "You're not thinking clearly. You don't need to show Gabriel what he did to your husband. He knows."

"Give me your hand," Uncle George shouted at me.

I stiffened my arms, squeezing my fists outside my thighs. I must have looked unreasonable and ridiculous—a stubborn girl, a brat.

"Get out of that grave, you fucking slag, or I'll bury you in it," Heathcliff said, raising his shovel.

Uncle George reached in and hoisted me out by the armpits. He tossed me so hard that I slipped in the mud and landed with a slap on my back. Neither man helped me to my feet. Instead, they worked the shovels, slamming the coffin lid and plopping muddy earth onto it.

Heathcliff stopped shoveling, glancing at the entrance.

"Where's she going?" he said to Uncle George.

"Where's who going?" Uncle George responded, still digging.

"Charlotte. She took the lantern with her. She's standing by the entrance there, waving us on."

Uncle George straightened. "Charlotte's standing right behind you." He pointed his shovel at me.

Heathcliff spun and looked at me. He glanced in the direction of the church across the street. "Who's that over there?" Heathcliff leaned forward, peering through the rain.

"There's nobody over there," I said.

"Heathcliff," Uncle George said. "The lantern fell into the coffin. It's buried with Émile. The lightning probably burned its image onto your eyes. It'll go away."

"No." Heathcliff pointed his chin at the entrance. "I saw someone standing right there."

"Maybe it was Émile's ghost," Uncle George said, laughing at Heathcliff.

"Someone was holding a lantern with one hand and waving us on with the other." Heathcliff looked at me. "I thought it was you. I had the feeling that you—or whoever it was—was rushing us along to get us out of the cemetery. It must have been your husband's ghost."

"It can't be Émile's ghost," Uncle George said, much more serious in tone, trying not to mock Heathcliff—not for his sake, for mine. "Émile only has one arm. How could he hold a lantern with one hand and wave us on with the other?"

"I know what I saw," Heathcliff said curtly.

They continued to dig without talking, and I thought about bashing in Gabriel's head with one of those shovels while he slept. Heathcliff drove his shovel into the mud, eliciting a sucking sound that drew me out of my murderous fantasy. When they finally covered the grave, we walked onto Church Street. I glanced back. They left the shovels sticking out of the dirt. I began to walk toward them.

"I'll get them," Heathcliff said, staring into the cemetery, maybe waiting for that ghost to reappear. "I'm staying here."

Uncle George shook his head. "*Now he'll outstare the lightning,*" he said, quoting someone, patting Heathcliff's shoulder. "You're one stubborn bastard."

Heathcliff slapped his hand away. "Leave off," he said meanly.

Uncle George and I walked down Church Street and stopped at Queen Street, which led to his house on Archdale. Though the rain continued to fall hard, the lightning storm moved inland, its explosions lighting up the clouds as if a cannon battle was blowing Heaven apart.

"Don't tell Gabriel you dug up Émile," Uncle George said. "Keep it a secret. Focus on our mission. We'll discuss Émile's murder, if he was murdered, with my mother. Jane Harris will decide what we do about Gabriel. That is the Wacataw custom."

"I can have that bastard hanged for murdering a British officer," I said in French, Émile's mother tongue.

"Gabriel's Wacataw, Crow," Uncle George said in Wacataw. "And Wacataw don't kill Wacataw. He's also your uncle. Your mother's brother. My brother. Wacataw certainly don't kill family. Jane Harris will decide. Not you."

"*I* wouldn't be killing him," I said in Wacataw. "The British Army would be killing him. *Your* army."

Uncle George paused, his face pointed at the ground.

I had offended him.

"My army?" he said, wiping his wet face with his big hand. "You are my army. I stayed on fighting with the British to protect you, to get you out of South Carolina. I was thinking of your future when we moved to Québec City, not mine. I knew you'd be out of the influence of Gabriel, who did nothing while your parents hanged. I wanted to keep you out of the coming war between the colonies and Britain. You'd get a French education in Québec City but spend winters in the Carolinas, where you'd retain your connection to our Wacataw people. If I had stayed here, I would have fought with the British alongside the Cherokee against the Wacataw. I'd cut my own throat before I ever fought against my people— or alongside a Cherokee. So I made every sensible sacrifice for you, for the honor of my murdered sister, and for your father. It was never my army I was fighting for, Crow. I was fighting for you."

He was not my father. This was not the life I would have had with my real father. This was certainly not the life he had planned for himself, either. Uncle George did everything a surrogate parent could have done, and I hurt his feelings and insulted him. I felt my tears leave my eyes and drip off my cheeks, tiny drops obliterated by the greater ones falling from the black sky.

Uncle George stepped toward me. He grabbed my shoulders and hugged me. The constant pelts of rain pounding on the puddles around us sounded like a fast-moving brook.

"Has anyone ever told you why Jane Harris named you Crow?" he said, blinking against the rain.

"I got a big mouth," I said, laughing childishly as I repeated what everyone said about me.

"No," he said, clasping my smaller hands in his big ones. "That was a joke someone started. Only it stuck. No. That's not why. When you were a child, there used to be a crow in our village, a big one. It used to live in the trees opposite our house. My mother used to cook outside in the summer and would leave the fire smoldering afterward. She went inside once and noticed when she came back out how that big crow had flown down to the fire. It had a twig in its beak, placing one end in the coals. It saw Jane Harris and flew into a tree. She backed off, and after a while, the crow returned and picked the burning twig up in its beak. It hopped across the ground to the forest floor, where it had gathered dead pine needles in a pile. That crow dropped the glowing end of the twig onto the pine needles and fanned them with its wings until the pile started smoldering. Then it arched itself over the smoke with its wings spread. My mother said the smoke chased all the bugs and fleas off its skin and out of its feathers, which was this brilliant crow's way of bathing. It was the smartest crow in the world, my mother said. She said you were like that crow, that you were the smartest child of all the children she'd ever seen. All your talking and jabbering and questioning was like that crow starting that fire and getting it to smoke by flapping its wings—that you flapping your lips was your way of fanning the fire inside you. That is why Jane Harris named you Crow."

He clasped my wet cheek with his hand and touched the padding of his thumb to my lips, not letting me say a word. His hand fell away as he turned from me. Though it was dark, I could still see him as he marched off. Normally, he would have grown smaller as he walked away, shrinking to a black dot as the distance between us increased. The reverse was true. He grew much taller and bigger in my eyes.

A fire usually burned in the kitchen house, so I went there to warm up. Removing my muddy dress, I stood naked before the fireplace and repeatedly stepped on the footbellows to excite the flames. I added a few split logs. I thought about Émile's journal, how he never mentioned getting the pox. That was because Gabriel was reading his journal. I remembered how Émile left that crossed-out passage in his journal about getting sick from the Duke of Norfolk punch. That passage had such a fine line drawn through it because he wanted me to read it. Gabriel wouldn't have known it would be uncharacteristic of Émile to leave a crossed-out passage in his journal, but Émile knew I would know. Émile wanted me to know that no food or drink had sickened him—that something else killed him. That something else was on the next page of his journal and in the hidden letter to me—in Drawer Four.

After I had warmed up, I lit a candle off the fire and sprinted to my room, slipping into a gown. I stepped into slippers and made my way to the third floor of Gabriel's hospital.

I had to know.

I stood before the glass cabinet and opened the door, grabbing one arm on the bottom shelf and pulling it into the light. Gabriel had treated these arms with chemicals to prevent maggots from eating the flesh. I examined the forearm and put it back exactly as it had been. I grabbed another one, one with large pustules.

That's when I saw it.

The wound from the lead ball in the webbing between his thumb and forefinger. The one Émile got fighting alongside Uncle George defending Québec City from General Benedict Arnold's attack in 1775.

I gripped Émile's right hand—the same hand that caressed my cheek, that tucked my hair behind my ear when he looked me in the eyes and said *Je t'aime*; the same hand that cupped my breasts and brought them to his mouth, held my hand, and hugged me close. Underneath the arm, where the muscle was, I noticed a large patch of darker bumpy skin where Gabriel may have sewn some other man's flesh onto Émile's—some other man with the pox. Burns surrounded the patch, scorches produced by Leyden jars. I put his arm back. The other forearms had identical skin grafts and burns. I closed the cabinet door, wondering in horror, *were they alive when he did this to them?*

In my room, I slipped between my bedsheets.

Why kill Émile so grotesquely? Maybe Gabriel killed Major Montcalm, Wragg, and Bancroft, too. Did he know Montcalm? Had they met in France? Was Gabriel in business with them as well? Did Pawsworthy want to frame Gabriel because he knew he was next on Gabriel's list and didn't have time for me to prove Gabriel's guilt?

Did Émile discover Gabriel killed Montcalm, so Gabriel killed Émile to silence him?

I fell asleep as dawn came. At some point, He Who Never Dies took me away, and I dreamt I was with Émile. In the dream, he was dead, I knew that, but he was also awake and walking around. He had the head of a crow and angel wings made of black feathers. He spread his wings and squatted over a smoky campfire. He said he didn't enjoy me trying to fuck him in the coffin because he was dead. I insisted that I wasn't trying to do that, that the thunder was vibrating him down there, not me. "That's the noise light makes," I told him. "It's so loud it shakes things. Even us."

"Well, I don't like it."

I knew it was vital for him to be comfortable. He permanently belonged to a place now where nothing would ever change.

"It won't happen again," I told him. "We put you back and closed the lid."

"Was that you? I couldn't see. I realized you had dug me up and thought I could see a light. A lantern. It was at the end of a long, dark tunnel. Was that you? Was that really you?"

I grabbed Émile's cold wrist. "When did you learn to speak Wacataw?"

Émile's forearm vanished from my grip, and the rest of him disappeared. I woke up, moving from my inner darkness to my sunlit bedroom. I hadn't drawn the curtains last night. I sat up, wishing Émile was beside me. I felt his presence still from the dream. Then I felt a tear leave my eye and snake along my cheek, cooling on its trail over my skin.

My grandmother, Jane Harris, first told me about the journey of the snake when I told her I was marrying Major Émile Savatier, a British officer and a lawyer.

"Don't worry," she said with her customary smirk, "we all make mistakes, Crow. On our journey through life, we go the wrong way many times. We correct for it, going back the other way, trying to get it right. You keep making mistakes, though, and you keep adjusting for them, and you lose yourself on a winding road with no direction. Then one day, you step back and see you haven't been slithering aimlessly left and right: Like the snake, you've been moving forward in a straight line all along. Follow the journey of the snake, Crow, and you'll see your mistakes will enrich you."

She was letting me know it was all right to marry a lawyer, though I was making a big mistake!

I laughed, remembering grandmother's charming cynicism—but gloom quickly returned: I also recalled I had to pretend I didn't know Gabriel murdered Émile. The wind blew, and the curtains by my desk parted as each half rose as high as angel wings, the breeze carrying the smoke of a nearby chimney fire. It was a clean, crisp smell, but one created by destruction. That sparked an idea: When I saw Gabriel next, I'd tell him to his ugly face that I owned both his houses.

Instantly, my outlook changed, swinging from gloom back to delight.

# CHAPTER SEVENTEEN

## *Holy Darkness*

I wasn't sure how atrociously I'd react if I ran into Gabriel, so out of respect for Uncle George and my grandmother, I didn't leave my room for two days (except to find a morsel to eat or empty my night pan). The following morning, I awoke watching the sunlight creep around the edge of my curtains, reflecting off the dark green ceiling cornice, casting everything in the room, including my arms and the off-white quilt blanket, in the emerald hue of pond slime.

Someone stirred in the chair at my desk.

I shot up.

It was Uncle George. Chuckling at my unease, he stood and handed me a harness made from deer hide. It supported a hunting knife in a stiff sheath that hung between the shoulder blades. He wore a similar one. His was bigger and held two knives, their wooden handles worn smooth and black from use. I got out of bed in my nightgown and handed him the harness back. I told him to hold it up for me, and as I turned, I raised my arms to poke my hands through the two round "sleeve" holes. It fit like a vest.

"I asked my neighbor, Mrs. Collins, to model for me last night," Uncle George told me. "I needed a woman model to ensure the straps fit around your boobs."

"And Mr. Collins didn't mind?"

"Mr. Collins was killed in the Battle of King's Mountain."

"And you're what?" I said, turning around. "Filling his shoes, so to speak?"

He wagged a finger at me. "I did try his shoes on one night." He nodded and frowned. "And the fit was perfect."

"I'm sure."

I tugged on the leather straps in front of my chest and fastened them together by tying two leather strings into one. I reached behind my head, feeling for the handle, and pulled out the long, thin knife.

"Wear that everywhere you go," Uncle George said. "Every moment of the day. And sleep with it. You can't trust anyone. Not Heathcliff. Not Gabriel. Not Dawson. Not John Peele, either." He shook his head. "I never thought I'd say that."

"Those two are up to something strange," I said, meaning John Peele and Gabriel.

Uncle George parted the curtains by the back window next to my desk. Standing at his side, I groped for the knife's sheath with my left hand to slide the blade back in without cutting my hair, skin, or gown. I succeeded. Uncle George pointed his chin out the window. Winslow and Mahala carried baskets from the market and brought them into the kitchen house.

"You can't trust them either."

I sat in the chair. I reached behind my neck for the knife handle and pulled it out.

"I want to cut Gabriel's throat. Why won't you let me?"

He gently took the knife out of my hand, walking behind me to slip it back into its sheath. He slapped the side of my head lightly.

"What if your mother wasn't alive?" I said, looking up at him as he walked in front of me. "What would *you* have me do?"

"Me? That decision would fall on you. The head of the family is the eldest female. You know that."

I did. I never thought about it, though. Jane Harris was such a looming figure. I reckoned she'd live forever.

"So what would *you* do, Crow?" Uncle George said. "As the head of the family? Would you slaughter a blood relative? How would that look to the other families in our village?"

"Our village doesn't exist."

"But our people do. So what would you do about Gabriel?"

I dropped my face into my palms, and in the darkness, I saw the lightning flash in the cemetery, and I saw Émile's maggot-eaten eye sockets.

"My heart says to cut his eyes out," I said. "But my head tells me not to listen to my heart." I looked at my uncle and mentor, who taught me never to act on emotion. "It's hard to hear my thoughts. My heart's pounding so loud. Can you hear it, too?"

My voice broke, and my tears warped my vision as if I were seeing my uncle's face from below the rippled surface of river water. His wide palm, hard with muscle, clasped my cheek.

"I want to kill that bastard," I said through clenched teeth.

"Crow." Uncle George hooked the tip of his forefinger under my chin and raised my face. "Think nice thoughts about Émile instead."

I switched from Wacataw to French, saying, "I can't. All I can see are the holes in his skull where the maggots shit out his beautiful blue eyes."

Uncle George put his hands on his hips. That usually meant a lecture was forthcoming.

"I've got bad news," he said.

I stared at him, sniffling.

"Heathcliff always has money," he said. "He doesn't ask you for it. He certainly won't ask me. So where's he get it? I thought he was mugging drunks, which could get him and you in trouble. So I followed him two nights ago. Crow, he went to Pawsworthy's house."

"He must be spying on Pawsworthy," I said. "He's convinced that cask is full of gold."

"He stayed for an hour. Then he and Dawson came out."

"Together?"

Nodding, he said, "He's got his own agenda, Crow. He's been keeping Dawson and Pawsworthy up to date on everything we've been doing."

"I bet that worm told them we're related. He told Pawsworthy our plan."

Uncle George scratched the side of his head—the one with no hair.

"I thought that, too," he said. "So I confronted them when they came out of the gate. I was going to kill them, but Heathcliff wasn't surprised or frightened to see me. He winked at me. I think he was discreetly telling me he was on a secret mission, but he could have been tricking me into putting my guard down. I couldn't tell. Dawson had a drunkard's bravery, saying if I was here looking for my French master—you—to try the Horn Works. He said he heard you were popular with the soldiers there. He and Heathcliff laughed, and I let them walk off. I followed them, though. They went to a tavern. Heathcliff didn't drink, but Dawson did. Eventually, Dawson stumbled back to Pawsworthy's house, and Heathcliff sat on Gadsden's dock in the cold, staring at the stars until the sun came up. I went home. He hasn't been back to the house since."

I walked over to the bureau to get dressed.

"Wait for me at my office," I said. "I'm going to the Watch House to order soldiers to go to Pawsworthy's house and bring Dawson to the Craven Bastion. In chains, if they have to."

He left. I tilted my head back to shake the stress out through my shoulders, and the stiff knife handle poked the back of my skull—always within arm's reach now.

～⌒～

Dawson came to my office on his own about two hours later.

"Sergeant Phillips told me you needed to see me," he said, stepping into the office. His face flushed when he saw Uncle George, perhaps remembering his crude comments about me. He greeted Uncle George with a nod, and Uncle George grunted.

"Please," I said, waving a hand over the chair opposite my desk. "Have a seat."

Dawson was in uniform. He removed his red coat, tossed it over a table behind his chair, and sat.

"Where's Heathcliff?" I asked.

"I haven't the foggiest." He jerked his head at Uncle George. "I thought he lived with him."

"George ran into you both at your uncle's house two nights ago."

"Yeah, and I haven't seen him since."

"Why was Heathcliff there?"

"I thought you sent him. To spy."

"Why would Pawsworthy allow him in? He can't trust him."

"He was more than pleased to see Heathcliff." Dawson glanced at the cabinets. "He cherished the opportunity to ask him questions about you and your investigation."

It was absurdly frustrating—having to ask a liar about the motives of another liar questioning an opportunist who was as big a liar as the other two liars.

"What did Heathcliff tell your uncle?" I said.

"That you're way over your head. That someone tortured Francis Wragg and Barnabas Bancroft to death, exactly as they did Montcalm. And that you haven't the slightest idea who this murderer is."

I stood, went to the cabinet, and took out the scotch decanter and a glass, setting them on the table next to Dawson. I poured him a *wee dram*. He toasted me before slugging the scotch. I walked back to my desk and sat.

I said, "Speaking of murder, why did you kill Mrs. Bancroft?"

He didn't flinch.

"Me?" The glass decanter clinked when he touched its spout to the mouth of his glass, pouring more scotch. "A thief must have done her in."

"She had nothing to rob," I said. "Soldiers brought her to Charleston in irons. You and your uncle are the only people who would profit from her murder."

"How would I profit from that hag's death?"

"Your uncle's spies listened to me interview her. He knew she told me he sells rum to the French. That's treason."

"So."

"So you'd kill her. You wouldn't want Balfour seizing Pawsworthy's property. Are you the beneficiary of your uncle's will?"

"I don't know."

"But you'd be in the running after Pawsworthy learned you saved his life by killing Mrs. Bancroft."

"No one will miss her." He sniffed the scotch. "So why am I here? If you wanted me arrested for suspicion of murder, your soldiers would have done that. Instead, they told me to come here. Which tells me you want something."

He was uncharacteristically cocky. Was it the booze—or something else?

"Who's killing your uncle's business partners?" I said.

"We have no idea. My uncle thought it was Wragg. You must have noticed Wragg didn't have slaves at his house that day you found him.

That's because he sold them. He was broke. His cabinet business was failing and he needed money. Donald figured he was killing everyone off to take complete ownership of the distillery, so my uncle was going to beat him to it. He planned on killing Wragg and framing Dr. DuBois."

"Why?"

"His intent was to place Wragg's dead body on DuBois's property and have witnesses say they were both rebels. Say they got into an argument and DuBois killed him. He wanted DuBois's houses—before you stole them out from under him." He slugged the scotch. "And now he knows he's wrong about Wragg being the murderer, so he's worried."

"Worried?"

"Donald thinks he's next."

"Does he have any idea who the killer is?"

"No."

"Is there another co-owner of the rum company that I don't know about?"

"No. But Donald tripled the soldiers around the house. No one can get to him. Hell, no one's been able to for years."

"You could be lying to protect him. I still think he's the murderer."

"You can believe he is all you want. You're wasting your time." He sat up and glanced along his shoulder at Uncle George, who had inched closer. "I'll let you in on a little secret. I hate my uncle. But I don't hate you, despite your cruel treatment of me. And I can prove it. I haven't told my uncle who you are—either of you—your true identities, that is. I overheard Harriette Garden at Balfour's party calling you Charlotte La Pierre."

I didn't balk at being exposed.

"You're lying," I said. "Heathcliff told you."

"Heathcliff wouldn't tell me the time of day unless he profited from it," Dawson said. "So I asked Dr. Garden, Harriette's father, about Charlotte La Pierre. Dr. Garden explained her history—your history. How my uncle got your parents falsely convicted of hiding runaway slaves in order to get their property. Dr. Garden won't have anything to do with my uncle. He thinks he's a mound of shit. My words, not his."

"You mound of shit, too," George said in his shoddy English.

"I also asked Harriette about her friend, Charlotte La Pierre," Dawson said, ignoring Uncle George. "Don't worry. I didn't lead her to believe that you were the same Charlotte. In fact, I convinced her you weren't. Anyway, Harriette said your mother was a Wacataw and her name was Gail Harris and that you had two uncles, Gabriel and George." He turned to wink at Uncle George. "Dr. Garden told me your father, Dr. Jacque La Pierre, married Gail Harris, George's sister. I don't know how Gabriel got the last name DuBois, but he looks a lot like this George Harris who's standing a little closer to me than I'd prefer. It's too coincidental that Gail, George, and Gabriel are all brothers and sister, but not related to you. Especially when you consider what Dr. Garden told me, that Gail and Jacque La Pierre had one daughter named Charlotte—you. He said you also had a younger brother and a sister, only they died as babies, so you were particularly cherished. You, Charlotte La Pierre Savatier, have come back to Charleston with your mother's brother to get revenge on my uncle. And I want to help."

"You want to help us? Why?"

"I have personal reasons."

"Such as a lavish inheritance?"

He shrugged.

"You'd better do more than shrug when I ask you a question," I said. "You're not leaving this room alive without proving you're of some value to us."

He raised his scotch glass to his nose and closed his eyes, his nostrils narrowing. "My uncle had my mother committed to the Poor House." He opened his eyes and sipped the scotch. "She wasn't insane."

"His own sister?"

"My grandfather named them equal beneficiaries in his will. Greedy Donald thought it should all go to him. Since my father had died of yellow fever a year earlier, when I was twelve, there was no one to stop Donald from committing his sister. It took several miserable years for her to die in there. Donald killed my mother. So you and I have that in common."

"Is he aware you know he had your mother committed?"

He shook his head. "He thinks I'm an idiot, that I simply accepted she was crazy. She was so afraid Donald would retaliate against me that she told me to play along and let him think I believed she was crazy, too."

I paused, watching him. He stared back, blinking lazily, patiently.

"Did Heathcliff tell Pawsworthy about the little needles, too?" I asked.

"What do you mean?"

"Did he tell you where they came from?"

"No. Who cares?"

"And you're sure Heathcliff didn't tell Pawsworthy about Uncle George and me?"

"You'd be dead if he did, trust me."

"So I'm right. You killed Mrs. Bancroft to ingratiate yourself with your uncle."

"I want Donald to think he and I are in the same boat and that I'm his oarsman."

"You realize you murdered my only witness that could have helped convict Pawsworthy of treason."

"You'll dig something else up," he said.

"What was in that heavy rum cask delivered to Pawsworthy's carriage house the other night? Gold or lead?"

"You know about that too, eh?" He poured himself more scotch.

"Well?"

"He moved it. I have no idea where."

"So it's lead."

"It could be gold. Don't be so certain."

"He wouldn't move that much gold out of his sight."

"I didn't say he moved it off the property."

"Tell me where the cask is," I said.

"I said I'd help you with your revenge. I want what's mine—what he stole from my mother. My inheritance. I need that guarantee."

I crossed my forearms on the desk and leaned forward, nodding as I spoke. "Give me proof that cask is filled with lead slated for the rebels, proof that I can show Colonel Balfour, and I'll arrest your uncle. I'll leave your brother out of it. I promise you I'll intervene and make sure you get that inheritance. I'll convince Colonel Balfour not to seize your uncle's properties, to have John Cruden give them to you as a reward for your loyalty." I sat back, grinning. "Look how I convinced them to give me my uncle's houses."

"But . . ." He flapped his hand between Uncle George and me. "But what do you want out of this?"

"Nothing," I said. "We want to see Pawsworthy hang, like my parents."

Dawson looked at Uncle George. "That's all you want, too?"

Uncle George hissed and grunted.

"What about Heathcliff?" Dawson said. "He doesn't care about your parents." He jerked his head at my uncle. "I don't want Heathcliff coming after me because you two betrayed him or cheated him out of something he's expecting."

"Where is he?" I asked again, thinking the scotch and our new alliance loosened his unwillingness to share.

"I have no idea. That's what worries me. He's a ghost. He shows up out of thin air."

Dawson glanced at Uncle George, who flipped his long hair over his shoulder. Dawson tilted his head back, drained his scotch, and slammed the glass on the table. He stood and grabbed his coat, draping it over his arm.

"If my uncle hears of this plot before I get Colonel Balfour's assurance that I'll get his entire estate," Dawson said with wet lips, "I'll deny it all and expose your true identities. My uncle will raid your homes with his troops, slaughter you, and make up false charges afterward."

"Fair enough," I said, standing. "I'll speak with Colonel Balfour about sequestering that property immediately."

Dawson smiled and turned to leave, nodding to Uncle George as he passed him. The free scotch and the promise of immense wealth appeared to put a little prance in his step. Uncle George followed Dawson to the doorway and watched him walk down the hall before addressing me.

"That man is a drunkard," Uncle George said in Wacataw. "And trusting a drunk is idiocy."

"I don't trust him. And I'll never speak to Balfour about sequestering that property for anyone other than us."

"Do you think he's telling the truth, though?" Uncle George said. "That Pawsworthy isn't the killer?"

"Maybe. But Pawsworthy has an established method of getting rid of people in his way. He sets them up and uses the courts or his militia to kill them off. Why would he change what works?"

"So Pawsworthy is the next victim?"

I shrugged, adding, "There's still something wrong here."

"What's that?"

"They're all getting killed in the same horrific manner. There's a reason for that. If Pawsworthy is the next victim, that means he knows what that reason is. Pawsworthy must be hiding something. Something awful. Something he's connected to."

I walked to where Dawson had been sitting to put the decanter back in the cabinet, but it was empty.

"Look," I said. "That hog drank all my scotch."

Uncle George raised one hand and spoke English to the tall ceiling so that his voice would amplify, "*Oh, that men should put an enemy in their mouths to steal away their brains.*"

I pointed at him, nodding confidently, saying in Wacataw, "That's got to be Shakespeare—or my name isn't Charlotte Crow La Pierre Savatier, She Who Never Shuts The Fuck Up."

"Yes!" Uncle George made a fist and swung it through the air. "You finally nailed one!"

I went home. Uncle George said he would search Charleston for Heathcliff. Gabriel's hospital was deserted. He went somewhere with John Peele. To their hospital ship? As the day wore on, I expected Uncle George to strut into the compound wearing Heathcliff's scalp on his belt. He didn't. I went for a walk in the late afternoon.

I strolled along Magazine Street toward the Ashley River, passing the area where the Poor House used to be. The grounds were in ruins. The damage wasn't from the recent siege. Plants had grown in the dirt lodged in the low areas of the crumbled brick wall, meaning the building collapsed long ago. As children, my girlfriends—Harriette Garden among them— and I used to crouch behind a huge smooth boulder on the grounds and giggle as we listened to the insane people inside the three-story building. They would howl obscenities and scream like red foxes.

One afternoon, a lunatic escaped from the Poor House, a naked man, running with his arms straight out and his private parts flapping as he tried to ditch his pursuers. He bolted toward the boulder—toward us. He stopped. We were huddled like frightened kittens. Our gazes focused on his black pubic hair, his nude tube, and his pear-shaped goolie bag sprouting wiry hairs. He looked right at us and pissed on the rock—and now we were screaming. He jiggled his pecker and the squiggles of urine brought out a black hue in the dusty gray stone, the splatter forcing us to crab-walk clumsily away.

Suddenly, three men tackled him from behind. The handlers wrestled the nude fool, subduing him and dragging him back to his cage. We girls had discussed penises before this event, how they got magically bigger and stiff to slide inside us. But after seeing an adult one for the first time up close, we all agreed we didn't want anything to do with one of those nasty things. Never, ever, ever!

The boulder looked much smaller than I remembered. Sitting against it was a teenage boy whose shirt and pants were rigid with filth. Pox bumps covered the tops of his hands and wrists. He raised his head, and his face was bumpy, too. I recognized him. He was one of Gabriel's red-headed musicians who played during our electrified-frog-leg dinner party. I squatted in front of him.

"Do you remember me?" I said.

"How could I forget you?" His voice was sad and weak. "You're Charlotte. The lady at the frog party."

His blink was as slow as someone drunk on whiskey and ale. The whites of his eyes were yellow. He had one hand on his raised kneecap, and I gently took it into mine.

"Come with me. You can stay with us in Dr. DuBois's house till you're better."

He pulled his hand out of mine, turning his head away by rolling the back of his skull over the smooth rock.

"He said he could help us before," the boy said, his voice husky. "He said he could make it so we never got the pox by putting pus in the cuts he made on our backs. But we got sick. He put us in a dark room in that hospital. He killed my brother, Ken—you met him that day, he played the piano. I snuck out after Ken died and went home, but my parents were dead, and so were my sisters."

"From the pox?"

He nodded, saying, "We gave it to them." He rolled his head toward me, and a slight smile parted his chapped lips. "Can I ask you something, Charlotte?"

"Of course," I said.

"My brother and I talked about you ever since. We both thought you were the most beautiful woman we'd ever seen. And the way you speak with that accent."

He stopped talking to muster the energy to inhale, exhaling slowly. His head drooped. I cradled his cheeks in my hands, and his face was cold.

"I'm fine," he said meekly. "I'm just tired."

I could tell by the heaviness of his head, by the lack of musculature in his neck and jaw, that he wasn't fine.

"Charlotte," he whispered. "Ken and I were wondering. We made a bet. Which of us would you ever kiss?"

I panicked. I didn't know his name. This was no time to ask for it, either.

"*Mon petit ange*," I said in French. "Ken wouldn't stand a chance."

I continued to clasp his cheeks when his eyes shifted rapidly. He was trying to focus on me. His nostrils channeled a burst of air that hit my forearm with the weight of a lover's whisper. That was his last breath. He died. I lowered my hands, and his head slumped so that his cheek hugged the smooth surface of the cold rock that was now his headstone. I remembered the snaky penmanship of that lunatic's penis on this boulder—that crazy script could well have been the writing on this boy's gravestone since it defined the *absurdity* of his premature and unnecessary death. He didn't have to die. Gabriel murdered him.

Not knowing his name, I had called him *mon ange*, my angel—what I called Émile—and a sense of loss, a void, opened within me. This was how Émile was found in the street, alone and without family. I missed Émile. He was gone forever. He was no longer a part of me. Is that why I couldn't remember his face?

What was I supposed to do with the boy's corpse? As I turned to go to the Watch House for help, my vision darkened rapidly. I groped for the rock and sat beside the dead boy, completely blind.

I inhaled deeply, frustrated that I couldn't see. This time, I refused to lay still and fall asleep. I wanted to understand why this was happening. It wasn't a medical condition. I understood enough about medicine to know an affliction by now would have either gone away or progressed and permanently taken my sight. I didn't see blindness as a turn in the journey of the snake. It wasn't a turn. It was a pause. A point where I stopped and recoiled, hiding in the dark. Hiding accomplished nothing. It served no purpose.

Was it God? Was He Who Never Dies talking to me when I was awake, as Jane Harris said? Or was it caused by emotions, as Uncle George claimed?

It wasn't either of those.

My grandmother was wrong. Out of all the people suffering world-wide, why would He Who Never Dies bother to talk with me? There wasn't anything special about me. And Uncle George was wrong. God didn't equip us with emotions, only to ask us to ignore them. That was as silly as giving us voices and then demanding we never talk to each other.

As a child, I would suffer bouts of blindness after Uncle George was called away from Québec City on military duty. He left me in the care of those sisters I had told Dawson about, my "mousy" aunts. They weren't my aunts, and they weren't blood sisters. They were Catholic nuns, and though they were exceptionally kind to me, I hated how they doted on me: It increased my self-pity and loneliness. That's when I would lose my sight. My grandmother never doted on me when I lived in our Wacataw village. Yet everything there reminded me of my mother, which made me miss my father—when my isolation intensified and blindness struck.

Now, whenever I longed for Émile, I went blind.

Loneliness, being reminded I wasn't living with the family that loved me, with the people I loved—people now dead—*that* must have caused these bouts of blindness.

I thought about my ever-watchful grandmother. You don't need light to dream, Jane Harris used to tell me. She said that was the power of God, enabling you to see in utter darkness, in dreams, inside your skull where there is no light. God was the darkness. That was where I felt my parents' spirit and their love—within me, in the dark. And that's where I found Émile's love, too. Inside me, in the dark. Maybe I was doing the opposite of God—trying to transport that inner dark outside—bring them and their love out here with me, where they used to be.

That thinking struck me as embarrassingly childish. It made sense, though.

Émile had once told me all children, with rare exceptions, began drawing pictures at the same rudimentary skill level: Sketching stick people. Unsatisfied with their ugly artwork, most kids eventually quit. If, as adults, they tried to resume drawing, their "skills" were at the same level as when they stopped years ago: Drawing stick people. I was older, but I was still drawing stick people. I was still, and always had been, blindly handling death and loss with the emotional skill of a ten-year-old child.

I slid my hand off my lap to sit up against the boulder, and my palm squished the dead boy's forearm. I held the poor boy's hand and clutched his chilly flesh to my breast. It reminded me of Émile's severed forearm in the cabinet, utterly disassociated, vaulted in isolation. I thought about that severed sailor's hand on *The Naga*. That hand was curled in on itself, withdrawn, alone in the shadows, no longer moving. Like a recoiled snake. Like me. No longer moving on my journey.

*I* caused my blindness.

Not God.

Look how I gripped this poor boy's dead hand. I still wanted my parents here in the real world with me. I wanted Émile at my side.

But that was impossible.

I put the dead boy's hand on the ground, pressed the back of my head against the rock, and stared wide-eyed. I didn't care how long it took to see. I wasn't going to lie down and sleep this off. I caused this blindness. I needed to see *through* the dark—through my eyelids if I had to.

I would outstare the darkness.

And I did. Eventually, I began to see a tiny light, a pinhole, as if I were peering at a lone star in the night sky. The little light reminded me of when I held that small round mirror up to my parents' mirror. Both mirrors reflected their images in a snaking tunnel that gradually shrank to a black point, a dark other-end off somewhere in infinity. Only now, from my blind point of view, I saw the opposite of that dark little point:

A tiny light at the end of a dark tunnel. That was what Émile would see from his side of the mirror, from his side of eternity. He'd look back at me on my side of my parents' mirror in the bright room with the candles and sunlight. I'd be that pinhole of light to him.

Strangely, I was looking at myself.

That's when the tiny light, the star in the night sky, grew bigger, and the black tunnel shrank as the aperture of light expanded more and more until I could see again.

For the first time, my sight returned without having to sleep.

And the first thing I did was blink. And when I did, I caught a glimpse of him. I squeezed my eyes and saw him clear as day in God's light.

*Émile!*

I finally remembered what he looked like. I could see his bright blue eyes, the same blue of a cloudless midday sky, and his white teeth filling out his handsome smile.

I loved seeing him smile.

*I* made him smile.

I opened my eyes. His image vanished. That didn't matter—I was happy to see him go. I would never forget his face.

I stared at the dead boy's ruined face. Gabriel killed him. Killed his brother, his parents, his sisters. Wiped out his family.

I jumped up. I immediately lost my balance. My legs had fallen asleep, and I stumbled left and right. I laughed at myself: I was moving like a snake. My chuckle didn't last, though. I knew what I had to do.

And there wasn't anything funny about it.

# CHAPTER EIGHTEEN

## *Heart Failure*

I walked through the gate and crossed the compound heading for Gabriel's hospital when the door to the kitchen house opened. Winslow stepped out carrying an armful of slender logs. I slowed my pace.

"These don't belong up there," he said, glancing back at the second floor of the kitchen house. "It's not kindling."

The skinny logs were bent and hairy.

"What's so special about those ugly things?" I asked, walking beside him as we approached the hospital.

"I use the smoke to suffocate rats in the hospital."

He had a towel between his bare arms and the logs.

"What are they?"

"Poison ivy vines."

"Have you seen Heathcliff around town?" I asked him.

"No, ma'am. Not in a week or more."

Those were the same hairy sticks I'd seen in Wragg's fireplace. Innocent, quiet Winslow wasn't so innocent after all. He said he stored wood in the hospital's back hall to keep it out of the rain.

I looked for Gabriel on every floor, in the stable, the kitchen house, the outhouse, and the main house. He wasn't anywhere on the property.

∿

The Gypsy Lady's carriage pulled along the gate in Price's Alley after dark. Gabriel stepped out, and The Gypsy Lady's pale face and hand moved into the weak light of the carriage's interior lantern as she handed him a small medical bag. He told her and the carriage driver to wait for him and strutted into the hospital. When candlelight illuminated the windows of his office, I crept up the hospital stairs. My heart was pounding, and it wasn't from the climb.

The candelabra burned in Gabriel's office at the other end of the long room. I stopped briefly at the glass cabinet. Gabriel sat at his desk, scribbling in his ledger. His bony face glowed in the gloomy yellow candlelight.

Smiling, he said hello in French. He immediately asked if I could get Winslow to come up and help him move his Leyden jars down to the carriage. I held Émile's forearm by the hand, exactly as you would when you begin a marriage vow. I tossed it on Gabriel's desk. It landed with a thump, causing the candle flames to jump, and as the shadows shifted over Gabriel's face, he lost his idiotic smile.

"That belongs to my husband," I said in Émile's beautiful mother tongue.

"So it does."

He clasped it with his left hand and set it in the margin of his desk as if it were merely a loaf of bread.

"Crow—"

"Don't call me that. And don't lie to me. I've had enough of your lies." I reached between my shoulder blades and slid my knife out. "Your brother knew I'd never have the strength of a warrior, so he taught me how to use this. There was a period after my parents died when I had a knife in my hand every day. He even tied it to my palm so I'd get used to it when I slept. Uncle George doesn't want anyone to hurt me, you see."

He nodded solemnly.

"I dug my husband's coffin up. You mutilated him. Why?"

"Émile discovered what I was doing here in my hospital." He interlocked his bony fingers. "He told me he would tell Colonel Balfour if I didn't stop. So I told him I would stop."

"Stop what? Killing people?"

"I've spent years studying smallpox. Trying to find out how it works. How it grows, if that's the right term. I use soldiers as test subjects."

"You poisoned those teenage musicians, Ken and his brother. They weren't soldiers. They were boys. It spread to their parents and sisters, too. They're all dead."

He sat back, raising one finger to point to the outer room.

"Can I show you what I've developed?"

I backed out of the office. He grabbed Émile's forearm and the candelabra and walked to the glass cabinet. When he set the candelabra on his operating table, we both jumped, spooked by a hissing noise that sounded like a snake. Uncle George emerged from the darkness and came into the flickering candlelight. He flushed air through his missing tooth, staring at Gabriel. He stood on the other side of the operating table.

"You scared me," I said to Uncle George in Wacataw.

"Me too," Gabriel said in Wacataw.

"Don't." I raised my knife level with Gabriel's lips. "Don't speak that honorable language in front of us. I'll cut your tongue out if you do. A true Wacataw doesn't coldly murder family." I lowered the tip of my knife to his throat. "Not without a proper cause."

He glanced at Uncle George.

"Something tells me if she has her way, brother," Gabriel said in French, "there won't be much of me left by the night's end."

Uncle George didn't speak. He just stared.

Gabriel removed several forearms from the cabinet and set them side by side on his operating table. He pointed at them from left to right, the last one being Émile's. I shifted to his left, standing with my back to the cabinet.

"This shows the gradual success I had," he said. "First, I got the pox to infect quickly. Eventually, I managed to form a new pox, or isolate a particular kind of pox, that also infected rapidly, but this one produced bigger pustules." He pointed to two forearms, one of them Émile's, with large black saggy blotches. "I used the electricity in my Leyden jars to excite the growth of the infection. Low shocks made them grow faster, whereas too high a dose killed the flesh."

"You electrocuted Émile?"

"Yes. To watch the growth patterns. I surgically removed the arms after my patients died."

"Patients?" I struggled to keep as calm as Uncle George was. "Isn't a patient someone you heal? Not someone you experiment on?"

"My experiments have produced a potent and contagious version of the pox. The welts get big. We might want to call it 'largepox.'"

"Those farmers south of Orangeburg," I said. "Those fathers and mothers and children. You killed them, didn't you?"

"I infected each family to study the effect of the largepox on white and black people," he said. "I couldn't get it to spread. I've had much better success with my smallpox. In fact, I've been infecting wounded soldiers in my hospital with smallpox and sending them back to their regiments. I've been doing it since the war started. I made real progress after the British Army came south. I've single-handedly sickened all their armies here, on both sides. I'm destroying them from within."

"So why develop this largepox?" I said. "If the small one is such a success?"

"The largepox's infection rate is quicker," he said. "I finally isolated a type that spreads quickly, too. That's why I've moved my injured soldiers at midnight, first to the warehouse, then onto my hospital ship the next night. No contact with people. I didn't want it spreading through Charleston. Not yet." He bit his lower lip, thinking, putting his long teeth on display. "I've sickened so many armies with smallpox that I hear Cornwallis might move them all north to Virginia before the summer brings yellow fever back here. Do you know what happens when Cornwallis goes north? The Yankees and the French will confront them. All the armies will gather. When they do, I'll introduce my largepox. It'll spread through every regiment."

"So you want to wipe both sides out with disease?" Uncle George said in French.

"Yes."

"I saw John Peele speaking with that tax assessor on the docks," Uncle George said. "So I asked Byron what John Peele was up to. He told me your ship is sailing first to New York City, then to London."

"I'm going to the naval hospital on Long Island," Gabriel said. "By the time we arrive, the entire crew will be stricken with largepox and admitted to the hospital. According to my calculations, the injured soldiers should already be dead or damn close to it. John Peele will hire a new crew and sail to Great Britain."

"To spread this largepox?" Uncle George asked.

Gabriel nodded at a forearm on the table. "He'll infect them just before landing."

"That's insane," I said. "You won't be able to stop it here or in England. It'll cross the English Channel. It'll spread through France."

"Exactly," Gabriel said. "It'll spread through them all. Every last European man, woman, and child."

"After all France has done for you?" I said. "They accepted you into their academy, a foreigner, an Indian, and treated you as an equal."

"Because of DuBois," he said.

"Whose name you disgrace," I said. "You will disgrace the Wacataw people, too. Every last one of us. They will think we were in on this."

"But you will be saved," Gabriel said. "You have been inoculated. Both of you. I shall inoculate all Wacataw. All Indian people. Join me."

"You weren't trying to save us," I said. "You were experimenting on us. You wanted to see what would happen to me, a so-called half-breed. You inoculated yourself and John Peele, but you were willing to kill your own brother to see if you could inoculate another full-blooded Wacataw."

"Very astute," Gabriel said.

"You succeeded in killing Heathcliff, a European," I said. "You brought him back to life, that's true—but you saved him only to see if it could be done. You're heartless."

"What about the blacks?" Uncle George said, no doubt thinking of his lost wife, Betty Polk, and their child. "They will all die, too. They're innocent."

"When the British invaded South Carolina during the French and Indian War," Gabriel said, sneering, "they nearly wiped out the Wacataw when they brought smallpox with them. By the end of that year, only five hundred of us were standing. Don't talk to me about the innocent getting wiped out."

"Émile figured out your depraved scheme," I said. "So you killed him."

"He left me no choice." Gabriel pointed to Émile's arm. "He escaped. Held the Gypsy Lady at gunpoint and forced her to drive him to the military hospital at the Gibbes House. As if they could've saved him. Ha! He was too weak and fell in the street. I brought him back here to pass peacefully."

"You fought with him in the street, you liar," I said. "John Cruden saw you. He told me."

Uncle George walked from behind the operating table and along the glass cabinet, stopping beside me. For the first time, Gabriel showed fear. He backed away from us, standing at the end of the table with his back to the dark room, no doubt scheming how he could turn and bolt out the door.

"What about my family in France?" I said. "My relatives in Beaune? They die, too, Gabriel?"

"He doesn't care about the Wacataw people," Uncle George said. "You were never part of our village. You left as a teenager to live with our sister and Crow's father in Philadelphia and later moved to France with Dr. DuBois. You turned your back on our people long ago. You turned your back on Crow's father and our sister when they were hanged. Crow's father took you in as a son. Introduced you to Benjamin Franklin, Benjamin West, and Jean-Paul DuBois. You have betrayed everyone who's embraced you. Even now. These British in Charleston have accepted you as one of their own, and you throw that trust away for some higher cause? You're full of shit, not honor. You're selfishly seeking redemption for turning your back on our sister—by murdering innocents. It's as Crow says. You will bring disgrace on the Wacataw people."

Uncle George stepped toward Gabriel, who inched back, almost out of the candlelight's reach. But Gabriel suddenly stopped. Or, more accurately, his body jolted forward and jerked to a stop, an unsuspecting rat snatched by a snake. Someone's bare forearm clamped Gabriel's throat.

It was Heathcliff, walking Gabriel into the light.

"What the hell are you lot carrying on about?" Heathcliff asked. "I don't speak a lick of frog."

I told him about Gabriel's murderous scheme.

"You'll not murder my Cathy Earnshaw," Heathcliff said, his white fangs shining brighter as the hands of darkness cupped his face. "I'm working on a plan for her. I don't care how long I wait. But she can't bloody die before then, now can she?"

"You're too late," Gabriel said in a choked voice. "John Peele has left the dock."

"You're lying," I said. "The Gypsy Lady's out there waiting to take you to your ship."

"I'll stop the ship," Uncle George said. "I'll get soldiers from the Watch House."

"You can't take soldiers aboard that ship," I said. "They'll spread this largepox through Charleston after they disembark."

Uncle George nodded. "But I'm inoculated. I'll go alone. I'll convince John Peele I've joined his fight. I'll tell him Pawsworthy arrested Gabriel again and we have to leave now. When we're far out in the Atlantic, I'll burn the ship. We can't burn it in the harbor because people can jump overboard."

Gabriel started to speak, but Heathcliff choked him. Grabbing a candle from the candelabra, I crossed the room and peered out the window overlooking Price's Alley.

"Come, Heathcliff," I said, beckoning him to join me at the window. "You speak the Gypsy Lady's language."

Heathcliff walked backward so he could drag Gabriel in the chokehold.

"Tell her one of the Leyden jars broke," I told Heathcliff. "And that it'll take Gabriel all night to fix it. Tell her to take George to the ship instead and come back tomorrow for Gabriel."

Heathcliff shouted down to her. I didn't have to tell him to tighten his grip on Gabriel's throat to prevent him from warning her. She opened the carriage door, poked her head out, and looked around with a raised lantern. She looked up at Heathcliff, whose face turned crimson as they hollered to each other in their language.

We walked back to Uncle George. Heathcliff enjoyed dragging Gabriel around by the throat, a panther toying with a kicking rabbit. I returned the candle to the candelabra. Heathcliff turned to Uncle George and me, glancing at us over the top of Gabriel's head.

"So you both know," Heathcliff said. "Pawsworthy's cask is full of lead, not gold. And he's got a half-dozen barrels."

"That's why you came back to us?" Uncle George said. "You betrayed us, only it didn't pay off?"

"I didn't betray anyone." Heathcliff jerked his head toward the window. "But your bride is waiting for you in the carriage, Giorgio."

Uncle George hesitated.

"Go," I said to Uncle George.

Tears magnified his eyeballs—tears from the man who hated emotions. I realized what was wrong: He was going on a one-way trip.

We would never see each other again.

I jumped into his arms. I owed my life to him. If not for this noble, brave, caring man, this poet warrior and killer, this contradiction, I'd probably have a bed right next to Eliza Breckenridge to this day. He hugged me so hard I felt the muffled snaps of my bones cracking along my spine. He pried himself out of my arms and kissed my forehead. He brought both hands up to his ear and removed his eagle feather. Grabbing my hand, he placed the feather in my upturned palm and closed my fingers around it.

"You fly without me from now on, Crow," he said in Wacataw.

"No," I told him, sticking the feather in the bun at the back of my head. "This is now an owl feather. I will fly with you every night in dreams. Look for me." I grabbed his big hands, smiling as I stared into his eyes. "Uncle George, I can see through blindness now. I can even see through closed eyelids and through mirrors, too. Darkness can't blind me anymore. I see everything."

"*Nemosahteh yehyeh, ee-ee,*" he said in Wacataw.

*Ee-ee* means *Crow*. You pronounce it slowly with the tempo of a crow saying *caw-caw*.

*Nemosahteh yehyeh, ee-ee.*

*I love you, Crow.*

I had never heard Uncle George say *I love you* to anyone.

"I love you, too," I said, and my tears blurred his face.

He reached up, rooted the feather deeper in my bun, turned, and walked away, his broad back merging with the darkness, the floorboards creaking under his heavy feet.

Heathcliff still had Gabriel in the chokehold.

I walked over to the fireplace. It wasn't lit. Kindling was stacked there. I grabbed a long splinter of thin wood and walked over to the three-tiered candelabra.

"Watch this," I said to Gabriel.

I lit the end of the splinter on one of the candles, picked up the candelabra, and faced the wall beside Heathcliff and him. The three candles had long wicks and were collectively far brighter than the little flame on the stick.

"Look at the shadow that the brighter candlelight casts on the wall," I said to Gabriel in English. "You can see the shadow of my arm, the shadow of my hand, and the shadow of the stick in my fingers. Look closer at the shadow of the burning stick. It's just a dark line. You'd never know the stick was on fire. You can't see the shadow of the smaller flame at the tip because light can't cast a shadow. God is the darkness, Gabriel. God, He Who Never Dies, *is* the shadow, and we are the little lights. When our little light gets blown out, we instantly become one with God, with the greater darkness. We dissolve into it. We become eternally invisible. We vanish forever in Him, with Him, in holy darkness."

I brought the candelabra closer to my face so the flames highlighted my Wacataw cheekbones.

"I've lost everyone, Gabriel. My entire family. I watched my mother and father die."

I blew out one candle, and as I turned the candelabra to bring the next flame closer, ultrathin ribbons of white smoke wound themselves in a ghostly braid through the black air.

"Then you took Émile from me."

I blew out the second candle, and darkness moved closer to us. Shadows filled his and Heathcliff's eye sockets, preparing them for blindness once the other flames went out.

"And soon Uncle George will die, too."

I blew out the third candle. Shadows filled the hollows of their cheeks. Heathcliff's ears and temples were no longer visible. God was all around us, closing in, and the closer He got, the more our physical features diminished. We were dissolving in His presence. I tried to put the candelabra on the tabletop, but the base set awkwardly on the meat of a forearm and fell over without a sound when dead hands caught it.

"Your mother, my grandmother." I brought my face near Gabriel's, keeping the burning stick's tiny flame close. "She once told me that when

I begin to feel lonely and wonder who I am, not to worry. She told me to think about the people who love me—not the people I love, but the people who love me. She said, *Our love makes you who you are, Crow. You are our love.* She said you can measure your value as a person by counting the people who love you, and you should use their love as the standard for how you behave in this world. *That* is who you are, she said. So who loves you, Gabriel? And don't say Mommy."

He said nothing. I moved the flame close enough to blind his eye. Heathcliff shifted his stance, pinching Gabriel's windpipe in the crook of his elbow, and Gabriel gagged.

"So the man no one loves is to be our Indian savior?" I said. "What a farce. Émile didn't believe in executing criminals. He believed people like you should spend the rest of your lives in prison, in the same windowless cell eating the same food, sleeping on the same bed, your only chair a chamber pot. I could let hatred sway me and have Heathcliff break your neck. But Wacataw don't kill family, Gabriel." His eyelids blinked rapidly, as if they could generate enough wind to blow out the flame. "So, in honor of my husband, I'm going to beg Colonel Balfour not to hang you but to imprison you for life in a dungeon in England instead. I pray when you eventually die that He Who Never Dies imprisons you in people's nightmares. I pray God casts you as a terrifying ghost who spends eternity scaring people in dreams. That way, everyone everywhere on earth will hate you throughout time."

I blew out the tiny flame, and darkness rushed in. Nothing moves faster than God.

We were all blind. I could hear feet scuffling, Gabriel trying to escape Heathcliff's grip. I heard a chortle and a muffled snap, and I knew the thump that vibrated through the bones of my feet was my uncle's skull hammering the floorboards. Heathcliff had killed him. Behind me, footsteps tapped on the stairs. Uncle George had stayed in the shadows to learn what judicial sentence his protégé would pass on his brother. His measured footfalls grew quieter in their descent.

I wasn't happy Heathcliff killed Gabriel. It happened so fast I couldn't have stopped him. Gabriel wasn't worth talking about anymore, though.

Groping my way to the other side of the room, I found the tinderbox on the mantel and brought it back. I lit the candelabra and nestled it on the tabletop between two forearms. Heathcliff and I stood on opposite sides of the narrow table. Gabriel's torso lay in a hideous, reverse fetal curl.

"Why'd you come back?" I asked Heathcliff. "Because the cask was filled with lead, not gold, as Uncle George said?"

"Even if it was gold, how could I move it myself? And where would I take it? I'd need your help."

I studied him. He didn't look away. We both knew anyone in Charleston would have helped him for a wage. Outside, the carriage driver's whip snapped a few times, followed by the clopping of horseshoes. The black horses were hauling Uncle George off on his one-way journey.

"I came here tonight," Heathcliff said, "to get rid of Gabriel once and for all. I didn't know you and George were going to be here."

"You wanted Gabriel out of the way because we're your only way to get rich."

"Accuse me of anything you want. The fact is, Gabriel was in my way. Now, he's not. Not in your way, either. We can concentrate on our mission." He brought his face closer. "I'll do whatever it takes to attain wealth. I'll suffer any indignity or hardship. I don't feel pain. Mind you, I don't seek happiness or contentment, not the way you lot chase after it."

"I was happy once," I said. "Very happy. With Émile. But Émile is gone forever. Uncle George, too. So tell me, how exactly am I seeking happiness?"

One or both of us breathed on the light, and the flickering flames made shadows hop around the deep walls of Heathcliff's eye sockets. His dark eyes sat back there, glossy black marbles, unmoving and wet—snake eyes.

"You, on the other hand," I said, "are trying to slither your way back to someone who has hurt you. This Cathy woman. She is your happiness, your bundle of joy, your one true love. We heard you talk about her when you had a fever in your sleep. Right here in this room."

His eyes were no longer visible under his scrunched eyebrows.

"She must be a dreary and nasty woman to want anything to do with you. Meaner than you, if that's humanly possible. After all, she abandoned you for someone else, right?"

He groaned, or rather growled. A teased watchdog.

"This other man is wealthy, yes?" I said. "You crave wealth so you can return to England and impress Cathy Earnshaw. But hold on a second. This rich man has the same last name as that soldier we disgraced. What was his name? Linton? You said you hated that name. Her name isn't Earnshaw, is it? It's Cathy Linton." I snickered. "Your bundle of joy chose a rich man over you. She sounds like a shallow slag to me."

He seized my throat, pulling me onto the tabletop, and I grabbed his wrists with both hands so I didn't suffocate under my weight as my feet left the floor. I thought he would strangle me. He didn't squeeze. He drew me so close we could have kissed. I preferred he choked me. He bared his white fangs.

"Who's given who the slip, you slut?" he said through gnashed teeth.

He cackled and released me.

He was laughing at me, at my loss—my loss was *permanent*, and his wasn't. Émile was dead, whereas Cathy was alive. Heathcliff pivoted, looking at the floor, at Gabriel's corpse, ultimately focusing on me.

"We've got to get rid of his body," he said calmly.

"We can't toss him in the river," I said, equally calm, both of us acting our parts. "People will recognize him."

"They won't recognize him if they think he's a soldier. I'll get a uniform—"

"Lay him out on the floor behind the desk," I said, pointing my chin at Gabriel's office.

He shrugged Gabriel's corpse over his shoulder while I cleared any evidence of a scuffle. It was an easy clean-up since it had been a bloodless killing. After placing the severed forearms back on the cabinet shelves, including Émile's, I joined Heathcliff in Gabriel's office.

"I'll tell everyone that Dr. Gabriel DuBois died of heart failure," I told Heathcliff. "I'll tell them he must have broken his neck in the fall."

# CHAPTER NINETEEN

## *Bedfellows*

Heathcliff headed home. I entered the back door of the house. Mahala was in the sitting room on the settee across from Winslow in a cushioned chair.

"Do you have a moment?" I asked them.

Sitting at the card table, I told them I owned both houses, a maneuver I made so the property wouldn't fall into Pawsworthy's hands.

"We heard," Mahala said, brushing something off her apron with the back of her hand.

"How?"

"People talk," she said.

"People at the Pawsworthy household?" I asked.

She shrugged. "So I have to look for a place to live," she said, planting a palm on the arm of the settee as leverage to stand.

I showed her my palm. "Please," I said. "You don't have to go anywhere."

She studied me, trying to figure out what I wanted from her. I had no underlying scheme.

"I got to ask you something, though," I said. "Both of you. Did you know Émile died of the pox?"

"Gabriel told me that he inoculated Émile," she said, "but it didn't work."

"He told us not to tell you," Winslow said. "He didn't want you hating him for killing Émile by mistake."

I told them why he killed Émile, about Gabriel returning infected soldiers to their regiment, spreading smallpox, and how he developed a nastier version. I pointed at her hands, at the pale spots there.

"He inoculated you both, didn't he?" I said, watching them nod. "He inoculated the people who worked for him because they could help him fulfill his demented goal. He wasn't trying to save you. He was experimenting on you. Did anyone he inoculated in this household die? Anyone black, that is?"

"Mary," Winslow said, "and her boy, Tom."

"Were their pustules large or the typical small ones?"

"Tom's were large," he said. "Gabriel said it was because the pustules got infected. He died immediately. Maria a few weeks later. He kept them in the hospital attic, away from everyone. The pox got bad here in Charleston. By September, hundreds of blacks were dead from it. The British forced them to quarantine a mile out of town in a camp."

"Why would he do that?" Mahala said, shaking her head in disbelief. "Try to kill off blacks and whites?"

"He's profoundly disturbed," I said, keeping it brief, "with deep personal guilt."

"Shouldn't we stop him?" Mahala said. "He told us he's sailing injured soldiers to New York."

"We're working on that," I said.

Someone rapped at the back door. Winslow opened it and a black woman stepped in, closing the door herself.

"This is Hannah," Mahala said to me. "Gabriel told you about her. Your parents' mirror?"

"Pawsworthy's planning a raid on this house," Hannah said. She was breathing heavily, probably from her run here. "With soldiers."

Mahala glanced at me.

"A raid?" I said.

"He's got a court order," she said, facing Mahala. "He was talking with some Board-of-Police attorney. I caught the tail end."

Pawsworthy must have lied, telling Colonel Balfour that Gabriel broke parole.

"When are they coming?" Mahala said.

"Any moment," Hannah said, looking from Mahala to me. "I got to get out of here before he shows up."

"I appreciate your risk coming here," I said to Hannah. "But in the end, it doesn't matter. Gabriel's left Charleston."

It didn't matter if the soldiers found him dead of heart failure.

Hannah gave me a surprised look, eyebrows up.

"They're not coming for Gabriel," she said. "They're coming for you."

"Me?" I said, feeling something slither in my gut, stirring bubbles.

"Which means you two got to find somewhere to live right away," Hannah said, looking from Mahala to Winslow. "You got to get out of here. He's seizing this house. He's going to say you're not free blacks and take you."

"He can't do that," I said. "I can prove in a court of law that they're free."

"Don't listen to her," Hannah said to them. "She can't take on Pawsworthy."

Hannah hugged Mahala. She embraced Winslow, and they kissed. Winslow followed her outside.

Dawson must have revealed my true identity to Pawsworthy. But so what? Being the daughter of Gail and Dr. Jacque La Pierre wasn't a crime.

However, he was an established master of proving nonexistent crimes.

They arrived a half-hour after Hannah left. Despite marching along the piazza, someone had the courtesy to knock instead of kicking the door in. I opened it with Winslow at my side. Mahala was smoking cannabis in the kitchen house to remain "calm." She was afraid of soldiers, she said. Five redcoats stood behind Pawsworthy in a line. Pawsworthy's hair was greasy and clung to his head.

"Good evening," Pawsworthy said to us.

We didn't return the greeting. He clicked his fingers, and a soldier handed him a legal document. Overly dramatic. I could see boldly penned signatures and wax seals.

"This is your late husband's will," Pawsworthy said, holding it up.

"No, it's not," I said, struggling to remain calm. "His will is in Québec City, in our office there."

"That will is null and void as of December 15, 1780," he said, pointing his dirty fingernail at the date. "This is his last will and testament."

"Impossible. Émile would've told me."

"Like he told you about his affair with Eliza Breckenridge?" He flapped the will. "I kept this a secret because I didn't want to distract you from your investigation. And, of course, it would've looked improper in front of the Board of Police."

"Improper? What are you talking about?"

"Seeing that you are nowhere near solving the murder of Major Montcalm," he said, "appearances no longer matter." He flipped through the pages, reading from the document. "*. . . and I hereby bequeath my property and all my holdings, including, and especially, the legal status of my wife, to Donald Periwinkle Pawsworthy; to be clear, I willingly give my wife, Charlotte Savatier, body and soul, to Donald Periwinkle Pawsworthy as his wife; he has her as my gift and permission to take her into his domicile as his lawfully wedded bedfellow upon my death.*"

At first, I wanted to laugh at the absurdity, but I had a vision, a memory, of my parents swinging on those ropes, their heads bagged in black hoods. My legs bent at the knees, my hand coming up, groping for something to hold on to. I stepped away from Pawsworthy, walking backward, deep inside the room. I saw my reflection in my parents' mirror, and my face was as pale and gray as one of Gabriel's severed forearms.

"You . . . you . . ." I stammered. "You can't transfer marital status like it's a deed. The marital bond isn't a possession."

"This document is legal," he said, standing in the doorway.

I walked toward him. He held it with both hands, gripping the margins so I couldn't snatch it. The signatures were bold, and their names were written in longhand underneath: Émile Savatier, with Alexander Wright and Egerton McClain as witnesses.

"The Board of Police oversees legal disputes these days." Pawsworthy handed the will to a soldier. "What with the war and all. I'll make sure a minor civil matter like this one never appears on the docket. And seeing as I now own everything you do, including this estate and everything back in Québec City, you have no money for legal representation anyway." He nodded to Winslow. "Get her a ginger beer or some rum, will you? She looks like she's going to puke all over my rug."

I watched my hand rise, reaching between my shoulder blades for the knife handle. I ran my fingers through my hair instead, scratching madly at my scalp.

"Pack your trunks, my dear," he said. "You're moving in with me."

Dizziness stole my breath. I inhaled deeply and exhaled slowly, trying to steady myself.

"I understand you'll need time," he said. "I'll be back in two days."

I had no idea what day it was suddenly. The room had a slight tilt to it, too; it may even have begun to spin. Or was I in a spin on my way to the floor? He saw my bewilderment and grinned at my defeat.

"I'll have you forcibly moved into my home in chains if I have to." He turned his head, saying to someone behind him: "Station two guards at the front and back of the house. My wife is not to leave these premises unchaperoned. And bring a Cherokee tracker here. No, bring two, in case she does run away."

I heard boots marching and felt them vibrate through my backside and spine—apparently, I was sitting on the floor, my dress spilled around me like a pool of blood.

～

Winslow discovered Gabriel's body the following day while I was rummaging through law books in the sitting room. He told me the body needed to go somewhere. It was attracting flies.

"Please put him in Price's Alley," I said. "Then inform the Commissioner of Streets that Dr. DuBois has died of heart failure and to have a city wagon come get the carcass."

That's what the sergeant at the Watch House told me to do with the dead boy slumped against the Poor House boulder. Winslow stood there, gawking.

"Would you prefer I haul my husband's killer into the street myself?" I said.

"No, of course not. I . . . I thought he left for New York."

"Heart failure has a way of changing your travel plans."

Winslow tottered off.

I wasted more time researching marriage law. I finally slammed the book on the floor. I'd never stand before a judge; Pawsworthy would ensure it. I looked out the back window and saw Winslow cradling Gabriel's corpse in his arms, stomping toward the gate to Price's Alley. Gabriel's arms and legs were so stiff they didn't bend, but his head, with its neck bones broken, swung with the same sway of a droopy goolie bag.

His stiff limbs reminded me of those frog legs at our dinner party. That gave me an idea.

At six o'clock that evening, I went to Colonel Balfour's house. Captain Benson came to the door, courteously asking how I was doing.

"Miserably," I told him. "I must speak with the colonel. My life is in danger."

He ushered me into a small sitting room. "Please be patient," he said and left.

The pendulum clock ticked for nearly an hour before Colonel Balfour entered the room.

"Charlotte," he said.

"I'm sure you're aware of my husband's will that suddenly appeared out of nowhere."

Discussing myself as someone being passed from man to man was embarrassing. My sweet Émile didn't want any woman to feel this humiliation.

"From what I can see," he said, "you have made no developments in this investigation. In a few days, an inquiry will arrive from His Majesty on one of the mail ships. I shall have to report back. And I have nothing to report, do I?"

"I am close."

I could see he didn't believe me. He pursed his lips and blinked, a look of sympathy for me softening his jaw muscles. He thought I was pathetic.

"I can do nothing for you, Charlotte."

"So you will have me whored to that jackass? That dirty little man? I know the law. A marriage cannot be willed, given, or sold to the highest bidder like a property deed."

"Your honorable husband signed the will. McClain and Wright both witnessed Émile's signature."

"It's a fake."

"McClain and Wright are prominent members of the Board of Police. What am I to do, publicly, call them liars?"

"My husband would never submit any woman to living a life against her will. He would have told me in one of his many letters if he had changed his will, and he is not the kind of man who would pass his wife off to someone else—to *Pawsworthy* of all people? Really, Colonel?"

I was near tears, not for my sake, but for Émile's: Pawsworthy was destroying Émile's reputation. Everyone had to be laughing at this will.

"Émile wanted to stay in South Carolina after the war ended," I told him. "He was determined to ensure slavery ended. He was a staunch advocate for abolition, Colonel Balfour. Does he strike you as a man who'd will his wife to another man?"

He threw his hands up. "If you had any idea what pressure I am under." He scratched his forehead. "You'd understand why I can't help you. Our armies are shifting. Enemy militias are, too, possibly moving south. There's talk of a massive French armada off the Carolinas. Small-pox is raging through the armies. And you want me to worry about your marital status?" He slapped the outsides of his thighs. "Really, Charlotte, you have to go. *I* have to go."

With that, he left the room—left me with my mouth agape.

I began thinking in Wacataw, saying my name, *Crow*, over and over and hoping every time I said it, I would grow wings and fly out of Charleston.

～

I spent that night in my bedroom utterly listless and unable to concentrate.

I owned virtually nothing.

*Nothing.*

I had no family.

*No one.*

Except for Jane Harris.

And the next time I saw her, it would be my doom. A Wacataw had a duty to avenge a murdered relative by taking the murderer's scalp. Once she learned I was responsible for killing her son, Jane Harris had every right to come for mine.

I picked up the round hand-held mirror from my desk and stared at my face, at my little black pupils. They were tiny portals. On the other side opened a vast dark world of God. I closed my eyes and floated in that darkness, in that inner peace where Émile lived. Where my parents lived. When your eyes are open, you bring the outside light, the outside world, inside you, and it never leaves. He Who Never Dies sees everything you do, remembers everything you forget, and He keeps it all vaulted in here.

And I realized the more you see, the more terrifying your inner world becomes.

In the morning, I visited Egerton McClain at his home on Tradd Street. He had a soiled reputation for a sex scandal involving his wife's fifteen-year-old sister, whom he impregnated and shipped off to England. The child was born and died on the voyage. McClain was never punished for his debauchery. As a member of the Board of Police and a magistrate, he influenced the civil court—as my husband's fake will testified. He also witnessed every one of Pawsworthy's acquired properties since the rebels surrendered Charleston in May 1780.

I was certain McClain would refuse to meet with me if I showed up at his front door, so I came in through the back. He sat at a round table at the rear of the house, spooning through a bowl of porridge. He spotted me and wiped the corner of his mouth with a napkin.

"You can't barge into my house unannounced, Mrs. Pawsworthy," he said.

"It's *Mrs. Savatier*, you slithering worm."

"How dare you?"

He pounded a fist, and silverware chimed against fine teacup saucers as a few walnuts hopped out of a shallow bowl. His fingers crawled after the nuts. He munched them slowly, concerned more with their flavor than my insult.

"Pawsworthy is blackmailing you." I slid into the chair opposite him. "That's why you signed my husband's forged will. You and Wright. I—"

"I did no such—"

"Yes, you did. I suspect Pawsworthy caught you in some disgraceful sex act and has you in a parallel vice." I reached for a piece of his toast and crunched into it. "Did you have anything to do with that naked soldier they found at Colonel Balfour's party? Sergeant Linton? Someone abused him sexually and left him unconscious. Was that you?"

He stared, curling his upper lip on one side.

I pointed the bitten end of my toast at that snarl. "See how angry you are? That's how I feel. Only far worse. As you can easily imagine, I hate Pawsworthy. He is our common enemy, sir. Relax a moment, and listen to my proposal. Take a look at France and Spain. They have a common enemy, too—us, King George's British Empire. So why don't you and I pretend we're France and Spain, and Pawsworthy, for argument's sake, is Great Britain? We can band together against him."

I told him about the barrels of lead I found. He stared, not saying a word.

"Help me, and I'll help you," I said. "He will never be able to blackmail you. I promise."

"If we fail, I'll deny everything," he said. "You'll be hanged."

"What is it the Yankees say? Give me liberty or give me death!"

He collected a glob of porridge into the well of his spoon and brought it to his lips, chewing faster so he had room to speak.

"Can I be Spain?" he said. "I simply love their sherry."

"*¿Por que no, Señor?*"

On the appointed day, Pawsworthy arrived with a half-dozen soldiers and a horse-drawn prison transport carriage to cart me off. I peeked between the curtains. Dawson was out there, too. Pawsworthy and four soldiers marched down the piazza. Winslow opened the front door.

"I have a certificate of probable cause and seizure in my possession," Pawsworthy told him. "And my men are prepared—"

"I'm sure your document is proper and legal," Winslow said, raising a hand and pumping the air to slow Pawsworthy. "Mrs. Savatier will only see you, sir. No one else is allowed inside her private parlor."

"It's my house." He grinned as he folded his warrant. "And her name is Mrs. *Pawsworthy*, not Savatier."

"If you say so, sir," Winslow said.

Pawsworthy shuffled into the parlor. I sat in one of two cushioned chairs, mine to the left of my parents' mirror, its back against that same wall. The other chair faced mine, a table separating the two. The curtains were drawn, and one candle on the table lit the dim room. I heard Winslow close the front door and come into the parlor. We had moved the other furniture out of the parlor, so Pawsworthy had to sit in the chair facing my parents' mirror. Mahala and Heathcliff were upstairs in the dining room above us. Winslow had drilled a peephole in the floorboards above the chairs, opening a view to most of the parlor.

"Can I offer you a cup of tea, Donald?" I said.

"I should love one."

He squinted, obviously wondering why I was being polite. I asked Winslow to prepare our tea, and he stepped into the hall, pulling the door shut behind him.

"Why is it so gloomy in here?" Pawsworthy asked.

"We are low on candles. On account of the war."

"That's not true. DuBois's hospital is well stocked. I know. I sell candles to the military and the military hospitals."

"We need to discuss what's going to happen between us," I said.

"What's there to discuss?" Pawsworthy sighed as he leaned back. "You have no say in the matter. The law is clear."

"I am not your whore. And I never will be."

"You have marital duties that all wives must honor. I read your letters to Émile. So I know which duties you truly enjoy."

"*The Royal Gazette* is full of advertisements for wives who've run away," I said, ignoring his smug grin, "because they refuse to perform said duties. However, I'm not going to run away, I promise you that. And I'll promise you something else. We'll never be bedfellows. I will stick you in the heart with my dagger before I ever allow you to stick anything of yours into me."

"Strong words." He chuckled. "I've had enough of you and your words. Playtime is over. No more talking about the law and how you and

Émile used to do this and that up north. That's all over with. From now on, you'll run my household, not your mouth."

The service bell down the hall chimed. In the dining room upstairs, to the right of the fireplace mantel, hung a cloth rope that was connected to a bell in the sitting room below. Heathcliff had sounded the alarm, my cue to leave the parlor.

"That bell means the tea's ready." I smiled as I stood. "I'll be right back."

I left, closing the parlor door. I crept up the stairs at the back of the house and joined Heathcliff, Mahala, and Winslow in the dining room. Mahala was on the floor, peering through the peephole at Pawsworthy. I knelt opposite her. She sat back, and I placed my eye over the hole. The candlelight was dim down there, purposely, but I could still see Pawsworthy in the chair facing the mirror, one of his knees pumping with impatience.

Behind him hung Émile's portrait of me—only we had hung a black curtain in front of it. We also sewed a string into the curtain and ran that string up through the ceiling through another drilled hole to the dining room, where we could pull on the string and draw the black curtain aside to unveil the painting.

I nodded to Mahala, instructing her to grab the curtain string. I looked at Heathcliff, who stood with both hands ready. We waited for the rat to creep closer to the waiting snake. At any moment, Pawsworthy would recognize my parents' mirror. Mirrors were like genitalia—a temptation to every person left alone with one, something you could ignore for only so long. Sure enough, he struggled to stand, leaning heavily on one of the chair's arms. He stepped outside the mirror glass, to the left, to avoid his reflection. He examined the mirror frame and, perhaps recognizing it, stood before it to get a better look. His head shifted right to left; he squinted, apparently not wanting to see his full reflection as he finally looked at himself.

When his hands came up to touch the metal frame of the mirror, to take it off the wall and repossess it perhaps, I turned my head and waved to Heathcliff. I quickly looked back through the peephole, hearing the Leyden jars' metal levers click as Heathcliff made the connections. White sparks exploded downstairs, and Pawsworthy shook as violently as those frog legs at our dinner party. I raised my hand and, not taking my eyes off Pawsworthy, pointed at Mahala to jerk on the curtain string and reveal the painting of "my mother."

We had hung the portrait so that her face would appear behind Pawsworthy when he looked over his left shoulder in the mirror. As the electrical flashes lit up the room, he couldn't help but behold the ghostly pale vision of "my mother," having returned from her stint in hell to avenge him. I heard more clicks. Heathcliff couldn't resist connecting the remaining levers. A small streak of lightning snaked from the metal frame and struck Pawsworthy's neck fat, and his body shook ruggedly as if he was struggling to stop a ram by its horns.

Heathcliff had described his electrocution as fire shooting through your veins, paralyzing your muscles by overwhelming them with pure agony. He said it froze your voice as well. Seeing my mother in the mirror, Pawsworthy had to have regarded the burn in his veins as the very fire of hell.

Suddenly, the floor began to shake. I sat back. Mahala was running across the room. She pushed Heathcliff away from the Leyden jars and pulled the levers back. Pawsworthy finally screamed—more, I hope, from the fright of seeing my mother's ghost than the misery of electrocution. A whack as loud as a horse kicking a barn door sounded through the house.

Pawsworthy had fallen.

"What are you doing?" I yelled at Mahala.

"Those soldiers will arrest us all if he dies," she whispered hoarsely. "It's gone on too long."

I looked through the peephole. Pawsworthy was on his side, legs scissored. The mirror was still on the wall. My intention wasn't to kill Pawsworthy. I wanted to scare him so badly he wouldn't want anything to do with me or this house: I'd finally tell him I was the ghost's daughter.

We ran downstairs. Two soldiers were in the room. Dawson was still out front by the carriage. Pawsworthy was on his side, drool pooling on the rug. Mahala stepped between the two soldiers, moving one aside by gently pressing on his chest, her other hand on his sleeve. She knelt at the soldier's feet, grabbing Pawsworthy's greasy hair and turning his head to lower her ear over his nose and mouth.

"He's still breathing."

She let go of his head and wiped her palms on his coat sleeve before standing. Pawsworthy's eyes were open, but he didn't seem to recognize anything. He wasn't talking either.

"What's wrong with him?" Heathcliff asked one of the soldiers.

"I dunno," the soldier said. "We heard this loud crash and ran in to find him on the floor."

Heathcliff nudged the seat of Pawsworthy's pants with his foot. No change in his behavior. Soldiers stomped down the piazza. Dawson stood on the threshold with his men behind him. Seeing Pawsworthy, he rushed into the room, pushing one soldier aside.

"What'd you do to him?" Dawson said, looking from Heathcliff to me.

"Nothing," I said. "I left the room to prepare our tea. When I came back, these two soldiers were standing over him."

Dawson questioned them, getting the same report.

"He's had some kind of attack." Heathcliff widened his hands over Pawsworthy. "Is the geezer prone to convulsions?"

"Not that I'm aware of." Dawson's voice was more relaxed, not so rushed. "Is he dead?"

"Very much alive, I'm afraid," Heathcliff said.

And he was. His chest heaved and sank rhythmically. But the increase in electricity had clearly done him physical harm. Possibly permanent harm. He struggled to speak. His mouth kept opening and closing, his wet red tongue appearing briefly before receding—like the bird in a cuckoo clock. Dawson clapped loudly.

"Stand back," he told us. "No one touch my uncle."

"That choice isn't yours," I told Dawson. "It's mine."

"*Yours?* Who the hell do you think you are?"

By now, the remaining soldiers on the piazza were crowding the doorway.

"You there," I said to them. "Come inside quickly."

They shouldered their way in.

"Each of you grab an arm and leg." I looked Dawson directly in the eyes. "Take my husband back to our house on South Bay Street. Take him in that prisoner's carriage out front. I'll meet you there with a doctor."

"*Your* house?" Dawson said.

"Yes." I winked at him. "*My* husband. *My* house. You're no longer welcome there. Or here in this one, which is also *mine*."

"You'll have to sleep at the Horn Works," Heathcliff said.

With his nostrils flaring and tightening, Dawson resembled someone who had to defecate desperately. I squeezed Dawson's elbow, affecting my very best British elocution.

"Do tell Harriette Garden that Charlotte La Pierre says hello when you see her next, won't you, my dear friend?"

"Get out," Heathcliff told Dawson, sinking his palms into Dawson's chest.

Dawson staggered back. He studied the floor, his face as crimson as the roses in the woven rug. Heathcliff stomped toward him, and he fled. I stepped onto the piazza, glancing over my shoulder.

"Come, Heathcliff," I said. "We have work to do."

# CHAPTER TWENTY

## *The Chamber*

Whatever thrills I might have enjoyed moving back into my parents' house were thwarted. Pawsworthy couldn't talk or walk, so we stripped him and moved him into a bedroom on the third floor. Pawsworthy couldn't answer my questions, either, not even with blinks or grunts. He could have been acting. Hannah employed a rotating shift of spies to observe him through the gap along the hinges of the open bedroom door. The sole movement anyone reported was from his bowel; however, I didn't want Hannah or anyone else cleaning Pawsworthy up, so I appointed a Royalist soldier to bed-nurse Pawsworthy once a day.

Pawsworthy had decorated one wall in my father's library with odd, esoteric memorabilia—items his victims once owned. A pair of shattered eyeglasses, for example, hanging from an ivory toothbrush stabbed into the toe of a man's shoe. A white shirt framed behind glass with three flattened dead mice and rusty blood stains over the left breast. An ornately framed portrait of a beautiful young blond-haired woman with a broken walking cane nailed to the wall beneath it. And, of course, a gilt-wood framed pen-and-ink drawing of the 1771 hanging of Jacque and Gail La Pierre that appeared in *The Royal Gazette*.

But what interested me was the two wooden casks of rum in front of this wall. Each stood on a marble pedestal. That meant they were important to Pawsworthy. Above the taphole ran the script *F & B Mount Gilboa Distillery* in a semicircle along the rim, with the word *RUM* in a semicircle below. Branded into the center was *No. 1* on one cask and *No. 2* on the other.

No one in the house knew anything about F & B Mount Gilboa Distillery. I asked at the meat market on Broad Street. No one had heard of it. I went to the fish markets on Queen Street, to the low market on Tradd Street, to tailors, cobblers, and taverns. I spent hours traveling from shop to shop, and no one knew anything about F & B Mount Gilboa Distillery. I was resting on Beale's Wharf on East Bay Street when I looked across the street at one of the city's oldest taverns. I went inside, plodded through the sailors and pipe smoke, and found the owner. He said he used to sell F & B rum.

"They made delicious rum," he said, stroking his long gray beard. "They made a dark one and white one but went out of business before the war."

"What does F & B stand for?"

"Frank & Becky."

"Frank and Becky who?"

"Beats me," he said.

"Why'd they go out of business?"

"They didn't. They sold it to Pawsworthy and Wragg. And it'll snow in Barbados before I ever sell those greedy idiots' rum, I promise you that, lassie."

I thanked the man and left. Pawsworthy wouldn't have those kegs of F & B rum on marble pedestals against his Wall of Victory unless he cheated Frank and Becky out of their company. Unfortunately, I could never find out anything about that company: Its deeds were in Barbados.

As I strolled along East Bay Street, I kept thinking about Mahala. One particular issue troubled me. She never wanted to be around soldiers, yet the moment Pawsworthy fell onto the floor in a state of paralysis, her "fear" of soldiers vanished. She gently ushered one aside with her palm on his chest and knelt at his feet. Not the actions of someone who feared soldiers. Also, at our electrified frog dinner, she had said she learned how to thicken almond cream from her father, who concentrated sugar into molasses by heating it to make rum.

I veered my investigation in another direction.

Mahala had a permit to buy at the markets. I decided to check the Board of Police records. Weeks ago, I got my permit, too. You needed proof of identity or someone of status to vouch for you to get issued one.

Slaves provided written notes from their owners, who were landowners with permits. If a person wasn't a landowner, he provided a parish record of baptism or marriage—evidence with names and dates. Since Mahala wasn't married, I hoped to find information about her birth—her baptismal record or a parish record of her parents' marriage with their names.

Mahala had the leanest entry in the ledger. Her first name, permit number, and issue date: June 5, 1780. That was it.

I marched to Gabriel's house and bluntly asked Mahala what her last name was. We were in the compound outside the kitchen house.

"Who wants to know?" she said.

"Me."

"Why?"

"Maybe I was thinking about giving you some property I'm having sequestered."

"Why would you do that?"

"Maybe I'm thinking about something else—issuing a warrant for your arrest, for example."

"Why would you—"

"Answer the question."

"No."

I felt my eyes squint on their own, suspiciously. "What's your father's name?"

"My father?"

"That's right."

"Harry."

"Harry?" I said, disappointed it wasn't Frank. "What's your mother's name?"

"Susanne." She planted a hand on her hip. "Are we done here?" She glanced at the kitchen house behind me. "I'm baking some rice bread with fresh ginger root and—"

"Where are you from?"

"England."

"I know. But where in England?"

"Dartmoor."

"What did you do there?"

"We own a sheep farm."

"Why are you here now?"

"To start a new life in America."

"Where did your father make rum?"

"At home." She scrunched her face. "In the barn, if you must know."

"Why did he make rum?"

"For the same reason you pour water into a glass."

"Why isn't there a last name recorded on your permit to buy at the market?"

"I'm starting a new life. I left the old me in the past."

"The old me? What the hell is that?"

"Let me ask you something. How many blacks in that register of yours had last names?"

"Some."

"And those that did, was it *their* last name or the name of their owner?"

"Their owner, from what I saw. But you're not a slave."

"So what? Last names are meaningless. Why don't you make one up for me? How about I take yours?"

I squinted, asking, "What was wrong with the old you?"

"She was tired of smelling sheep."

I suspected it was more than sheep she was leaving behind. "Why isn't a pretty woman like you married?"

Maybe she was one of those wives who ran away from *marital duties*. She stared at me. I didn't look away, and neither did she. I saw no connection between F & B Mount Gilboa Distillery, sheep farming in Dartmoor, Pawsworthy, Harry, Susanne, or The Old Me. The snake needed to veer back the other way.

I leaned in close to her neck.

"I smell ginger," I said, sniffing. "Did you rub some on your skin as perfume?"

"Of course not."

"Then you'd better go check on your bread."

"You're bizarre," she said.

"*Bon appetit.*"

I stomped out the gate.

～～～

Each morning, I held a glass of water up to Pawsworthy's lips so he wouldn't die of thirst, but much of the water leaked back out. He could munch on morsels of bread and minced meat, but the left side of his mouth drooped, and his lips couldn't purse. By day four, Pawsworthy still wasn't moving. Heathcliff and I were at his bedside. Pawsworthy watched us. I reached in and closed his greasy eyelids with the padding of my thumbs. His right eyelid struggled to reopen, fluttering.

"I dare say the electrocution has rendered him an invalid," Heathcliff said. "Do you think his condition is permanent? How will he ever tell us where the gold's hidden?"

"Pirates hoard hidden gold, Heathcliff. This turd collects property. He'd rather steal your house, horses, and guns."

"And buy gold with it."

"He may never be able to tell us anything." I raised a forefinger. "Watch." I pinched the skin on Pawsworthy's forearm and stretched it several inches without letting go. "He can feel the pain but can't react to it. Place your fingers on his neck to feel his pulse."

He knew where to feel his heart pound.

"It beats faster when I abuse him," I said, stretching his skin even more.

"The electricity must have cooked a vital organ," Heathcliff said, stepping back.

I stepped back, too.

"I've been wanting to ask you something," I said. "You paid Eliza Breckenridge not to tell me whatever she told you on the way to the Craven Bastion that day we interrogated her. What was it?"

He pointed his chin at Pawsworthy. "She said this fat cow loved to torture anyone that crossed him—before he killed them."

"And why'd you want to keep that from me?"

"She told your husband that, too—after swearing him to secrecy. She made him promise he wouldn't even write it in his notes. Anyway, I feared if you found that out, you'd suspect he killed your husband, and you'd try to prove it. And as it turned out, I was right. That would have been a colossal waste of time."

"You know what I think?"

"You regret involving me in your plot," Heathcliff said.

"Oh, no. You're helpful—so long as we're both working toward a common goal. No. I was going to say, I think it's time we send these South Carolina Royalists away. They're reporting everything we do to Dawson."

Heathcliff winced. "But if we get rid of the soldiers"—he pointed at Pawsworthy—"who's going to wipe his arse?"

"I'm not emotionally capable of handling that task." I closed one eye and scratched behind my ear. "So that leaves you."

"I'll strangle him first."

"How about this? If we don't feed him, there won't be anything to clean up."

"Well done," Heathcliff said.

Pawsworthy's right eye popped open.

We left the room, and I locked Pawsworthy in.

That night, Hannah summoned the Royalists on the front walkway. I read them my Order of Compliance and dismissed them. Each day, Heathcliff or I monitored Pawsworthy's condition. He could move his right arm and right leg with limited range and blink his right eyelid. His left eyelid didn't open fully. He was still unable to speak.

One morning, Heathcliff and I checked on Pawsworthy together. I put Émile's leather bag on the bed, pulling out papers. His eyeballs shifted between us.

"I have something that might interest you," I told Pawsworthy. "It's your last will and testament. I struck a deal with McClain and Wright. We even got the man who forged Émile's signature to forge yours." I held the last page up, showing him his signature and wax seal. "You're leaving everything you own, all your holdings, the immense debts owed to you, the contents of your warehouses, every ship, every plantation and farmhouse in South Carolina, including your five homes here in Charleston, the mansion in Philadelphia, the tobacco farms in Virginia, all your slaves, all your holdings in Barbados, including your precious Narraganset Pacer horses, your sugar plantation and the total ownership of the rum distillery there, too—all of it, you heir to me, your beloved wife, bedfellow, and admirer." I grinned. "I shall own *everything*." I pointed to the will. "And, look closely—come on, I'm not talking to a horse, swing that other eye over here—see? You had the foresight to appoint me your guardian and legal representative in the event you are so incapacitated that you're incapable of thinking for yourself, such as the wretched state you're in now."

I glanced at Heathcliff, who stood with his jaw set and black eyes unblinking.

"All you got to do, Mr. Pawsworthy, sir," Heathcliff said, "is fucking die."

Pawsworthy stared at me. No wiggling. No blinking. Nothing.

"This paralysis must be awful for you," I said. "Like hanging from a noose with your hands tied behind your back and a black hood over your head."

A painting of Charleston Harbor hung on the wall opposite his bed. I replaced it with Émile's horrible painting of me. Pawsworthy's right eyelid fluttered.

"That's my mother," I said. "I'm the proud daughter of Gail La Pierre and Dr. Jacque La Pierre. I watched you hang my parents across the street when I was a little girl."

I could tell Dawson never told him who I was. Panic pried his right eye open even more. The right side of his face, the side that worked, twitched, and his fatty neck jiggled. His right arm flopped against his left leg, edging it off the mattress. Heathcliff slapped it back onto the bed, hard.

"My uncles are Dr. Gabriel Harris DuBois and George Harris. You didn't know Gabriel was a full-blooded Wacataw Indian, did you? He wasn't a French Catalonian."

I reached behind my head for the knife and pulled it out. As I moved toward him from the foot of his bed, I spoke Wacataw.

"I am called Crow, She Who Never Shuts Up, and I am here in full sight of He Who Never Dies to retake the honor of my parents who you murdered."

I bunched the hair at the front of his head and pressed my blade horizontally against the top of his forehead, intent on cutting from front to back to take his scalp. That's when Heathcliff clamped his muscular hand on my shoulder.

"Someone's here," he said; he had the exceptional hearing of a guard dog.

The distant knocking of shoes on floorboards echoed through the hall.

"My dinner guests are early," I said, backing away but looking into Pawsworthy's gray pig eyes. "I'll be back to tuck you in afterward, dear husband."

I returned my knife to its sheath.

"Come, Heathcliff," I said. "We have guests to entertain. Be sure to lock the door."

Behind me, Heathcliff slammed the door so hard I felt my hair move.

~~~

I had invited Winslow, Mahala, and Hannah to dinner, telling them I wanted to discuss changes in the households. I had freed the domestic slaves. I also invited Byron, the tax assessor, and asked him to bring some documents. We sat around the dinner table in the second-floor dining room. Hannah had prepared rabbit stew and rice bread.

"Heathcliff wants to move into Gabriel's house," I told them. "He now owns that property and the hospital, too, which he plans to rent to German officers. But I have plenty of room for Mahala to join Hannah and me in this house if you want. Hannah has agreed to run the household with a paid commission."

"She'll be my boss?" Mahala said, nodding toward Hannah.

"You can work that out," I said. "How about you, Winslow? There's plenty of room for you, too. Just don't kill us with your smoldering poison ivy logs."

Winslow eyed me, squinting suspiciously. "This is a clean household," he said, flashing his lightning-white teeth. "I doubt you have anywhere near the rats Gabriel's hospital had. Bloody clothes and bandages were always piling up." He raised his spoon, prodding the air with an afterthought. "But they might need my services at the military hospital next door."

"You wouldn't have a problem with Pawsworthy living here, too?" I said. "He's in a crippled state. He's utterly defenseless."

"I couldn't care less about him," he said, sipping stew from his spoon.

"The other day," I said to Mahala. "I saw Winslow bringing poison ivy vines down from the second floor of Gabriel's kitchen house. He said *these don't belong up there*. Which meant you put them up there, Mahala. He told me he suffocated rats with their poisonous smoke. I had seen a few butt ends of those hairy logs in Francis Wragg's fireplace after finding him tortured to death. I remembered how you sedated that raccoon in your smokebox before cutting its throat. Mushrooms, cannabis, opium. Your knowledge of plants is impressive. It's what makes you such a great cook—and a great teacher, too. You taught Winslow how to kill with poison ivy smoke."

She lowered her head, but I saw her glance up to make eye contact. She slid her hands off the table as she sat back.

"You stopped Heathcliff when he was electrocuting Pawsworthy," I said. "You didn't want Pawsworthy to die. Was that because you wanted to kill him yourself? How about when Pawsworthy collapsed on the floor? You suddenly lost your fear of soldiers—which meant you were never afraid of soldiers in the first place. It was a ruse. You were hiding from Pawsworthy, using his ever-present entourage of soldiers as an excuse."

I looked at Byron. "Did you bring the information I asked for?"

He handed me a piece of paper, and I read through the transcribed details he acquired from the Board of Police. He had written her first name, her permit number, and the date it was issued. His handwriting was sloppy, barely legible. I tapped the page.

"It appears," I said to him, "that you discovered exactly what I did about Mahala's background: Nothing. Everyone in Charleston except for Mahala has shown documentation proving their identity. It's as if someone paid the clerk off—someone who *knows everyone*, like you."

Byron glanced at Mahala, who didn't look away. She blinked sadly at him.

"And why not include a last name?" I asked him.

Byron didn't answer. He examined his rabbit stew, which he hadn't touched.

"I know how Pawsworthy behaves," I said. "That depraved ghoul keeps things that belong to the people he destroys as a souvenir. Take the rum casks from F & B Mount Gilboa Distillery that sit on their own marble pedestals in his library, for example. F & B stands for Frank and Becky. Or that's what I thought, not having seen those names written out. I also thought they were first names. Who wouldn't? So my attention snaked in another direction, in the opposite direction, moving from first to last—from first names to last names. What if Frank and Becky were last names? Surnames that represented two families, not two people? That means *Frank* would be your last name, Mahala, making your father Harry Frank. That means Becky is your mother's maiden name, her family name. Only it's not Becky, as in B-E-C-K-Y, as I had assumed." I faced Byron. "If you anglicized the pronunciation of your French name, *Bêche,* you can get the sound, *Becky.* Over time in England, that's what happened to your family name. Foreign speakers have difficulty pronouncing written French. I remembered my uncle's Wacataw friend, John Peele. He was learning English and wasn't proficient at pronouncing written words. He read your name and pronounced it as *Beck-ee.* Your actual English name doesn't have the French pronunciation, does it? It's written as *Beche* with plain English spelling, but it's pronounced *Becky.* So if you were to read what the letters *F & B* stood for, say, on a deed, they would read *Frank and Beche,* not *Bêche.* It's Frank and Beche Mount Gilboa Distillery. And that would make Susanne Beche Frank, Mahala's mother, your sister."

I remembered what Colonel Balfour had said when I first met him: *Everyone seems to be related to everyone else these days.*

"What drew my attention to you," I told Byron, "was your improbable claim of having a blacksmith craft *five* of Mahala's smoking ovens. Because of the war, there's such a shortage of metal that the army is confiscating iron fences and wagon wheel rims to melt them down for horseshoes." I pointed my chin toward the ocean. "They even took the iron door that used to hang in our stone wall out front."

"Bully for you," Byron said, reaching inside his coat; he pulled out a small pistol and laid it next to his stew.

"My goodness," Heathcliff said, banging the table with his fist so violently that our bowls and the pistol hopped. "Look, everyone, Byron brought his own bloody dessert!"

"Put that away," Mahala told her uncle.

"It would be rather difficult to pull that trigger with those tiny needles in your finger," I told Byron. "You said a palmetto palm cut your finger. But that would have sliced you. You have no cut. Even if you did, it would have healed by now. You mishandled the suicide plant when you killed Wragg." I held up his transcription. "It's why your handwriting is sloppy. You have to write with your left hand."

"You wouldn't believe how much these things hurt," he said.

"A German doctor told me the pain can last for years." I faced Mahala. "I found out F & B made two brands of rum. No. 1 and No. 2. No. 1 was dark rum. No. 2 was lighter."

"The longer you age rum," Mahala said, nodding, "the darker it gets."

"So I'm guessing from your skin color and Uncle Byron's skin color that the two rums represented more than your parents' surnames. The dark and light rums mean your father was black and your mother white, yes?"

She nodded, tears wetting her eyes. "I'm pretty sure—"

"She had nothing to do with this," Byron said. "I asked her to put those poison ivy vines aside for me. I told her I would use her smokebox and poison ivy vines to threaten Pawsworthy. To get him to talk. She didn't know I had killed anyone. Those rats deserved it. Every one of them." He smiled nervously at her. "I couldn't risk Pawsworthy discovering her last name was Frank. He'd have slaughtered her."

"That's also why Mahala lived with Dr. DuBois and not you," I told Byron.

He nodded, saying, "When I came to Charleston, I started pronouncing my last name like the French to keep Pawsworthy and the others unsuspecting. I doubt he or Wragg or Bancroft even know what the *B* in F & B stood for anyway, but I couldn't risk it. So I introduced myself to everyone using the French pronunciation of *Bêche*. But you're right. We pronounce it *Becky*."

"My father was a free man," Mahala said. "He had developed a popular rum recipe in Dartmoor, which he sold to local taverns at first, then a few in London. Since my mother's family owned property in Mount Gilboa, Barbados, they thought they'd try producing it. I was twenty-five when they moved to Barbados. My parents always wrote to my sisters and me, but they abruptly stopped. This was right before the war started."

"So I went to Barbados to check on them," Byron said. "Harry and Susanne had disappeared. Locals thought that they sold everything and went back to England. I found out that a group from Charleston owned our property. Two of them, Pawsworthy and Montcalm, already owned sugar cane plantations there—one, Pawsworthy's, was next door. So I went there and spoke with the slaves. When I told them I was Suzanne's brother, they spoke freely. At the time, Pawsworthy was back here in Charleston, trying to protect his properties from rebels. I found out those bastards murdered Harry after he refused to sign over the property."

"What bastards exactly?" I said.

"Montcalm, Bancroft, Wragg, and Pawsworthy. They shot him in his own house. Harry Frank was one of the finest men I've ever met."

"We don't know what became of my mother," Mahala said. "That's why I didn't want Heathcliff killing Pawsworthy that day. I want Pawsworthy to tell us where my mother is."

"Which brings up the matter of torture." I faced Byron. "Why did you torture *everyone?*"

He didn't answer.

"You don't torture *every* victim that brutally." I shook my head. "The first man would tell you everything, including his innermost sins. Nor is this a tit-for-tat for shooting a man. It's been over five years. Everything in equal measure. You're getting revenge for something far more sinister."

Byron's eyeballs were glossing over. He planted his elbows on the table and lowered his face into his palms. After a while, he raised his head and glared at Mahala.

"In Barbados," he said, "they told me what happened to your mother. I didn't want you to know how she suffered." He paused, sniffling. "Fishermen found Susanne floating in the ocean with her wrists and ankles tied to an armchair, naked, with little needles all over her skin. The needles come from a poisonous plant Montcalm grew on his plantation, on the other side of Pawsworthy's." He looked at me. "The people on Pawsworthy's plantation showed me where those plants grew, and I collected several of them before I left Barbados. I used them on Montcalm.

He told me how he had discovered the plant on a trip to New Holland. He took it back to Barbados so he could use it in place of the lash on slaves. The pain was far more memorable, he told me. Trust me, he told me *everything*."

Mahala's hope turned to anger as she set her jaw and tightened the muscles in her face; she wished her uncle hadn't kept that secret from her.

"In London," Byron said to me, "my friends in the military told me in February of last year that they were planning to attack Charleston. I immediately asked for a transfer. I was here by May. Mahala came later. I was determined to wait for however long it took until all those murderers were together in Charleston, and when I found out Montcalm snuck into town, I struck."

I glanced at Hannah.

"She's your paid informant, right?" I said to Byron. "She told you Montcalm was at Pawsworthy's that night he came to town."

He nodded.

"I followed Montcalm to The Jester's Mate," Hannah said. "That's where he met Francis Wragg. I told Byron they were there."

"You got Montcalm arrested," I said. "You told the soldiers a French spy was in town. If you wanted him dead, why'd you get him arrested?"

"Montcalm was arguing with Wragg," he said, nodding. "Wragg demanded money immediately. Montcalm stormed off. He said he had to return to a privateer ship that was taking him back to Martinique. I didn't want that bastard getting away. So I told the soldiers he was a French spy. If I had to, I'd bribe all the guards in Charleston to get at him in his jail cell." Byron paused, breathing deeply. "I wanted them scared. So I killed Montcalm exactly as they had killed Susanne. But instead of water, I drowned him in smoke. I couldn't drag him to the ocean without being seen. I wanted them to talk with each other. To talk about the suicide plant. To wonder who was going to get it next. To stir distrust among them."

Mahala spoke up, addressing me. "If you knew my uncle was killing these murderers, why'd you invite him here tonight? Why not arrest him at his office earlier?"

"I wanted to understand *why* you were killing these men," I said to Byron.

I explained how Pawsworthy murdered my parents, too, and stole this house from them. He lowered his eyes.

"Now what?" Mahala said.

I told them how Pawsworthy was supplying lead to the Yankees. "I'll turn Pawsworthy over to Colonel Balfour. He'll be tried for treason."

"After what he did to your parents?" Byron asked. "You're going to let Balfour hang him?"

"I can't influence Balfour's decisions," I said. "I'd prefer to see Pawsworthy linger as an invalid on a prison ship."

"Let me have him," Byron said. "What's the difference if I kill him or Balfour? You can arrest me afterward. I got my tools hidden outside. I've been watching your house. Waiting."

"Tools?" I said.

"The suicide plant. The smokebox. Mushrooms. Poison ivy logs. Poison ivy leaves, too."

"Why mushrooms?" I said. "And why upside down in the chair?"

"If they're upside down, I can fit their head into the top of the smokebox and tie the box to the chair leg. The poison ivy smoke burns the throat and lungs."

"And the mushrooms?"

Mahala spoke up. "Those mushrooms make you see things. Fantastic designs in the woodwork of a door or a table top or even a rug. You see things according to what kind of person you are. A nice person will have pleasant exotic visions while an evil person will suffer terrifying hallucinations."

That made me think back to Pawsworthy seeing an Indian woman—my mother—in the mirror.

"Did you know about these mushrooms?" I asked Hannah. "Did you secretly feed Pawsworthy them? To help him see things in his mirror?"

She darted her eyes at Mahala, which was as good as a confession.

"The last thing you want to do under the influence of mushrooms," Mahala said, "even if you're a good person, is look at yourself in the mirror."

"It's true. I've eaten them." Byron pointed his chin at me. "I almost went crazy seeing myself in the mirror. It's as if your face isn't yours. It's a mask. All the parts seem absurd. My nose started moving on its own, how a candle flame wiggles. I felt trapped behind this ridiculous mask. So I looked away. But then things changed for the better. I had the funniest full-on conversation with my palm."

I looked at Hannah. "Did Gabriel know you gave Pawsworthy these mushrooms?"

"It was his idea," she said.

"Did Gabriel know what you were up to?" I asked Byron.

He shook his head. "I first met Gabriel on the docks back in June. He was looking for a shipment of medical supplies that arrived on Pawsworthy's ship. I told him Pawsworthy was stockpiling them in his warehouse to raise the price. I could tell he hated Pawsworthy, so I helped him with shipments whenever possible. That's how I became his patient. When I learned he needed a cook, I got Mahala the job."

I studied him. "That way, she could spy on the investigation. Warn you if Émile figured you out?"

He nodded.

"So you positioned them upside down with their heads in the box," I said, "gagging on poison ivy smoke while they see hellish things on account of those mushrooms while their skin burns from the needles?"

"I also tie a plant stem in their mouths so they can't scream," he said. "Give me Pawsworthy, please. I want him to go through the hell they put my sister through."

Mahala lowered her head and wept quietly. Hannah stood, holding her hand out across the table to Winslow.

"I think it's time you and I go for a moonlight stroll, Winslow, and leave these folks to their machinations."

"A great idea," he said, clasping her hand.

"You, too, Mahala," Hannah said. "Come on."

Mahala looked at me, and I nodded. After they left, I noticed something was amiss.

"Where's Heathcliff?" I said.

Chairs and floorboards squeaked as we stood and looked for the elusive Brit.

"I never noticed he left," Byron said.

A bang upstairs shook the ceiling. Heathcliff shouted.

"Dear God," I said. "What's he up to?"

We ran upstairs.

We could see from the hall that Pawsworthy's bed was empty. He was gone. For a moment, I thought Heathcliff had thrown him out of the third-floor window, which was open. Heathcliff stood on the other side of the bed by the fireplace, clutching a rope.

"Where'd he go?" I asked, coming into the room.

Pawsworthy was on the floor with a noose around his neck. Heathcliff said he had dragged him out from under the bed—a rather stupid hiding place, he noted.

"I'll get him to tell me where the gold is," Heathcliff said, "by dangling him out the window."

Byron clasped his hands. "Mr. Heathcliff, sir," he said. "He weighs too much. He won't be able to talk. You'll only succeed in suffocating him. If he owns a hidden stash of gold, I shall find it for you. No one is better qualified to extract such information than I." Byron turned to me. "Charlotte, let me get my tools. Please, arrest me afterward. Please, I beg you, let it be me, not Balfour, who kills this wretch. For my sister's sake."

If Pawsworthy could have spent the rest of his life in prison, how Émile would have wanted him to, I would have said no. But that wasn't going to happen. Balfour would hang him for treason. He'd told me he had enough of this insurrection.

"He's yours," I told Byron.

Byron hurried out the door.

"Jolly good decision," Heathcliff said.

We hoisted the obese little man onto the bed. Heathcliff sat him up, setting his back against the headboard. We waited—until I realized Pawsworthy would be hanging upside down over smoldering embers. I walked to the other side of the bed and got my knife out when Byron entered the room. He set the smokebox on the floor by Heathcliff and placed a woven basket on the mattress—his tools. He eyeballed my knife.

"What's that for?" he asked, jerking his head at Pawsworthy. "You said he was mine."

"Not quite all of him." I held the knife up. "I'm not going to kill him. But I need his scalp. It's a family obligation."

"You can have his scalp when I'm done. I can't have him passing out from blood loss. And that blood dripping off his head might put my smoke out."

"Charlotte," Heathcliff said gracefully, appealing to me with upturned puppy eyes and the joined hands of a monk. "Byron has proven methods and procedures we shouldn't fuss with."

I reached over my shoulder and returned my knife to its sheath. Byron pulled on a pair of white gloves that officers and gentlemen wore. He winced when he tugged the glove over his injured finger.

"Come, Heathcliff," I said. "Let's adjourn to the library." I looked across the bed at Byron. "Promise me you won't burn any of his hair. And don't worry. I'm not going to arrest you."

"But I will," Dawson said, standing in the doorway, pistol in hand.

Pawsworthy started to bounce as if riding a horse and gasped excitedly at the sight of his nephew—his savior. Dawson wiggled his pistol at Heathcliff.

"Step back against the fireplace," he said, looking at me. "You stay where you are, or I'll blow another hole in your face."

I raised my hands level with my ears.

"Go ahead and work your magic on this crippled fool, Byron," Dawson said, jerking his head at his uncle. "But I'm going to turn you all over to Balfour afterward."

"You have one shot," Heathcliff said.

"And it's going between your black eyes," he said, cocking the hammer and aiming at Heathcliff.

I reached behind my head and squeezed the handle of my knife, bringing the blade down in a stiff arc and following through so that the knife tip hit the mattress. Exactly as Uncle George taught me. Dawson's severed hand fell on the blanket, still holding the pistol, his forefinger curled around the trigger. Dawson reached for the pistol with his other hand, and I turned my wrist and drove the dagger into his throat, feeling the steel vibrate as the tip struck the bone at the base of his skull. Holding my palm over his mouth, I yanked the knife out fast, blood spurting far enough to sprinkle Pawsworthy's bleached face.

Dawson collapsed on the floor. I grabbed his severed hand, leaving the pistol, and stuffed it inside Dawson's shirt.

"Come, Heathcliff," I said, squatting by Dawson's head. "Help me throw him out the window so he doesn't bleed all over my house."

"Stop saying that," Heathcliff said through gnashed teeth.

"Saying what?"

"That *Come, Heathcliff* rubbish. You make it sound like I'm your lapdog."

"Aren't you, though?"

We struggled with the limp body and dropped it out the window. Blood painted the wall. I tapped Byron's shoulder.

"Don't you need a bigger chair—since you're putting him upside down in it?" I pointed my chin at Pawsworthy. "He's rather thick. We can get an armchair from the library."

Byron shook his head. "That chair there will do fine."

"But that's a chamber chair," I said.

"I know," he said. "It's perfect. It's been used already, yeah?"

"Twice."

"Who used it?"

"I did."

"And you left it there beside him, full?"

"Yes."

"Brilliant," he said.

# CHAPTER TWENTY-ONE

# Three Tongues

I never appeared before the Board of Police to deliver my final report to Colonel Balfour's committee. He said he was too busy with the war. He wanted a written report. I blamed everything on the greedy nephew, Sergeant Andrew Dawson.

I described the ownership arrangement of the rum distillery in Barbados, how shares of ownership would pass to the other owners should one of them die, and since Dawson had killed them one by one, Pawsworthy ultimately acquired the entire business. Dawson murdered his victims, including Pawsworthy, in such a bizarre manner as to make it resemble the work of a lunatic, a mental disorder all too familiar to Dawson: His mother was committed to the Poor House for lunacy when he was a boy. Dawson thought he would inherit his uncle's vast estate; however, I, Mrs. Donald Pawsworthy, was named the sole heir in Pawsworthy's last will and testament, which McClain and Wright witnessed. Dawson was killed in the scuffle when Heathcliff and I caught him torturing Pawsworthy, whose life we could not save. I never mentioned the valuable lead casks.

Colonel Balfour wrote to me saying he had reported my findings to King George, recommending that parliament give me the highest possible accommodation for my service to the Crown.

In the end, I did what I said I would never do at the beginning: I framed a man for a crime he didn't commit.

～

A few weeks later, while I sat at my library desk one night, I heard heavy feet marching up the stairs. Mahala had taken Hannah and Winslow to show them her new farmhouse on the road to Moncks Corner, which I had John Cruden sequester from the rebel owner. The house stood on a broad "creek" and had a spacious barn—perfect for distilling rum, Mahala's new undertaking. I was happy to help her start a new life—she had finally left her "old me" in the past. Heathcliff was away recruiting sailors for one of our pirate ships (we weren't licensed for privateering—yet). I was home alone. By the intensity of the stampede, I estimated three or four soldiers were marching up the stairs. My library door swung open with enough force that it hit the wall.

My grandmother—Gabriel's mother—Jane Harris, strode into the room flanked by two shirtless Wacataw warriors. They had painted their heads and torsos red with solid black circles around their eyes. The warriors were so big and muscular that I couldn't believe we belonged to the same species.

My day of reckoning had come: Jane Harris would avenge her dead son.

I sat erect in my chair, facing her on the other side of my desk.

"Hello, Grandmother," I said in Wacataw. I pointed to the globe of the earth on my desktop. I had Pawsworthy's greasy scalp draped over it. "That's for you. It belonged to the man who killed your daughter, my mother, Gail Harris La Pierre."

She grabbed it, shaking the dried blood out of it, and handed it to the man on her left, who placed it in a deerskin carrying bag. One of the warriors removed the journal I was writing in and put it on a nearby table. He took the quill out of my hand and reached for my inkwell, putting them on the table. The other man took the globe and my books from the desk. The top of my desk was clear.

"Get up," Jane Harris said.

I stood. The warriors flanked me, grabbing my biceps, their other fingers crawling over the low collar of my dress. They tugged in opposite directions, ripping my dress down my torso. I stood naked from the waist up.

"Peeling your top down is part of the ceremony," my grandmother said. "Like a snake shedding skin or removing the husk of corn to expose the true inner self."

Removing the husk to expose the inner self meant Jane Harris would scalp me for killing her son, and afterward, one of the warriors would stab me intermittently to allow me to show my bravery and Wacataw pride as I bled to death. I saw this happen to a Cherokee when I was twelve or so. I was with Uncle George and other warriors when a skirmish with Cherokees broke out—some old score to settle. We Wacataw won, capturing a Cherokee. They tied him to a tree, and that man laughed every time Uncle George stabbed him, then he sang in his language as his blood left his body. His voice stopped working when his heart did. Uncle George said he hoped he would show that much bravery when his turn came.

It was my turn now.

One warrior moved my chair aside while the other pushed between my shoulders, forcing me to bend over the desktop. One man stood behind me. He muttered something. The other man walked to the front of the desk and stood next to Jane Harris.

"Give him your hands," Jane Harris said.

I reached for that man, and he grabbed my wrists. The man behind me also walked to the front of the desk. He took one of my smaller hands into his big ones. Jane Harris put the leather bag on the desk beside my ribs and walked into the middle of the room, looking around. She grabbed an ottoman in front of an armchair, brought it to me, and told me to sit on it. The men pulled as I sat, keeping a tight grip on my wrists so that my breasts were squished against the edge of the desktop—miserably so.

Jane Harris dragged the chair I had been sitting in closer and sat beside me. She reached for the leather bag, and metal clinked as she searched for her favorite skinning knife. If they didn't stab me to death and only scalped me, I would live the rest of my life looking like Benjamin Franklin. I could get a pair of those fancy round wire glasses. I tried to humor myself. I knew I was doomed.

"Crow," Jane Harris said in Wacataw. "This is going to hurt."

*Really?* I thought. I squeezed my eyes.

I felt her palm on the top of my head.

"Keep your head high," she said. "Be proud."

I couldn't have been prouder of what I had done. "I love you, Grandmother."

She patted my head.

"George survived his journey," Jane Harris said. "He waited several days until that ship of death was far enough out to sea, then he set it on fire. He said John Peele and all the other contaminated souls sank with the ship. He got away in the lifeboat and ended up in Virginia."

I tried to look back at Jane Harris. I wanted to cry. I did cry. But not for myself.

*Uncle George was alive!*

I tried to talk, but one of the warriors grabbed my face and squeezed. His fingers sank into the hollows of my cheeks.

"Stop talking," he said.

I was going to talk even if it was the last thing I did. "Where is he?" I shouted into the warrior's palm, and my hot spittle smeared my nose and cheeks.

The warrior let go of my face and wiped his palm on his deerskin pants.

"Grandmother," I said, "at least tell me—"

Jane Harris yanked on my hair. "Shut up, Crow, or I'll mess up. Your tattoos have to look nicer than the ones I gave George. It will be good that he is jealous of you. General Big River and I have agreed to give you two black snake tattoos. You and George saved the honor of our Wacataw people. We would have been mocked throughout history as the people who tried to murder humanity. He told me everything, Crow. About Émile. About putting my disgraceful son to rest."

"Is he in Charleston?" I grunted, straining to counter the warriors' pull on my arms.

"He's still in Virginia," Jane Harris said. "He's staying down the street from General Benedict Arnold. He said to tell you he has some score to settle with him."

I began laughing, and it was the most painful laugh ever.

"Grandmother," I said. "This desk is killing my tits. Can I at least have a pillow?"

"Shut up."

Metal tapped on metal, and I felt a bee sting. I forgot about my breasts hurting because that bee kept stinging me for hours. Eventually, I had to stand so Jane Harris could wind the snakes' tails around my hips and partly across my stomach, ultimately curling their tails around my belly button. She returned her attention to the snakes' heads that were on the balls of my shoulders.

"The black snake," Jane Harris said, tapping the final touches on the tattoo, "is the shadow line between light and dark. It's the umbilical cord connecting day with night." She instructed me to turn left and right as she examined the snakeheads, their tongues sticking straight out, pointing in the direction I walked. "One snake guides you through this world, and the other is the form you take navigating the dream world of He Who Never Dies." She laughed. "Now you have three tongues to talk with, Crow. God help us all."

I slept on my stomach for over a week while the tattoos scabbed and itched.

Byron's interrogation of Pawsworthy revealed a trunk of Spanish gold coins in the basement, where we also found Pawsworthy's blackmail ledger. That book named the men and women Pawsworthy had dirt on throughout the southern colonies and a few who fled to England. The roster included plantation owners, slaves, constables, tavern owners, farmers, sailors, prostitutes, officers, and soldiers. He paid slaves on plantations to be informants, using the fact that they were informants against them to gain more influence. He listed corrupt officials, possible spies, and loyalists trading with rebels, including Norman's contact for his lead casks. He logged sexual encounters of every scandalous order. I was on that list. He had quoted (poorly translated) sentences from my letters to my husband, intimate fantasies of what we'd do to each other when I arrived in Charleston.

Heathcliff and I were wealthy, but this ledger could generate more prosperity.

Early one morning, we met to discuss the possibilities. We were seated on my second-floor piazza, looking over Charleston Harbor. We watched a three-mast ship sail out to sea.

"What do we do with our Book of Sins?" Heathcliff asked, nodding at the ledger in my lap.

I raised the book. "How we handle these sinners defines who we are, Heathcliff."

"In that case, I'll seed all their flower pots now with the suicide plant so I can torture them later."

"No. We can't victimize good people like my parents, innocent lovers unlucky enough to fall prey to Pawsworthy. I'll find the devious and depraved people in here and unleash you on them."

"I shall happily pay them a visit."

"I don't ever want to depend on anyone again," I said. "I had to beg Colonel Balfour to save me from an unlawful marriage, and in the end, he denied me. Pawsworthy denied me access to the courts, too. An unmarried woman is far more liberated than a married one, and the only thing that guarantees me that independence is more wealth."

"Something we both want," he said.

"But I suspect your loyalty—like your sincerity—exists on this side of your teeth."

"Likewise," he said.

"You don't trust me?"

"I don't trust anyone."

"I keep my word. Your newly acquired assets prove that."

"We are on the same side, Charlotte. My riches increase with yours. That's what matters."

The ship in the harbor had to sail against the wind to reach the Atlantic Ocean. It navigated left, tacked right, sailed left again, imitating the journey of the snake. My thoughts shifted direction, too.

"Are you aware you can purchase a commission as an officer in the British Army?" I asked Heathcliff.

"You don't say."

"I do. I also know from experience that having soldiers at your command gets people's attention." I leaned forward and opened the Book of Sins, and my dress rubbed against the remaining scabs of my snake tattoos. The flakes tickled as they sprinkled my lower back. The snakes were shedding, being reborn. I loved the tattoos. I had never been so comfortable in my own skin. "That's a personal confidant of Lord Cornwallis's."

I pointed to a name on the page, Sir Edward Crumley. "Look at the dirt Pawsworthy has on Crumley. I'm sure we can persuade him to get Cornwallis to sell you a commission. If we apply enough pressure, Crumley can get Cornwallis to make exceptions to the regulations and sell you the rank of major."

"I'd rather be a colonel."

"Only the King can appoint a colonel," I said.

"Major Heathcliff it is, then," he said. "I hear the South Carolina Royalists just lost their major."

"Wouldn't you fancy your very own militia, Major Heathcliff? I'm certain Sir Edward could get a new militia chartered with soldiers of our choosing. How's Heathcliff's Rangers sound?"

Heathcliff's grin revealed his fangs. He relished the sound of Heathcliff's Rangers. So did I.

The morning sun cast the shadow of a piazza column over me. I sat back in the soft chair, and the sunlight crept around the column. I closed my eyes, enjoying the warmth on my face. I licked my lips and tasted something sweet in the light.

# About the Author

**ADAM SMITH** is an award-winning author and a graduate *cum laude* of the University of Arizona. Born and raised in New England, he lives on Cape Cod. He's an accomplished chef and avid runner. He regards being handpicked by Dennis Lehane for his novel-writing workshop at Writers In Paradise as a prized writing honor.